PENGUIN BOOKS

THE KING OF KINGS COUNTY

Whitney Terrell was born and raised in Kansas City and attended the Iowa Writers' Workshop. He is the *New Letters* writer in residence at the University of Missouri–Kansas City. Terrell's debut, *The Huntsman*, was a *New York Times* Notable Book. He lives in Kansas City, Missouri.

Praise for *The King of Kings County*

**Listed among the best books of 2005
by *The Kansas City Star* and *The Christian Science Monitor***

"In a neighborhood that includes Richard Ford's *Independence Day* . . . Tom Wolfe's *A Man in Full* and Jane Smiley's *Good Faith* . . . Whitney Terrell's *The King of Kings County* brilliantly dramatizes the . . . racial tensions, family ideals and local shenanigans that created the places in which most of us live and work. With another novel this good, he'll put Kansas City on the literary map with Anne Tyler's Baltimore and William Kennedy's Albany."   —*The Washington Post Book World*

"A big, fat juicy novel of conflicting values and elusive dreams . . . like *All the King's Men*'s Willie Stark or even Huck Finn, [Alton Acheson] reminds us that any search for the meaning of America starts with a warts-and-all portrait of Americans."   —*The Atlanta Journal-Constitution*

"Youthful alliances and tragedies; city politics; racial showdowns; the prairie eviscerated by the highway; honor trumped by greed . . . Terrell evokes [the 1950s] with wit, lyricism, and an admirably jaundiced eye."   —*The Boston Globe*

"Half coming-of-age tale and half tangled history of a modern American city, Terrell's second novel manages to be both intimate and epic."   —*The Baltimore Sun*

"Painfully realistic . . . Fans [of] Jonathan Franzen's *The Corrections* . . . will take to *The King of Kings County*."   —*People*

"[Terrell's] saga of real-estate ambitions and corruptions may be the great American novel of Midwestern suburbia."
— *The Kansas City Star*

"Combine J. D. Salinger with Mark Twain and you'll have some idea of the irony, humor, and harrowing sorrow in Whitney Terrell's tale of the improbable rise and fall of a farcical, con-man father and his watchful, melancholy, embarrassed son. *The King of Kings County* is the finest novel of delusional lives in Kansas City since Evan S. Connell's *Mr. Bridge*."
— Ron Hansen, author of *Mariette in Ecstasy*

"*The King of Kings County* is a scandalously convincing novel and Whitney Terrell writes prose as smooth and quietly sparkling as that of the finest old masters. He follows a small cast of privileged Kansas City characters who are alive enough to kiss, or maybe punch on the nose, and through them conveys with convincingly intimate detail the thumping hearts and cold logic of the powerful as they congregate and connive to change forever the future of a fine city. His eye is sharp and his sentiments firm."
— Daniel Woodrell, author of *The Death of Sweet Mister*

"Terrell is an astute, sensitive, and funny writer with the ability to pull readers into the story . . . Highly recommended."
— *The Library Journal*

"A powerful story about the birth of the suburbs and the death of the American dream. . . . A grand work of fiction, epic in scope and intimate in detail."   — *Kirkus Reviews* (starred review)

"*The King of Kings County* is Whitney Terrell's second novel, and with it he claims his province as a writer: the heart of the heart of the country, both physically and philosophically. . . . This is a portrayal of people and place that . . . becomes iconographic, a map of all our messy allegiances and sprawl, the shaky ground of American business ethics itself."
— *The Charlotte Observer*

The
King
of
Kings County

A Novel

Whitney Terrell

PENGUIN BOOKS

For Gayle

PENGUIN BOOKS

Published by the Penguin Group
Penguin Group (USA) Inc., 375 Hudson Street, New York, New York 10014, U.S.A.
Penguin Group (Canada), 90 Eglinton Avenue East, Suite 700, Toronto, Ontario,
Canada M4P 2Y3 (a division of Pearson Penguin Canada Inc.)
Penguin Books Ltd, 80 Strand, London WC2R 0RL, England
Penguin Ireland, 25 St Stephen's Green, Dublin 2, Ireland (a division of Penguin Books Ltd)
Penguin Group (Australia), 250 Camberwell Road, Camberwell, Victoria 3124, Australia
(a division of Pearson Australia Group Pty Ltd)
Penguin Books India Pvt Ltd, 11 Community Centre, Panchsheel Park,
New Delhi – 110 017, India
Penguin Group (NZ), cnr Airborne and Rosedale Roads, Albany,
Auckland 1310, New Zealand (a division of Pearson New Zealand Ltd)
Penguin Books (South Africa) (Pty) Ltd, 24 Sturdee Avenue,
Rosebank, Johannesburg 2196, South Africa

Penguin Books Ltd, Registered Offices:
80 Strand, London WC2R 0RL, England

First published in the United States of America by Viking Penguin,
a member of Penguin Group (USA) Inc. 2005
Published in Penguin Books 2006

10 9 8 7 6 5 4 3 2 1

PUBLISHER'S NOTE
This is a work of fiction. Names, characters, places, and incidents either are the product
of the author's imagination or are used fictitiously, and any resemblance to actual persons,
living or dead, business establishments, events, or locales is entirely coincidental.

THE LIBRARY OF CONGRESS HAS CATALOGED THE HARDCOVER EDITION AS FOLLOWS:
Terrell, Whitney.
The king of Kings County : a novel / Whitney Terrell.
p.   cm.
ISBN 0-670-03425-8 (hc.)
ISBN 0 14 30.3769 2 (pbk.)
1. Kansas City (MO.)—Fiction.   2. Suburban life—Fiction.
3. Teenage boys—Fiction.   I. Title
PS3570.E692K56 2005
813'.6—dc22   2004061188

Printed in the United States of America

Jack

When I was a kid, my father took me every fall to watch the Bowen family switch on the holiday lights at their Campanile shopping center. This was a big-time spectacle for Kansas City, and in preparation, they covered a grandstand with flag bunting and towed it out onto a bridge named for John Wornall, a slaveholder who'd owned a brick mansion up the hill. My father claimed that John Wornall's whole importance stemmed from the fact that his house was the only old-time building the Bowens hadn't demolished yet, but history didn't seem to matter much on Thanksgiving night as the shops closed down, the police barricaded off the streets, and the crowds poured into the Campanile. Then he was a great American, and we revered him, and that grandstand was set up where his bridge crossed Brush Creek and intersected with Bowen Boulevard, which made for a symbolic joining of great Kansas City names.

It would be hard to overestimate the crush of this great event. To get out on the bridge you needed a ticket, which, as an "associate" of the Bowen Company, my father wore clipped to his hatband. He also made reservations at the Campanile Steak House six months in advance. My mother was a southerner and disliked the cold, so we lingered over our creamed spinach and prime rib, watching TV crews unload cameras the size of freezers (I'm talking the early sixties here), and planes buzz overhead, until my father wiped his mustache and said, "Let's get in the thick of it." He knew something about the thick. He went about 260 in those days, one of those formerly athletic men whose size allowed dandifications that others might not risk. He had long, white-blond hair, he affected foulards and straw boaters long after they were out of date; he could be observed in tan seersucker and white oxfords in the spring—a hell of a wardrobe, which embarrassed me greatly. But his favorite outfit was a yellow suit of baggy linen with a black string tie and a kid gray fedora. Following him in that getup, as he elbowed his way down Bowen Boulevard that cold November night, his hair all glittery gold against his neck, was like following a crazed Custer through a welter of black-hatted braves.

And what a crowd it was. I didn't give a damn about any of it. Once we'd showed our ticket and gotten Mother, who was short, to a place where she could see, all I cared about was looking at Geanie Bowen, Prudential's granddaughter, who'd be sitting between her brothers on the stand. I knew she was in pain. We'd seen the whole Bowen clan out there at five o'clock when we drove to the steakhouse, already screwed down into their folding chairs with nobody around except for a few members of the Ladies' Auxiliary stapling up the bunting. By now Geanie's lips were green—she was a skinny girl, a redhead—and she had secretly slipped her arms inside her dress. Being skinny myself, I assumed a sympathy between us. The creek that we stood over, for instance, had a concrete floor and grassy banks, but in its ice-rimmed trickle, toilet-paper flags and turds floated past. I knew that Geanie felt the same contempt that I did for the woolen-coated crowd who stood down there in their own mess, cheering her family.

Nobody else recognized these incongruities. Or rather my father did, but he thought they were great. I saw his eyes get swoony when Prudential Bowen stepped up to the podium. He both loved and hated the old bird. "How the hell can you imagine that?" he'd say afterward to my mother, loud enough that I could hear it in my room. "That crinkly bastard getting thirty thousand people to come out and clap for him in a hayfield. It's like Khrushchev reviewing troops. Not a single ounce of charisma, but he's got all the strings tied up backstage." He always said these parts about craftiness or cheating loudly, so I could hear. My interest in rectitude was a worry to him constantly. "You know why Brush Creek stinks, don't you?" he had more than once asked me. "Because Prudential bought all the land along it upstream, then told the city if they wanted to run their sewers to it, they'd have to build him a system, too, for free. Think of that: free sewers, and then you just float all your crap out and back to the city. That's how a real businessman does it." It was important, in his eyes, that I know such things.

Another of my father's observations: "If you can convince people that a parking lot looks like a doge's palace, then why can't you convince them that shit smells sweet?"

This, of course, was in reference to the actual shopping center, the Campanile, whose buildings had been built as three-quarter-scale models of famous architectural sites in Florence—with the doge's Venetian palace thrown in as a bonus. It pretty much looked the same as it does today, with "strada" this and "villa" that on every corner, and red tile roofs slanting around crazily. (They're really six-foot sheets of plywood with tiles glued on, and thus have no peaks.) The fountains also haven't changed: Neptune riding horses through the sea, old Bacchus eating grapes, Iphigenia on her altar outside Swann's Women's Wear. The boy who pees on a pigeon. His little cork, as the joke goes, was the only competition Prudential would allow on the premises, which is why you'll find that Neptune's and Bacchus's presumably more hoary packages are smoothed away.

But I had to admit, standing there with my parents, that the sweep of the whole thing was out of the ordinary. Up onstage, the mayor had spoken, and Prudential and his son Henry (Geanie's father) took the podium. You could hardly imagine they were related. The old man's head flattened like a bottle cap and had a wild halo of white hair flurrying around it, as if someone had beaten chalk erasers there. Henry, on the other hand, had a skull like a watering can, bald on top, with wisps of carrot color in the side yards and the back. "The true honor here, which humbles my son and me, has been the public embrace of our little development," Prudential was saying in a horse's whinny. I felt sorry that Count Basie had to listen to this kind of stuff, lounging up there onstage behind his white-enameled grand. Finally the TVs took a commercial break, and then they turned the mike over to the Count, who was going to do the "*Count*-down"—a joke that made me hold my ears in sadness—to the moment we'd all come to see.

It was on this particular night, during my junior year at Pemberton Academy, that my father stepped into the first intimations of his success. That, as the crowd counted down from twenty, Prudential wobbled to the edge of the stage, his hair like a half-blown dandelion. "Alton Acheson," he called to my father. "I need to talk to you, *please*."

And so that is how I like to remember him, the crowd parting suddenly now, all respectful-like, around his yellow suit. The Bowens huddle with him on the back corner of the stage, against the painted scrim of a bandstand shell. The crowd chants, *Five, four, three, two, one!* with the Count accompanying on the upper keys. A switch is flipped. And in a series of flickers, strings of lights bang on all over the Campanile, white lights, multicolored lights, lights that are all red or all blue, outlining every building, every window, as well as the shafts of the bell towers that poke up against the sky—an electric, X-ray city—above which firecrackers burst overhead and peal off brick. Everybody cheers, except my mother and me. We are watching my father on the floodlit stage, being talked to by Prudential Bowen. It's clear Bowen is serious. His nostrils are flared BBs. Never once does he so much as glance at the exploding spectacle he has brought all these people here to appreciate. But my father does. He looks off across the grandstand, his head tilted toward Prudential's bellow, as if he's listening, but his eyes, as I can see even at a distance, are filled with the reflection of these colored things.

When the cheering stops, the old man shakes my father firmly by the wrist and pats his back, smiling now that the crowd's attention is turned his way again. And the faces of the Bowen executives in the front row—none of whom had bothered to say hello when we came in—turn to follow my father as he descends, grinning at him now cheerfully. And onstage I see Geanie Bowen's mossy eyes, gazing down at me.

My father had left Kansas City after he finished high school. He'd joined the navy in '44, learned to operate destroyer guns, and then shipped quietly off to watch the Japanese surrender in Tokyo Bay. He'd been on leave, visiting a shipmate in Asheville, North Carolina, where he met my mother, who at the time was seventeen but said that she was twenty-two and a graduate of Sarah Lawrence. They were introduced on the back terrace of a piney country club, tucked into the shadow of the Blue Hills, because my father was claiming he'd gone to Boston U. They lied contiguously. "I'd seen him tee off that afternoon," my mother said metaphorically, "and here was this blond man—twice the size of all the men he was playing with— who hit this enormous drive. And it went perfectly straight up, as high as you could imagine, with a cute little draw at the end." There was no ceremony. My mother (her name was Alabaster Mann) was due in senior year social studies at Carl Sandburg HS in Hendersonville that fall. She was five foot even, wore her hair cut short and parted to the side, and when she quit Asheville with my father, she left behind her cheerleading skirt, her bathing cap, and that spring's yearbook. Her father, a traffic engineer in Hendersonville, retrieved these things in grief.

"I know I'm going to be something," her new husband had told her, driving, his fingers gripping the wheel. "I know I got it in me to do *something* great, make a mark someplace. All I ask is you be patient with me till I find out what it is."

By the summer of 1954, my father's greatness still remained a phantom, believed in by no one but my mother and me. We were back in Kansas City then, where my father was looking for work and spending his evenings on our apartment's white-columned porch, thumbing through biographies. "Look at this," he said, reading simultaneously from *The Story of a Fortune* and *The Last Billionaire*. "Jay Gould, at age twenty-four, was working for a leather tanner in Delaware—huh? Huh? That's not so great, and twenty-four isn't that much younger than me." I was eight. I sat in a canvas butterfly chair wearing a revolver and a Lone Ranger hat, but my father addressed me as if I were a professor from the university he'd never attended. "You know when Henry Ford's name first appeared in a paper?" he asked. "He was twenty, and a whirlwind blew him off a hayrick in Dearborn, Michigan. Hell, he was thirty-two before he even saw his first car—listen to this, Nugget [his nickname for me]: 'I didn't often know if we'd have the rent,' Ford said of his early days. *But,* in the same breath, as if the incongruity had just hit him, he added, 'I just paid seventy-nine million dollars in taxes.' Imagine that!"

I was counting. "Twenty-six, twenty-seven, twenty-eight—"

My father chuckled, snapping his book closed. "You're gonna have a tough time getting to seventy-nine million that way."

"If he was twenty and you're thirty," I said, "then the difference is . . ." I held all my fingers up in the air.

"No, no, no, that's not the point here." My father's hand closed over mine like a baseball glove over a couple of peas. "The point is that Henry wasn't anything at twenty. He didn't really get started *until* thirty-two, which puts me two years ahead." He showed me this number on his fingers. I flashed my ten back, and he whipped his robe tail around the great hairy columns of his legs, looking wounded and betrayed.

At school I tried my best to cover for him. Every year since I'd entered Pemberton Academy, we prepared for the spring Field Day, timing dashes, measuring broad jumps, and in all categories I ranked in the last heat. This was how I'd met Freddy Prudhomme, along with Ozzie Tubman, Larry Stark, and a deformed boy, Elton Bunglehoff, whose father owned the city's largest dry-cleaning chain. Elton's left foot turned in perpendicular, and his right wrist bent down permanently, so he ran as if carrying a bag. Even the teachers called him "Jungle Jim." By comparison the rest of us looked normal: Freddy with his sinus problem that left dried crust around his nostril rings, or myself, dark and scrawny with my mother's upturned nose and feet that looked like seal flippers. It was in the service of my father's reputation at that school (his face grinned out at me from photos of the varsity football and golf teams in the gym; his name was etched on the Missouri State football trophy from 1943) that I dragged myself to the track every day, that I wore only what the boys wore in the *first* heat, that I never mentioned that my grandfather, not my father, paid my tuition. I even tried to rig the races in the last heat, explaining to the guys that if we let a different person win each time, everyone would get one blue ribbon, at least. "You got that, Elton?" I said, crouched among the rusted tackling sleds at the far end of the field. "We let Larry win the first race." But as soon as the gun went off, Elton bolted like a sea horse, his arm madly swinging its invisible bag. No one wanted to lose to *him,* and so off we went, the turf bumping past me like a conveyor belt and the jeers of the other racers, pulling for Jungle Jim, echoing in our ears. I came in third every time that way.

It would have helped if my father had even been slightly aware of these efforts I was making to protect our family's reputation. In the fifth grade, I spent the entire semester explaining to my teacher, Mr. Franz, that my father traveled every weekend, to New Orleans, Salem, Asheville, Omaha, and thus would be unavailable, under any circumstances, to address our class about his profession, as everybody else's father did. However, Mr. Franz must have decided to go behind my back and call my father directly, because on the last Friday of the year, he stood up before the class and announced, "Today, children, we are going to hear from Jack's father, Mr. Alton Acheson, who has offered to lecture on the history of American business today."

My father's first rhetorical gesture had been to crack the cover of his favorite book, *A Railroad to the Sea,* and display the frontispiece photograph of Tom Durant, slouched in a coat with a mink collar thick as a tire tread and his hair grown long and curly past his ears. "Anybody in here recognize this guy?" he asked.

Preston Petersen had his hand up immediately and with a sly look at the rest of the class, said, "Well, sir, he looks a lot like you."

My father gave a Bronx cheer. "I wish," he said. "Try again."

Others guessed the names of European kings or characters in Shakespeare—these being the only other men they'd ever heard of with long hair.

"Franz, you want a crack?" my father said, turning the photo to my teacher.

Mr. Franz must have guessed that this question was going to be coming around sooner or later and he tried to play along with it engagingly, polishing his glasses, putting them back on again to squint. "Sorry, Mr. Acheson—stumped me."

"Nugget," my father said, turning to me. "Tell them who it is."

He had to wait for an answer until the class stopped breaking up at this introduction of my nickname. When they finally seemed to settle down, Preston shouted out, "Go on, answer him, Nugget!" breaking everybody up again.

"Never mind these morons," my father advised me from Mr. Franz's lectern. "They haven't been taught right. Just tell Franzy what you know."

Thanks to my father, I knew plenty about Tom Durant. I knew that he'd grown up in upstate Massachusetts. That, unlike Ford or Edison, who invented things, or Rockefeller and Carnegie, who'd traded in new commodities, Durant had found his true genius in his ability to exploit the value of undeveloped land—the one natural resource that we'd been provided with in Kansas City. And I knew that around the time my father began studying Durant, he had also stopped cutting his hair.

Instead I made a face, widening my eyes and pulling my lips back in a grimace, begging my father to lecture about something else.

"*Please,* Nugget," someone said behind me.

"He was the president of the Union Pacific Railroad," I said resignedly. "He drove the golden spike, connecting the first train tracks across the country."

Once I got started it wasn't so bad. With my father's help (and hoping at the same time to distract attention from several cigarette burns I'd noticed in his lapel), I went over what he'd taught me of Durant's history: How he'd gotten hold of the Union Pacific in the first place by buying up all the stock under a false name, then electing himself treasurer. How Durant, needing a way to siphon off the money that Congress gave him, formed his own company to supply the railroad and then paid double or triple the actual cost to himself for the materials he might need, making sure that enough senators and congressmen had shares in the supply company. How Durant, knowing that he was getting paid per mile of laid track, had laid the tracks in a wiggle across Iowa to increase his pay. It was all done perfectly brazenly and in the open, my father explained—"This is the great tradition of American commerce, boys. The question is, What do we do with it?"—statements that caused me to sink lower and lower in my seat. But not my father; he had points he wished to make. If this *was* the American way, then shouldn't it be taught practically? Why even mention the Transcontinental Railroad if students never learned Tom Durant's name? Or studied the brilliant methods he'd used to build his empire.

"I am sure, class," Mr. Franz said, hoarsely, "that Mr. Acheson is by no means trying to suggest that all American businesses are run this way."

"Only the ones that work," my father said. "The rest are just a dream."

My father waited for me excitedly after class. There were, apparently, certain secret conclusions to his speech that could be explained only to me, and on our way to the streetcar, he handed me a bulging manila folder of newsprint, its cover scribbled with the words "National Highway Defense Project." As usual, my father was immune to the embarrassment of this. "Before you answer," he instructed, "remember that the key to Durant's success wasn't in building the railroad. It was in purchasing farmland out *ahead* of his railroad, then building tracks through his *own* property, so its value went through the roof." We were walking then down the school's front drive, my classmates filing into their parents' Cadillacs and Packards on either side.

"So what do you think?" he asked, as I pretended to read.

"Dad, I really don't think most of those guys were listening," I said.

"No, about the article," my father said. He flipped through the newsprint in the folder, framed by shoe ads and women in slips, to one that proclaimed:

EISENHOWER ADOPTS FUNDING FOR INTERSTATE ROAD

Sends Bill to Congress

"See this, Nugget?" he said. "That's *my* railroad." But what I saw was the window of a burnished Fleetwood, filled with Preston Petersen's cross-eyed face.

One year later my father put on his best pair of brushed oxfords and a panama hat and rode the streetcar to the Bowen Company offices on the Campanile. Prudential Bowen had turned seventy-five that year. His picture hung in every shop, Khrushchev-style, and banners fluttered with the legend 1882–1957, THANKS FOR 75 YEARS OF EXCELLENCE, MR. B! Did my father see any danger in these things? If he did, he didn't show it as he marched straight past the secretary and down the long hall to the old man's office, where he tossed President Eisenhower's highway plan on his desk. "Sir," he said, "this road Ike's proposing is for real. National highway, coast to coast, Canada to Mexico. The ensuing demographic shift"—he stumbled, opening to a page not necessarily related to his comment—"is . . . well, it's a little bit ha-ha-hard to find. But what troubles me, sir, is that no one at your company has so much as broken wind on how an interstate highway might affect real estate, which I happen to think is an important thing to know."

In the silence my father mouthed a cigarette with trembling fingers. Many a disgruntled store owner, or competing developer, had sat here and cried, cajoled, and cursed the Bowen family, only to be met with the snowy crown of Prudential's head as he scratched away at his correspondence. But when my father burst out, "It's going to be the biggest land grab since Tom Durant stole half of Iowa for the Union Pacific, and I'd like to run it for you, please," the old man looked up, curiously.

"Do I know you?" he asked.

"I'm the messenger of destiny," my father said. He lit the cigarette.

The old man made a snorting noise, like a dolphin clearing its hole. He was also famous for having a live electric wire woven into the cushion of his visitor's chair that could be operated by a button under his desk, which was why my father put his briefcase down before he sat. "Why are you sitting on your briefcase, Acheson?" Prudential asked.

"Rumors, sir," my father said.

"Doesn't seem like much," the old man said. "Acting stupid on account of a rumor." As if by radio signal, his secretary slipped through the office door. "Get Livingston to check on this," Prudential told her, shoving the highway report her way, and then he returned to writing. For a time my father just sat listening to the wet ruffle of the old man's breathing. There were complications here, ancient and dangerous reasons for mistrust—but my father shook them off. He stuck his hand out. "Give my best to Henry," he said. (This was the old man's son, whose office was two doors farther down the hall.) "And remember, it won't be a rumor when Ike sends the bulldozers in."

"Squirrels, Acheson," the old man said, without looking up.

"Excuse me?"

"It's the squirrels that I electrocute," Prudential said. "Little bastards. Problem is, they get so hungry, they don't care about the pain."

"I don't get it," my father said.

Prudential grinned with corn-kernel teeth.

"You will," he said, and then gestured to the door, which was already opening behind my father, the next supplicant edging inward, nervously.

The next day my father made a lunch reservation at the Grotto Restaurant, downtown. I always liked going downtown better than going to the Campanile, because when you crested Gilham Hill and saw first City Hall and the courthouse and the Warburton Building, with their fire escapes etched against their sides, it felt like something was *coming up*. The trees dropped away, and sunlight glared off the glass fronts of Western Auto and Chapin Hardware and Sewall Wallpaper and the newspaper building where the presses churned behind barred windows. And then finally, after waiting, you crossed Fourteenth Street, and the sky darkened as the buildings closed in overhead, and the streetcar wires made a black net above the street, and the pigeons fluttered up from them. When I was a kid, the driver had let me hold the switch, the brass cool and wet beneath my fingers, but now I just watched, sitting beside my father, as the signs peeled out from the building fronts like flags for Gribble's and Kresge's and Emery, Byrd, Thayer's, for Baker's Qualicraft Shoes, and Rothschild's, founded in 1855.

The Grotto was at Twelfth and Baltimore, and we walked there. It had rows of red-checked tablecloths and brass-riveted booths under white trellises woven with plastic vines and a waitress came and led us to our seats. Usually the owner, Joey Ramola, escorted people in, and I could tell that my father didn't like being ignored by the way he lit his cigarette and blew his smoke toward the front of the restaurant, where Joey was standing. We were also having lunch with my grandfather, Big Alton, which rarely made my father happy. These two thoughts wiped out all the excitement at what might be *coming up,* and I began looking around at the other tables, trying to imagine who would see if my father had a blowup, and whether or not I recognized anybody. There was no real way to prevent or hide one of my father's blowups, and so when I felt one coming on, I tried to concentrate on things I *could* control. I folded my napkin. I rearranged my silverware, my father's silverware, and my grandfather's silverware so that all the pieces were as close together as they could be without touching. Each table was provided with a basket of peanuts; the previous inhabitants of our table had left a semicircle of crushed shells on the floor, and as I bent down to sweep them away, my father reached across the table to grab my arm. His touch was light, but his blue pupils looked fried. "Nugget," he said in a low voice, "I want to apologize to you ahead of time. The only way I could get your granddad to meet me was to bring you, too."

"All we're doing is having lunch, right?" I asked, hopefully.

"No," my father said. "No, I'm afraid it might be more important than that." Briefly I saw his attention shift to the doorway, then back to me.

"Are we going to ask him for money?"

My father did, at least, grin at this. The one good thing about his blowups was that they were never directed at me. "Not this time," he said, adjusting my tie. "This time all we have to do is pretend that someone's giving us money."

"I don't see why *that* should be a problem."

"I hope it won't be," my father said. "But this is a very important deal for us, so right now, when your grandfather comes, I need you to promise me one thing."

"Don't worry about me, Dad," I said. "I know how to act." I'd stuffed the peanut shells in my pocket and was now dusting the pieces off my hands, but my father curled his finger under my chin, so that I was forced to look up at him.

"Whatever happens," my father said, "just don't say anything."

My grandfather arrived in surprisingly good spirits. He had a bad knee, sometimes a war wound (he'd fought in 1918), others a riding injury. Unlike my father, he wore a gray English suit, shoulders square, and as he hobbled toward us across the restaurant, Joey Ramola scurried after him, shouting about the ponies—"Charolais, what a beauty!"—in his ear. When he sat down, he brushed off his coatsleeve where Ramola had touched him. "All I can tell you, Jack," he said, scooting in next to me, "is that I hope you never reach a point where it matters what a man like that has to say. The idea of a city councilman selling his independence for spaghetti on a plate . . ."

Fortunately, it wasn't necessary to say much around my grandfather. He reeled off the names of politicians at the surrounding tables, and then showed me the conditions under which an "elected official" could eat for a dollar—order placed between 1:30 and 1:45 on Tuesdays, Thursdays, and after 12:00 on Mondays and Wednesdays, except bank holidays, choices only from the front side of the menu, no chipped beef, soup an extra $1.50 except when on special, no specials—which my grandfather claimed confirmed the corrupt nature of the place. I tried my best just to listen, though it didn't help to know that whatever blowup my father had planned would be witnessed by half the politicians in the city. My father did the same, avoiding the subjects that he and my grandfather normally argued about (except when the waiter came to take our order and my father, nodding at Big Alton, said, "He'll have the dollar spaghetti, I think"). Toward the end of lunch, I saw my father check his watch, his gaze roving among the tables, and then he leaped up and collared a bandy-legged man in tortoise-shell glasses, wearing a suit the color of sand. "Colonel," he said brightly, pushing the man into our booth, "my father and I have agreed that you would be the perfect man to share our surprise."

"A surprise?" the colonel said. His mustache tips were the yellow of used cigarette filters, and his eyes rolled soapily. "Alton, what's he talking about?"

"Whatever it is," my grandfather said, "I'm not involved."

My father, at that moment, lifted his leg and drove his heel so hard into Big Alton's knee that the breadbasket jumped. Or rather, this is what I believe must have happened. I saw only the sudden surge of blood to my father's cheeks, his tongue pressing the corner of his mustache, followed by a thump under the table and a gasp from my grandfather, who bent over beside me, his cheek white as his bread plate.

"I've instructed Pops not to comment," my father said.

"*That* seems irregular," the colonel said, trying to get up. "I think I'll—"

My father grabbed a half bottle of Chianti and three water glasses from an abandoned table, shoving the colonel fondly back in his seat.

"A toast," he said. "At least stay for that."

The colonel fingered his glass as if it were sticky.

"I'd still like to know what we're talking about," he said.

"*It's his birthday,*" my father whispered, and then stuck his thumb in his mouth, making a drinking motion. To my surprise, the colonel's face assumed a hooded look, and he chucked Big Alton's shoulder. "Alton, old man, congrats," he said.

I later learned that the whole conversation was a pretense, designed only for Tyler Livingston, whom Prudential Bowen had assigned to read the highway plan. His starched white shirt and maroon-and-blue Bowen Company tie swept past us in the middle of our toast, ten minutes late for his usual table but just in time to see what my father intended him to see: namely, himself and Colonel C. J. Pickering, a retired banker and possible investor, raising a glass of wine with conspiratorial smiles.

After this my father stood, reached across the table, and lifted me by my armpits over Big Alton's bent neck and onto the floor. "Gentlemen," he said, "there's nothing I'd rather do than stay around and talk shop, but I've got a streetcar to catch." And giving his father's shoulder a squeeze, he whispered, "Tell Joey to put it on my tab," and led me straight out of that place and back to the melting tar of Twelfth Street.

As much as I'd looked forward to my father's success—to his finding the thing that would make him great—beating up on my grandfather didn't do very much to improve my confidence that he was, as he claimed, finally on his way. Nor did our activities over the next two weeks, which my father and I spent having lunch at the finest restaurants in Kansas City. Or perhaps I should say we *attended* lunch at the best restaurants, since my father never actually had enough money for us to eat. We failed to eat in the Aztec Room, atop the Hotel President, where highballs and steak sandwiches were served beneath two-story-high effigies of the Sun King. We failed to eat in Woolf Brothers balcony, in the tearoom at Emery, Byrd, Thayer, at the pool hall in the Dixon Hotel, and at the Rendez-Vous Club in the basement of the Muehlebach, where Coon-Sanders and the Nighthawks played. All of these restaurants were downtown in what my father would call "the thick." They were filled with businessmen, men his father's age, like Ezra Sayers, Puffy Arenson, and Leo Sturges, young up-and-comers like Jimmy Peterson and Clive Jones, who knew my father from their Pemberton days. He hailed them all jubilantly, using me as a conversation piece. "Leo, have you met my boy? Kid woke up this morning, and I'll be damned if he didn't say he wanted to come downtown for a drink." He was always casual with these men, always smiling, always at ease. If you looked at him from a distance, you would get the feeling he was posing for a photo shoot, an exposé on the good life, there in his starched peach shirt and his suspenders, his hair swept back from his face. And in fact he *was* posing for something, because at each of these restaurants, about ten minutes after his arrival, white-shirted executives from the Bowen Company showed up to eat. He gave them a wink and a cheery wave. He called them by name. And he was always, when they passed by, talking cheerfully to men who had money. And who were known to invest in real estate.

He never mentioned his interest in developing land around the interstate to these men. When asked what he was up to, he raised his eyebrows and looked away. Once, feeling their skepticism, listening to the way they muttered behind his back, I blurted out, "He's going to build a *million* houses by the highway," he lowered his heel atop my arch, enough to remind me of my grandfather's knee.

It was a tough business for a kid who got easily embarrassed. As much as I wanted to help my father, I dreaded the moments when these men smelled out our act and forced him to order drinks, then watched through slitted eyes as he acted surprised to find his wallet empty. I hated being poked and prodded like Charlie McCarthy at his side—enough so that I began to evaporate at lunchtime, drifting off to the public tennis courts with the Tiller boys, who lived downstairs. My mother called me in one morning before I could leave. She had my father's sandwich fixings—roast beef, red onion, lettuce, tomato, Swiss cheese—lined up like accusations on the kitchen counter, facing me. "Jack," she said, "how come you quit on your dad?"

"I didn't quit." I cradled my three best, used tennis balls in a paper bag. "All he does is sit around and talk to people. It's not like he needs me for anything."

"There's a lot of kids who'd feel lucky to eat lunch with their dad."

"We don't eat," I pointed out. But that wasn't the problem. The problem was that I wanted my father to be a success *without* me—to go to work and leave me out of it, without ever mentioning Prudential Bowen or Tom Durant.

"Would you want to go?" I asked.

My mother looked up at me. The backs of her hands were red with peel. And though she always dressed in color-coordinated outfits and applied her makeup every morning, I realized that I'd not seen her leave the apartment in a week. "Well now, *ho-ney*," she said. Her smile was crooked. "What do you think?"

And I was out there the next afternoon, standing hungry with my father at the corner of Twelfth and Grand. When the streetcar squealed up, my father rifled his pockets sheepishly, then said, "Well, ol' Nugget—you got any change?"

One unexpected consequence of my involvement in my father's business plans had been the dissolution of my parents' moral authority. The summer before, I'd been forbidden to leave our neighborhood after dinner, but now when my father and I returned from our downtown lunches, I did as I pleased—whether or not the Tiller boys were there to accompany me. The early evenings were the best time for walking anyway. Armour Boulevard was still, in those days, a swank and wealthy street, and the apartment buildings along it rivaled and in my opinion outdid those that Prudential Bowen had built farther south, on the Campanile. Even their names sounded mysterious to me—the Sombert, Clyde Manor, Windsor Manor, the Newberry, the Brownhardt, the Bainbridge, and in particular the Chalfonte, whose beautiful rounded windows and carved stone pediments hovered invitingly over the sidewalk, curtains flapping.

The Hyde Park courts were tucked down in a sunken glen of hickories and white oaks, through whose upper branches glittered the windows of the wealthy homes that surrounded the park like the walls of a canyon. Toward dusk, when I got bored with serving my three balls, then walking around the net to serve them again, I'd sneak into their backyards and spy. My interest in these homes and their families was intimately connected to my own concerns and worries about my father, and I compared the fathers that appeared behind the lighted glass with him. I wondered if they, too, lectured their sons on the criminal activities of Tom Durant or went out to lunch and kicked their relatives in the knee. This is not to say that I thought my father was crazy—I had the clear sense that his goal was to end up living in a house just like one of these. My real concern was whether or not he was going to make it. I had no way of judging this. On the one hand, whenever I expressed doubts about my father's success to my mother, she seemed entirely calm and confident, unwilling to suggest that my father's methods might be abnormal in any way. "Don't worry, honey," she would say. "Trust me, from the outside any business looks like it's all crazy." On the other hand, if I had sat down next to these fathers inside the window, unfolding my napkin at their dinner table or laughing at Jack Paar on TV, and given a point-by-point accounting of what my father had been up to that summer, I had the distinct feeling that they would have disapproved.

Evening after evening that summer, I crouched in the bushes of Hyde Park and debated these things. One night I had the sudden feeling that I wasn't alone, and when I spun around, I saw my father standing in the yard behind me, smoking a cigarette, as he peered into the same lighted window I'd been looking through.

"You ever think about knocking on the door?" he said.

I flattened myself beside the window's shutter and shushed him so fiercely that my father raised his arms like the victim of a holdup. Backlit by the streetlamps along the park, his face in shadow, he spat out his cigarette and sank quietly behind the bush. "I still think it's a fair question," he said through the evergreens.

"You can't just go up and knock on strangers' doors, Dad," I said when I'd crawled back through the bushes. My father was still kneeling there, arms out.

"Why not?" my father said. He motioned, in mock seriousness, toward the lit cigarette he'd tossed away. When I nodded, allowing him to retrieve it, I had to bite my lip to keep from cracking up. "You could argue that the whole point of life is getting strangers to talk to you. Your mother was a stranger when she met me."

"It's *not* the same thing."

"Or your grandfather," my father said. "When your grandfather moved here, after the war, he didn't know anybody. All he did was knock on strangers' doors and pretend to be someone they'd want for a lawyer."

"Is that why you don't like him?" I asked.

"The difference between your grandfather and me," my father said, avoiding the question, "is that he pretends he isn't pretending."

"And you don't?" I said. "What about when we have lunch?"

A shadow bent against the ceiling inside.

"That's business." My father stood up. "The goal in business is to convince everybody else that you know something they don't."

"Is that how everybody does it?" I asked.

"I can tell you one thing," my father said. We'd left the yard by then, strolling backward, looking back at the shadowed mansions along the park. "Nobody ever got inside one of those joints by just standing around in the bushes looking in."

In mid-August, Tyler Livingston phoned from the Bowen Company and asked my father to lunch. In a burst of confidence, my father had agreed to the meeting only if Prudential himself came, and then, when his confidence wore off, he arranged a simultaneous interview with Horace Cogle of Cogle & Sons Mortgage, certain Prudential wouldn't show. I liked Horace Cogle; he was a fat-legged, white-haired man who'd always been friendly to us during our trips to the Grotto, and as he talked with my father, I found myself imagining what would happen if my father took a job with him. No more posing, no more sneaking in and out of restaurants; my father would accept a position at Cogle & Sons—"I expect regular hours, eight to six," Horace was saying—and work his way up like everybody else. Which perhaps explains the prickle of despair, rather than elation, that I felt when I saw Prudential Bowen swooping toward us through the Grotto's gloom, with Joey Ramola trailing off his wing. "Horace!" Prudential said gruffly when he was still several tables away. "What are you doing with that kid?"

I assumed that the phrase referred to me, until Horace said, "Offering him a job, Pru."

"Can't do that," Prudential said.

"And why the hell not?"

But Prudential's rooster tail of white hair was already veering away. He carried a walking stick at its center and tapped our tabletop with its end. I could see dust in its rubber scallops. "Come on back when you're ready," he said.

In a few minutes, my father and I followed Horace Cogle down a hallway past the kitchen, through a curtained doorway marked "reserved," and into a long and narrow chamber, like the belly of a ship. It was decorated like the whorehouses in cowboy movies. Red velvet curtains shaded hidden alcoves; vine-clotted mirrors tilted above the diners' heads, so that we walked through a gallery of reflected skulls: dark-whorled, candied pink, gray as an overcooked egg. Prudential Bowen ate a grilled cheese sandwich at the far end of a banquet table, accompanied by his son, Henry, and a group of men whose presence caused Horace to grip my father's elbow surreptitiously.

"Have a seat," Prudential said, pointing his butter knife at my father. "You, too, Horace—and don't whine about it either. Just order something."

"*Homo homini*," Horace said, rotating his eyes ceilingward.

"No!" The old man jabbed at Horace with his knife. "Down!"

"Dad, I *told* you," Henry muttered in his ear.

"Aut deus aut lupus." This was the kind of lingo I'd heard Horace use out front with the politicians. "Which is to say," he continued, grinning slyly at me, "that one man's God is another man's devil."

But I was more concerned with the menu. I couldn't find a hamburger. The "entrées" cost more than we spent on groceries for a week. And when I turned to the waitress for help, I found a pair of bare breasts beached atop the cork lining of a tray.

Beyond them Horace's white tufted eyebrows poked up. Used limes, chewed straws scattered in between. "Try the steak," he whispered seriously.

"I'll have what he's having," I said, pointing at Prudential's grilled cheese.

Later on, Prudential himself stood up. His eyes stared out at us like spoons of skimmed milk. You couldn't tell what was behind them. His voice had a squeaky tremble to it, not at all like the voice I imagined spoke for J. P. Morgan and Henry Ford in my father's books. He told us about the importance of this new highway for the growth of the region and to keep us a city of first rank. "And since nobody here other than Mr. Acheson seems to know a damn thing about it," he informed the table, "we at the Bowen Company have decided to give him twenty-five thousand dollars in investment capital to *explore* the opportunities for residential and commercial development along this new highway, and I suggest you men consider doing the same." There was a power to it. He made it sound as if the idea of building houses along the new highway—despite the plaid sport jackets, despite the oxford shirts and pointy ties, despite (or perhaps because of) the plum breasts of the waitress penduluming over Prudential's water—was every bit as daring as financing the Union Pacific. By the time the speech had ended, I'd rearranged my silverware five times and cleared away all the crumbs from around both my and Horace's plates. Fortunately, Horace paid no attention to this; instead he raised a fat paw and said, "Well, that's fine—I like young Acheson here, and it sounds as if you've rounded up a nice bunch of rummies to give money away." He indicated the table generally. "But about thirty minutes ago, I was thinking about hiring this kid to answer phones. So what makes you think he can suddenly manage all this cash?"

In response Prudential Bowen waved a bony hand at the Grotto's owner, Joey Ramola, who was wandering around on break from his maître d' duties, his tie undone, his comboyer rumpled, a cigarette burning in his lips.

"Fellas," he said, coming over. "What's this?"

He held up a hairy middle finger, covered it with his left fist, then jerked the fist away to reveal a flat row of knuckles. "That's a Japanese fuck-you!" he said, slapping Prudential's shoulder with his free hand.

"Mr. Ramola," the old man said with a quick smile, "will be keeping the books."

And that was how my father made his leap. I could see him, sitting up at Prudential's right hand, a stunned expression on his face. He must have known that by offering him his own company, as a surprise, Prudential had his own bluff going, would be attaching to this deal his own invisible strings. But my father *wanted* this chance. The offer could be withdrawn so easily. . . . And so he wrapped his arm around Joey Ramola's shoulder and said, "I think I speak for everybody here when I thank Joey Ramola for donating our lunch here today—and . . . *and* for being, as I've just been informed, the second investor in this company, to the tune of ten grand."

Then he went ahead and named the company "Alomar" in honor of Joey's contribution. And also so the other men could make out their checks.

As for me, I took a piss. In the john I met a dark-haired man who wore an argyle cardigan and a black polo shirt buttoned to his neck—the only outfit I'd seen more striking than my father's yellow suit. He came toward me at the sink, zipping and tucking with a vigorous rhythm, each movement timed to accent his words. When he fastened his belt, he looked like a jockey hauling on his cinch. "Sounds like a sewing circle in there," the man said to me. "What are they doing, fixing up world peace?"

"My dad's having a business meeting," I said as if this happened every day.

"Is that right? A business meeting," the man said as if this were funnier than I'd intended it to be. "And which one of these guys is your dad?"

"He's Alton Acheson," I said.

"The *loud* guy? Are you kidding me?"

"My father's going to be the greatest developer this city has ever seen," I said, drying my hands. "You'd be lucky to work with him."

"Hey, no offense. I never said he wasn't. I just mean that you and him . . ." He gestured to my reflection in the mirror. It was true; with my dark hair and my mother's olive skin and thin nose, I looked nothing like my father's son.

"Not that there's anything wrong with being a little different, either," the man said, as I inspected myself in the mirror. "The rest of these guys, they're all worried about how *they* look and sound to everyone else, right? But you—I kept an eye on you in there—it's like you're invisible. You just sit, watching everything." He had a meticulous appearance: his collar ironed (oddly for a polo), his hair a deep and purplish black, yanked back from his forehead geometrically. But when he straightened his finger beneath his eye, you could see that his nose curved hard beside it, like a reversed C.

Outside, he stuck out his hand. "My name's Nick," he said.

"Jack Acheson," I said.

"So, Jack, my daughter's starting at this girls' school next to yours—you keep that eye on her, hey? Her and her brother." And that was how I met my father's future partner, Nick Garaciello—or "Nicky Garbage," as my classmates, by the end of the first week of school, had already begun calling both him and his kids.

The Garaciellos

After so many years of simply talking, reading his books, and theorizing, my father's life was, following his meeting with Prudential Bowen, populated by a completely new world of business partners and concerns, many of them only partially explained to me. I approved of Nick Garaciello more than most. He was not an investor in the Alomar Company, as far as I could tell; my father's explanation for his presence was that he'd been assigned by Joey Ramola to "help out." And yet, by the fall, his partnership with my father seemed a necessary thing. One hot, one cool. One a talker, another a watcher, as Nick had described me. I had no idea when or how this friendship had been established—I was back in school by then and thus didn't keep track of my father during the day. But by the time Nick showed up at our apartment in mid-September, carrying two yellow cardboard tubes of maps, and sat there on our porch drinking an Old Milwaukee, my father knew him well enough not to say thanks. Instead he wrenched these tubes apart as if it had been Christmas Day. There would be two interstates running through the city, he showed us on these diagrams: I-35 and I-70. Drawn up, they looked like a gunsight, centered on downtown, one (I-35) running north-south, the other (I-70) running east-west. "But seriously, Nick," my mother said, "Alton's been calling the highway department for weeks, trying to get these plans. How'd you do it?"

"Nothing but bureaucracy," Nick said, folding his fingers together so they interlocked. "One guy touches another guy touches the guy you want—most boring thing in the world. Your husband's the guy with the original ideas."

For the rest of that month, my father and Nick Garaciello spent their time looking for the highway. It didn't exist yet—none of it. But whether it was visible or not, my father had already made his decision by the New Year. He chose the spoke of I-35 that ran south-by-southwest out of downtown and on a diagonal through the farmland of Kings County, Kansas. And this led to a spring morning in 1958 when my father, my mother, and I drove in a newly purchased Fairlane 300 through that great green expanse of territory, followed by the Garaciellos (Nick, his wife, and their two kids, Nikki and Lonnie) in a station wagon. We were truly in the sticks. I watched as my father wove a series of dirt back roads, stopping every so often to check the green rills of his map with Nick. I watched a single farmer in railroad overalls, so still against the horizon that he appeared welded to his tractor seat. I watched cows in mud holes; I watched Nick Garaciello wink back at me through his windshield as he followed us patiently. But most of all I watched my father, sopping like a spa-goer in his yellow suit, driving with his head stuck out the window, as if this helped him see. "Once the highway comes, all of this will be ten or fifteen minutes from downtown," he said, sweeping his arm out the window. "It'll be quicker to get there from here than from our place."

It sounded like wishful thinking to me. The regular city map that my mother and I were studying did a good job of listing the streets in Kansas City, from downtown south to Seventy-fifth Street. It covered Paseo, Troost, Main, and Broadway; it showed the Campanile on Forty-seventh Street and even the three small developments in Kings County, all done by the Bowen Company and all hugging the county line—but the space where we were driving, or where I thought we were driving, was nothing but green. As a consequence my father spent the next two hours making three-point turns on narrow gravel roads, whisking the Fairlane back past the Garaciellos' Roadmaster, grim-faced, refusing even to wave. Finally he pulled into a field of thistles that rose above the Fairlane's grille and unpacked what appeared to be a miniature telescope—it was a surveyor's theodolite, I later learned—from a leather case. My father was the kind of man who, the less he knew about something, the more decisive his actions would be, and he assembled this piece of machinery like Jackson Pollock going after a canvas with some paint. His big thumbs fiddled screws and dropped glinting pieces of things. As the rest of us waited in a battened area of weeds, I saw Lonnie tilt his head and whisper something in his father's ear. "Hey, Al," Nick said, "isn't there some kind of time limit on this? Like, if we don't get set up before noon, it's no good for the rest of the day?"

"Why the hell do you think I'm hurrying?" my father said. "It's not like I see anybody else around here rushing up to help."

"I thought you'd done this before," Nick said. He checked his watch and after a few more minutes squinted at my mother. "*Has* he done this before?"

"I hope so," my mother said, smiling nervously.

Then, with a nod from his father, Lonnie stepped up to the theodolite. He was dressed in a pressed Boy Scout uniform, and to my amazement he twisted a box onto the eyepiece, adjusted the controls expertly. The boom of the telescope swiveled to face the sun; the box swelled white against the bone of his eye. I watched the blood drain from my father's face as he removed his watch and sternly counted the seconds down to noon, and I decided what I figured everybody else there must have already decided, including Nick Garaciello himself, who was at this moment squinting at the sun directly, his fingers pinched to hold it like a grape: I decided my father had gone insane.

Even before this performance, Lonnie had been a mystery to me. He was a tall, morbidly pale kid whose utter lack of survival instincts had been apparent from his first day at Pemberton Academy. We'd taken gym class on the football field, just across Bowen Boulevard from the creek. In kickball there he was, hair upright in a black blade, strutting and exhorting the captains to pick him by pointing a finger at his head and saying, "Hey, get *this*!" Of course the captains had picked anyone other than Lonnie, even boys from the last heat, until he'd been left standing alone, at which point someone said, "Sorry, Garbage—even teams." Lonnie, however, had decided to go out and play anyway. If the team had a weak shortstop, say, he simply shadowed him and, when the pitch came, stepped in front to do the fielding. Brawls flared up, particularly once the other team started kicking the ball to Lonnie deliberately, then running the bases while he and the real position player wrestled over it. As members of the last heat, we resented the popular boys, of course, but our hatred of Lonnie came from kinship. Freddy Prudhomme could barely make himself say his name. He watched this game with us from the sidelines, a twisted expression on his snot-ridden face. "That dirty greaser," he said. "We could drown him, except that hair would just bob up and float away."

"Forget the hair—he's got grease all over him. It's like a sheen."

"Why don't we just light it off? Acheson, you got a match?"

"Come on, guys," I said. "He just got here. He doesn't know anything."

"You know what a moron like that does?" Freddy said. "He gets the rest of them all excited. First they go after him—and then next it's you and me."

As we said this, our classmates had begun to shake the chain-link fence around the field, chanting, "Garbage is a faggot," and waving the bird in Lonnie's face. There hadn't been much I could do to help him—nor had Lonnie asked for my advice on how to avoid the beatings and dog piles that had quickly become a part of his life. And yet, in the country, he'd responded to our "introduction" in an offhand, slangy way, as if we'd always been the best of friends. "Oh, yeah, Jack and I hang out sometimes," he'd said to my father. "He's an all-right kid." I wasn't sure which shamed me more, knowing that I'd failed to stand up for him at school or being forced to pretend that I had.

As for Nikki, I was amazed to find that she saw the chance to hang out with me as a social opportunity. She thought a lot about opportunity, in particular social opportunity (a trait that earned her, perhaps unfairly, the reputation as a "climber"), because she liked her new life at the Briarcliff School for Girls, the sister school to Pemberton—but also, I recognize now, because she could see in the lives of the girls around her an escape from the world her father had to offer. Perhaps this accounted for what otherwise might have seemed like an obsessive awareness (even more than most girls) of the forces that affected grade-school popularity. For instance, there was the notebook that she carried in her back pocket where she kept track of the "crushes" of the boys and girls in the sixth grade—a tabulation that surprisingly included me. Or the fact that, unlike her brother, she wore a new outfit to every picnic, trying skirts, Peter Pan–collared shirts, cuffed shorts, before finally settling on the properly casual look of too-short jeans, saddle shoes, and a violet bow to hold back her hair.

I wondered if it also accounted for the scarlet rawness of her chapped skin, which, particularly around her bitten nails, resembled the hands of nurses or the women in the cafeteria—anyone who washed herself too frequently.

Nikki and I spent those first weekends together in Kings County idling along hedgerows grown thick with black oak, playing a spying game.

"Okay," she would say in a stage whisper, once our picnic site dropped out of view. "The deal is, my dad's got us covered if anyone comes in the front, right? So our job is to keep an eye on the back." However, once we both climbed into those hedgerows and settled in a nettled pocket, knee to knee, Nikki abandoned all talk of spying and instead opened up the notebook that she'd been carrying in her back pocket, pen tip at her teeth. And began to ask me how certain other, more popular boys—just out of curiosity—would rate her friends on a scale of one to ten. "Say, for instance, Sarah Worthington," she said.

"What about her?" I asked. I leaned back, hands clasped behind my head, embarrassed because I knew that my own name wouldn't appear on this list.

"How do you think Brad Marsh would rate her?"

"Are you kidding?"

"If you can't give a number, just give a plus or minus."

"Two," I said.

"Oh, that's not right." Nikki drummed her pen against the notebook's page.

"If it's not right, why don't you rate her yourself?"

"Because that's not the game."

"Whatever happened to spying?" I asked sarcastically. "Any minute some Apaches might come charging up, and here we are just rating girls."

But Nikki was entirely unfazed by this behavior—seemed attracted by it, actually, as if pointing out her contradictions only affirmed my interest in her in the first place. She would slap her reddened hand against my chest, eyes blinking in false modesty at my boldness, and then say, "Okay, Mr. Smarty. I guess I'll put down that you *are* interested in Sarah Worthington but don't have the guts to admit it."

I distrusted the hothouse flavor of Nikki's comments, her air of manufactured gossip and intrigue—the very opposite of her brother who, with his studious eyes and pale skin, avoided such things. "Besides," I asked, "Don't you feel disloyal for sitting with me in the first place? You know the guys in my class are pretty rough on your brother."

"Why else do you think I'm here?" she said. Her expression was a parody of eroticism, lips parted, voice breathy, though also on the verge of breaking into a laugh. "If it wasn't to get you to stop treating my poor brother in that way."

On a Sunday morning in early November, Nikki and I strayed farther than usual from the picnic site. Harvest was over. The fields smelled of phlox, of Queen Anne's lace, of cow shit; the sun was still white and cool early in the day, and we crossed a creek that ran along the edge of a baled-alfalfa field, then picked our way up through larch whose trunks shafted like harpoons at a forty-five-degree angle to a steep hill. They suddenly gave way, at the very top, to a bare open meadow whose camber caused its brown grass to curve away indefinitely—no sign of danger, no reason to worry in the middle of this open field. Nikki was walking slightly ahead of me, her head turned back my way, chattering something about how "I don't care if Trudy McIntyre is technically going out with Angus Wallace. If she lets Brad Marsh French-kiss her, that's not a technicality" when, in my peripheral vision, I noticed a shadowy gulf just beyond her cheek and then reached out, grabbed her sweater, and pulled her back toward me.

The size of the drop-off was impressive; only a few steps from where we'd stopped, the field ended in a perfectly straight line, the meadow's grass tufting out into space, and sixty feet below I could see a chalky pool of water filling the nearest three-quarters of the pit. Pallets of white rock lined the adjoining walls, along with patches of moss, the occasional tree that had taken root and poked out sideways from the wall's cracks. Meanwhile Nikki had mistaken my grab for something else. A sound came from her throat like a bike gear coasting, and she had tilted her skinny lips to mine, a bouquet of wet string. I was considering ways to move her without embarrassment when a voice behind me said, "It's a quarry," and as I spun in surprise, Nikki opened her eyes, took one look at the dark void beyond my shoulder, and screamed.

"Mostly Bethany Falls limestone," this same man's voice was saying about twenty minutes later. By that time Nikki had calmed enough for her to creep up to the quarry's edge, wrists pressed beneath her chin. "With a top layer of Winterset—some sandstone, some whetstone, if you look at the records." The man had a delicately featured, pinkish face, and the fringed leather jacket he wore, along with matching moccasins that laced up to his knee, made him look like an extra in our school's Thanksgiving Day play. He tossed a stick, and we sat waiting, waiting, for the dry click on the rocks below, followed by the magical ripples of frogs along the water's edge.

"Doesn't look like anybody uses it," I said.

"My father had to shut it down," the man said. He stood up very carefully in his moccasins, as if concerned about hurting his feet. "Access trouble."

"Why would anybody want to come here in the first place?"

"You look at any paved road laid around here before 1920, and a good number in the city, you're looking at this quarry. Plus there's this." He dug around in the pocket of his jacket, his eyes tilting skyward, and tossed a chip of rock to me.

It was a reddish delta shape. "Cool," I said, handing it to Nikki approvingly.

"Chert, actually," the man said. "That's what the Shawnee came here for—lots of it in the Winterset band, places where the topsoil wore away. Used it to make their *warheads,* which that is. We're in their ammunition dump."

While the man walked on ahead, Nikki widened her eyes at me and made silent cutting motions across her neck—meaning, I could only guess, that this man was exactly the sort of dangerous person we should be spying for. But the guy hardly looked dangerous to me; he was too nicely dressed, the leather nap of both his boots and jacket unscarred, store fresh, the wing of a sour-apple-striped oxford (a color that my father would have liked, actually) visible in a crumpled wedge beneath his satchel strap. Besides, he was the first person I'd met, other than myself, who admitted to Kings County's ugliness. "It's a prison, really," he explained as he led us down into the trees and onto a limestone outcropping overlooking the creek. "The Shawnee didn't want to be here in the first place—hell, they weren't even from here. They'd been evicted from Ohio, from Pennsylvania, from Georgia. Their ancestral lands were long gone—traded in for 170,000 acres of Kings County. Same for the Delaware, the Wyandot, and other tribes that moved here. But you're a kid smart enough not to be imagining Mr. and Mrs. Wahoo running around in headdresses and staring off this rock at pristine country. I can see that." The man's voice had an odd seep to it, as if he knew that his words were only the outer markers of some larger secret that was already known between us, but the view itself had silenced me momentarily. The land was far less dramatic than even the land back in the city: neither flat nor hilly but a rolling compromise of plain, without a single hill or tree line higher than the one I stood on currently. In all directions, except behind me, the land didn't seem to end but merely fluttered out of sight into a pale blue haze.

"You see that railroad?" The man pointed off into the middle distance, just slightly to my left, where a pair of tracks wound atop a coal black bed. "That's the Santa Fe Trail. In 1840 a Shawnee standing here would have seen six hundred wagon trains pass by per week. He knew he was watching his own extinction, if he had any brains. Which is why I come up here." The man poked me in the ribs with that same implicit sense that we shared a secret. "To make sure *I* don't get extinct."

"Why would you go extinct?" I asked, hearing as I spoke the crackle of Nikki's footsteps atop the remaining winter leaves as she came up behind us.

The man stopped then to examine me. The hair that hung down beneath the edges of his weird cap was a waxy blond, the yellow less like a color than a stain. The flesh underneath his chin was white as the belly of a fish. "Well, I don't know, son. If I knew your name, I guess maybe I could ask you . . ." He paused here, theatrically.

"Jack Acheson," I said.

"Oh, well now, that's a *fine* name. Scots, is it?"

I nodded. "On my father's side, at least. My mother's southern."

"MacVess," the man said, squeezing my hand. "Royce MacVess is my name. And speaking of your father, I wonder if that might be him? In the field on the left?"

"Sure," I said, following his gaze. "That's him."

"I don't suppose that you . . . um, know what he's doing, do you, Jack? Besides, of course, bringing up such a bright, upstanding young man . . ."

But Nikki refused to let me answer this. I saw her switch the arrowhead to her left hand, so it lay flat against her palm. "Hey, mister?" she said, tossing the arrowhead up near MacVess's eyes. "You want this arrowhead back?" When he lifted his arms instinctively to catch it, she swatted him hard along the zipper—right where it counted, as we would have said at Pemberton—causing MacVess to gasp as my grandfather had the day my father kicked him, then drop to a knee. "Go!" she said to me.

It was a pure sprint after that, my greatest weakness, even downhill. Nikki and I pounded after each other, past larch trunks, over small cliffs of limestone, through piles of scaly leaves. She passed me early on, sprawling from tree to tree like a mad cat, while I plodded after; at the bottom we dove into a patch of briars, peeking back along the creek to see if MacVess was following. "Don't you," she gasped, as we hunched over to catch our breath, each spitting dryly into the dirt, "know *anything*?"

"Know anything?" I sawed at the thicket's branches for a better view, dropping down a rain of twigs. "Like I'm supposed to know that it's a smart thing to go around hitting farmers in the nuts? That it's normal to go around lying to everyone you meet? I'm not the one that hit that guy— he seemed okay to me."

Nikki didn't answer this immediately; she just blinked her hollowed-out brown eyes. Then she said, "Okay, Mr. Smarty," and clambered through the underbrush to the edge of the field we'd overlooked with MacVess. "The guy who also thinks it's funny to chase my brother around with thirty other guys—"

"Hey," I said, chasing after *her*. The idea of her father knowing this worried me, seriously. When we came out of the woods, we could see my father along with Nick and Lonnie, all working as a team far off across the dusty turf. My father held up white-and-red poles for the surveyor to aim at while Lonnie sprinted athletically between them, dodging cow patties, rolling out a long black measuring tape. Nikki pointed beyond them to the hornet dab of the Fairlane parked in a ditch on the back side of the property. "And what's your dad's car doing parked there?" she asked. "How come they moved it, instead of leaving it with the rest of the picnic?"

I had no immediate answer (though I spent some time trying to come up with one): the Fairlane clearly had been reparked intentionally.

"I'll tell you why," Nikki said. "Because that car is the *getaway*."

The word itself seemed like a joke; my father was not the kind of person who could own something as ridiculous as a getaway car, any more than he might pack a "heater" or be in trouble with the "feds." And yet when Nikki and I reported our sighting of MacVess to her father (a report that Nikki delivered without mentioning that I'd talked to him), Nick jumped up and gave a long wolf whistle that caused my father and Lonnie to stand upright immediately at the far end of the dusty field. The picnic also sprang into action, as Nikki, Mrs. Garaciello, even my mother began folding up picnic blankets and stashing utensils and plates in the station wagon's back end, while Nick took a pair of binoculars from the front seat and scanned the trees. No one spoke to me, nor did I offer to help. The whole thing seemed absurd to me—all of it, that is, except for my father's foreshortened figure that I could just make out, running full speed for the far back corner of the field. I watched him scale Royce MacVess's barbed-wire fence, one hand clamped atop his hat, and then leap into the Fairlane with Lonnie and speed away, their dust lifting in a white contrail, and it was then—as my mother called, "Come on, Jack, we're leaving"—that I knew I'd been deceived.

I don't mean to make these trips sound overly sinister, or to give the impression that what we did out there in Kings County was in any way equivalent, say, to robbing a bank. The goal of this amateur surveying project was simply to figure out exactly which fields bordered on the route of the new highway, a project that, by necessity, involved trespassing on private property. The picnics that my mother and Mrs. Garaciello set up were merely decoys, designed to allow us to distract any approaching farmers long enough for the members of the survey crew to break down their equipment, hustle off to the Fairlane, and make an escape. Nick's job was to provide security, and the way he and my father handled the whole procedure—even the more rigorous changes made after our encounter with MacVess—made it seem like a game, a comedy. One would have felt like an idiot to resist. They painted a bedsheet with the words MASON FAMILY REUNION, which we strung between two trees (carefully, so as to attract no attention from the roadway) at every site. They brought paper party hats, which everyone was required to wear in the "picnic area" despite the irritating pucker of their rubber bands beneath our chins. They purchased a folding table and a red-checkered tablecloth, noisemakers, and metal whistles to be blown whenever we spotted a farmer or his truck.

It was hardly threatening to see Nick Garaciello seated there in his folding chair, a party hat tilted sideways on his Vitalis-ed hair, a cup of Kool-Aid in his hands—a sentiment that most farmers who drove into our picnics seemed to share. The problem was that nobody had bothered to tell me what was really happening.

But even this couldn't completely explain the mysterious emptiness I had felt as I watched my father scurry over Royce MacVess's fence, hat in hand. It is important, I think, to explain that this feeling was not primarily moral. As a matter of fact, in the evenings that followed my encounter with Royce MacVess, my father and I spoke more openly about the Alomar Company than we ever had. I listened as he read me passages from Durant's biography in which he did exactly the same things. Attempted, as he lay there on the bed smoking, to follow his logic as he said, "Look, Nugget, I could tell you that I bullshit these farmers about the survey for a competitive edge, okay? But the real truth is, these guys don't *want* to know about this highway. So long as you are decent and respectful and avoid waking them up from whatever dream—Jesus, or Rock Hudson, or the communist threat to freedom—is occupying them currently, they'll let you do pretty much whatever you want. It's when you break down and try to be honest with most people that they fetch a rope and start looking to string you from the nearest tree."

However, if truth be told, I could have lived with the idea that my father had chosen to deceive the farmers of Kings County. What bothered me more was that my father's stories of Tom Durant—how, for instance, he had traveled west in Abraham Lincoln's lead-lined Pullman car, eating boiled trout à la Normande and watching a tribe of Pawnees do a war dance on the Nebraska plain—made our own efforts seem pathetic and useless by comparison. Listening to them, I felt a terrible dullness; the sight of my father's long, prone body there on the bed, the scuffed shoe soles largest, tapering down to his smoke-wreathed head, would at times fill me with a feeling that resembled the emptiness of hunger, though very often we had these discussions immediately after dinner. It got so bad that I began, for the first time in my life, to find excuses to avoid listening; I would at times begin to yawn, deceitfully, waiting for my father to notice, and then pretend over his protests that I was awake enough to continue talking, saying, "No, Dad—it's great, I'm fine. I'm not tired at all," when in fact I hoped he would send me to bed. My father enjoyed this show of persistence every bit as much as he had in the past, when it had been real. He would haul me out of my chair and lead me across the apartment and into my bedroom, ruffling my hair and saying, "Looks like you've had enough, Killer—hey, Allie, we got a bed for Killer, here?" Then he put me to bed as he had once done when I was younger, making a great show of finding my pajamas in the dresser, of returning my dirty shirt to the clothes hamper (though now he looked away slightly as I took down my pants), and of turning down the bed to tuck me in. And as I lay there, the recoil that I suppressed at my father's whispered benedictions—"You're a good man, son. We'll get 'em tomorrow, won't we?"—as well as the bristle of his mustache, the caress of his fingers, felt to me like the stark betrayal of a thief.

The Alomar Company

I'm not sure how my father survived, quite honestly. For months he spread his maps over every flat surface in the apartment, pinned them to couch backs, used them as tablecloths on the kitchen table, kept particularly compelling sections folded up beside the can. During the week he disappeared into a shadow world, out the door before I woke, home long after dark, with lines of sweaty dust around his collar seams. On a June day, a few weeks after the survey was completed, we rode the streetcar downtown together, tufts of cottonwood seed drifting in the air. We were going to buy new suits. "You understand that what I make now will be yours someday. That's why I've included you in all of this," my father told me. I could feel his emotion clamping down on me right there by the Viceroy sign. "Business is about originality. It's about results, the brain. It doesn't matter in business how fast you can run the forty or what girls write in your yearbook." By now he'd splayed his hand on my head like a doormat.

"So what you're saying, Pops, is that I might not screw it up in business, even though I'm slow and I'm a bad athlete?" I said.

This was meant to be a joke, but my father flinched. "I said no such thing," he protested. "I was using the forty as an example. What if I had said archery?"

"But what you meant was how I do in track. How do you expect me to be any good in business if I can't even see that?"

"See what?" My father glanced at the women shoppers as if they might answer.

"I just don't want to embarrass you, is all," I said.

It was the speed of my father's reaction that frightened me more than its actual force; I was still talking as he grabbed my armpit and hauled me off my seat.

"Have I ever said that?" my father asked. His teeth were clenched, and when I shook my head, I could feel the whistle of his breath against my averted cheek. "All right," he said, relaxing his grip. "There's not one kid in a thousand who'd stick with his father like you have. Don't you *ever* forget that."

I loved my father's praise, ferocious or not, but I also knew that he rarely gave these pep talks by accident. The survey that he'd completed—correlating the highway's spine and future exits with the actual topography of Kings County—had provided him with a "bible" of the lands he wished to buy, and my first view of how I factored in to that part of the procedure came in a few weeks. The scene was a clapboard farmhouse whose kitchen window looked out over an eroded side pasture, clumped with stunted evergreens—and beyond this, in the distance, the same hill where Nikki and I had first met Royce MacVess. My parents wore costumes: my mother, the secretary, in a drab gray skirt, my father in a double-breasted sharkskin suit that I'd seen him measured for on Petticoat Lane. I'd refused to put on the yellow suit my father had bought me for the occasion ("Try the seersucker," he'd said that morning. "We need to look rich"), which meant that I was wearing a blue blazer with an ascot tucked underneath a golf shirt, certain all of Kings County knew me for a swish.

"Thirty thousand for the property, Mrs. Wilcox," my father said. "To be honest with you, these offers tend to go down rather than up."

The woman he spoke to was in her sixties and had, after a burst of jittery welcome, descended into abrupt silence, head bent at the kitchen table, staring at her veined fists. Her son, Toby, leaned on the sink. He wasn't far past my age, his chin curled with a few ginger whiskers, his boots muddy. He finished an apple and put the core in his shirt pocket. "Ask how come he wants it," he said.

"Why do you want it?" Mrs. Wilcox asked.

"Well, to be honest, ma'am . . ." my father said. He smoothed his mustache as he had smoothed his hat. "We want it to lose money."

The young man snorted. He was also sucking on a wad of snuff. "Tell him he won't have no trouble with that," he said.

But Mrs. Wilcox folded her hands around her bent head.

"Show her the papers, Alice," my father said.

My mother shuffled papers from a briefcase and slid them in front of her; at the same time, my father jerked his eyes, and I stood to tug his sleeve. "You said we could have lunch, Dad-dy," I said. "I don't want to stay out here in this . . . *place.*"

It wasn't a bad performance. I laid it on thick, figuring I had nothing to lose in Toby's eyes. I wondered if I'd seen him in the crowd, when the country schools came to play our basketball team. "Just a minute, son," my father said. He patted me.

"But you *promised*," I said miserably.

He checked his watch. "Alomar is a diversified company. As you can see from our brochure, we are involved in meatpacking, corrugated siding—"

"I never heard of it," Toby said.

"—based primarily in Minnesota," my father said. "We see this property as a tax *hedge*, if you understand what I'm saying. A concern intended to lose money. Therefore, since we understand also that this property is mortgaged to the . . . um"—my father inspected the papers—"the Bank of Missouri to the amount of . . ."

"Fifteen thousand and fifty cents," my mother said.

"My husband was born here," Mrs. Wilcox said.

"We will assume this, of course, it being a prerequisite of our properties that they bear"—my father licked his thumb—"such an attractive load of debt."

"I mean in this same room," Mrs. Wilcox said, and I thought it was over then. We were all looking at her with the furious smiles of golf tournament sponsors, and with these same smiles we followed her black eyes over the décor of that kitchen, imagining the birthing scene of a man whose gravestone could be seen overgrown with chickweed out back: two windows whose screens looked to have been rubbed with charcoal stick, a stove with one burner, and two sinks that stood on metal legs and were blue tin with a white foam pattern worked in. Down the brass catch basin, flies buzzed atop some oatmeal spoor, and Toby spit chew on them; even my father was picking his hat up to leave, and I thought it was over, I prayed that it would be over. "Oh, Lord a day," the woman said, blinking back tears. "I thought I'd never get free of this godawful place!"

My father froze. He was already out of his chair and stopped his hat on its way to his head. "Our offer is now fifteen thousand," he said. "Plus the debt."

"Goddamn it, Mama," Toby said.

"What?" Mrs. Wilcox repeated. Her face jerked, turning back and forth, like someone had stuck a needle in it. "But you promised . . ."

My mother spread the papers out before Mrs. Wilcox. "He's not kidding," she said. "I've seen him get like this."

"I think it seems fair to try twenty," she said.

"Fourteen thousand," my father said.

"Quickly now, honey," my mother said, and she slipped a pen into Mrs. Wilcox's hand. She signed while my mother whispered her fingers through the thick pad of papers, saying, "This is the mortgage paper, this is the loan, the title, and this is the disclosure statement which says that you may never talk to anyone about the terms of this deal." I saw Mrs. Wilcox's mottled hand shaking and scribbling over the pages like a cheerleader who hadn't studied for her chemistry test, my father standing over her in teacherly equipoise, his sleeves rolled up. . . . All of us seemed different then, not just my father, but also my mother and I, because only we felt the invisible lines between us, and later, as the wind crackled in our windows, my mother pulled out the contracts and handed them around the car, and I rubbed the paper where the pen tip made a dent.

It is one thing to know that all real estate is done this way—to know that if the farmers of Iowa had been aware that Tom Durant intended to build a railroad through their cow pastures, they wouldn't have sold them to him in the first place. But it is quite another to see it happening right in front of you. I got better at this eventually. I had to, since my father would go on, over the next six months, to buy some fifteen pieces of property along the proposed route of the highway—sales for which I would dress up and play the son of a church pastor looking to establish a youth-group camp or, on a farm owned by a man named Brian Arburry, a message boy for an oil prospector.

I am sure that my mother knew that our activities were a few points shy of stealing, if that, but her presence had a cleansing effect on me. It was impossible to feel like a thief around my mother. Thieves in the movies were tall, ugly men, not five-foot housewives with bobbed black hair. They wore dark suits, not navy striped blouses and matching deck shoes; they carried

Tommy guns, not roast beef sandwiches and Ritz crackers in a wicker basket. As for my mother, I think, she'd made her bets, she'd escaped North
Carolina and whatever drab future awaited her there, and her moral calcu-
lations involved what was necessary to help our family—a position that
she arrived at intuitively and, unlike my father, without needing to resort
to the life of Tom Durant. "I know this is tiring, ho-ney," she said to me,
on days when I resisted dressing up for another pitch. "Trust me, I used to
work in the grocery before I met your father, and there were days when I
thought I'd have to kill myself if I shelved another can."

"We're not running a grocery store, Mom," I said.

"Well, it's sales, isn't it? We're your father's representatives; if he was in
the grocery business, would you go around telling people they didn't need
to eat?"

Her gaze, however, as she knotted my tie, was far more straightforward
than her logic; this business, any business, was better than the Hendersonville grocery. And she didn't need to tell me that it represented my father's
last big chance.

I didn't mind the veneer of respectability she brought to our trip; I was
overjoyed by it, in fact. But I also felt curious about this cocoon of innocence she wove around us, as a kid might feel compelled to touch a spider's
web—and besides, the skeptic's position was open in my family. One of
my father's more outrageous projects in those days was to sort through the
dumps of Kings County farmers, hoping to find mortgage statements,
bills, and any other financial documentation that would help him convince them to sell. These dumps were often the most beautiful spots on the
property, untilled, overgrown, set far enough away from any houses to be
safe. One day, my father rattled the Fairlane down a well-worn truck path
wedged between a bean field and a grassy hill owned by the Jackson family. Pheasants burst from the grass ahead of us, so fat and lazy they looked
like winged basketballs. On the back side of the hill, we pulled up beside a
ravine, surrounded by rosebushes and a wild carpet of lavender clematis
that had grown over the frame of a fallen windmill. "Hey, what about
Mom?" I said as, having donned a mechanic's jumpsuit from my father's
trunk, I followed him down into the trash.

"Looks great, doesn't she?" my father said.

My mother did look great. She was wearing a tight tan-and-white argyle sweater, and a white golf skirt whose pleats opened to reveal tan darts. She grinned at us from the windmill's strut, where she sat lacing a pair of tan-and-white golf shoes.

"It's pretty easy to look good at the dump if you don't have to go through the trash yourself," I said.

"You think it would be better if your mother went through the trash and you watched?" my father said.

"I think it would be better if nobody did it."

"What if nobody cooked dinner?"

"Cooking dinner's normal," I said.

"Speak for yourself," my mother said. She had removed a secondhand Louise Suggs driver and a bag of balls from the Fairlane's backseat and was hitting them tentatively and without much success back along the path. Golf was the newest habit that my mother had picked up as a way of "stepping in" to society.

"*This* is not normal," I said, standing atop the trash pile. "Do you realize that? Do you know that most people don't look through dumps on Saturday afternoons?"

"Careful," my father said. "The best stuff's on top."

"That," I said, pointing to my father, "is not normal."

"I don't see what's so unusual about trash," my mother said.

"You," I said, pointing to my mother, "are not normal."

"Did we feed him this morning?" my father asked.

I had climbed up to the highest point in the dump. My parents watched me from below, my father in a pair of fishing waders, his tie tucked into the bib, my mother leaning on her golf club, her hips cocked to one side. If I had to pick one thing I loved most about my mother, it would have been her expression just then. She was not upset about my accusations; instead, her lips were already forming a smile, as if she was anticipating a great line. "We may not be normal," I went on, improvising, playing to her now directly, "but what people don't know is that here, in this lowly dump"—I blessed my parents with a rotted umbrella—"were born the true *kings* of Kings County."

When I finished, a small landslide of cans rattled downhill. My mother glanced at my father dryly. "Where does he get *that* from, do you think?"

But there were also times, as I sat in these country kitchens, and watched families like the Wilcoxes or the Jacksons sign away their properties, when I found it hard not to think of them as members of their own last heat. Or to consider the lectures that my eighth-grade English teacher, Mrs. Finchley, had given us that fall semester. Poor Mrs. Finchley. She was the only member of the Pemberton faculty who tried to convince us to stop picking on Lonnie. The false eyebrows she'd penciled high up on her forehead gave her two expressions, one as happy as a cocktail hostess, the other pale and desperate underneath, and this face, pleading with us, became the backdrop for a winter collage of abuse—Lonnie with his head buried in yellow snow, his shoes untied, heels sprung, sticking out from beneath an evergreen bush. Mrs. Finchley may have been right that no wall should separate one man from another, but her face said something different. Oppose, it told us, and you'll end up like me. The other problem was that she passed gas when she read Frost's poetry, due to the relaxation it gave her, I think. And so instead of considering the way we treated Lonnie Garbage when she read

> The work of hunters is another thing:
> I have come after them and made repair
> When they have left not one stone on a stone,

my friend Freddy Prudhomme passed a note to me that said

> Something there is that doesn't love a stink.

That spring, the highway came. It had been working its way up slowly from the south, across the plains of Kansas, and when it arrived in Kings County, my parents and I went out to meet it in a windy, piebald field. The wind had its own agenda on that day. It cupped and growled at the podium microphone and sent roars through speakers mounted on two flatbeds, and when the Olathe High School marching band—farm boys like Toby Wilcox in long white pants—tried to play "Semper Fidelis," the wind snatched the notes from their trumpet bells so they sounded like a wind-up box tinkling far away. We stood with about thirty people in a tire-torn strip of grass, facing a buckboard dais set up in between two long tongues of bulldozed dirt, the sod cut fresh enough that it showed yellow roots. They had in fact started work on this road two years before, three hundred miles south of this exact point, we were told by the highway commissioner, whose comb-over flapped in mated strands. And you could see a little bit of what the process really looked like if you ignored him and tried to get a peek between the line of dignitaries across the dais's back. There was a whole valley of dirt back there, ziggurat piles of it, strafed across a bare valley about half a mile across, no grass anyplace. It was a sight that tightened me up, quite honestly. Huge yellow machines crawled in the distance, lifting and piling up matchsticks of forest where they lay smoldering, and every so often the wind would bring a curl of ash above our heads. In the face of this, I found my gaze returning again and again to Henry Bowen's daughter, Geanie, whom I recognized from school. She sat calmly on the dais in a navy skirt with a fine, long grass stain along her shin, but I imagined her in jeopardy, the great slow slide of dirt and rock bearing down on her thin back and braids like the lavas of Pompeii.

Somewhere along in here, a disturbance began. The mayor of Lenexa, Kansas, was talking then, complimenting Prudential Bowen for his hand in creating "Kings County's two newest cities, Mission Hills and Prairie Village, as well as his willingness to donate his advice on the placement of this highway," when I noticed a few surprised glances from the dignitaries in their seats. "Son of a bitch," my father spit out angrily beside my mother's ear, so I could hear, too. "That's Royce MacVess."

He had got through a fence somewhere and snuck up quietly, if it is possible to be quiet leading a horse eighteen hands high. He stood in back. I had the idea he was attempting to give the impression of politeness and impartiality, that he was a man who listened carefully to things. He was wearing a fringed suede jacket buttoned tight up to his neck, with a yellow cavalryman's scarf knotted underneath, black knee-high boots with the cuffs of his pants tucked in. I thought I smelled a whiff of cologne, but this was covered up by the horse, which lifted its tail to do some business in the grass. Women stepped away, holding handkerchiefs. The highway commissioner (the same man my father had argued with about the highway maps) came up and whispered in the mayor's ear during this and the mayor smiled out at the crowd. "I'm told that we are joined by the owner of the surrounding property, Royce MacVess, a descendant of our county's most *historic* family. As well as a donor to the Shawnee Mission Indian

Museum, so as we take this step forward in our county's progress, I guess there's no one who it would be more fitting to have—oh, I don't know—drop by? Is that what brings you here today, Royce? Maybe we could all give Mr. MacVess a hand. . . ."

The applause was light and uncertain, as the mayor's voice itself had been, but the rancher took it grandly, lowering his chin against his chest. "Don't let me interrupt, please," he said. Meanwhile I saw my father edge off to the side of the gathering, where the construction workers who'd put the podium together were squatting in the grass.

"Well, is there something specific we could help you with?" the mayor asked.

"I'm just waiting," MacVess said airily. His horse shifted beside him, and he moved with it. "You see, I was hoping Mr. Bowenstein would speak, and I thought perhaps it would be instructive to the crowd."

"Excuse me?" the mayor said. He looked back at the line of dignitaries, all of whom wrinkled their foreheads collectively. "I'm sorry, Mr. MacVess, I don't think we have a—" He turned back again, covering the mike, and said, "Bowenstein?"

MacVess held one gloved arm straight out, his finger aimed at the thin frizzle of Prudential's white hair. "Him," he said, decidedly. "Maybe the great *financeeer* can tell us all really what this federal *hiiiiighway* project is supposed to mean? Is it the interstate, Mr. Bowenheimer? Mr. Wittenburg? Or is it the end-to-states? What does *Waaashington* think we need to have imported here so badly that they want to spend thirty billion of our own money to do it?"

"Mr. MacVess." The mayor folded and unfolded his glasses like a speaker caught in a perpetual rerun of his introduction. "I think the actual bill is twenty-five billion nationally, not just in Kings County. So let's not get too far out ahead on that."

MacVess barely noticed this correction. He was crafty, I'll give him that; I saw a tiny pull of fear at the corner of his lip as he noticed my father rounding up the construction men—he certainly wasn't any match for them. But neither had the crowd turned on him quite yet, there being no lack of curiosity among them about someone who had the guts to call Prudential Bowen names. "I'll tell you one thing they'd like to import on this highway, folks," he said broadly. There were women coming up now with their children to pet the horse and he tipped his hat and petted gently above the children's hands. "All you have to do is head over to Topeka to see that."

There seemed to be some perk of interest among the men when he said this, even in the line of black knees and tie clips up on the dais. He had a bit of the Christ-touch to him did MacVess, leading his mule on in to Bethlehem, and he lifted up a little girl in an embroidered one-piece dress and lace-edged underpants and set her in the saddle, his freckled hand atop her leg. "We all know what happened in Topeka," he said. "We all know what Judge Earl Warren did to our schools there. We all know how the judge feels about a people's right to educate their children as they see fit . . . to educate a beautiful little girl like this." He was holding hard now to the girl's knee and I saw a wiggle of fear go through her face as the horse made a sideways twitch. "With Negroes. That's Judge Earl Warren's plan for Topeka. I know it's not pretty to think about or to say, ladies and gentlemen, but that's a fact. So you have to ask yourself, how do Negroes travel in Judge Earl Warren's plan? If your answer is 'by bus,' then you have to ask, 'How do buses travel?' And if your answer is 'the highway,' then what do you think Mr. Bowenstein and his friends plan to import to us here in Kings County on the end-of-state highway?"

Something had gone wrong with MacVess's eyes during this. They cleared out, as when you drop a dab of soap into an oily sink. My father was giving directions football-style to the construction workers to form a ring around the crowd, and MacVess pointed him out, saying, "Why doesn't someone ask a question of him—ask him if he told Irma Wilcox or Brian Arburry or the Cushmans when he bought their property that he planned to be standing here two years later at a highway ribbon-cutting party!"

It was hard to tell what spooked the horse. All I know was that the muscles along its back rippled like a snake's and then, just before it reared, MacVess alertly snatched the little girl away. The confusion was general after that—I saw a brunette in a knitted turtleneck sink down beneath the animal's revolving rib cage, holding her handbag above her head—but what I remember most was this horse's ass. I had a clear view of it once the horse dropped its forelegs and, instead of moving into the open field where it was facing, it began to back toward me. I backed with it. Gradually I could feel people fall away on either side, so it was just me and this pair of haunches reversing together in some sort of tango step. It felt for a moment (incorrectly, of course; all moves were chance) like it had a homing device, the horse changing direction when I did. But I was also fascinated by it. I'd never been this close to any single physical thing that seemed quite as charged with speed. Its two moons flexed independently, in a slow, luxuriant manner, muscles the size of truck tires, and the coat—pure white before the gray began—looked smooth as ermine with all this power underneath. I had reached out to touch it when a voice said, "Don't!" and two hands grabbed my shoulders, jerking me away. It was just in time, too. The horse's butt grazed the red ribbon up before the dais, waiting to be cut; then there was a bang, and the horse surged, whinnying. As I sprawled on the ground I felt two things for the first time: the age-old awe of looking up at a rearing horse, its forelegs pawing like two clods of iron, and the press of Geanie Bowen's skirted thigh between my legs as she rolled on top of me. "What the hell are you doing?" she said in actual anger. "You never stand behind those things."

But nothing truly bad had happened yet to me.

The Bowens

After Royce MacVess's appearance at the highway opening, something significant changed in my and my father's attitudes toward the Bowen family. Mine primarily had to do with Geanie Bowen, whom I'd met again a few weeks later at a "coed" field trip to the Westbrook orchard. The trip was heavily anticipated by both Briarcliff and Pemberton students, who rarely got to see each other in anything so wild and open as an orchard (my hikes in the country with Nikki were exceptional this way). It also involved a peculiar form of one-upmanship: a green card, passed out in advance, listing the "donation" cost per bushel of apples and explaining that any excess between what a student picked and wanted to take home would be passed on to charity. This led to a bidding war between the parents, competing to see who could write their kid the biggest check, which in turn led, once we reached the actual orchard, to something like an apple orgy: Kids shaking trees. Kids staggering under stacks of forty empty bushel baskets. Kids racing from the bus to "save" certain blocks of trees that would, after that, be off-limits to slower kids, kids from the last heat, like Freddy Prudhomme and myself . . . the usual thing, quite frankly. As for me, my father had refused on principle to pay for what he referred to as "apple ransoming," so I had slipped away, edging outward toward the borders of the group until I crossed through a tree line after which there were *only* trees. The branches hung there, drifting in the breeze. Their apples were bottle green . . . and I had wandered crosswise through the groves until I'd seen Geanie.

She was in the next open alley over from mine, separated by a screen of leaves. I heard her first, a grunt and a curse, and then pushed my way in through the branches to find her bent forward at the waist, her right elbow resting on her bare knee (she had her hockey skirt on) and her left hand curled behind her back, holding an apple that she spun idly, testing her grip. It was the iconic position of a pitcher looking for a sign. That there was no catcher and no sign—only a turned-over bushel basket, sixty feet away—seemed completely natural to me. Any boy my age had spent hours pitching imaginary games this way. The orchard was a perfect spot, I recognized immediately: an endless supply of "baseballs" and no need to chase the ones you threw away—which was what I was thinking when Geanie turned to the apple tree where I was hiding, shaded her eyes, and said, "Hey, in there. You want to do something useful?"

"I'm . . . um, picking apples," I said from inside my tree.

"No you're not. You're just standing there."

I pushed my way out into the light.

"Actually, I was kind of spying," I admitted.

"Don't worry about it," Geanie said, cutting me off. She dragged me to a makeshift mound (the rubber marked by a broken piece of fence) and handed me an apple. The sweat looped beneath the armpits of her shirt. "Show me what you got," she said.

I threw the apple hard, on a line. It missed the basket but skipped and rolled about forty feet past the range where Geanie's pitches lay.

"Great," Geanie said. "Purr-fect." She shaded her eyes again to follow the apple's progress, then dropped her hands, her irises wide and bright, as she turned back to me. "Now do it again," she said. "But at half speed. I mean, I want you to go through the motion"—here she pantomimed for me her own delivery, an absurd cross between a shot-putter and a waitress lifting a drink tray—"only slower. Pretend like you're underwater or something."

"What exactly are we doing here?" I asked. Throwing was fine, but this acting business caused me to stick my hands deep in my pockets and scan the trees.

"Watching you throw," Geanie said.

"Yeah, okay, I'm getting that—but why?"

"Because you're good at it."

"I am?" Secretly this set a chord off in me.

"Well, it's not like really *great*. But you at least throw like a guy, which is all I need to see. When I try it, it's all jerky."

"All right, I'll do it," I said. "But you have to go next."

I knew a little bit about Geanie Bowen already, since she rode her bike over to take chemistry at Pemberton twice a week (and with good reason, given that the Briarcliff lab doubled with home ec and very often had chocolate cakes in the ovens and beakers full of powdered garlic in the racks). Along with field hockey, she played tennis, basketball, squash, and she swam. She had tried and failed to organize a Briarcliff track team. She had knock knees. She sold ads for the yearbook. She was hardly what you'd call a beauty—five foot seven, a beanpole of a girl who attended class in her hockey skirt, cleats, and shin pads to save time. She was also the only student on either campus whose family not only paid tuition but had *created* both schools, donating the land and buildings from their holdings around the Campanile. ("Prudential's not stupid," my father once told me. "He's got every potential rich kid in Kansas City addicted to his department stores before they even know how to drive.") But it was the fact that she'd skipped out on the apple picking that interested me. Other than my father, I didn't know anybody else who could have, but chose deliberately *not* to, fit in.

"There's this pond where we used to swim before the Westbrooks opened the orchard up," she said after we'd worn ourselves out with throwing. "There's, like, a million tadpoles we used to dive and catch for experiments."

"What kind of experiments?" But she was sprinting off down the orchard's alley, glancing back in challenge. My last-heat status was revealed finally—feet tangled, ankles rolling on rotted apples, I went sprawling while Geanie's skirt nipped easily between the trees. I found her nearly twenty minutes later in the shadowed fold of a small farm pond, hunting for tadpoles in a stand of cattails. I watched from the bank and then confessed, "You know I made up all those rules on how to throw. The truth is that when my dad taught me, he'd just buzz one at me then say, 'There, do it like that.'"

"If your dad's even half an athlete, you should feel lucky," Geanie said, splashing in the shallows. "In my family *everybody* throws bad, even the guys."

"I'm kind of slow myself. . . ." I was saying.

"The worst part is, they think I should be shopping," Geanie said. She turned to me, hands cupped beneath the water's surface, as if to emphasize this. "I mean, can you believe that? How are you supposed to prove you're any good by just buying stuff?"

"What about selling?" I said. This was half joke, half test.

"Don't get me started."

"On what?"

Geanie yanked her hands upward with a splash and turned to me with a speckled animal wriggling in her palm. "Look, don't get me wrong—I love my dad. There's something wrong with you if you don't love your dad. But he has no idea what it's like to be a girl." She had come up out of the water, showing the tadpole to me, its drumlike ears, the wet balls of its eyes, its tiny black ribs flexing. "How would you like to spend your whole life talking about which guys were *cute,* instead of learning anything? I bet you'd go jump in a lake. I'm serious." Her face was close to mine, her green eyes overlarge, her voice a whisper to draw me in. "If that ever happens to me, you can just do this." She folded her hands together, not a clap, not hard, but with just enough pressure that when she opened up her palms the thing was lifeless in between.

And there, to me, was the flash of knowing—the private expansion of her pupils as she looked at me across her open hand, the faint parting of her dry lips, that allowed me to imagine Geanie Bowen as a partner, someone who didn't care about the last heat.

My father's change in attitude involved a reevaluation of his agreement with the Bowens that gave them the right to buy any land he purchased at cost plus 50 percent. This clause was something my father had missed (in part because he'd refused to let any lawyer—like, say, my grandfather—look over the contract), and its fairness became a subject of great debate within the family. Even my mother, who had thus far refrained from saying anything about my father's spending habits, believed that her husband should just shut up and take the money. My father, not surprisingly, wasn't having any of it. "Do you understand what this land is going for out in Kings County?" he asked me. "A thousand dollars an acre. Which is about what it would cost to buy the ground you're sitting on right now."

"But this is the city," I said. We were parked on the store-lined alley of the Campanile's Brunetto Latini Way, the summer sun pouring through the windshield and the backs of my bare thighs stuck to the leather of the Fairlane's front seat.

"What do you think it was fifty years ago, Nugget?"

"Why are you asking *me*?" I said. "I wasn't around."

"In 1910, this was a pig farm," my father said. "Twenty-five cents an acre, if that, for land that today is twenty-five dollars a *foot*. Which means?"

"It means we can't afford it," I said.

"It means that every time Prudential Bowen walks outside and looks at his bell tower or the Jack Henry Building"—he crouched down next to me, pointing out the rooftops of the buildings, the humped back of the theater, over by the Campanile tennis courts, McClain's Drug on the corner just across from us, the minaret of the Campanile's signature bell tower—"he's looking at fifty million in profit on an investment of maybe ten grand." His expression seemed wistful and he reached up with his thumb to smooth the center of his forehead, as if these figures amazed even him.

"You think you can make that much in Kings County?"

"That's how you start," my father said. "Let's say you take an acre of that Wilcox property and put ten houses on it. And let's say those houses—because, all of a sudden, the people who buy them can get on the highway—are worth twenty grand apiece? The county kicks in sewers, since they'll be getting taxes, and the gas company and the electric company do the same. All you put up are the construction fees—five grand on houses that are going to cost twenty, a fifteen-thousand-dollar profit on each of ten houses, on a single piece of land that only cost you a grand. What is that, a fifteen-hundred-percent profit? While your mother here wants to settle for fifty?"

He ran through these totals angrily—without the mixture of awe and admiration that usually attended his stories of the Bowen family—his eyes roving the passing crowds as if working himself up to something. He must have been, because when Prudential's snowy head rounded the corner just down the street, followed by his son Henry's red-edged melon, my father wrenched his door open and jumped out. "Hey, *Bowenstein,* ol' partner!" he shouted, while attempting to squeeze around the Fairlane's front bumper. "How about returning a guy's phone call one of these days?"

The Bowens were only ten feet away when my father shouted at them—close enough that a woman who'd just passed them whirled around to look at my father, covering her mouth with a tiny black purse. But the Bowens themselves took no notice of my father's voice or of the whirling woman, or of my father himself, whom they simply skirted as if he were a fire hydrant or a tree. Even my father seemed amazed. It was like watching a small and entirely unplanned illusion, these two men passing by, gazing mildly at their storefronts, still chatting in hushed voices on the otherwise frozen street. Through the Fairlane's open window, I heard Prudential say, "You can send Millie out to Wyoming if you want, but I'm going to need you here," and then they were past, my father openmouthed at the Fairlane's front fender, reduced to stepping onto the sidewalk behind them and saying, "I know you heard me!" before he limply threw his hat, which flared and skidded in the Bowens' wake.

Curiously, this was what stopped them, the soft thump and scrape of my father's fedora against the sidewalk's sparkling concrete. Henry pulled up first, as if this sound were more offensive than anything my father had said. Prudential touched his son's arm lightly as if commanding him to stay in place. He retreated two steps, scooped up the hat, and checked the band.

"Where'd your father buy this hat, young man?" he said in his high, cracked voice. It was the closest he'd come to acknowledging my father's existence, his watery blue eyes focused not on my father but through the Fairlane's window, at mine.

"At Shipley's downtown," I said, which was the truth.

"And those suits of his," Prudential said. "That . . . yellow thing. I don't suppose you know where he buys *them,* do you?"

"Downtown," I said. "I mean, that's where he buys his clothes in general, but I don't know about the yellow one—he's had that as long as I've known him."

I felt odd answering these questions, since my father could have done a better job himself, and yet it seemed that Prudential Bowen had deliberately constructed the conversation this way, addressing me instead of my father—who stood hatless on the sidewalk off to my left—as if I were the parent and he the child. Once I'd accepted this role, he granted me a wan smile. "You sound as if you don't approve," he said.

"They're different," I said. I glanced at my father for help but he'd stopped about ten paces behind the Bowens and appeared as confused as I was.

"Well, good—see, he cares about his father's welfare. That's a good sign," Prudential said. "Every son can improve a father—just ask Henry. He's certainly improved me." He pointed at his son, though it was hard for me to imagine how a huge lunk like Henry, with his steamed-lobster face, had improved anybody. "Is that right, young man? Perhaps you'd be interested in some advice on how your father might succeed."

"I'd like to see you talk to him," I said. "We've been waiting all morning."

"Perfect, then. Come here."

I got out of the car warily. I understood that up to that point Prudential Bowen had done me the favor of taking my answers in the best possible light. And I have to admit that, having watched how the Bowens had magically erased my father from the fabric of their reality, I felt an almost hypnotic desire to be recognized, to fit in, to appear reasonable and of the right sort—a desire only increased by the presence of Henry Bowen, who was Geanie's father and thus a man I wanted to impress. I shook Prudential's hand when he offered it and answered clearly when he asked my name, an answer that provoked the response (as it did in almost any introduction in Kansas City society), "I've worked with your grandfather, son—Henry, you remember Alton Acheson of Acheson and Ketch. One of the great firms of the city."

"Thank you, sir," I said.

"I liked him," Prudential Bowen said. "And because I like him, I'm going to do you a favor—what do you think of that?"

Tucking my father's hat beneath his arm, he pulled a small business card and pen from the inside pocket of his blazer. The card read BUY ON THE CAMPANILE, and on the back, as Prudential flipped the card over, were printed the names of businesses that rented store space from the Bowen Company. "These are our stores," Prudential said, marking the names with the tip of his pen. "I have certain rules for my employees, don't you see. And it's important to explain to your father that all of us at the Bowen Company respect these rules—even my son Henry and I, even my granddaughter Geanie, who I believe is about your age. This issue of respect is very important in business, where, in order to be successful, the employees must all work together as a team, something that does not include yelling at people on the street. Do you understand what I'm saying, young man? Do you understand the issue of respect?"

"Yessir," I said.

"Then you can understand why I consider it necessary for employees to buy things from our own stores," Prudential said. He held the card out to me. "I've circled the names of our men's clothing stores here. Maybe if your father would take the time to buy his clothing here, on the Campanile, people might feel more friendly toward him. You understand, it's not just me. Everybody feels this way—the secretaries, the individual agents, our mortgage officers. It's a team effort, everyone on the same page."

The card, pinched between Prudential's thumb and forefinger, hovered near my chest. "Go on, take it," he said, and then, with a nod over his shoulder at his son, he added in a whisper, "Besides, Henry and I think it wouldn't hurt your father, as our representative, to move up the ranks in *taste*."

That comment by Prudential Bowen, delivered with a quick, rabbitlike lift of his lip over his upper teeth, decided it for me. Instead of accepting the card, I turned around to my father. He was standing on the sidewalk behind me, his jacket tails rumpled from the time we'd spent sitting in the Fairlane's front seat, his forehead beaded with sweat.

"Hey, Dad," I said. "He's got some card here with all the Campanile men's shops on it. Do we *need* anything like that?"

My father had been examining his shoes, smoking, in a strangely resigned position. It strikes me now that he might well have been expecting me to side with the Bowens—that his posture was one of prepared humiliation, of a man waiting to hear something bad. Which explained, perhaps, his slowly dawning grin. "No, son," he said, "I can't really think of what use it would be. Unless you've got any ideas."

"I'm sorry, Mr. Bowen," I said politely, turning back around to the old man. "We'll skip the card, I think."

Prudential Bowen gave a lemony smile, his lip lifting again briefly above the edge of his front teeth, and studied me over the card's edge, as if he were making sure not to forget my face. "Fine," he said, shrugging. "Just a suggestion." Then, despite his legendary hatred of litter, he let the card drop. I watched it flutter down the sidewalk—and with it, in my overheated imagination, any chance of Geanie Bowen's admitting me into her family. When I looked up, the Bowens were already leaving.

"Mr. Bowen," I said, "I'd like my father's hat back, please."

———

On the drive home, my father tousled my hair until the roots hurt. The Fairlane's radio was tuned to WHB—whose announcer, Lew Brock, was interviewing Andy Williams in the Jones Store lunchroom downtown— and every so often, I would sense a silence beneath Mr. Williams's voice and the clink of silverware flowing through the Fairlane's speakers, and I would turn to find my father grinning and staring at me from behind the wheel. When I noticed him, he would silently punch me in the arm, and silently I'd punch him back. At home he retold the story to my mother over lunch, complete with reenactments. He told it to our downstairs neighbor, Mr. Tiller, to the doorman at the St. Regis Apartments just down the street, and to the bartender of the Palms Tavern, where my mother sat and drank a Sazerac. "What do you think the kid says?" my father boomed into the phone as I lay in bed. "He says, 'Well, it seems to me if you understood respect, sir, you would have called my father back a week ago.' "

There was a pause, during which my father lit a match.

"This kid," my father continued. "No, now, wait a minute—this is a story about *your* grandson. Yeah, some balls is what I'm talking about." Silence.

"Okay—" My father's voice sounded younger than I was used to. Silence.

"Yeah, but if you'd just listen—"

Silence. The receiver clicked back in its cradle.

"Well, fuck it, then," my father said.

It must have become clear fairly quickly to my father that freezing out the Bowens was hardly a good way to get them to talk to you—though, to his credit, he never complained about this to me. Instead, after a few more days of silence from the Bowens, he loaded me sternly into the car and drove south down the Paseo to Fifty-fifth Street. Our neighborhood was a mix of big houses, apartment buildings like the Gramercy, along with dry cleaners, schools, corner groceries. Everything, even the big houses, hugged the street, which was what made spying in Hyde Park so easy. By comparison, after my father headed west on Fifty-fifth into the "Campanile district," the block where we parked looked entirely empty. Instead of sidewalks I saw driveways where the curb tapered down to meet the gutter, each flank marked by a stone pillar. On the left side of the street, these driveways made long, sleek curves up to gloomy-looking houses that seemed at least a football field away, while to my right I couldn't see any houses at all: only a high, spear-topped fence backed by a hedge and then a driveway, just behind where we'd parked, that led through a closed gate.

"Remember that time we talked about knocking on doors?" my father said. "I thought you might be interested to see how that applies to negotiating." He climbed out of the car, circled around to the trunk, opened it, and reappeared on my side holding a pitching wedge and a green canvas bag bulging with golf balls.

"What doors?" I asked.

My father walked up to the closed gate and tilted his head back, as if inspecting its high wings. A box mounted on a metal pole, just at a car window's height, rose up beside him, and, flipping up the lid, he pressed a red button in the center of it. Nothing happened at first, and then the gates swung inward with a grinding hum so loud I felt sure it could be heard by the entire street.

I followed him down a drive that dipped through a grove of walnut trees, chips of their green-and-black fruit mashed against the asphalt, and then soared up through a sea of grass before dividing into two arcs—one left, one right—that ended before two of the largest houses I'd ever seen. You couldn't call them houses, really. True, they were brick; they had front doors, windows, white stone corner markings, chimneys, awnings—but all of this was done in such profusion, with such a multiplicity of doors and windows and moldings and strangely shaped upper rooms that it seemed impossible to give either building a single name. It was also terribly quiet going up to them. No matter how steadily I stared off into the distance at the stone porticoes that fronted them, at the chalk lines of color that suggested flower gardens in the back, I saw nothing move. I was curious, really, rather than worried or embarrassed, and my father, as we veered off across the still-damp lawn toward the right-hand house, turned and gave me a wink, as if he'd personally arranged this spectacle for me to see. And I stayed curious until he emptied his bag of balls on a flat spot in the lawn, pulled a wedge from his bag, addressed the ball, and fired off a shot miles high against the blue sky.

"The first principle of negotiating," he said—this conversation began during his backswing and finished with the ball hovering over the slate roof of the second house—"is to make sure that you know why your opponent wants to do a deal with you in the first place. Which, of course, is the same thing as finding out why he's weak."

Distantly, I heard the metallic crack of the ball hitting slate and then, a few seconds later—like a punch line—the *plink, plink, plink* of it bouncing on the front portico's concrete. "What the hell are you *doing*?" I asked.

My father squinted at me over the white cylinder of his cigarette.

"Negotiating," he said, clipping another ball from his pile.

My father had lost the svelte physique he'd had as a quarterback at Pemberton Academy but, standing over a golf ball, he still looked like an athlete. His thighs flexed as he squatted down in his stance, the sinews in his forearms shifted beneath curled blond hair. There was a beautiful combination of threat and grace in the way his meaty hands maneuvered a golf club, culling a ball from his pile, daintily teeing it up and then, after a hitch or two for balance, triggering the sweeping violence of his swing— enough violence that I made sure to wait for his follow-through before I ran out with my arms raised. "Do we even *know* these people, Dad?" I asked as the ball rose and disappeared, this time in silence, behind the pillared porches and buttressed wings of the house.

"Pushed it," my father said regretfully. He clipped another ball with the blade of his club. "Hope nobody's weeding back there."

I picked this ball up and heaved it into the walnut grove we'd walked through originally. This got his attention, at least. He culled another and watched as I rifled it toward the street. The yard was so big that even my best throw didn't reach the fence. By this point my father was following my movements with a sly, complicit grin that only infuriated me all the more. He served up the third ball with a slight, maître d'–type wave, as if inviting me to throw it, and so I kicked it instead. It's hard to kick a golf ball, and after a home-run windup, the ball shanked off the side of my foot and dribbled listlessly some ten feet away. "You finished?" my father asked.

"Are you?" I asked. "Come on, Dad—give me a break."

"I'm not knocking on any doors, am I?"

"You're not shooting a cannon either," I said. "That doesn't make it right."

"It *is* just an eight iron," my father said.

"People don't hit golf balls at other people's houses." This was such an obvious thing to say that, having said it, I couldn't look at my father with a straight face.

"And what about them?" my father said, gesturing to the house with the heel of his iron. "Why is it okay for Prudential Bowen to ignore me, to refuse to take my phone calls—refuse to explain why some farmer whose property I'm trying to buy already knows who he is and shows up at a highway ceremony just to yell at him?"

"This is the Bowens' *house*?"

"Henry's," my father said. "I'm a little afraid of the old man."

I held my head and walked away, which was a mistake, because I immediately heard my father take a swing behind my back.

"Who else have I been trying to talk to all week?" he said.

"That's business," I said. "You don't go to somebody's personal house to settle business. You call them on the phone, you go to their office, you send a letter."

"I tried that," my father pointed out. "Besides, we're in the real estate business, aren't we? What the hell do you think we've been doing in all those kitchens out in Kings County? And who do you think's been paying me to do it?"

"I don't *know* anybody in Kings County," I said.

"So who do you know so good here?" my father asked.

At that moment, to my great dismay, a strong female voice carried down to us along the green slope of Henry Bowen's lawn. I'd actually heard this voice earlier in our discussion and, standing as I was with my back to the house, had tried to ignore it—had hoped, in fact, to convince my father to leave this property before the owner of this voice could recognize me. I had also tried somehow to shrink during the conversation, pulling in my shoulders and speaking increasingly in a whisper, as if this might make me less noticeable from a hundred yards away. Now it was too late. "Hey, down there!" the voice called. It was clearly Geanie's. "You guys missing something?"

My father raised his eyebrows at me and pulled his lips back so that his cigarette was clenched dead center in his smiling teeth. "Ah, so?" he said to me.

"No, Dad," I said. "No. No, no, no—I'll do anything. Just let's go. Please."

But the angle of his gaze had already lifted—without any change in expression, his eyebrows up, his cigarette smilingly clenched—past me toward the Bowens' house. As he began to raise his club in greeting, I yanked down hard on his sleeve. "Hellooo yourself," my father called. "Am

I speaking to the greenskeeper or the lady of the house? Sorry about that shot. My partner distracted me. Is it playable?"

"Never mind," I called over my shoulder, still wrestling with my father. "You can keep the ball—we were just leaving. There's been a mistake."

"Never mind?" By then I was draped across my father's chest, holding down one arm and pulling on the other so that my chin was tilted toward his. From a distance it must have looked as if I were giving him a kiss. "Are you kidding?" my father said. He staggered just a little with my weight, and I hooked my heel around his calf and dropped both of us into the grass. It was the first time I'd ever tackled my father, but I didn't stop to celebrate; instead I scooped the balls into the canvas sack and heaved the strap of his golf bag around my chest, making sure I kept my back to the house. My goal, I think, was to look like a caddie. I'd caddied before for my father, when he snuck in to play on the various country-club courses where he did not have a membership, and I clung to the illusion that if I pretended he'd just hit his shot and headed for the car with his clubs, he'd follow me as if I were heading for the green. Instead my father watched me from a seated position, his pants hiked up so I could see the tops of his socks. He was wearing oxfords rather than golf spikes. "Son," he said as I left, "I got to ask you if this is how you go after all the girls you're sweet on. Because the one thing I know about life"—he stood up, dusting his pants—"is that no matter how little chance you have, you got to at least make an offer. Nobody's going to give you anything for just wanting."

"This is not," I said, "a business deal."

My father frowned and tilted his head sideways, plucking his pants where they'd bound about his thighs. "What kind of deal is it, then?" he asked.

I was saved from having to answer this by Geanie's voice. "Hey, mister, are you coming up here or not?" she said. "I had to dive into the pool to get this thing." Looking up for the first time, I could see her standing there behind a stone railing, a little flicker of pale arms and green bathing suit, waving something above her head.

"*Uno momento*," my father called, sprucing up his hair in a way that made me want to strangle him. He widened his eyes inquiringly, and when I shook my head, he shrugged and tossed me his car keys. "Wish me luck," he said.

———

I carried the clubs back to the street. The bag's strap had been spooled out to fit around my father's chest, which meant that it dragged against the ground while I was walking and caused me to fall twice as I lugged it through the walnut trees, my heart filled with generalized black hate. I especially hated the bag. It looked like a cross between a Christmas tree and a dead cheerleader, what with the plastic tags fixed to the zippers from my father's amateur tournaments—the Trans-Texas Regional, the Bayou Four-Ball, the Charlotte Pro-Am—and the fact that he had considered it fashionable to have his bag made of marbled red leather the color of a bar banquette with the name ACHESON stamped in gold along the ball pocket. To say nothing of the pom-pommed woods. I would have loved to throw the whole thing out in the street, or abandon it to rot beneath the Bowens' walnuts, but that would have meant leaving verifiable proof that we'd been here in the first place. Nor did it help, as I opened my father's trunk and arranged the clubs properly atop the tire iron and the spare, that I found my own golf bag in there. This was a plain canvas number that I'd inherited from my grandfather, big enough to hold just the three or four clubs instead of the arsenal of twenty clubs (three putters alone) that my father had.

It didn't matter that I only knew how to use three clubs. The sight of the bag proved the accuracy of my fears that I, in my plain casing—I was by then in the Fairlane's front seat examining my own face in the rearview mirror, my plain brown eyes, brown hair with a cowlick, an unrisen pimple on my right cheek—would never be able to compete with my father, even for a girl like Geanie, who was my own age.

As I sat in my father's car comparing myself to a golf bag, a shadow fell over my shoulder, and I turned to find a long, curving wall of cream-colored metal drifting past my window. It moved so smoothly that for a moment I thought the Fairlane had started rolling backward; then four chrome windows appeared, and I saw that it was the same white Buick Century station wagon that followed Geanie at a distance on her bike rides over to the boys' school—the only chauffered station wagon that I had ever seen. There, in the third window, was Henry Bowen himself, shading his eyes and looking back into the sun at me. I could see just the sunlit lower half of his face, the turned-down corners of his lips, but I could tell that he recognized me, and, having done this, Henry Bowen pressed his long hand against the window glass, approximately where my face must have been, and hard enough that the flesh whitened along the palm's edge. That hand stayed there, trembling and dead, as the creamy Buick jolted into the shadows of the Bowens' walnuts. Then I got out and followed it through the gate, figuring that when it came to Henry Bowen, at least, my father and I were on the same team.

"The way I see it is this, Henry," my father said, "you can't fire me, since you don't pay me a salary. And if you're not going to withdraw your investment, or cancel the contract we signed and buy this land yourself, then you have to talk to me."

"Oh, I'm planning to talk to you," I heard Henry Bowen say. "I've got a couple of things on my mind."

"Well, that's an improvement."

"Get out? Would that do it?"

"Oh, Henry, Henry, Henry," my father said. "Didn't we just go over that? If your dad didn't cut me off after I called him dirty names, then why should I think that *you* can do it?" I could see the two of them through the hedge that bordered Henry Bowen's backyard. My father sat on a woven deck chair, his legs spread so that his feet pressed flat on the brick terrace, while Henry was stretched out in a lounger, a glass of iced tea balanced on his zipper such that, when he lifted it to sip, it left a pornographic target. My father's tone of voice was close to being friendly, intimate; there was a drawl to it that he almost never used, and for one terrific moment, I thought he was going to lean forward and pat Henry Bowen on the knee. As for Henry's face, I couldn't see it; because of the way the hedge parted, I made out only broken colors in that direction, though what was most notable was the silence, the sound of sparrows in the hedge. Then Henry said, "Get some peanuts for us, will you, dear?" and I saw Geanie's red hair and bare shoulder flash past, a towel wrapped around her waist, followed by the sound of a door slamming. I decided to take this as my cue to go in.

"Another one?" Henry said when I pushed through the gate. His hands were folded across a small lump of belly. "Do you follow the logic of this man?" he asked, squinting up at me. He appeared truly mystified, the question genuine.

"Sometimes it's easier than others," I said. I sat on the arm of an upright chair, trying to pretend that I wandered into Henry Bowen's backyard every day. The chair tilted on the bricks, and I nearly fell, grabbing it.

"*He* claims I have to answer questions," Henry said. "He says that because I don't want to talk to him, that's proof I have to."

"They're not tough questions," my father said.

"Aren't they?" Henry said. He lifted his eyebrows. They were the braided orange and white of the lane ropes at the downtown Y.

"Here's one, Henry," my father was saying. "You and I both know that Royce MacVess owns the biggest and most important piece of property in Kings County. The highway goes right through the middle of it, so any developer that wants to build out there will have to control that property—I *know* you and your father want to buy it. What I don't know is why you'd ask a jerk like me to do it, instead of just going out and making an offer yourself. Unless, of course, you knew ahead of time that the owner of this property wouldn't sell to you in the first place." During this, Henry's eyes were moving, and his cough-laughs were timed to something other than my father's conversation, as if he were watching cartoons high up in the sky. Then I noticed squirrels up there in the elm trees, two of them chasing each other, winding around the branches. Their nails scrabbled. When finally they shot off, out of sight, Henry stopped watching.

"How many employees do you think I have," Henry said to me, "who come in and tell me I'm stupid for spending twenty-five thousand on one of their ideas?"

"Not very many?" I ventured.

Henry gave me a significant look over his iced tea.

"Do you want to know what's really funny?" my father asked. "The real whopper? Ask Henry if he really plans to move Negroes into Kings County."

Personally, I didn't think this sounded like it would be funny at all. Besides, I was only interested in the back door, where Geanie had presumably disappeared to get peanuts. Watching it, I felt my palms begin to sweat. "That's okay," I answered, and then quickly corrected myself. "I mean, sure—I'd like to hear."

"Mr. MacVess's comments on the Negro Question," Henry responded angrily, "show a complete ignorance of decades of Bowen Company policy."

"And they're *funny*!" my father said. "I mean, come on, Henry, the largest landowner in Kings County rides a horse to a highway opening? So he can yell at your father about Earl Warren and school busing? Bowenstein?" He did his own cough-laugh, like a man sniffing pepper, a red swell coming into his face as he bent forward across his parted knees. This laugh was the first sound he'd made that rang false. "That's a whole lot of things. Ill informed? Yes. Embarrassing, quite possibly. But it is definitely funny. And when I notice that this guy whose property *we* want to buy, is yelling at *your* father about bringing Negroes in"—a laugh here again, nearly teary—"it makes me think that my involvement might be worth more than fifty percent."

My father leaned a little bit too hard on this last line, and it clattered around against the window banks of the Bowen house in a way that embarrassed me. Henry continued staring and smiling. It was the same magic trick of obliteration he'd pulled with Prudential out on Brunetto Latini Way, only his silence seemed less a show of wizardry than an admission he had no other defense. Then Geanie came out the back door with a towel around her waist, a green bathing suit on, and bare feet. She was carrying a bowl of peanuts. I would have thought that anyone else walking into the silence we had going on that terrace would have had to stop and readjust, like someone going through an airlock, but she didn't seem to find it worth noticing. She balled up some peanuts in her fist, tucked a couple of them in her cheek like ballplayers did with chewing tobacco, and said, "Daddy, Myrna wants to know if you're going to need sandwiches while you're still here."

"Sandwiches?" These seemed a remarkable invention to Henry; he stood and patted his big white palm on Geanie's back, a bluff grin of hunger on his face. "Very good, very good. We'll have them in the study, I think." Then he trooped off through the back door without hesitation, as if we'd been discussing tiddlywinks.

"I think he probably means you, too," Geanie said to my father. "The study's down the front hall on the left."

We were alone after that. Geanie sat down in one of the upright chairs and crossed her legs, still chewing peanuts. "That's where your father's ball landed," she said, pointing to a dusky green pool by the patio's edge. "Tom

Pendergast poured it out of the same concrete he used to pave Brush Creek." All I knew about Tom Pendergast was that my grandfather had described him as the crookedest politician he'd ever known. But at least the comment gave me an excuse to look at Geanie. You could still see little bits of Henry all over her—in the feet, I thought particularly, which were maybe longer than they ought to be. They had scarlet rub marks on them. But there were also her breasts, not much of them but more than Henry had, behind the green webbing of her suit, and the way her calf filled out when she propped it across her knee. I decided that I'd like to hear her dump on her old man again. "So what's your dad so mad about?" I asked.

"You're the one to talk," Geanie said.

"Excuse me?"

"You heard me all right, buddy," Geanie said.

"But I don't understand what you mean." I tried to keep out the sound of begging. "I just got here."

Geanie sat there with her eyes blinking and her nostrils flared and her crossed leg ticking, as if counting off the seconds I had to come clean. Then she threw her peanuts over into the lawn, stood up to clear her father's iced-tea glass, which she dumped straight on the bricks, and went inside.

It took me twenty minutes to find her. It wasn't a pleasant game of hide-and-seek either. These houses that Prudential Bowen had thrown up in the thirties with Irish labor and bricks that he had mined from the clay of eastern Kansas and timber shipped in from the Ozarks are still more impressive than any private residence I've ever seen. Even the house of the governor of New York State, which I used to drive by during my college years, looks flimsy and jerry-rigged by comparison, the kind of house you'd build if you were running out of trees. No, the real Bowen mansions from the old days were filled with so much lumber and masonry that they seemed like some private distillation of all the midwestern forests that had gone into building them. You didn't imagine parties or Hollywood stars or chorus girls drinking champagne when you walked through them; instead what you felt—in their high spaces, in their empty dining rooms with out-laid silverware; their coat closets; their fireplaces; their arched windows, voussoirs, and embrasures copied, according to brass plaques, from the Palazzo Pitti—were the gusts of wind over wheat fields and the weird, magnificent emptiness of the continent's middle, which no one ever expressly comes to see. At the time this feeling seemed like an insult, and I took it personally, believing that Geanie had left me there to get lost in this abundance simply to remind me that I was out of my league.

I wandered twice through a front hallway, where what I eventually identified as a radiator was hidden by a polished brass screen of fleur-de-lis, and where the ceiling was white plaster that went up into curved peaks, like a bishop's cap. Finally the cook, Myrna, back in the kitchen—a modern place, with stainless steel sideboards—took pity on me and showed me the rear staircase, explaining that "Miss Geanie's room" was the third door on the left upstairs. When I hesitated, she said, "It's all right. Her mother's out now—ain't no one to hear." And so I went up those stairs, carrying a plate of sandwiches she gave me that were the size of squares on a checkerboard. When I knocked on Geanie's door and went in, calling her name, nobody answered me.

"I got sandwiches here!" I said loudly. I set the plate on a carved white chair in the middle of her room, which was normal size, with hockey clothes and graph paper and athletic photographs tacked up to a corkboard above the desk. "Lunch delivery!"

"I'm in the john," Geanie's voice hissed through a closed door. "Shut *up*!"

I went to the hall door where I'd entered. "Hey, pipe down!" I shouted. "We got a girl in the bathroom, and she needs *total silence* for this kind of thing."

My voice bounced off the bishop's-hat arches of the hall below with the shrill, speeded-up timbre of the squash courts in Pemberton's gym. "Total sssssssi-lence," I repeated. This was an imitation of what I'd seen other Pemberton boys do with girls, where the foolproof method was to humiliate or tease a girl you liked—but when I returned to Geanie's room, the door she'd whispered through was still closed. It had a mirror mounted on it, floor length, and I saw myself there, my hair sticking straight up around my cowlick, the pimple on my cheek having finally come to a head.

Retreat was the only option I could think of. It ran counter to my father's advice that I make a demand, but how was I supposed to make demands through locked doors? I went back into the hall. My yells had summoned nobody. The next door down on my left was open, and I pushed in. A wispy filament brushed my arm as I entered, a feeling that in my parents' house suggested a cobweb, but as my eyes adjusted—this room's lights were off—I found that it had been caused by a dry-cleaning bag. In fact, three of the room's four walls were lined with dresses, women's jackets, skirts, blouses hung on metal bars and sealed in plastic. There were, additionally, shoes on shelves underneath, a pair of wicker chairs, and a white wicker table (as if someone came in here to *look* at the dry-cleaning bags), and in the room's far left corner, I noticed an open door through which I could see the back of a bare calf. Walking in farther, I found Geanie standing on top of a toilet lid, her head stuck in a medicine cabinet that opened behind its tank. "What are you doing?" I said.

Geanie jerked her head up so it hit the shelf above and then she whirled around at me, holding a finger to her lips. Then she stuck her head back in the cabinet.

I tried to wait quietly. There were things to look at, including the rear end of Geanie's swimsuit, but after I'd paced the bathroom and opened the locked door on the other end to peer into her bedroom, where I'd started out, I said, "Look, if you want me to leave, just say so. That's fine. But I don't get what I did to you."

From inside the medicine cabinet, I heard a wooden clunk and Geanie withdrew her head again, closing the mirrored door behind her. "Do you even know what I'm doing, before you go around getting upset?" she said.

"No." This was a cross between a shout and a whisper, choked up in my throat. I was so furious and confused about the meaning of this conversation that I swung my arms as if fending off a crowd of bees and knocked over a toothbrush cup, which broke loudly in the sink. "No, I don't know what you're doing," I hissed as I fumbled around, making even more noise as I tried to pick up the broken glass. I said this in such a way as to include not just Geanie, or the room filled with dry-cleaning bags, or the glass, but also the house itself, the goddamn Palazzo Pitti windows, whatever the hell it was that had put together this house in the first place or had caused my father to come here and hit golf balls over its roof. "I don't know what anybody's doing. How am I supposed to know what anybody's doing if nobody's doing anything that makes sense?"

"*You* don't know what anybody's doing," Geanie said.

"I don't!" I was brushing glass off my pants, and little shards tingled in the palms of my hands. Geanie seemed, watching me from her perch on the toilet lid, to be amused at least slightly. "I'm ruining your sink," I said. "That's what I'm doing."

"I'm *listening*," Geanie said. She faced me with mock composure, biting her upper lip as if daring me to laugh at this.

"Okay," I said. I scanned the room—cotton balls, dental floss, a box of tampons on the radiator—trying to figure out what she was listening to.

"Do you promise to be quiet?" Geanie asked. When I nodded, she climbed on top of the toilet again and opened the medicine cabinet. The skin of her back was freckled like some patterned piece of silk, and below that I could see an area where the webbing of her suit pulled away just under her waist, levered out by her rear end. Looking at this caused my nose to run, as if I'd been punched in the face. When Geanie waved at me, I climbed atop her porcelain toilet, with the entire length of her leg, hip, and ribs pressed against me. The cabinet smelled of menthol, and on the floor was a trapdoor, which Geanie pulled back to reveal a shaft.

"It's a laundry chute," she whispered, as if sensing my confusion. "It goes right past my dad's office—listen."

I leaned in; the chute seemed to go down forever, the sides galvanized, the light from the bathroom petering out into darkness. When I turned my head, I heard nothing at first, and then faintly, knocking its way up the metal walls of the shaft, Henry Bowen's vacant cough-laugh reached me.

"Cool, huh?" Geanie whispered.

"Yeah, yeah—real cool," I said, trying to muster a smile. I felt her eyes on me.

"Can you make anything out?"

I tried again, using a finger to plug my topside ear. I thought, just possibly, that I heard my father say, "A sandwich is fine with me." After a few seconds, the shadow of Geanie's head disappeared and I felt her step down, away from me.

"You don't have to tell me," she said, when I came to find her in her room. "I know it's crazy. You can hear parts but not the whole thing."

"I don't think you're crazy," I said. This was partly true.

Geanie rested her chin on her knees. It was the first time I'd ever seen her look sheepish, or in need of reassurance.

"You would if you knew how often I used to stand there."

"Why?" I said. I sat down on the bed and then, with what I thought was surely transparent casualness, let my arm drop from my thigh to the neutral space between us on the bed. To my relief, Geanie didn't flinch.

"To listen to my father talk business," Geanie said. "Or mostly pretend I was listening. Sometimes you really can hear things."

"If you want to know what he's talking about, why not just ask him?"

"Is *that* what you'd do?" Geanie scowled at my hand, which lay between us, palm up, like the fake rubber hands that kids brought to school on Halloween. But rather than deter me, this glance allowed us both to acknowledge that the hand existed, and I lifted it and placed my fingers on the small of her back.

"In case you haven't noticed," Geanie said, "girls aren't supposed to discuss business in the Bowen Company. Girls are supposed to go fetch peanuts. They are supposed to go shopping, like my mom. They're supposed to pay attention to directions, get dressed up for parties, sit around at ribbon cuttings, and raise money for the symphony." She said "symphony" with such disgust that we both laughed.

"C'mon," I said. "It can't be that bad."

"Do you know what my father used to do when I was little and wouldn't eat something?"

"Send you to the symphony?" I said.

"'Eat it or wear it,'" Geanie said.

"Don't kid me."

"That's what he did. It was beans for me. I liked beans, really; what I thought was stupid was the game. But my father used to always tell this story about how, when he was a kid, his dad's rule was 'eat it or wear it.'"

"*That's* crazy," I said.

"No, it really was that way. He used to tell it to company," Geanie said. "And so one time after he told this story, I just quit eating beans."

"What happened?"

"What do you think? I went through a whole summer of having beans dumped on my head. In that tub in that same bathroom where we just were—because after he did it to me once, you know, there was no way I was going to give in."

"That's a funny story," I said. I leaned across then and gave her a kiss. The movement was awkward, more a dart than the confident lean I'd seen Spencer Tracy use in the movies, and because Geanie did not turn her head to meet me, I caught only the corner of her mouth. But neither did she pull away.

"It's not a funny story," she said when I'd finished. When she said this, she *did* turn her face toward me. "I bet your father tells you everything," she said. "So my question is, if I kiss you, how much of it will you tell me?"

When I left the Bowens' house, it was late afternoon. Neither my father nor Henry had called upstairs to interrupt Geanie and me—not that I'd wanted them to—and so I was surprised to find that Henry Bowen's cream station wagon and uniformed driver had already left. Out on the street, I thought my father had left as well until I noticed the Fairlane parked down at the far end of the block and my father himself leafing through a copy of the afternoon paper in its front seat. Reading a paper in your car was an unremarkable activity in our neighborhood, but here he stuck out like a sore thumb.

"Hard for the paperboy to get a good toss over the fence," he said, indicating the wall of iron that fronted the Bowens' yard. "So I told him to give it to me."

"Meaning that you took it," I said, climbing in next to him

My father gave me an appraising stare, as if trying to remember whether he knew me. "Among other things," he said. He folded the paper slowly and handed it to me. "Henry wouldn't change our contract," he said. "But I did accept his offer—designed, I suspect, to prevent me from going to another company—to become a *salaried* member of the Bowen Company . . . at three hundred a week."

It was enough money to shock even me. It was enough money for us to actually become members of the Mission Hills Country Club.

"What about you?" he asked. "Did you take anything?"

"Take?" I said. "What do you mean, take?" But I was flushed. I realized that my father must have pulled down here in order to give me more time with Geanie.

"Oh, I don't know," my father said. "Henry was a little worried about where you and Geanie had gone. But don't worry—I explained it to him."

My father grinned at me as he nosed the car down into the tangled, crisscrossed streets of Mission Hills. I could tell that he wanted to get a rise out of me, that he was pleased I'd been the one to do something that required a cover-up. Despite my instinct to ignore whatever fib he'd invented for Henry, I was happy, and so when I finally turned to look at him—the car was stopped by then at a stop sign—and saw him sucking his mustache and watching me with an expectant air, I couldn't help but laugh. "All right," I said. "For God's sake, I give. I give. What'd you tell him?"

"You promise not to get mad at me?"

"WHAT DID YOU TELL HIM!" I shouted.

"Well, son," my father said. Now that he had me on the hook, he was in no hurry to let me off. Though another car had pulled up behind us, he removed his pack of Luckies from his shirt pocket, shook one out, and pushed in the dashboard lighter, deliberately. "It seems only fair, if *I* was honest about what happened to me—"

"There's people behind us," I said.

"Oh, really?" my father said, not looking. "Well, maybe you better hurry up and talk." He lit his cigarette and rolled down his window and gestured on the car behind us. There were three of them lined up there, and each passed with the driver glaring across the passenger seat at my father, who waved pleasantly back. It was exactly the kind of thing that drove me crazy, especially in Mission Hills, where there was a better-than-even chance that the drivers of those cars had kids at Pemberton. "I kissed her, okay?" I said finally. "Is that what you want? First base! That was it! Is that what you told Henry when you were doing me such a big favor? That I was upstairs getting to first base with his daughter? Isn't it possible for anyone in this family to have a little privacy? Or do we just have to yell everything out in the street—is that it? Is that what you want?" I rolled down my window, though not before I checked to see that there weren't any more cars behind us. "I got to first base with Geanie Bowen!" I shouted out the window to the shrouded lawns and gabled roofs that surrounded us.

"Close enough," my father said. "I told him you had tennis practice."

What I didn't tell my father was that I had seduced Geanie by talking about *his* business, or some of it at least. I had told her, for instance, about the founding of the Alomar Company and the room with the naked waitresses in the back of the Grotto, as we had lain there side by side on her bed, in between our first and second kisses. In fact, despite all my complaints and worries about my father's practice of lying, I had discovered that a lie, or at the very least a story about a lie—since everything I told her was true, actually—could be in certain cases a useful thing. It had been the lies, or the truths that sounded like lies, that had caused Geanie to wrestle with me, that had given her an excuse to be shocked, and to pin my arms back, and to sit on top of me, pelvis to pelvis, in her swimsuit, saying, "My father in a topless restaurant? Run by Italians? You're full of it!" And so, feeling each other in this way while actually pretending that we were only talking, I had told her my stories. I had told her the story of meeting Royce MacVess up at his quarry (a story that was a slight lie, since I didn't mention Nikki); I had told her the story of going to restaurants with my father, told her the story of how my father had kicked his own father in the knee.

"It's not fair," Geanie said. "How come I never get to go out and see any quarries? How come I never get to go to lunch with my father anyplace—unless it's something terribly boring?"

"I didn't go to lunch," I pointed out. "I was hungry."

"I'd rather be hungry than bored," Geanie said on the pillow next to me.

The only drawback to the entire afternoon had been the way Geanie and I parted. After lying there on the pillows for a while, we'd started kissing again until Geanie had suddenly leaned back and said, "What's it taste like to you?" I'd been thinking about this myself because kissing Geanie did taste like something—like the peanuts she'd been eating out on the deck. "It tastes like mouth, I guess," I said. "Your mouth. And since it's your mouth, it tastes good to me. What's it taste like to you?"

"Kind of funny," Geanie had said guiltily. "Not *real* bad, but I was just wondering if it might be better if you brushed your teeth."

I had rolled out of bed, angry that I'd been nice enough not to mention the peanuts, and gone into the bathroom—where I had found the pieces of the glass I'd broken still in the sink. When I came back out, Geanie had slipped on a T-shirt and shorts over her swimsuit. "Are you glad that we kissed?" she asked. When I nodded, she said, "So am I. I'm glad that your father hit a golf ball at my house. I'm glad that you followed me upstairs, even though I got mad. I'm glad you told me your stories, and now, before we argue or ruin a perfect day, you ought to leave."

"So I really didn't taste all that bad," I said.

"Of course not," Geanie said. "But there's one other thing: I'm going to be gone most of the summer, and when I am here, I'm going to be very busy practicing."

Practicing what? I thought. *How about kissing?*

"So I don't want you to call me," Geanie had said. "It's not because I don't want to see you; it's because I *do* want to see you, but just not in the wrong way. I can be rude when I'm gone or when I'm practicing—okay? Do you understand?"

And then she had kissed me once more before I left.

"I'll tell you one thing and one thing only on this subject," my mother said three weeks later. "That one thing is that the way people are in the beginning of something, that's how they'll be. And the most foolish thing you can do is expect them to change."

This conversation took place deep into the month of August, when every window and door in our small apartment was open and we had fans blowing the same hot air back and forth in crisscross patterns across the narrow space. The idea that it was possible to ruin a good thing by trying it too often was something that had made sense to me, at least originally. I'd been willing to believe that there was something special between the two of us, something that needed to be guarded and protected, something that could be spoiled by exposure to the everyday. Besides, here had been something *exhausting* about the whole procedure of kissing Geanie Bowen, as my mother would say. This feeling had lasted about two weeks, a period of time during which I had secretly believed that Geanie Bowen would break down and call *me*. When that illusion failed to come true, then my feeling about the entire experience began to unravel, until the idea that Geanie and I had any understanding between us at all—an understanding that I had enjoyed precisely because it had not been overexamined, like everything else in our family, to the "nth degree"—fell apart completely, and I told my mother everything.

"Maybe my breath was bad," I said to my mother, who, unlike my father, didn't mind talking about sex.

"I can tell you one thing for sure," my mother said. "Whatever happens between you and Geanie Bowen will have nothing to do with your breath."

"Or maybe she just really didn't like me," I said.

"Did she *say* she didn't like you?" my mother asked.

"No," I admitted.

"What *did* she say?"

"She said she was going away for part of the summer and that she didn't want to spoil things. Plus, she said we weren't in a hurry."

"She's right—you're not in a hurry," my mother said. "But I don't know about the spoiling part. It's my opinion that it's best to get the spoiling part over right away."

"So do you think I should call her?"

"I think you need a *hobby*," my mother said.

The Trojans

Every student at Pemberton Academy had one absolutely unavoidable responsibility to his alma mater, and that was to play tackle football on the freshman team. It didn't matter if you were a hemophiliac or a pituitary case or, in the case of Jungle Jim, an actual cripple—when that bell rang for the first day of practice, the trainer handed you a helmet and tossed a mouthpiece into a vat of boiling water that he'd rigged up on a charcoal stove, so the plastic could be fitted steaming to your teeth. It was an "enormous boost to class unity," according to the literature the school sent out, along with the medical releases that parents were to sign, protecting the school in the event of their son's injury or death. But the real attraction was the betting. In freshman football, we didn't schedule other schools but instead divided the class into four squads—the Marauders, Crusaders, Trojans, and Warriors—who played a series of seven-on-seven matches. The familiarity of the rosters added a personal element to the handicapping, especially for those who believed they had some unique insight into the hearts and minds of Pemberton students, and consequently most of our faculty and staff wagered serious money on the games. This had always included the black members of the cooking and cleaning crews, who'd watched peacefully from the east end zone, until Shelly Petersen, the mother of Carl and Preston Petersen, spent a season with her binoculars trained on their dark faces. She'd then presented a report on their use of "unfamiliar African terms" and "what appear to be hexes and/or voodoo" against the players, in particular singling out Elmore Haywood, the middle-school custodian, whom she had seen throw a doll down on the ground and stomp on it during one of her son's games.

Fortunately, the principal knew that his own wife had made the dolls—

G.I. Joes dressed in the uniforms and colors of the Crusaders—which she had passed out to supporters of the team. Second, he knew that both he and Elmore had bet on the Crusaders. Third, Mrs. Petersen's eldest son, Carl, had blown the Crusader's season by muffing a snap late in the game, and the principal knew that if he'd had a doll at the time, he would have stomped on it, too. And so as "punishment," Elmore and the other blacks were invited into the stands, where presumably they'd act more reasonably.

I and the other members of the last heat had for years made sure to sit near Elmore when the freshmen played. He was a giant, shambling man whose pant cuffs were always frayed and who wore a parka with a moth-eaten fur ruff even on warm September days. His normal voice was elastic, sliding and slipping over octaves like those pull whistles that, on the radio, signaled something was falling through the air. But when he cussed at football games, he did it as a white man. I couldn't figure it out at first. There would be Elmore writhing and twisting on his bench, agonized peeps escaping his lips as his team's defense all but turned and hid behind the yard markers. And then, right when the opposing team scored a touchdown and their fans stood up to cheer, you'd hear a voice in what sounded like exaggerated Cockney—the sort of voice that the drama club used to signify poor people in plays—ringing out above the parents' heads:

"The bloody stupid bastards! That lad there on the corner—send 'im back to nursery school if he can't tackle anything. It's a disgroyce, a lousy disgroyce! Ask those fairies to take their bras off, Coach, so they can hit somebody!"

The language in these tirades was so unexpected that when the parents surveyed the crowd for a source, they refused to consider Elmore as a possibility.

There came to be, for me, a strong convergence between Henry Bowen's "Negro question," Elmore Haywood, and my own life. The full meaning of this convergence was not apparent to me immediately—just as the full meaning of Royce MacVess's shouts had seemed like nothing but nonsense when I heard them at the time. In fact, I and most of my classmates had no idea that Negroes posed any kind of question at all. We knew who Negroes were; we understood with a diffuse guilt—but also, if the truth be told, a certain kind of pride—that they, not we, had once been slaves. But this is about as far as anything resembling what might even remotely have been called the "civil rights movement," or even the term itself, came to penetrating the world of Pemberton Academy, or Kansas City in general. That was all the business of the South and not our responsibility. And yet those two words that Henry Bowen had spoken from his backyard deck chair, staring up at the squirrels in his elm's leaves—and the subsequent meeting that he'd had with my father—had, even more than the words "interstate highway," changed my father's life. His new "salary" was accompanied by a new, more secretive project for the Bowen Company. Now he was up at night paging through maps of the city, rather than Kings County. And he seemed more critical than ever of our neighborhood, citing the occasional stray paper cup or older-model car parked along the curb of the Paseo as evidence of decline. I had decided not to ask my father about these things, believing it was a bad idea to ask questions whose answers you don't care to hear.

But when I fumbled in my team's first football game and heard Elmore Haywood's Cockney voice shouting out above the crowd—"It's rigged! It's rigged! Why not just pick our pockets, guv'nor, instead of fixing the games? It'd be more fun to watch than this nasty thing!"—I was surprised to find my father's kid gray fedora two or three rows up in the crowd, his back turned to me, and a pair of field binoculars aimed directly at Elmore in the right-hand corner of the stands.

I was even more surprised, and curious, to find the two of them waiting together on the cinder track, just below the stands, when I left the locker room after the game. Actually, I was surprised to see my father there at all. I'd always assumed it pained him to watch me play sports; my memories of past field days mostly involved searching for his skulking figure underneath the bleachers or amid the trees at the far end of the field. "He wants to be there to watch," my mother told me in such instances. "But at the same time, he worries that his being there puts too much pressure on you. Because his father used to do things that way." I had never believed this, not for a minute, and so I was relieved as I walked up to my father and Elmore Haywood that he seemed interested in talking about something other than the game. "Son," my father said, "I'd like to introduce you to Elmore Haywood, one of the finest defensive linemen ever to come out of

Kansas City. And probably one of the only actual professional football players that you are ever going to meet."

I glanced between my father, dressed in his version of football-going clothes—a full-length camel's hair coat, silk scarf, gray fedora—and Elmore, with his shoulders hunched forward beneath the green canvas of his parka.

"Does he always get that excited about meeting folks?" Elmore asked my father.

"Don't insult the man, Jack," my father instructed. "Shake his hand. If you're lucky, maybe he'll give you an autograph." And then to Elmore he said in an undertone, "He's just woozy. Took a couple shots." He tapped his forehead.

"But I know you already," I said to Elmore. His hand, when I shook it, felt as thick and heavy as a loaf of bread. It was also, I realized, the first time in all these years that I'd touched him. "You *work* here."

"That's what I keep telling this guy," Elmore said.

"He *was* working here," my father said. "But that was before someone came along and told him how he could get rich."

"You're leaving?" I said to Elmore.

"You see that?" Elmore said to my father, pointing at me. "You've gone and scared the kid." Then he squatted down so we were at eye level and leaned his head forward until I felt the tickle of his hood's ruff against my forehead. "Listen, man," he said. "I don't know what Rockefeller over here is up to, but I can tell you in the twenty minutes we been standing here, he hasn't said one true word to me."

"Wait till he tells me I played a good game," I said.

I saw my father wince under the shadow of his hat brim; Elmore lifted a hand to his face. "Let's go," my father said, heading for the parking lot.

"Are you telling me that you run this fine-looking boy down?" Elmore said, following him. "That you aren't fully complimentary?"

"I heard what you said about me, too," I told Elmore.

"Heard what who said about who?"

"'It's a disgroyce, a bloody disgroyce,'" I said, imitating his accent. I and most of the boys in the last heat had learned to curse by imitating Elmore.

"I never heard anybody say *that*," Elmore said. To my father, he said, "Did you hear anybody say that?"

"Do you know what I tell him about football?" my father said. "I tell him football is a stupid game." He had his hands thrust into his coat pockets and led both of us across the white grid of the now-vacant lot, bottle glass and sand crackling under his feet. "It's just he never pays attention to me."

"Disgrace? I never heard anything like that," Elmore said. "Nope."

We'd reached the car by then. Elmore had, as we walked, kept glancing at me over his shoulder, goggle-eyed, as if asking me to be quiet. But, having started, I found I couldn't stop running through a greatest-hits parade of all his curses, sotto voce—Ballocks! Ya bloody poofter! Crikey!—not maliciously, necessarily, though I had been hurt to hear Elmore yelling at me, but because they best expressed how I felt about the game, which my team had lost 28 to 0. The car ended this routine. It was a brand-new Buick LeSabre convertible, blue, with full chrome, whitewalls, and batlike rounded fins, purchased by my father on credit, the day after his first check from the Bowen Company arrived. It gleamed top down in the far corner of the parking lot, facing an empty baseball diamond, and, upon seeing it, Elmore cupped one of its rocketship taillights and said, "Son of a bitch—somebody did get rich," in pure, uninflected American.

My father hunted through his pockets with a studied calm, watching Elmore run a finger along the trunk. When he found his keys, he dangled them at arm's length.

"You want to drive it, El?" he asked.

We ate dinner with Elmore in our apartment. My father made this suggestion as Elmore gleefully jerked the LeSabre to a stop outside the Gramercy. One of our neighbors—Dr. Campbell, a notoriously sullen bachelor dentist—passed by our car, headed for the corner grocery just up the street. His face looked clammy in the elm's shadow and I noticed that as he approached us, he kept his stare steadily on Elmore, his head rotating as if hypnotized, until my father said loudly, "Maybe we should invite Campbell, too, if he's so interested," and the dentist suddenly hurried away.

"Does he always do this?" Elmore asked me.

"Do what?" I said. "Bug people?"

"Have bad ideas," Elmore said.

"You're coming in, my father said decisively. "If you can't eat in my house, you're definitely not going to be able to do this job."

"What job?" Elmore asked. "I've already got a job!"

"Or you can walk," my father said, gesturing after Dr. Campbell.

In all the years we'd lived in that apartment, we'd never had a black man to dinner, and only rarely had we seen one on the street. I was also fairly sure, for all the years he'd spent working around the white students at Pemberton Academy, that Elmore had never eaten in any of their homes. This apparently hadn't occurred to my father, however, who delivered a blunt introduction to my mother—"This is Elmore Haywood. He's interested in the place"—and then disappeared into their bedroom to change, leaving us alone in the front room. My mother was better at handling my father's surprises than I was, and so while I fumed and rolled my eyes at the ceiling—gestures intended to convey to Elmore my awareness of my father's rudeness, but which probably only made things worse—she shook Elmore's hand directly and said in her most hospitable North Carolina accent, "Well, welcome, Mr. Haywood, to our humble abode. I do so love it when Alton brings his friends by. Would you like me to take your coat?"

This kindness only tightened Elmore up more. He *was* in his work clothes, naturally—a burgundy-and-blue jumpsuit whose stained legs showed beneath the hem of his jacket, along with a pair of hobnailed boots—which he probably wouldn't have worn to his own table, much less someone else's. When he snuck off to hang up his coat, my mother caught him and they traded a fusillade of no-thank-yous, you're-welcomes, and I'm-sorrys as if they were trying to levitate the jacket onto its hanger through a torrent of sheer politeness. Then they couldn't figure out how to leave the front hall. "After you, Mr. Haywood," I heard my mother say.

"No, really, please—you go on ahead, Mrs. Acheson."

"I'm sorry, I have to insist. It *is* my house, isn't it?"

My father refused utterly to notice any of this. He breezed from the bedroom in a fresh cardigan, cracked a beer from the fridge, offered Elmore a chair, and, when Elmore refused, he simply shrugged. With a great exhalation of air, he plopped down on the living room sofa and put his feet up. "So what do you think of the place?" he asked, waving his hand. "It's not bad, as far as apartments go. Neighborhood's quiet. In a little bit, if you want, I can have Jack take you on a tour of the place."

I stared at my father. "Dad," I said in protest.

"What?" my father said. He had just lit a cigarette and spread his arms wide, like a ballplayer disputing a score, leaving contrails of smoke squiggled in the air. "Are you embarrassed to show Elmore our house?"

"No," I said through my teeth. "It's just that—"

"It's just that what?"

It was just that I figured that Elmore, being a janitor, probably didn't have as nice an apartment as we did, and it seemed impolite to rub his nose in it, as my father had done with the LeSabre (though, to be honest, Elmore had seemed to enjoy *that*).

"I like it," Elmore said noncommittally.

"So you like it, but not enough to move in," my father said.

"Did I say that?" Elmore said, looking around for another speaker.

"So you would move in," my father said.

"Who?" Elmore said. He'd relaxed some since my father's entrance, allowing my mother to get him a beer, telling her a few harmless lies about how well I'd played, which I'd let pass out of politeness. But my father's repeated questions about the apartment alarmed him. "Is he deaf, or does it just seem that way?" Elmore whispered to me.

"He practices selective hearing," said my mother. She was hurrying past us carrying plates loaded with sliced roast beef and buttered spaghetti, heading to the porch, where she'd set the table. "Especially on subjects that he hasn't bothered to discuss with his family."

Elmore had intended the "deaf" comment to be heard only by me and now made a surprised, buttoned-up face, with his lips crinkled together and his teeth open beneath them. Then, under his breath, he said, "How about some selective talking?"

"That doesn't seem to work," my mother said to Elmore, who could not have known, as I did, that my mother heard *everything*. "Sometimes the only way to control it is to give it something to eat. Outside, everybody, please!"

We all filed to the porch to eat. Elmore looked gray at this exhibition of my mother's hearing and, I noticed, cut his slices of roast beef into very small pieces—pieces smaller than any a man his size could have regularly eaten and survived—as if he figured my mother might be able to hear him chewing, too. But my father attracted most of my concern. He spoke for a while about how he and Elmore had met; they'd played high-school football during the same years, in the early forties, and had even played against each other once in an exhibition game, pitting the best white team in the city against the best black team. But I knew that his discussion about Elmore's moving into our neighborhood—in fact, Elmore's entire presence at our dinner table—fell into one of his favorite conversational styles. In this style he brought up a premise that made everybody present uncomfortable (Elmore's moving into our apartment) and then proceeded to treat it with utter seriousness, until someone would be forced to explain to him *why* it made them uncomfortable, at which point he would feign surprise.

Meanwhile Elmore was talking about his experiences playing defensive line for the Boston Yanks in 1948, a conversation that had evolved into a discussion of the difference between the NFL and the AAFC. "So you have experience working around white people," my father said after Elmore finished his story of being traded from the Boston Yanks to the Cleveland Rams for fifty dollars, plus the cost of his train ticket.

"I also have experience with getting my head knocked in," Elmore said to my father. "That don't mean I want to do it again."

"But you don't think it's right," my father said, "that you should have gotten your head knocked in more because you were black instead of white."

"My head doesn't hurt less."

"Or that Dr. Campbell should have stared at you that way?"

"Dad," I said, "is there some reason why we *can't* just talk about football?"

"Is there a reason why we can't discuss this?" my father asked. "You all laughed at the idea of Elmore living in our apartment because he's black, right? And this neighborhood is white—just like the football teams used to be."

"As far as right goes," Elmore said, "there wasn't any team I played on ever won anything by being right. In football *nobody* is right."

"I agree with you completely," my father said, scooting his chair forward eagerly. "Now we're getting someplace."

"Uh-oh," Elmore said to me.

"Beecause I'm not going to lie to you, El," my father said. "The proposal that I have in mind has nothing to do with being right."

"Why am I not surprised?" Elmore said.

"It has to do with making money," my father said.

"How does he make money by living in our apartment?" I asked.

"He makes money by selling our apartment," my father said.

My mother laughed from clear out in the kitchen. "Oh, that'll make him rich," she shouted. "Selling an apartment that we only rent. Millions

have been made that way. I'm sorry, Elmore, if that's what he's been leading up to all this time. The only good news is that I made a cake. I'll give
you a piece in consolation."

"Does she hear everything?" Elmore said to me.

"I mean the *whole building*," my father said, in a voice that my mother
would be sure to hear. "But that was just an example. What I really meant,
if anybody *cares*, was that he'd start selling several other properties closer to
Elmore's own *neighborhood*."

"How do you know where Elmore lives?" I said. Derailing one of my
father's conversations was a rare feat, and I wasn't giving in so easily.

"I'll bet you and your mother a hundred dollars that Elmore lives between . . ." My father sucked his mustache, figuring in his head. "Independence Avenue and Twenty-seventh Street on the north and south, and
Central and Prospect on the east and west." He held his hand out to shake,
as he always did when certain to win a bet.

I looked at Elmore. "Is he right?" I asked.

"That's where the black folks live," Elmore said offhandedly, but he was
watching my father with an expression that did not match his voice, his
eyes narrowed, in a mixture of suspicion and astonishment.

"But they don't have to," my father said.

"You ever tried to get a black man a mortgage outside of there?" Elmore
asked.

My father banged his palm on the table. "Say I took care of that. Say
you *could* get a mortgage. Say you rounded up all those black people who
have been stuck living in that one square of the city for, what, forty years?
And you told them, all of a sudden—and I mean you, Elmore Haywood—
told them that you were the one man who could get them a house *and* a
mortgage outside of there. I'm talking the immutable laws of America
here, El. If I can get the supply, I want to know if you can furnish the demand."

Elmore leaned forward, stretched one heavy arm across the table, and
plucked one of my father's cigarettes from the breast pocket of his shirt. He
tapped it on the tabletop, softly, as my mother served dessert. "Anyplace?"
he said.

"No," my father admitted. "I'm afraid we'd have to leave any Bowen
Company houses out of this, for the time being. We'd start here, on the
east side."

Elmore raised his eyebrows as if this at least made sense. He was staring now, off beyond the railing of our porch, not toward the street, where the elm's leaves obscured everything, but north along the side of our apartment building, where you could see the fronts of the other apartments and houses that lined Paseo Avenue. It almost seemed as if he were trying to imagine black people living there. "What you're talking about," he said to my father, "is a whole lot more dangerous than *football.*"

"But more profitable," my father said.

Like most things that involved my father, our dinner with Elmore Haywood created more questions than it answered for me. Anyone who had ridden the old Paseo streetcar line, as I had, knew that black people had their own neighborhoods in Kansas City, but I had no idea how this had come about or why it would be, as Elmore put it, "dangerous" for a black person to buy a house outside them. Nor could I figure out what any of this had to do with Henry Bowen, much less the land that my father had spent so much time buying in Kings County, or even the still-unbought farm of Royce MacVess—the very person who, as far as I could tell, had *started* this whole "Negro Question" business in the first place. In fact, once Elmore agreed to work with my father on an "experimental" basis (which meant, in essence, that he refused to quit his day job at Pemberton Academy but instead waited at three-thirty in the school parking lot for my father to pick him up), my father seemed to forget about Kings County entirely and instead talked incessantly with Elmore about what members of the custodial staff wanted new houses and what properties they might want to see.

Fortunately—or unfortunately, depending on how you looked at it—I had other, more significant distractions going on that fall, especially my responsibility to the "institution" of freshman football. The masterminds of this league were our history and English teachers, Mr. Gristead and Mr. Fichte. They'd invented it ten years earlier, back in '50, as a substitute for the smokers that Gristead had organized while a supply sergeant with Patton's Fifth Division on the Marne, where Fichte had met him. We considered it glamorous that they'd seen fighting, since very few of our own parents had. (Henry Bowen, as my father liked to point out, had enlisted in the Hawaiian National Guard in 1940 in an attempt to avoid war.) And in response Gristead and Fichte ran the third floor of Ashley Hall—where they had their "rooms," along with Pope, the math teacher—like a barracks. You'd see them leaning in their doorways during classes, discussing players, Gristead with his mop of curly black hair that always seemed slightly damp, his wash-and-wear slacks, and a series of ludicrously mismatched ties and jackets. And just down the hall, Fichte, in a pair of patent leather wingtips and a three-piece suit, carrying a pocketwatch, the pits of acne scars along his bleak sniper's cheeks.

On the first of September, they had held their draft. By then we'd been in school two weeks and they'd had time to "scout" us, showing up at gym class (along with Pope and a new teacher named Lewis, who coached the other teams) to check our physiques and running us through a series of drills—forty-yard dash, push-ups, pull-ups, tire courses, pass catching— whose results they noted down on mimeographed sheets.

"Acheson, front and center," Gristead had said, calling me out of the line on the first day. He was chewing on his tie as he wrote on his pad. "Have you ever been laid?"

I'd looked around to see if this was serious. Fichte was standing there with his aerated cheeks, smoking a cigarette and looking somber. He said everything under his breath, half an inhale and half a choke. "Maybe he doesn't understand the question."

Gristead was still chewing on his tie, and a stain of spit had begun to darken the backing. "Well?" he'd asked.

"Nossir," I said. "Not really."

"You don't get the question?"

"I haven't been laid, sir."

"Ask if he's got a dick," Fichte said.

"I'm asking if he's got hair on his balls. Half these kids we've got are still ninnies, but this one looks like his anchor's dropped."

"Is that true, kid?" Fichte said.

"My anchor?" I checked the back of my shorts. "What the heck is that?"

"Oh, for chrissakes," Fichte said. He stepped up, pulled back the elastic band of my gym shorts, and looked down at me. "Sprouts," he said.

"Congratulations, Acheson," Gristead said. "You're a prospect."

Gristead and Fichte had built me up as a future star this way for about two weeks. I had potential suddenly. I'd tried to walk in the broken-down way that I'd seen the varsity athletes do, my knees rounded out and my shoulders swaying, as if I'd been thrown from a horse recently and hadn't had time to check for injuries. It had been hard cheese, too, for my old buddies in the last heat, particularly Freddy Prudhomme, who'd slammed his shoes into his locker the day that Gristead had announced my time in the forty-yard dash. While I meandered the campus in my new football cleats—à la Geanie Bowen—I felt a vague and distant sorrow, as if from a parapet, when I imagined how difficult my success must be for Freddy. "Heard Fichte wanted to know if you had a dick," Freddy had said one day. His sinus problem thickened his saliva, and as he held his mouth open to breathe, little harp strings quivered between his teeth.

"Yeah?" I said. "Did he tell you what he thought of it?"

"He did, but it must have been metric," Freddy said. We were learning about that in science class. Freddy kept giving me an appraising eye that I didn't like. "He look different to you fellas in any kind of way?" he asked the members of the last heat. "There's a kind of glow around him, don't you think?"

My stardom turned out to be a ruse, as Freddy had suspected. When Gristead and Fichte discovered that the new coach, Lewis, had drawn the first pick on draft day, they'd chosen me as a "Trojan horse" to get him to waste it. The plan worked perfectly. In fact, Gristead and Fichte had bamboozled Lewis so completely that our team—the Trojans, naturally—had ended up with every member of the last heat. "Meat!" was how Freddy Prudhomme put it when we went down to look at the rosters posted on the athletic director's door. "Meat! We're dead meat! Who is this idiot Lewis? All I wanted to do was sit on the bench for a good team!"

"But look who's *with* you," said George Belcher. He was one of the fattest and meanest kids in our class and had been picked by Gristead to be a lineman on his team.

"Meat!" Freddy was saying. He'd gone off into a corner of the weight room, which was outside the athletic director's office, to lie on a pile of gym mats. "Meat, meat, meat," he repeated sorrowfully.

"I think you forgot somebody," Belcher said. He tore the list off the athletic director's door and carried it over to Freddy.

"Who's there to forget?" Freddy said. "That idiot Lewis picked every goof and retard in our entire class. He didn't forget *anybody*."

"No, seriously, there's somebody here you need to see," George Belcher said. I knew who he meant. After Freddy had walked away, I'd noticed

Lonnie Garaciello's name penciled in at the bottom of our list, out of alphabetical order. (This was the result of another trick by Gristead and
Fichte, who had claimed that he was injured and then *given* him to Lewis
at the end of the draft—to be "friendly," they said.)

"Leave him alone, Belcher," I said. But there wasn't much force to this.
I had slumped on the bench of our Universal gym and begun to unlace my
cleats, which I'd realized now were yet another embarrassment.

Belcher sat on top of Freddy and wiggled the paper in front of his face,
pointing to what I figured was Lonnie Garaciello's name. "Come on,
buddy, take a look," he said.

Freddy made a gurgling sound.

"Maybe he'll even let you hold his mouthpiece," Belcher said.

"Don't choke him, for chrissakes," I said. "It's bad enough as it is."

"I'm not choking him," Belcher said.

He wasn't. In fact, frightened by the dire sounds that Freddy emitted,
Belcher had climbed off the gym mats and stepped away. I came over, and
we stood together, looking down at Freddy. His face had gone white, his
eyes bugged out, and his nose, as usual, was a mess.

"G-GG-rrr," he said to me.

"What?" I said. When Freddy motioned me to come closer, I knelt and
put my ear beside his mouth, so he could whisper to me.

"I CAN'T TAKE IT!" Freddy screamed.

I jumped away, covering my ear. "Jesus," I said. "Take it easy."

"I CAN'T TAKE IT AT ALL!" Freddy screamed. He was lying spread-
eagled on the shiny blue mat, his thin chest heaving. "DO YOU REAL-
IZE THAT SINCE *KINDERGARTEN* WE'VE DONE NOTHING
BUT LOSE AT THIS GODDAMN PLACE? I'M SICK OF IT! I HATE
IT! AND DO YOU KNOW WHAT ELSE? MY PARENTS ARE PAY-
ING FOR THE WHOLE SHITTY THING!"

"It's true," Belcher said, looking again at our roster. "I really don't see
how you guys are going to win any games."

"FUCK YOU, BELCHER, YOU FAT PIG!" Freddy screamed. "I
HATE YOU! I HATE FOOTBALL! THERE'S NO WAY I'M GOING
TO PLAY!"

"Gentlemen?" a voice said from behind us. It was Coach Lewis, standing in the now opened door of the athletic director's office. I realized that
he must have heard everything—and so had probably also just figured out

that Gristead and Fichte had screwed him royally. But nothing in his smile suggested this. It was a grim, pasted-on smile designed to insist that he'd heard no such thing or, if he had, it wouldn't change his determination. "I want to welcome you to the Trojans," he said to Freddy and me. "I want you to know, first thing, that on my teams *everybody* gets to play. The key to football is participation and teamwork. We may not have stars on the Trojans—but we will have a family. I'll see you at drills today."

Then he walked away. The athletic director's office was on the second floor of the gym, and we listened as his sneakers squeaked down the staircase. It was silent for a moment, save for the sound of Freddy's sniffling.

"WHAT A MORON!" Freddy said.

To be fair, Coach Lewis was a decent man in his way. He smiled through the catcalls about drafting "All-Pro Acheson" during practice, as well as the realization that he was going to spend the next year, if not the next decade, with two colleagues who'd just fleeced him of five hundred dollars (the coaches' minimum bet—"To ensure a good-faith effort," as Gristead said). But he was also one of those men who put great stock in the *spirituality* of a football game. He saw no reason the precepts of the New Testament ought not to be applied there, and he believed sincerely, like a man clinging to a board in deep water, that righteousness, fairness, and a quiet but vengeful sense of being wronged would score more touchdowns than talent in the end.

The only person who bought into Lewis's theory that football could be affected by right and wrong was, interestingly enough, Lonnie Garaciello— though not in the way Coach had intended. After our first week, Coach Lewis (having realized the depths of his mistake) gave a pep talk on how Christ, at least in technical terms, had never really won anything, especially against the Romans. But, by sticking to his principles, he had become a great man anyway.

"So what you mean," Lonnie had said, "is that even if we don't beat these guys, we can try to hurt them at least."

"No, Lonnie," the coach had said, "that's not exactly what I mean."

"Because the way I look at it," Lonnie said, "there's a lot of guys on this team who owe a lot of these other guys some pain."

"I thought you were *already* injured," Coach Lewis said, flipping through his draft sheet.

"Mr. Lewis," Larry Stark said, raising his hand, "weren't the Trojans Roman in the first place? So if it's true that we're not supposed to be like the Romans, don't you think that maybe we should change our name?"

"A Trojan is a condom, fool," Lonnie said. "Which is Gristead's way of saying we're all a bunch of dickheads."

"That doesn't seem like a very good name either," Larry said.

"Sprints!" Coach Lewis had shouted, wearing the smile that meant he hadn't heard anything. "We're going to run sprints now!"

We had gotten creamed in our first game—the game after which my father and Elmore Haywood had met me on the track. And the creaming looked like it was only going to get worse, since we'd been beaten by the third-best team in the league, the one coached by Mr. Pope, and had not yet even attempted playing the Crusaders or Marauders, coached by Gristead and Fichte respectively. My tendency was simply to go through the motions. I studied the blocking schemes, learned the proper way to take a handoff, but when I actually went into the game to run the ball, I didn't think about gaining yards. Instead, I ran straight to where the hole was supposed to be (but never was), ducked my head, and accepted the punishment that was waiting for me—losing yards but remaining, according to my way of thinking, blameless of any embarrassing mistake. My father occasionally tried to speak to me about this. Once, riding home from our second game, he'd turned to me suddenly and said, "Son, when that quarterback hands you the ball—don't *think*."

I'd responded by asking if what he meant was that I might as well be unconscious when I ran. But the real truth, the one he didn't understand, was that my style of running reflected the entire ethic of the last heat: We *always* thought. We'd invested years into studying the art of going along with things; we had carefully negotiated our exile status, had politely traded the occasional wedgie, spitball, dogpile, and nickname for the right to be ignored by the boys in the first, second, and third heats. Faced with Gristead and Fichte's treachery, our goal was to think our way into surviving the season with our bodies all in one piece. It was for a kid like Freddy Prudhomme, at 114 pounds, lined up to block the 175-pound George Belcher, to make a lunge at George's shoelaces and then lie safely in the dirt until the end of the play. It was for Elton Bunglehoff, eyes bulging with fear, to make four consecutive offsides because the opposing team's defensive end had shouted "Move!" into Elton's face mask before our center could get the snap away.

The only person who resisted this was Lonnie. It had come out that he was not the same age as his sister, but a year older than her and everyone else in our class—the giveaway being the fact that he now drove his father's green Impala to school every day. Consequently, he was the only member of the Trojans who might strike some fear into the other team. He shaved. He ran fast, had a sculpted chest and biceps, and stood right at six feet. This is not to say he was an athlete. He still ran in a far too upright and spasmodic style, hands flattened out and flapping beside his thighs. He never followed plays. Once Lonnie knew he would be carrying the ball (and after my first few runs, he nearly always did), he would pick out someone in the defense and promise to run over them. Sometimes the results were amusing. Once, after Lonnie singled out Preston Petersen for a beating (a boy who hadn't grown much since sixth grade), Preston had sprinted toward our own end zone to escape, causing Lonnie to run backward with the ball and knock Preston down fifteen yards behind the line of scrimmage—which statistically meant that Preston had registered a sack.

This all came to a head during our third game against the Crusaders, Gristead's team. From the very start, the players on the Crusaders taunted Lonnie in an effort to get him to telegraph our plays. "Hey, Garbage, give this to your dad," George Belcher shouted, tossing an orange peel over our center's raised rump. "And by the way, the next time he comes by my house, tell him to take the trash *away* instead of just standing there? My dad came home and found a big grease spot by the curb the other day."

"Lay off him, Belcher," said the Crusaders' linebacker, Tommy Thompson, a boy who was rumored to have dated Nikki. "Lonnie's dad's not a garbage collector. He owns the dump. Nikki showed me. There's a whole special section where she and Mrs. Garbage throw out their used tampons."

And so on until, on the next play, Lonnie simply ignored the handoff from Billy Eckstein and rushed straight after Belcher and Thompson, leaving Billy Eckstein and me alone in the backfield with the ball, where we were dogpiled immediately.

"That's it," Eckstein said after he and I were finally plucked from the turf at the bottom of the pile. Instead of handing the ball to the referee, he threw it at Lonnie, so that it glanced off his shoulder pads—his best and longest pass of the year. "I'm sick of you, Garbage. Why don't you shut up or get off the field?"

Lonnie ignored the ball entirely; it was probably the least painful hit he'd taken all day. Instead he just limped silently back to the huddle, put his hands on his knee pads, and waited for Billy to call the next play.

"He's right, Garbage," I said. "You're out."

Lonnie spit through the bars of his face mask, a long, viscous string that dangled in the grass between his feet. There was blood in it, I could see.

"Garbage is a faggot," Freddy said.

"At least I *play*," Lonnie said finally. From the creaky way he talked, I guessed he'd had the wind knocked out of him in the pile.

"But you don't *follow* the play," I said. "That's the whole problem. You're the only one of us big enough or fast enough to run against these guys—but it's never going to work if you tell them where you're going to be."

"If Garbage isn't running, who is?" Billy Eckstein asked, in a tone of voice that suggested it definitely wasn't going to be him.

"Let Acheson do it," Lonnie said. "He can run as fast as I do."

"I can't either," I said. I'd had a bad feeling the discussion was heading this way.

"You ever try?" Lonnie said.

The answer to this question was that I *had* tried, which was why I no longer played running back, but I felt the eyes of the whole team on me. "Okay, I'm in," I said.

"It's your call," Freddy said. "But whichever direction Garbage is going, I'd run the other way." Which was how we'd developed our one and only successful play. As we stepped into formation, Lonnie slapped me on the pads and then put his hands on his knees and began to yell across the line at the other team. "Hey, Thompson," he shouted hoarsely. "Yeah, you— the one my sister says has a little dick. How come you ain't calling out a Garbage Hunt now, fool? You want one, you jive suckah? Come on, let's hear you *call* for a Garbage Hunt because the Garbage Truck is coming right now for *you*."

"Shut up, Garbage," Tommy Thompson answered, not very convincingly, in part because he also hadn't grown nearly as much as Lonnie had since the sixth grade

"What's a jive suckah?" Freddy Prudhomme asked.

"Whot the bleeding holdup?" Elmore Haywood shouted from the stands.

"A jive suckah," Lonnie Garaciello said, "is any fool who gets in the Garbage Truck's way. The Garbage Truck is coming, Thompson. You hear me? The Garbage Truck is gonna take your white ass to the dump!"

Freddy was not the only one of us to notice that, during football games, Lonnie Garaciello's vocabulary began to turn black. Nobody cared enough to ask him why he spoke this way, but for the first time I appreciated its effect: Nothing offended white prep-school boys more than being cursed in the tongue of a black man by a classmate who wasn't actually black. The Crusaders' entire defensive line shifted in their stance, their own taunts silenced, focused entirely on tackling Lonnie. Billy Eckstein took the snap and pivoted away from the center holding the ball clasped, top and bottom, like the turnstile in a parking lot. With a yell, Lonnie ran straight through this turnstile and into the Crusaders' line, preceded by every blocker on our team—including, I noticed to my amazement, Freddy Prudhomme himself, who threw his tiny body into the hole with a cry of "MEAT!"

For a second or two, Billy Eckstein and I stood alone in the backfield. Billy was facing our own end zone, his back turned to the action and the ball cupped against his chest. Then he casually handed me the football, which I tucked against my hip and began a slow jog toward the right sideline, as if I were leaving the game.

It was a simple ruse, one that any kid who has played pickup football has tried a million times. And yet, because of the Crusaders' dislike for Lonnie Garaciello, it would have worked perfectly had it not been for one slight miscalculation—the sideline that I ran toward was occupied by the Crusaders, not my own team. "Ball! Ball! Ball!" Gristead began to shout, running down his sideline in the gold suit and vest he wore on game days, as if he were going to tackle me. By then I had only one man left to beat. This was Shaun Lambert, who, like the first-round draft pick that he deserved to be, had stayed in his position on the left end. Once Gristead started shouting, he took two faltering steps in my direction, and then all at once—"Hit Acheson!" Gristead was screaming—we both began to sprint. I'd been running parallel to the line of scrimmage up until then, so that as I turned upfield, Shaun still had an angle to catch me. I don't know why he didn't. I wasn't faster than Shaun Lambert—though I was, as Lonnie Garaciello had suggested, faster than I believed myself to be. I do know that as I turned up that sideline, with Gristead chugging along beside me bellowing, I didn't think about how I looked. I thought about keeping up with Gristead. It was Gristead who'd made me believe that I'd left the last heat, and as I strained every muscle to keep up with him, I felt Shaun Lambert dive and miss, and then I was *just* running, crossing the very same grass and hash marks where, for the past ten years, I'd run in the last heat—only now, for the first time in my life, nobody was ahead of me. "You fuckheads! You idiots!" Gristead was shouting to my right, but I just kept on running.

Lonnie

Lonnie was still the outcast he'd been since sixth grade. He continued to wear precisely the wrong clothes, to comb his hair straight back instead of in a crew cut or a side part, even to curse incorrectly. In the process, he'd managed to avoid fitting into any heat at all, which at Pemberton was a difficult thing to achieve.

He also had a theory on life, one that he expressed to me gradually, like some dangerous and incendiary revelation, during the fall and winter of freshman year. He was an objectivist. I do not mean to suggest that either of us knew this term, or that, given his preference for science over English, Lonnie had ever read Ayn Rand (the English teachers at Pemberton tended toward Tennyson and Hopkins anyway). But the philosophy that he laid out for me contained enough parallels with that of Howard Roark that I would define him as the only *self-made* objectivist I have ever met—though the suggestion that his ideas weren't original would have disappointed him tremendously.

The first and primary point in Lonnie's philosophy was the belief that if you didn't make something, then you were a waste and a drag to society. Car dealers (like Bobby Jackman's father), lawyers, doctors, judges, insurance executives, and bankers—*especially* bankers—all of these were dismissed in one fell swoop as "unproductive" and thus nothing more than leeches on society. The second objects of his scorn were people who lived off an inheritance of any kind, which served to eliminate as viable citizens most of the remaining boys in our class, whose ancestors might have actually made something. Dorian Straithwaite's great-great-grandfather, for instance, had founded the largest paper mill in the state, but since Dorian merely stood to inherit the wealth left over, he was a "freeloader" and nothing more than that. These were prejudices that I could admit to feeling myself, at times, since there were many boys at Pemberton whose popularity seemed to derive from some fortune their family had acquired in the distant past. At the same time I was uncomfortably aware that, with a father in real estate and a grandfather who paid my tuition, they might also apply to me.

I learned most of this philosophy during the rides that Lonnie gave me home from football practice. This arrangement started out as a practical necessity; if my father picked Elmore up to sell houses, and my mother was busy, Lonnie's green Impala was my only ride home. We would usually stop off in the Briarcliff parking lot to pick up Nikki, and while we waited for her to quit gossiping and come out, Lonnie would offer amazingly concise summaries of the income that lay behind the pastel skirts, the "done" hair, the shining new Chryslers of the mothers whose cars lined up with us, waiting for their daughters to appear. "Look at that one, the blonde?" he said to me one day. "Bridget Gilman. You see that big rock on her hand? You want to guess how she got that? Her great-grandfather used to own shares in the Kansas City Southern railroad. That's it."

"But a railroad does something, doesn't it?" I asked.

"Not for two generations," Lonnie said. "What do you think her husband does? What do you think pays for all of that?"

I looked at Mrs. Gilman, a sandy-haired thirty-year-old woman who was at that moment leaning against the door of her car, chewing rather prettily on the earpiece of her sunglasses, and tried to figure out—other than the car and the ring, which were nice—what exactly Lonnie meant by "all of that."

"Does he work for the railroad?" I asked.

In response Lonnie pinched his right thumb and forefinger together, making a circular motion, pinkie lifted, as if stirring a drink. It was a gesture meant to suggest that all Mr. Gilman really did for a living was to stir around someone else's money.

"But he can't just do nothing," I said.

"Advertising," Lonnie said, as if this and nothing were one and the same.

Very often Lonnie would single out one of the mothers and then, once Nikki arrived, tail her out of the Briarcliff lot. This was both a harrowing and a fascinating procedure for me. Lonnie made absolutely no pretense about this tailing. He would run stop signs and take left turns in front of oncoming traffic in order to keep up with his chosen mark, and he tailgated these mothers as they brought their children home along quiet, leafy streets, the Impala's bumper—looming a foot behind theirs—all the more ominous for the fact that the fancier their neighborhoods became, the emptier they seemed to be. This was especially true in Mission Hills, where the white stone replicas of Michelangelo's *David* and Ghiberti's *St. Matthew* that Prudential Bowen had erected on the traffic medians were the only human forms one might see. In the best cases (from Lonnie's point of view), the mother's agitation at being followed would be transmitted to her kids, whose moonlike faces would stare back at us over the passenger seat until the mother reached over and pushed them down out of sight.

It also terrified his sister Nikki. The Impala's windows were tinted so that, with the top up and the air-conditioning on, these mothers couldn't see who was following them—a fact that took some getting used to, since under the direct stares of these women, many of whom I knew, even I tended to flinch away. But for Nikki the windows provided no protection. She was convinced, not without reason, that Lonnie's car would be recognized anyway as the one she climbed into after school every day, and so Lonnie's determined tailing was accompanied by a string of desperate pleas from Nikki, who would spend the entire episode crying on the floor of the backseat. "Please, Lonnie," I would hear her say, sobbing. "Please don't do this—you promised me." Had it been a case of insults, or merely vanity, I might have been able to withstand this more easily. But though Nikki knew of her brother's unpopularity and though she had, under normal circumstances, the sharpest tongue in our class, she always treated Lonnie with delicate respect, as if he were her older brother (which he was, I guess). "Maybe you should lay off," I'd say to Lonnie when Nikki's pleas reached their peak and her skinny red hand had reached around the side of the front seat to squeeze my forearm.

Lonnie was having none of it. His expression during these chases was invariably focused, his broad mouth with its faintly mustachioed upper lip pursed in concentration behind the wheel. Any suggestion on my part that we quit elicited a mocking grin. "Quit what?" he would say. "This is a free country, isn't it? So since when did it become wrong to drive under the speed limit on a public street?"

We finally got busted by the Mission Hills police. Lonnie followed a woman named Mrs. Amberson and her two middle-school daughters to a house on Tomahawk Road, only a few blocks west of the Missouri line. Clearly he'd been mistaken about the mountains of wealth that he claimed Mr. Amberson had put together by "investing in banks out east." The Amberson house was in fact pretty ragged by Mission Hills standards—a small, dun-colored ranch whose shutters had orange seams of rust blooming through the paint. Lonnie glowered at Mrs. Amberson as she hustled her children up the walk with the furious expression of a boy who'd missed a question on a test he expected to ace. Then, as the poor woman fumbled for her keys, he slammed the Impala into reverse, and squealed his tires as he swung around in the street.

Mrs. Amberson must have been quick about calling the police, because by the time we'd retraced our path along Tomahawk Road, a Mission Hills cruiser pulled us over a block west of the state line. There, just beyond the parapet of the small bridge, was a wild, overgrown hillside of day lilies along the edge of Indian Creek. It was the closest thing you could find to wilderness in Mission Hills—a motley, late-blooming bank of yellow that shimmered behind the cop's back as Lonnie rolled down his window to talk to him, embellished by the burgundy leaves of sweet maples. "Mr. Garaciello," the cop said when he'd inspected Lonnie's license. "How nice to have you visiting our little city of Mission Hills. Would you step out of the car, please?"

"I was driving on a public street," Lonnie said through his teeth.

"I didn't ask what you were doing, did I?" the cop said. The man's voice had a loose, jaunty pleasantness to it that was obviously fake. He leaned in through the window and said to Nikki, "Hello, Miss! Maybe you could step out too, please."

"I don't have to do anything," Nikki said furiously.

The cop punched the handle on Lonnie's door and opened it so hard that the door rebounded on its hinges and slammed. "Let's try that again," he said. At which point, *I* got out of the car and waited on the curb until Lonnie and Nikki followed.

"Garaciello," the cop said after Lonnie handed over his driver's license. "Boy, that name sure sounds familiar to me. You think it's just chance that we pulled over some other Garaciello acting like an ass?"

"Could be," a second cop said. He'd arrived late, as "backup," and hooked his thumbs in his belt, perusing Nikki. "Maybe they got an epidemic of 'em in Missouri."

"I was driving on a public street," Lonnie repeated slowly.

"I know, I know," the first cop said. He wrapped an arm around Lonnie's shoulder and pointed down Tomahawk toward its intersection with State Line Road, and the streets of Kansas City, Missouri, beyond it. "But, you see, these aren't really public streets at all," the cop said in his nice, fake voice. "Not for you anyway, or Miss Garaciello, or your thumb-sucking friend over there. In fact, they're really private streets. They're owned by a man named Mr. Bowen, who you've probably never heard of, living where you do, who is also the guy who owns city hall, and the police station, and who pays my bills. I'm not a public cop, you understand. It doesn't work over here like it does in Missouri. This man pays me to protect the people who buy houses from him, and so when one of the people who owns those houses tells me that you did something . . . well, then that's the way I see it. And if you think that's unfair—do you think that's unfair, Mr. Garaciello?" Lonnie was staring straight ahead, his head slightly lowered and his chin stuck rigidly in place. "Well, if you do," the cop continued, "there's a couple things you can do. One, you and your sister here can buy a house in the neighborhood."

This struck the second cop as funny, and he stomped his boot, wiping his nose with the back of his hand.

"Or," the first cop said, "you can go right back there into Missouri where you belong, and keep your wop ass out of here."

"I would," Lonnie said, "if you'd give me my license back."

The cop held the license out and then, as Lonnie reached for it, flicked it like a playing card underneath the Impala. "Jeez," he said. "I'm sorry."

I thought for sure that Lonnie would snap as he wriggled on the asphalt of Tomahawk Road, groping for his license while the two cops leered down at him. That he didn't, I realize now, was probably a sign of how minor a traffic stop must have seemed in comparison to the real trouble that he and his sister had seen. Whatever the cause, he got through it without incident, moving very slowly, as if the effort of being polite had made him delicate in the joints. When we were all back in the car, Lonnie stuck his head out the window and said something so softly that the officers immediately stepped up close to the Impala's door. "What was that?" one said.

"I was just asking whether or not Mr. Bowen gave *you* a house to live in here," Lonnie repeated. "Because if not, guess I'll be seeing you in the city."

Then he peeled out, running a red light, back across into Missouri.

The better question, at least from my perspective, might have been to wonder why I felt so *good* about speeding through that light with Lonnie. After all, I'd spent three years trying to keep my distance as he slugged it out with the popular boys, making sure his reputation didn't tarnish me. I was no great fan of the theory, embraced wholeheartedly by my father, that a person could suddenly arrive at a new understanding of the world and decide to change his life overnight. And yet that fall, it seemed as if something— or at the very least a constellation of somethings—had left me more open to Lonnie's philosophy than I had ever been previously.

The first of these somethings was Geanie. Before school had started, I had found the Bowens' home number in my father's desk and walked up to Tiller's grocery on Forty-seventh and Paseo to use the pay phone, my fingers shaking as I dropped my dime in. I'd always liked that grocery; it was owned by Mr. Tiller, who lived below us at the Gramercy. I'd played innumerable sets of tennis with his boys, Ernst and Jacob, who attended Paseo High School down the street. But once the phone call had gone through, the awning over Tiller's grocery had suddenly appeared ragged in comparison to the awnings over the high-end grocery on the Campanile; the fruit stacked in wooden boxes had looked old-fashioned, unclean, the curb and sidewalk dirty with gum and cigarettes, compared to the Bowens' long, clean, empty street. When a voice had answered on the other end, I'd hung up immediately and, by the time school started, I had lost the self-confidence that had given me the guts to kiss Geanie Bowen in the first place.

Part of the problem was that I worked better as a wingman. I'd grown up waiting for my father to make the first move, to show up at a party where he'd not been invited or at a restaurant where he didn't have the money to pay. My job then would be to follow along, presenting myself as the reasonable member of our team, explaining and apologizing for his actions—and all the while letting the glow of his wildness reflect indirectly off me. But my father seemed content with the Bowens these days. Though they'd refused to change the terms of their investment, the salary that they'd agreed to pay him meant no more impromptu visits to the Bowen house on Fifty-fifth Street. Once I tried bringing Freddy along to meet Geanie as she rode her bike over for her science class, but when she appeared, I glanced to my left and saw that Freddy had dropped back ten feet. He stayed there, making rabbit ears and Chinese eyes—until at last Geanie stepped around me and asked, "Can I help you with something?"

The football season had solidified my interest in Lonnie. It just wasn't that he'd been responsible for the single most successful athletic endeavor of my career—though I would never forget the feeling of standing there in the end zone as a ragged wave of Trojans picked themselves up off the turf and ran, very slowly, down toward me to celebrate. Or the way Lonnie had grabbed my face mask, swiveled my head toward Gristead, and said, "Hey, Coach, *now* you want to come over and check his dick?" That was not reality; the reality was that, as members of the last heat, my friends and I had invested years of effort into separating ourselves from Lonnie Garaciello, making fun of his clothes, taunting him into fights, expecting that in return we'd eventually be allowed to blend in. And yet we'd *still* ended up grouped together with him on a single, God-awful football team. If anything, the success of my touchdown run actually made things worse by giving my teammates and me a reason to *believe*. I remember a series of events from our second game with the Crusaders: Lewis's face all red and swollen, shouting in my face mask, "Take down the doubters, boys!" Then lining up to block with Freddy Prudhomme, who charged into the line beside me, his arm held out like a battering ram with a closed fist. And finally how Shaun Lambert rammed that fist with his helmet, doubling Freddy's fingers back toward his wrist, until I heard a crack.

I fell on top of Freddy as he curled up over his broken wrist, fetus style, so our helmets ended up face-to-face. Because his mouthpiece forced him to breath through his nose, his face guard was an explosion of wet and slimy things, and he kept saying excitedly, "Did we get it? Did we get it? Did we win?"

I waited as Lewis laid hands on Freddy's shoulder pads and prayed, and Gristead came out and toed his rump, suggesting he'd just lost his wind, but in the background what I was listening to was a marvelous Cockney voice, shouting out:

"It's rigged! It's rigged! Why not take 'em out back and shoot 'em yourself, Gristead? Wouldn't it be easier that way, you bloody prick? If the games is fixed, 'ow's anybody gonna get decent odds to bet? Whot's in it for the common man?"

When I came home from the game that night, I found an entire line of people stretching from the front door of the Gramercy Apartments, along our sidewalk, and out into the gutter of the lamplit street. Lonnie and I had just spent an hour driving up and down the streets of Mission Hills, so depressed that we hadn't tailed *anybody,* and now we sat staring at this crowd in amazement through the Impala's tinted front windows. "What the hell is this?" Lonnie said, squinting. "Some kind of party?" The tinted windows made it hard to see outside at night, and so it wasn't until I rolled the window down that I saw that every person standing there in the front yard was black—black women in heavy overcoats holding children by the hand, black men in black wool suits and Sunday ties smoking cigarettes and coughing nervously. As we watched, a young black couple pushed out the door, the man clutching a sheaf of papers that he held up like a trophy. "Down payment!" he said. "Preapproved! I'm moving up, now, y'all don't touch me!" But this was said jokingly and it seemed instead as if he and his wife on their way out touched everybody, shaking hands, laughing, hugging as if they'd just won some terrific prize. "Brother Lawton," said a fat woman, her feet bulging in a pair of tight red pumps at the end of the line. "What kind of paperwork was it they said they was gonna need?"

"Pay stub, Social Security card, copy of your lease," said the man with the paperwork, in a tune that suggested he'd committed this to memory. "After that they just give you a couple forms, you fill 'em out and—zip!—you go ahead and sign."

"Which means," said another man behind the fat woman, "that if you didn't have that little wife with you, you woulda been there all night."

Lonnie turned to me. I'd already explained to him about my father's business plans with Elmore, an idea that—though he liked my father—he disapproved of wholeheartedly. "If Henry Bowen's got the Negro Question," he said. "I guess your father's trying to come up with the Negro Answer."

I would, in a few years, come to a much clearer understanding of what my father and Elmore Haywood were doing on that night. I would come to understand that they had not expected that so many black people would want to leave their neighborhoods so badly (Elmore was not yet the salesman that he would become, and so perhaps downplayed the interest to my father, for fear of disappointing him) or that they would show up by the dozens on a cool October night merely for the *chance* to get on a waiting list for a new mortgage. I would come to feel, as I feel now, that the people outside my apartment had far worse things to worry about than a lost football game, that in fact these black clerks and mechanics and secretaries and gas-station owners and musicians and kitchen workers who paced and waited in the cold atop the fallen yellow leaves of our elm tree *were* the answer to Henry Bowen's "Negro Question." And that, furthermore, my father's effort to sell these people homes in white neighborhoods of the city's east side was simultaneously the best and worst thing he ever did with the Alomar Company.

At the time, as I stepped out of Lonnie Garaciello's car and retrieved my still-damp shoulder pads and football jersey from his backseat, I did not feel this way. I was fourteen years old and had lost a football game. And, having lost, I brought into the house my own spiritual as well as physical stink. It was the physical stink that got people's attention—the shellfish-and-salt smell of my pads and jersey. I had to hold these up above my head in order to squeeze past the line on the staircase. This caused quite a few comments—"Man, something in here smells funky"—in the kind of language Lonnie Garaciello tried to imitate. Other people in line elbowed and hushed these complainers, as if they recognized me, then I recognized *them*. They were members of the Pemberton Academy kitchen and cleaning staff (a natural source of recruits for Elmore, though I didn't think of this then), and I realized, horribly, that they had seen me play.

"Shhhh, now," I heard one woman say as I passed, "that's the boy that lost that game. I have never seen such a whooping—*mercy!*"

"Is that the one they took to the hospital?" somebody else said.

"If they took him to the hospital, fool, you think he'd be standing here?"

"He sho' as hell didn't stand up much during the *game*."

I didn't answer any of this, but even listening to it, I could begin to smell my own spiritual stink. At the door to our apartment, I saw Elmore Haywood in a forest green suit, a brown tie knotted recklessly beneath his throat, and his flattened nose bent over a clipboard, which he swung automatically to stop me. "Hold on, brother," he said, peering back into our apartment, "We got a system here—" but then he turned and saw my face. It was still possible in those days for a young white man—for a white person of any age—to ruin a black person's day due to something as tiny as a fit of pique, and I was far beyond that. A subtle shift in Elmore Haywood's expression, a flicker in his brown eyes, caused the people in the line behind me to quit talking, a silence that spread backward, as if by magic, down the staircase. I pushed past him into the kitchen and tossed my pads hard against the door that led to our rear landing and the laundry. Then, with carefully measured gestures, I opened the oven and found the foil-wrapped plate of food that my mother normally left for me when I came home late.

Our apartment had an open counter that separated the kitchen from the large front room, and as I stood there eating, I overlooked the black couples who had graduated from Elmore's line and were now poring over forms on our sofa, at our dining table, and on nearly every other available chair. It is amazing how much can be communicated wordlessly to people who are used to being forced to read the gestures of white people in order to avoid trouble. In the slightly violent way that I tore the tinfoil off my food, rattled the silverware drawer, gave the refrigerator door an extra push after I'd poured myself a glass of milk, I notified Elmore Haywood and everybody else that I was hostile to their presence there. And furthermore that I could, merely by expressing this hostility to my parents—whose voices I could hear, interviewing applicants in my father's office—immediately have this room cleared and ruin, on a whim, the hour or two they'd already spent waiting to get in. I ate quickly at the counter, and during the few minutes that it took for me to bolt my food, nobody returned my scrutiny.

It was a regrettable display. The only justice that I can find in the situation came after I'd finished eating and had, with furious deliberation, cleared my plate and utensils exactly as I would have done had I been eating alone. Then I went to my room. Its door opened directly onto the living room, which meant that, as I stalked to it, all the people there must have known what I would see. I am also sure that it didn't hurt them not to warn me. Because when I slammed my bedroom door behind me, I confronted a woman sitting on my bed, her blouse unbuttoned, holding a baby to her naked breast.

"I'm so sorry," she said softly, looking up at me. "He's really almost full."

But I was the sorry one, because I had no choice but to turn around and step back out into that silent living room, aware of what an ass I'd been.

An hour later my father came to find me. By then I'd returned to my room, which I'd recently redecorated to suit my new tastes. Certain things had been impossible to change—my father's childhood coverlet, for instance, in a checkerboard pattern that repeated some mysterious English crest. Two matching throw rugs, a lamp painted like a barber pole, a desk in whose front drawer my father's childhood hand had carved his name: PROPERTY OF MR. ALTON ACHESON II, ESQ., an effort that I suspected had taken more time than the actual homework he'd done there. But around these I'd added shrines of objects from our trips to Kings County: The slick back scales of a gar, found in a drained pond. Pieces of fool's gold, flint. Blue apothecary bottles. A deer's skull into whose nose socket I'd jammed a candle which I lit, after putting a Hank Williams record on my turntable and turning off the lights.

"Well, now." My father inhaled deeply through his nose, as if the two of us had just hiked a couple of miles to meet. His eyes twinkled as they did at the beginning of a sales pitch, but he seemed to forget what he'd come to sell and the twinkle faded until his vision went slack. "You mind if we turn that down a sec?" he said, indicating the record player. Then he rubbed his thighs and said, "Your mother, as well as various other people"—he pawed the air vaguely—"has suggested to me that you might not have found this particular night to be the ideal night for our . . . registration drive."

"Why would you think that?" I asked. "I'm just a little worried about your turnout. Maybe I should've asked Coach Lewis if he was interested in a place."

"No, no—really, we're doing fine." My father was generally unresponsive to sarcasm like this, his conscience basically at peace. "Look, Nugget, you know that you can talk to me, don't you? I mean, I know I seem busy—hell, I seem busy because I *am* busy—but I want you to know, no matter what I'm doing, I'm still available."

"We're talking now, aren't we?" I said.

"Yes, of course, son. We're talking."

"So is there something particular you want to ask?"

"Well, *I* don't know. Your mother . . ." Then he leaned in close to me. "Look, I know it's a tough time of change for any young man when he has to go through poo-berty, and I'm wondering if you have any questions."

"Poo-berty? What's that?" I knew perfectly well what he meant, but my father seemed to have mangled the word intentionally, as if the soft *u* somehow made it less embarrassing, and I was too angry to let him off the hook.

"Well, it's just a medical term."

"I don't feel sick," I said. "I do have a business question, though."

"Excellent," my father said. He collapsed against my footboard, relieved. The walls of our apartment were fairly porous, and during this conversation—especially during the embarrassing part about poo-berty— I had been able to hear Elmore's booming voice in the next room, talking to my mother.

"I was just wondering, " I continued loudly, "if you ever talked to Elmore much about Tom Durant."

My father's expression, rather than the worry I'd expected, contained instead a guarded smile—quite possibly pride.

"Because, you know, in this book about him"—I produced from the far side of the bed a copy of *A Railroad to the Sea,* the story of how Tom Durant had gained control of the Union Pacific, which my father had given me, inscribed, when I was eight. I had not actually been reading the book; my father had told me enough of Durant's story already, but I cracked the pages and thumbed them for effect—"they say he made all his money by owning land near the railroad, right? Or in your case near the highway. And that, in fact, land that wasn't near the railroad—or the highway— actually got cheaper once the railroad, or the highway, started up." I snapped the book closed with one hand, in what I considered to be an impressively self-confident gesture; it was also, I realized, one that Lonnie might have made. It was difficult to read my father's expression with the candlelight flickering off his full cheeks. The pride remained, I think, a smile tucked back somewhere along the corners of his lips (though his mustache always hid the wrinkles that would give this away). But there was still a vagueness to his stare as if, pleased with my reasoning, he had also caught sight of something—or someone—whom he mistrusted just behind me.

"And why should I tell Elmore that?" he said.

"Because," I said, "houses that you and Elmore are selling these people, they're not anywhere near the highway. I mean, if you think about it, they couldn't be farther away. So I'm just wondering how you figure it, if the land that you bought in Kings County is going to go *up* in value, then what's going to happen—"

"Did you apologize to that boy?" Elmore's bass voice jolted suddenly through my door, overlapping my sentence in a way that suggested he hadn't overheard.

"I am making our apologies," my father said.

"*I* ain't got nothing to apologize *for*," Elmore said.

"Elmore has asked that I make clear that he suggested I check with you, or at least inform you of tonight's event ahead of time," my father said. "Which I forgot to do."

"And that Gristead's an ass," Elmore said.

"Good night, El," my father said. He aimed his placid, salesman's smile at my door until we could hear Elmore, his voice excited in triumph— "buzzed," as my classmates would say—move away, saying good-bye to my mother in the hall. Then my father turned back to me, staring again in his queer, distant way.

"It's just a theory," he said, "what Mr. Durant says."

It was also the first time I knew for sure that my father had lied to me.

Lonnie's voice, among all these voices, became the only one that made any sense to me. The truth was that when I sat beside him behind the tinted windows of the Impala, I enjoyed the fear that I saw in the eyes of the Briarcliff mothers as they glanced back at us in their rearview mirrors. I enjoyed my invisibility. It would have been better to chase home the mothers of the boys on the Crusaders; it would have been better to chase home Gristead or Fichte (and Lonnie and I developed, in our private fantasies, many plans for doing just such a thing). But they would have recognized Lonnie's car for sure, and so, in our clouded logic, frightening the mothers of sixth- and seventh-grade girls—girls who would grow up to date boys on the Crusaders—and removing for a few minutes that certainty that they were safe, seemed to us the next-best thing.

I can see, in retrospect, that there were reasons for this darkness of mind—reasons I could not have explained to myself back then, much less to my father, no matter how many heart-to-heart talks we had. I agreed with Lonnie, Freddy, and Elmore; as members of the last heat, we were losing a rigged game. And while I'd felt sorry for Freddy, squirming there on the ground, at the same time I had wanted desperately to get away from him, to avoid touching him or looking again into his snot-ridden face, for fear that I would end up injured, too, before I had a chance to escape.

Which was where Geanie Bowen came in. That fall and winter, I occasionally walked her back over to the girls' school after her science classes, but I couldn't summon the courage to do much more than that. On a rainy January afternoon, I followed her out to the parking lot, only to find Mrs. Bowen and her driver waiting in the cream station wagon. "You want a ride?" Geanie asked. It was a mistake to accept. The Buick's seats were of a pale white leather, buttoned and hand-tufted, and climbing up on them was like getting in atop a mattress. Up ahead I could see the shell of Mrs. Bowen's hair as shiny as a cricket's back and a single curl along the bottom edge; underneath, a white neck. After two blocks she called out, "Geanie, is there somebody else in this car?" as if we were all lost from each other, in the dark corners of an immense cave.

"Yes, Mom," Geanie answered. "I'm surprised you noticed, but this is Jack Acheson, a friend of mine, who sometimes walks me over to our campus."

"Well, how in heaven's name does he get back? Can he walk?" Mrs. Bowen said. This was something of a problem, a fact that I did not care to admit.

"No, he can't walk," Geanie said. "He's crippled."

"I've got something to pick up," I said. "A test. If you want, you could let me out right here." Geanie kicked me for this, with a scrunched-nose look that implied cowardice—or at least that she expected me to stand up for myself better than that. But there was a strange, frantic calm in that car that seemed dangerous to disturb. I had felt something like it on a trip to St. Louis when my parents and I had taken a tour of a cavern whose ceiling rustled with nervous bats. "Well, I hope he has an umbrella," Mrs. Bowen was saying. "I'm afraid I simply can't spare the car today, even for someone dead."

"Why don't you ask him yourself, Mother?" Geanie said. She spoke in a calm, overdetermined voice that didn't do much for the tension. "Jack, my mother here is very busy and seems concerned that you're going to steal her car. Would you like to reassure her, given that never once in this conversation have you suggested that?"

I would be lying if I did not also admit that a portion of my interest in Lonnie stemmed from the fact that he had a car. One day in March—a day warm enough that Lonnie had decided to put the Impala's top down and peruse the homes of the idle rich directly—we picked up Nikki at Briarcliff and followed the curves of Briarcliff Drive from the bluffs above Brush Creek to Geanie's street. "Westbrook," Lonnie said authoritatively, pointing to a pillared stone palazzo on the corner that looked more like a museum than a private home. "And that one's Pickering," he said, indicating the house across from it, whose upper floors flickered with rubies of stained glass. "The banking family. They built it anyway—I think one of the kids might be living there." At the end of the block, we began to pass the familiar wrought-iron fence that bordered the Bowen property, and through it I could see the walnut grove and the sunny, pale green slope of lawn where the summer before my father had dumped out his bag of range balls and taken his stance. "Whose place is that?" I asked Lonnie.

Lonnie squinted his eyes and cocked his head at me, dropping from travel-agent diction to his own version of black speech. "You kidding me, fool?" he said.

"Even I know this one," Nikki said from the backseat.

"Why would I be kidding?"

"Are you telling me that your father works with these people and you don't even know where they live?" Lonnie asked.

"My father works with what people?"

"That's Geanie Bowen's house," Nikki said, leaning forward so her chin hung over the Impala's red leather seat. There was a mocking, teasing tone to her voice, directed at her brother. "Lonnie has her in *chemistry.*"

"Bu-u-ll," I said, drawing out the word. I'd turned to stare at the house myself, in part to prevent the Garaciellos from reading my expression.

"Bet me," Lonnie said.

"Don't do it," Nikki said. "He never bets unless he's sure of winning."

Nikki did not know, apparently, that her brother was in fact famous at Pemberton for making bets that he couldn't hope to win—foolish bets, desperate bets, bets based on his desire to rearrange the unfortunate truth of things.

"Sure, I'll bet," I said, holding out my hand. "What for?"

"Five," Lonnie said.

"For that money you've got to prove it."

"Prove what?" Lonnie said. "There's the house! We're *lab* partners. What do you want me to do, look it up in the phone book?"

"We gotta go in," I said solemnly.

Lonnie smiled. He had, by that time in his career, traded in his mother's suits for a uniform of translucent silk shirts (nobody at Pemberton, even the mothers, wore silk anything) printed with vaguely Hawaiian designs, their already short sleeves rolled up to reveal the tops of his biceps. The wind had blown his hair more straight up than usual, and as he sat there studying me, there was—in the flatness of his nose's bridge, in the smallness of his dark eyes—an almost Asian cast to his face. As an answer he threw the Impala back into gear. "Oooh," Nikki said from the backseat. "Lookee!"

I had spent the last six months trying to imagine a scenario in which I somehow "by accident" ring Geanie Bowen's doorbell without also imagining that I would, in the process, seem like an utter loser. But sizing up our group, as we waited on the Bowens' doorstep—Nikki in her corrupted-schoolgirl outfit, tartan skirt, blue oxford rolled up at the sleeves, a pair of her father's tortoiseshell Wayfarers (the kind whose glass was green) propped up on her windblown black hair; the Impala gleaming out there in the drive, engine purring; even Lonnie in his wild silk shirt, who, stone-faced, had jammed a toothpick between his lips—I realized that we looked pretty cool. Compared to everything else we'd done together, conning Geanie Bowen suddenly seemed like a piece of cake.

"Just don't act like idiots, okay?" Nikki said, the spring wind whipping black spines of hair about her cheeks. "And whatever you do, don't tell her we're here on a bet. That would be too mean."

The door opened, and the face of Myrna, the cook, frowned out into the windswept brightness where we stood. "We came to see Geanie," Lonnie said in a lazy voice, and behind Myrna I heard the thud of feet down a staircase and Geanie's pale, gangly figure coming toward us through the main hallway.

"Hey," she said, a little breathlessly—as if, just before Myrna opened the door, she'd been running instead of walking. "Lonnie? Jack?" She squinted into the light.

"It's Nikki," Nikki said tartly.

"Yeah, wow . . . so that's cool. Did you guys just drop by?" When she smiled, her teeth gave off a metallic flash that she quickly covered with her upper lip.

"We came to give you a ride," I said.

Nobody objected to this idea. Geanie seemed both pleased and flustered, though it was hard to read her expression, given the way she kept her lips pulled down over her teeth. "Bring a swimsuit—and an extra one, if you've got it, for Nikki," I continued. "We're going to go swimming in an old quarry."

The words leapt out as if they'd been waiting there all this time.

My father had never given me any books on how to entertain a girl like Geanie Bowen—the kind of girl who, according to Lonnie's philosophy, we ought to have been tailing home rather than inviting her to ride in the front seat. Even the short drive we made from Geanie's house to Kings County Boulevard, on our way out to the highway, testified to this. On our left we passed the rolling fairways of Mission Hills Country Club golf course; we passed the clubhouse of the Campanile Racquet Club and its compound of private courts—crowded on this sunny day—and then took a left on Forty-seventh Street (also named Bowen Boulevard) past the grounds of Pemberton Academy. All of this was or had been owned by the Bowen Company. So perhaps it is not surprising that, as we cruised down Kings County Boulevard (a continuation of Bowen Boulevard by another name), that Nikki leaned over the Impala's seats and began to tease Geanie. "So when did you get the braces?" she asked. "Was it, like, surgery?"

I had never known Geanie Bowen to get embarrassed about her appearance, and yet it was clear, from the tension in the soft white tendons of her neck, that these "braces"—a fairly new invention in those days—made her self-conscious.

"I'm sorry," Nikki shouted into the wind. "I can't hear you! I was asking about the braces. On your teeth. Not that I think there's anything wrong with *your* teeth, but I heard they were really good for correcting an overbite."

Geanie had turned around by now, her face so flushed that her freckles had nearly blended in. But since she could not shout without removing her lips from her teeth, her answer was buffeted away from us.

"What?" Nikki said, cupping her ear.

"She said her mother made her get them!" Lonnie shouted testily.

"You must have a really nice mom!" Nikki pounded Geanie's shoulder in mock appreciation. Then she lifted her chin and retracted her lips, curling her tongue back over an uneven spot where one front tooth overlapped the other. "Mine are a *little* crooked, but for you—those things are supposed to do wonders with an overbite."

By this time I was hauling on Nikki's elbow while trying to maintain a neutral expression, as if I hadn't heard anything.

"Well, it's true," Nikki protested. "I'm not saying she looks bad or anything, but why else would you get braces, if you didn't have something to fix?"

That spring, the interstate was still unfinished. Though the road had been paved through Kings County, no one had figured out how to weave it through downtown and so we got on it west of the city, in the middle of a vast dirt valley. As Lonnie goosed the Impala up to eighty, it felt like we were speeding down the bed of a river whose water had been sucked away. I was fairly sure my father had bought some of the fields that shimmered hazily on either side of us, but looking at them from the highway was like watching land on television; they seemed too distant to be real. When we pulled off on a gravel exit (the ramps were not yet built) near Royce MacVess's ranch, we saw that the country itself had changed. In the backyards of the farmhouses we passed, clotheslines blew and rattled emptily and the doors of these houses had been left open, banging in the wind. In many fields the hedgerows—perhaps the same hedgerows where Nikki and I had hidden, though by then I'd become disoriented and couldn't say— had been cleared, the brush from them pulled out into burn piles in the center of the fields, some of which were still smoldering. After a while the fields themselves, the milo stubble and the gulleys along the road darkened gray with soot, and bits of cinder blew down the roadway toward us. When the road crossed a small creek, I could see over the girders of the one-lane bridge how ash had gathered in billows along the bank, and occasionally the wind blew a chunk out, which spun like soap suds across the water's surface.

We all went silent, seeing this, including Geanie, who must have wondered why we'd brought her to such a place. Then Lonnie took a left, and we rolled up to what I recognized, belatedly, as the Wilcox homestead. I had worn an ascot and sat in a kitchen there staring out at the back paddock as my father signed papers on that property, but the back paddocks no longer existed, nor did the kitchen. The house in fact was gone entirely,

leaving only an open foundation in its place, and the grounds themselves—
the paddock fencing, the barn and outbuildings—had been replaced by an
equipment dump for the highway crews (who had paid rent to my father
for the privilege, I would learn eventually). Their trailers were emblazoned
with the name ANSI CONSTRUCTION, and the lawn around them had been
worn down to tire ruts and was strewn with stacks of rebar and iron joists,
piles of lumber, front-end loaders, backhoes, chains, cement mixers, iron
pipe—a football field of objects, as if some great oceangoing vessel had
been run aground and dismantled there. Lonnie slowed the car down
briefly, and we all just stared at it, grasshoppers lifting and buzzing from a
single strip of grass that remained between the road and that property.
Then we drove on to where the road ended in a cattle grate and a gate
marked with the sign FLATROCK RANCH—PRIVATE, and I hopped out to
free the latch and waved the Impala inside onto Royce MacVess's land.

When I got into the car again, I saw that Geanie had hooked her index
fingers into either corner of her mouth and, lips pulled back, was giving
Nikki a full view of both rows of braces, upper and lower. With her mouth
stretched, Geanie tried to say something, without much better results than
she'd had trying to speak with her lips closed. Then she took her fingers
out—they were wet with spit—and said, "So you want to touch them?"

Nikki was taken aback only for a moment; then she glanced slyly at me
and shouted, "With what?"

"You can use your hands," Geanie said.

But it was Geanie's reaction to the quarry that, for all of us, I think,
somehow saved the day. Lonnie found a shallow place in the creek where
we had camped with our parents originally, and from there we followed an
old dirt road that curved behind the quarry's hill and spilled out into the
open meadow up above. "My God!" Geanie said, as we pulled in. "How
did you find this place? It's like a church or something."

"It's the oldest quarry in the county," Lonnie said, with an authority
that surprised me, since, as far as I knew, he'd never been here.

"They used to take the stuff out by wagon—that's what this road must
be here for, don't you think?" Nikki said.

"Had to be," her brother answered, screwing up his eyes judgmentally.

"Amazing," Geanie said.

"But there were Indians before that." I was pissed that Lonnie had
stolen my story. "You can pretty much find arrowheads anyplace."

"Hooo!" Nikki shouted in her version of a war whoop. "Hooo! Hooo!"

"You mean these?" Geanie said, picking up a piece of gravel from the rim.

We changed (the girls into swimsuits, Lonnie and I into gym shorts) and climbed down in our tennis shoes toward the quarry's base. The walls towered overhead, blocking out the surrounding trees until glitter was just a cavern of sky above and we were engulfed by a strange stillness, the only sounds being the spatter of water down the cliff walls and the echoing scuffle of our feet until we reached the bottom, beneath the ledge where Nikki and I had met Royce MacVess. At the water's edge, I eased my foot down into the pool, feeling for the bottom and then saw Geanie's sneakers flash past. I pivoted just in time to see her hit, hands raised above her head, the pale water closing over her head. She surfaced a few seconds later with a triumphant gasp, shouting, "Oh, my God, it's *deep*!" Nikki went in next, shouting, "Son of a b-i-i-i-tch!" as she plunged over the edge. Then, emboldened by their laughter, I took a run and hurled myself into space, doing a cannonball right between them. The three of us spent the next fifteen minutes alternately clambering back up the rocks to the roadway for another jump and backstroking lazily around the pool, discussing the perfections of the place. "There's no mud," Geanie pointed out. "I think there's some mineral things with the water, too," Nikki said. "It feels clean." "I bet in the summer it stays real cool," I said, "being shaded down here like it is." "So nobody else knows about it?" Geanie asked.

"Nobody except this old weirdo that Jack and I met on our first day," Nikki said. "He was one of the first settlers."

"And he doesn't care if you use it?"

"Not after Nikki hit him in the balls," I said. I decided not to mention that this "weirdo" had *also* cursed Geanie's grandfather at the highway opening.

"It's abandoned," Nikki said.

"So it could be like a club, then," Geanie said. "I mean, we could keep it a secret and just come here and never tell anybody."

"If it's going to be a club, it should have a name," Nikki said.

"It's the Surveyors' Club," Lonnie said. He'd avoided the water and had instead climbed down the rock ledge, looking for "fossils"—or at least pretending to do so. Against its pallor, his eyes were dark and glittering. "We call it the Surveyors' Club because we found it when we were surveying, and to get in, each one of us has to do something that we were afraid of doing before we came here."

"How about just the Idiots' Club?" Nikki said.

Lonnie ignored this. He dipped his hand into the pool and splashed his face, smelling his palm, as if the water itself might make him sick.

"And since I'm the oldest, I go first," he said. He stood up, waved one foot over the water, then stumbled and fell back against the shifting rocks. "Which means I'm going to swim," he said sheepishly. "Or try to. But the other rule of the Surveyors' Club is that the other members have to help each other conquer their fear."

As soon as he stepped off the rocks and into the water, both Geanie and I swam toward him as quickly as we could. "He doesn't know how," Nikki called, dog-paddling behind us. "Be careful, he starts grabbing things."

When Lonnie bobbed back up to the surface, he held himself completely stiff, his hands flat out to his sides in the same odd position he used for running—as if by remaining still he somehow believed that the water wouldn't notice him enough to drown him. When Geanie and I caught him beneath the armpits, I could feel his muscles quiver, a frightening sensation, since those muscles—the flare of his biceps and his strong back—could have easily dragged down both Geanie and me, had he started to panic. As we towed Lonnie out to the center of the pool, the limestone walls leaned in toward us and a high prairie sky arched and brightened beyond them, a dome of white and blue glass. He was truly a terrible swimmer, and the small waves our bodies made in the pool's surface kept filling up his mouth. "So what we're going to do, for my test," he said, shivering, "is go down and touch the bottom."

"That's nuts," I said. "Come on—this is good enough. You're out here, right? Even Geanie said she couldn't touch the bottom jumping in."

"I did later," Geanie said.

"Still, what's that going to prove?"

"It's only going to count," Lonnie said, "if it's something that makes you really afraid. Besides, it shouldn't be all that hard. You guys just grab my hands and take me down. I'll hold my breath."

"Close your mouth," Geanie said. "And whatever you do, keep breathing out through your nose as we go down."

It was foolish, as I'd said; we had all outgrown the age of secret clubs and magical promises of friendship—though perhaps the fact that we'd never been asked to join such clubs or make such promises when we were younger made this seem more reasonable in some way. We joined hands there in the middle of the pool, Geanie and I on either side of Lonnie, and we counted to three, inhaled, and dropped beneath the surface. It was hard to make any progress while holding on to Lonnie, so I let go and swiveled around into a dive. When I opened my eyes, I saw Lonnie with his chin tucked against his chest, sinking down into the pearly grayness below, and across from me, her hands palming the water gracefully, was Geanie, her green eyes open, knifing after him.

Moving Day

During the summer that followed our first trip to Royce MacVess's quarry, we made a dozen more outings, deep in the midwestern heat, when the limestone walls beaded with sweat like a refrigerator and the four of us sunbathed on towels down along its rocky beach—and returned home, often as not, with our knees and ankles blistered with poison ivy. We toyed with Lonnie's idea that we should do things that frightened us, but none of our phobias seemed practical (Nikki, for instance, said she was afraid of getting fat) and finally Geanie came out against it. She was, in her peak form, a great appreciator. It is possible to argue that this ability to see the best in something was, at its heart, a Bowen quality—that only a man of insane optimism, like Prudential Bowen, would claim that a shopping center built on a former pig farm should be a model for shopping centers all across the world. But Geanie, I'd noticed, applied this talent to people instead of real estate. During that summer, it felt as if she was slowly transforming us, singling out aspects of our personalities that we'd taken for granted until, as she'd done with me in the Westbrook orchard, she managed to create for us roles and abilities that were far from normal—that were, in her estimation, "purr-fect."

Two weeks before the start of school, I organized a fishing trip along the creek that bordered the quarry's hill. It was a cool, late summer's day and as I perched on the limestone ledge that I'd first visited with Royce MacVess, peering through my father's binoculars at our campsite below, I could already see evidence of the changes that Geanie had instituted. Nikki, for instance, had abandoned fishing early on and was, despite the temperature, laid out on the grass in a skirted bikini, working on her tan. I hadn't considered Nikki much of a beauty, even when I'd nearly kissed her beside the quarry, but under Geanie's appraising eye, she'd begun to *act* pretty, at least. She was also the only one of us to date outside the group, and her stories about Tommy Thompson (many of them unhappy, since Tommy wouldn't officially agree to go out with her) had become, in Geanie's hands, evidence of her siren status. Meanwhile, Lonnie had buried his nose in an issue of *Popular Mechanics*. I'd known about his interest in science for some time. For years, his notebooks had been covered with drawings of planes and rocket ships. But Geanie, who shared his advanced science classes (as I did not) had transformed these drawings into evidence of his bright future as an "aeronautical engineer." Against all odds, Lonnie had become our brain.

My role with Geanie was similar to the role that Nick Garaciello had laid out for me, back when I'd first met him in the Grotto's john. My creativity—i.e., dreaming up a fishing trip—as well as my powers of observation seemed to be what stood out for her, made her laugh, and caused her (so I hoped) to be attracted to me. And it was through the license of this attraction that I'd convinced her to sneak up to the limestone ledge with me. "So what do you think?" I asked, handing her binoculars. "Right about here Nikki hit this guy and we both had to *fly* down this hill."

Geanie stuck out her lip as she squinted into the eyepieces.

"Sorry I'm not quite as exciting," she said.

"Are you kidding?" I said. "I didn't want to be here. I felt like I should have been going to tennis practice instead of running away from a nutcase."

"What about Lonnie and Nikki?" Geanie asked. "What did they think?"

"Look at them," I said. "Do you have any idea what we were like back then? Lonnie was getting beat up at school every day. Nikki was giving me rate calls in the bushes. I had no idea what my father was doing, really. I'd heard of the Bowen Company, but I'd never met you. Trust me, everything that's happened since then has been an upgrade—including the fishing."

"I guess your stories just make it sound so much more exciting," she said. "Before you upgraded to fishing."

"You're the upgrade," I said. "We were like some sort of lost tribe before this summer—hell, we didn't really know enough to like the quarry before we brought you here. The only thing that worries me is what I'm going to do with them when school starts and this all has to end."

"What do you mean?" Geanie had flushed beautifully at my compliment. "We've got tons of time. I'm not going anyplace."

"Last year I barely saw you once classes started."

"Was that my fault?" she asked.

"I know I wasn't the person who said not to call."

"I said not to call during the summer."

"Well excuse me for not getting the message," I said. "It's not like I wasn't around. It's not like I didn't drag Freddy out to wait for you when you rode over for class. I mean, that's something Nikki would do, right? Tell a guy not to call and then wait around for him to read your mind?"

Geanie was laughing by now; she covered her face with her hand. "Fine," she said. "Fine, you got me. Guilty as charged. Although"—she pointed a finger at me, still laughing as I grabbed it playfully—"you've got to admit it worked."

"What worked?" I said.

"You eventually showed up, didn't you?" Geanie said.

"Maybe I shouldn't have."

"Are you kidding?" Geanie said. "I was bored stiff that day. Do you know that you are the only friend, in all the years I've been in school, who's ever just dropped by my house?"

"So what are you complaining about?"

"*I'm* not complaining."

"So what are you doing?"

"I'm giving you another chance," Geanie said, leaning in toward me.

"To do what?"

"Read my mind."

Which was how, nearly a year after our first encounter in her bedroom, I managed to kiss Geanie Bowen again. As for what I'd said, every word of it was true. The view from the limestone ledge, which had seemed so drab to me when I had visited it with Royce, seemed transformed when I imagined it through her eyes—the fields broader and more majestic, the vast stands of corn alive with light. Even the new scar of the highway off to our right seemed impressive. By the time school began, Nikki and Lonnie seemed to be used to looking the other way when Geanie and I wandered off to the limestone ledge, or held hands, or climbed underneath a blanket to make out at the drive-in movie—or when, as we all sat talking on the submerged rock ledges in the quarry's pool, Geanie slid up between my legs and pressed her back against me.

We weren't quite dating, technically, but it felt close enough to me.

Sex, however—real sex—was a more complicated issue. Geanie was the first girl I'd ever met who seemed completely unembarrassed about the subject. At the Pemberton and Briarcliff schools in 1962 (a place where the sexual revolution of the sixties didn't arrive until the early eighties, when Republicans began to have sex, too) this was about as common as finding people who were willing to discuss the speeches of Malcolm X. At Briarcliff even the girls who were rumored to have sex—Nikki Garaciello herself being one of them—never admitted it openly. While at Pemberton we generally felt comfortable talking only about homosexual sex. It was natural, and considered funny, to tell a fellow classmate to "suck my dick" or to inform a squash opponent that he should "spread his cheeks and grin"— all phrases that Lonnie, who was often the recipient of such comments, was deeply familiar with. The closest thing we had to a technical discussion of sex with women could be found in a crawl space under the football stadium press box, called the "bad-word house." There, on the underside of the press box floorboards, generations of Pemberton boys had drawn intricate diagrams and scrawled exhaustive vocabulary lists on the subject, which meant that you could always find three or four sixth-graders huddled in its shadows during football games, contemplating the mysteries overhead.

Geanie had no such reticence. She discussed sex scientifically, in much the same curious way that she'd asked me how to throw a fastball in the Westbrook apple orchard. It was hard not to imagine, as she asked these questions, that she did not practice by herself in some way. "What's it feel like when a guy has intercourse?" she asked us once as we sat in Lonnie's car at Winstead's drive-in. "Do you think it feels different than it does for girls, or the same?"

Nikki immediately handed her banana split to Lonnie, who set it back on the tray that was hooked to the Impala's window. "Does anybody have any idea why she always asks these questions while we're eating?" she asked.

"I don't see why it should do anything to your appetite," Geanie said. "People are supposed to like sex, right? Isn't that why everybody's here on dates?"

She had a point. It was a Friday night in August, and most of the cars around us (other than ours) were occupied by couples.

"The reason that they're all here in their cars, instead of eating at their parents' house—which would cost less—is so they can have sex later, right? So why should they be disgusted to talk about it beforehand?" Another of Geanie's habits when talking about sex was to speak loudly and clearly, even in public places. The day's heat still lingered in the air; the Impala had its top down, and yet the woman in the car next to ours—someone who *was* on a date—had started furiously rolling up her window.

Lonnie and I both leaned out that way. "Excuse me, miss," I said. "We have a friend here that would like to ask you a couple questions."

The window sealed, and the woman, who was in her twenties, her long black hair falling in a curtain over her delicate upper arm, shook her finger at us, and then, just when a male hand reached across the car to grab her wrist, winked.

"I *think* she's disgusted," I said.

"She winked," Geanie pointed out.

"Her date sure doesn't seem disgusted," said Lonnie, who'd begun clearing soda glasses from the tray beside his window so he could get a better view.

"But that's my question," Geanie said. "Why should she be disgusted and not her date? Is it because it *feels* more disgusting for a woman to have sex and not a man? Or is it just something that people made up in their heads?" Discussing sex did not affect Geanie's appetite, and so she asked this question with a full bite of double cheeseburger in her mouth and a squiggle of ketchup on her chin. "Jack?"

My strategy in these situations, since I had no experience to go on, was to attempt to be more graphic than Geanie. "To do that I guess somebody would have to describe to you what it felt like to have a dick."

"No plumbing!" Nikki said from the front seat.

"But that's what I'm trying to ask," Geanie said. She wore the false-innocent smile, eyebrows raised, that usually accompanied her more outrageous suggestions. "If you look at the ganglia in a woman's clitoris—"

"I SAID NO PLUMBING!" Nikki shouted.

"—it's really just like a smaller version of what a man has. In the book that I was looking at, they called it a 'nascent penis.'"

"Nascent!" Nikki said, making gagging sounds.

"I bet her date has more than a nascent penis," Lonnie said.

"I'm just saying if it feels different when we do it, do you think it affects the way we act?" Geanie said. "If a woman's thing is smaller—"

"Nascent," I repeated, for Nikki's benefit. She was holding her ears.

"And if sex is something that she has done *to* her, something she's supposed to avoid and be ashamed of, like Nikki here, then do you think that makes her see the world differently? Do you think that's why all the men get to run the companies, because they're used to doing it *to* somebody, instead of having it done to them?"

"Men run companies because they're better at it," said Lonnie, whose objectivist theories did not apply to women. He detached the food tray and hung it on the Winstead's menu beside the car. "The people in control are the ones who *take* control. They don't think about it, like you're doing—they just do what come naturally."

"But maybe after all that doing"—Geanie balled up one of her napkins and, in a perfect motion, threw it over Lonnie's head into the trash can—"they might like it if, every once in a while, a woman did something to them?"

The person I worried about, during all this sexual discussion, was Lonnie Garaciello. It seemed logical to me—and had since that first day when I'd tricked him into entering the Bowens' drive—that Lonnie was himself interested in Geanie. I remembered the way that Nikki had leered at her brother when she said, "Lonnie has her in *chemistry*," and how when Geanie had come to the door, Lonnie had refused to look at her directly but instead stared out at the lush Bowen grounds with a frozen expression on his face. Once I got over the blindness caused by Lonnie's unpopularity, I realized that in many ways the two of them made more sense as a couple than Geanie and I did. They at least got to spend some private time together, up in the sweltering fourth-floor science lab in Ashley Hall, amid the black slate dissecting tables and tapered gas flanges and the formaldehyde jars that the biology teacher, Jack "The Butcher" Maslin, kept filled with fetuses, livers, and brains. It wasn't much more romantic than a hamburger restaurant, I admit, but it was more regular; plus, the need for "inclusion" that applied to the meetings of the Surveyors' Club did not, for some reason, apply to studying. She and Lonnie spent a good deal of time working together on problem sets, physics workbooks, differential equations for their advanced science courses—business of such seriousness that when I caught them together in the library, they had blank stares for me. They studied at Geanie's house, too, a fact that I discovered when I called over there one day, only to have Lonnie answer the phone, saying "Bowen residence," peremptorily.

"What the hell are you doing over there?" I asked.

"Eating," Lonnie said. Recognizing my voice, he took another bite of something crackly and forced me to wait while he finished chewing. "This kitchen, man, I'm going to tell you something—it's better than what you'll find at most hotels."

"Is Geanie even there?" I asked, trying to control my voice. It seemed even more intimate that Lonnie might be sitting around the place alone.

"Gone. Her mom took her to buy a dress, some crap. I'm going to tell you something, partner—you have definitely got some balls working your way into *this* family. I hope Geanie appreciates it."

"What the hell is that supposed to mean?"

"I mean *appreciates* it, appreciates it, man."

"Fuck you, Garaciello," I said.

"I'm just saying, I like to work with Geanie, okay?" I could imagine him there, his voice echoing off the Bowens' stainless-steel counters, his feet up, a bowl of Henry's peanuts at his elbow—an image that infuriated me. "I know you get all bent out of shape about this science-fair thing that we've been working on—"

"What science-fair thing? Geanie never said anything about that."

"This thing. Never mind the specifics, the point I'm saying is that it's one thing to do problem sets with a woman who's got a boss on like that—even though I'm the one who does most of the figuring—but as a wife? A woman to have around the house? I got to hand it to you, you're a better man than me."

This attitude was the most frustrating aspect of the whole thing. Despite the fact that Geanie Bowen was, other than Nikki, the *only* woman in all of Briarcliff School for Girls to give Lonnie the time of day—much less attempt to understand him—Lonnie took great pains to disavow any interest he might have in her, at least when he talked privately to me. I don't mean that he spoke of her coolly; I mean that he made fun of and spoke violently against not just Geanie but the whole concept of "dating" in the first place, and of its usefulness in helping a man get somewhere—again, another element of the objectivist creed that he seemed to have stumbled upon naturally. "No offense to you, Jack, and your thing with Geanie," he would say to me. "Having a woman early might help *your* career. But look at my dad, getting pegged even by a woman as beautiful as my mother, as early as he did? Not to be negative, but that pretty much killed all his choices, if you ask me.

Here he was, what—two, maybe three years older than you and me, and he's got two kids already. That's the kind of crap that gets you working for Bobby Ansi, adding up the profits of cigarette machines. If you want a girl now, what you want is sex—with a Trojan." At Pemberton, Lonnie was known for having the pale ring of a condom rubbed into his wallet's leather; he sold them to other boys, too. "No romance, no stupid ideas about saving it, and especially no bullshit about future plans. You start playing around with a girl and *not* fucking her, that's when she starts imagining a future with you—and in the process, you get so fogged up from wanting her that you start thinking it's a good idea. But if you nail her right away, then she knows what you came for, your head's clear—in *both* senses, man—and there doesn't have to be any of that sad crap about 'Where is this all going, honey?' "

But future plans, romance, a sense of where things were going—all of them stupid ideas, perhaps—happened to be exactly what I wanted from Geanie. I had tried to explain this to her in numerous conversations during sophomore year, mostly under the guise of asking her whether or not we should officially begin "going out."

"Personally, I think it's dumb," Geanie told me as we wandered beneath the stands during a home football game. "Even the words don't make sense. When you say two people are 'going out,' doesn't that mean they haven't left yet?"

"It's a commitment," I said.

"Marriage is a commitment," Geanie said. "I don't think we're ready for that."

"I don't want to get married either," I said, though the truth was, secretly, I'd thought a lot about marrying Geanie. "I'm just saying how are we ever going to know if we like it if we don't practice? Going out is like doing all the things you'd do in a marriage, only if you decide you don't like it, you can still quit."

Geanie was staring out at the football field through the slotted openings between the bleachers. A band of light from the stadium floods illuminated her eyes and the warped shadow of a man's ankle bent across her cheek.

"I thought you'd be happy that I asked," I said.

"I am happy, Jack," Geanie said. She came over and kissed me on the lips. "Nobody's ever asked me before, so I guess I'm curious about how it works. For instance, what do people who are going out do that we don't already do?"

"Well, I guess they agree not to see other people," I said.

"But I do see other people," Geanie said. "I see other people all the time. Does that mean I'm not supposed to go out with the girls on the hockey team?"

"I think it applies to boys, mostly."

"So does it mean I couldn't study with Lonnie?"

"No," I said, though I wished it *did* mean that.

"So I don't see what the point is," Geanie said.

At a loss, I canvassed the underside of the bleachers. High up in their gloom, I noticed the calves—and then, on the back side of a bench, the pooched rear ends—of two boys under the bad-word house. Only instead of studying the drawings, the white smears of their faces were peering down at Geanie and me.

"I guess the restrictions apply mostly to sex," I said, lowering my voice.

"But we don't have sex *now*," Geanie said loudly.

"I guess I'd feel better if you had some protection," I said.

"Protection from what?" Geanie asked.

At this point the boys above us began to chant in unison a limerick that I'd first read in the same bad-word house when I'd been their age:

> There once was a freshman named Marion,
> Whose cunt always smelled just like carrion . . .

"Yeah, yeah, yeah," I said, picking up a rock. "'*The guys loved her until she would bury 'em.*' That's hilarious, Walters. Now fuck off."

"You sure you know how?" one voice said, but I'd already heaved my rock by then, a perfect shot that missed the kids but drilled the tin siding of the press box, causing a boom that echoed over the PA. The kids scattered immediately, and I grabbed Geanie's arm, hustling her away.

"That," I said, angrily. "You need protection from that."

"All I'm saying, Jack," Geanie said, "is that if we like each other enough to have sex, why would we care about a limerick?"

My feelings about sex were more complicated than I was willing to admit to Geanie. I had known for some time, for instance, that my grandfather, Big Alton, had conducted "affairs"—a piece of information that my mother had given me in order to explain why he and my father did not get along. Once I'd figured out what the word "affair" meant, this had impressed me with the idea that having sex outside marriage had disastrous consequences. But I was also frightened about sex itself, especially if it involved Geanie. On the one hand, I wanted to try it; on the other, I was worried that I'd be just as bad at sex as I was at running sprints. Even more than practicing marriage, I wanted to practice sex *before* I tried it with her. This fact became clear during a garden party that my parents and I had attended at Henry Bowen's house in April of my sophomore year. Geanie and I had snuck away to kiss in her mother's room-size closet, whose window looked down over the party, and I ended up with my belt and the zipper of my seersucker pants undone and our bodies hidden under a double row of dry-cleaning bags. "Are you okay?" Geanie said to me.

It was a difficult question to answer; in one sense I was terrific, as happy as I could possibly be. But I'd also had to roll away from her before I lost control of myself all over her mother's shoes. "Look, I want to make perfectly clear, first of all, that I'm not stopping because I'm not attracted to you," I said.

"Why are you doing it then?" Geanie asked.

"Do you remember how you were asking if sex is something that's done *to* a woman? I mean, in the sense that if it's done *to* them, it makes them feel different?"

"I remember you didn't answer me," Geanie said.

"What I'm saying is that I don't want that to happen to you." I'd shifted onto my stomach so I could look at Geanie directly. Her breast was still bare, exposed as if through a venetian blind—white lace bra below, wrinkled blouse above.

"Jack, just a minute."

"I'm serious about you for the long term," I said. "I don't want sex to be something that I just *do* to you. If that's all it is, I'm willing to wait."

"Jack, could you zip up real quick?" Geanie bolted upright amid the dry-cleaning shrouds, slipped her bra back into place, then grabbed my arm and pulled me back along the far wall, behind the floor-length gowns. I heard the door opening and Mrs. Bowen's disembodied voice, as from her chauffeured car's front seat, saying to one of her maids, "I was thinking maybe we'd try something in blue?"

Even Geanie, who rarely passed up a chance for a good laugh, never mentioned the awkwardness of this encounter—"Oh, my word," her mother had said at one point, "Look at my shoes. Is that a stain?" Instead, once her mother left and we returned unnoticed to the party, Geanie was extremely gracious, squeezing my hand, admitting that she, too, thought about me "in the long term," though it was hard for me not to hear in her voice a note of contempt, or at least pity. A few weeks later, passing through the corridor on the fourth floor of Ashley Hall, I stopped at Mr. Maslin's door and watched her and Lonnie going after a frog together. Her face was filled with stubborn desire, a will to know, that I recognized from the day she'd crushed the tadpole out in the Westbrook orchard, only now she went about things more purposefully, not killing but dissecting. The two of them maneuvered together with scalpel and forceps to open the frog's belly, their foreheads touching casually as they peeled back the whitish cords of muscle—and I saw a look of triumph in her eyes, far more excited than any she'd recently given me, at taking a blade and cutting down to the true bottom of things.

That same year, my father and Elmore spent most of their time sifting slowly through the names of the black families that had applied to them for mortgages (with funding provided, at least according to the paperwork I saw, by the Bowen Company's mortgage division) and trying to find them houses to buy on the east side of the city, south of Twenty-seventh Street. It must have been at least somewhat dangerous, as Elmore had suggested, since it was the first of my father's business ventures that he hadn't tried to include me in. Twice he returned from these sales trips with the LeSabre's passenger-side window smashed; another evening he staggered home with a bruised cheek and a gash across his knuckles that he soaked quietly in salt water, refusing to comment on what had caused his injuries other than to say it had been a "rough day at the office." My mother and I were mystified by the entire process; we continued to be polite to the smartly dressed black couples who would sometimes appear in our living room, waiting for my father to fill out their paperwork or escort them to see a house someplace. But at the same time, we feared for his safety and I, at least, wondered what this had to do with my father's dream of building houses out in Kings County or why the Bowens would pay him to move black people into neighborhoods that they hadn't built, didn't own, and seemed otherwise not to care about at all.

The final straw came on a day in early August, just before my junior year, when my father moved a family into a modest brick house on our street. For several months, a for-sale sign had languished in the front yard of this property, and the night before, my father had strolled down the block with me, pulled up the sign, and hustled quickly back to our apartment, where he'd tucked it in the front closet. The next day, when Lonnie dropped me off from school, a crowd had gathered outside this house and I walked down with my book bag to see what was happening. A group of about ten people milled around the lawn, nearly all of them neighbors—Mr. Tiller, Dr. Campbell the dentist, Mrs. Meyers from next door—holding signs that read DON'T PUSH US OUT.

"I'm not pushing, I'm telling you, off the lawn," my father said from the house's porch. He was holding a rolled-up newspaper and as he descended from the porch, he shook it at our neighbors as you might at a stray dog. "This is private property—you know the rules. Don't make me call the cops. Campbell, I'm ashamed of you."

"Ashamed of me?" Campbell said. He flapped his sign back at my father. "This is our neighborhood, you son of a bitch. I've got my life invested here."

"It's still your neighborhood," my father said mildly.

"And what's going to happen to our property values when these people move in?" Campbell asked. "You're a realist—you know what this means."

"It's America," my father said. "A free market. I've got a right to sell these people whatever house they want. They've got a right to buy it, if they can pay."

My father must have gotten wind of this protest ahead of time, because he left his audience standing on the sidewalk and strolled back toward me. "Don't feed the animals," he warned, chucking me on the shoulder, and then led me back upstairs to our apartment, where the new owners of the house were waiting on the sofa, along with Elmore Haywood in his forest green suit. They were a light-skinned couple, a Dr. Stephen Randle and his wife, the doctor bald on top with a tight, lamb's wool tonsure of gray around the sides, and his wife taller than him, big-footed, holding a black velvet purse. Other than my father's "Don't feed the animals" comment, I don't remember anybody saying anything the entire evening. I did my homework and came back, and they were still there, sitting on the sofa without letting the cushions touch their backs, my father and Elmore sprawled out beside them in easy chairs, their feet up and their ties loosened.

At around eleven o'clock, my father checked his watch, said, "Okay, let's go," and the six of us walked down to the street. It was the first time that I'd ever scanned the shaded stoops and upper porches of my street with suspicion or searched the ribbed shadows of the elms for a hidden threat. A moving van and five black men waited at the corner. My father led the couple inside, then returned, and my father, Elmore, and I pitched in with the movers, carrying furniture across the lawn in darkness, as if robbing the house rather than possessing it. Halfway through, it began to rain, but we kept on ferrying sofas and varnished tables in to the couple, who waited inside with rags. Toward the end it was so cold I couldn't close my hands. This did not prevent Campbell the dentist from coming out to watch from under an umbrella, and when we'd finished and the couple came out on the porch to say good-bye, he started up their walk. Elmore blocked his way, hulking and drenched—I saw one reason my father employed him, at least—but the doctor said, "It's all right. He's a neighbor. Let him come up if he wants."

Campbell stalked around Elmore through the wet grass and up to the bottom of the porch steps. "Welcome," Dr. Randle said. "My name's Stephen, this is my wife, Ellen. We're moving in, as you can see."

"Welcome?" Campbell said. He refused to touch the doctor's hand. "Is that what you think? Well, I can tell you you're sure welcome to pay back the fifty thousand dollars that you're going to steal from me, before you offer to shake."

The next day a for-sale sign appeared in Campbell's yard; by the end of the week, ten picketed the block, none from the Bowen Company. On Monday, when my father and I went downstairs, there was a dog turd on the LeSabre's hood, and another on the driver's windshield, which had slid down against the wiper blades.

For the next two weeks, my father and my mother picked me up at school and drove me through Prudential Bowen's Campanile District, where Lonnie and I used to cruise. Many of these neighborhoods were only a stone's throw away from our own, a slight ten blocks west of Troost Avenue; the homes, though nicer than our apartment building, still couldn't match the stern grandeur of the old mansions along Hyde Park, where I used to play. But for the first time, they had an aura of cleanliness and safety compared to our old street. "Too shady?" my father would ask as we dawdled along Briarcliff Drive, a leafy road that traced the bluffs above Brush Creek. My mother's hand went to her neck as she peeked, then turned away. "Come on Owl-ton, quit it. That's not funny."

"Who said anything about funny?" my father asked. "We're looking around at houses, aren't we? All right—so look, at least."

One day, passing a familiar fork in Briarcliff Drive and the large wedge of land that filled it, my father pulled into a driveway. An old stone wall backed by thick holly bushes screened whatever lay beyond, and as my father drove through the gate, my mother grabbed his arm and said, "You can't do that—this is private property," which caused my father to glance in the rearview mirror and ask, "Nugget, what's the Alomar Company policy on private property?"

Inside, there was a stone house. I'm not going to say it was larger than the Bowens', because it wasn't, but in the twilight that had fallen, it seemed somehow competitive, mysterious and haunted-looking, with the honey-combed glints of leaded windows in the upper stories, a high raked tile roof, third-floor dormers—three floors! I counted them. We pulled beneath a columned stone carport to a pair of French side doors, across which, oddly, a velvet sash had been strung.

"Does anybody even live here?" my mother asked. My father was groping in the pocket of his madras jacket. Crickets in the yard beeped outside our open car windows, and when he handed a pair of scissors to my mother, she began to scream.

Bobby Ansi

That house on Briarcliff Drive represented more than just a new address. It was the mold my father had selected for our future, and he had determined that we would expand ourselves until we fit—a painful process, given the size of the place. On the morning of our moving day, I woke, tossed my pajamas and my toothbrush into a box labeled "miscellaneous," and then gave myself a final tour of our Gramercy apartment, viewing the porch where I'd first heard of Henry Ford and Tom Durant, its cracked concrete now bare, the wicker rug tied up and hauled away. My parents' bedroom had empty nail holes in the place of familiar pictures, and movers with screwdrivers were already breaking down their bed. The apartment, though stripped, appeared fuller than it had ever been, the boxes stacked three high along every wall, the bedrooms barricaded with steamer trunks and bedsprings. But when I walked to the new house after school (it was only a few blocks away across the creek), all of what had seemed to me like an adequately full life had been fit easily into the first-floor parlor, piled up in a mound that failed even to reach the chandelier.

I was thrilled with all of this; to me the size and space of the new house, its ranks of empty rooms and leaded windows meant we were finally safe. I assumed my mother would feel the same way, that such a house was exactly what she'd imagined as the corollary to her faith that my father would in fact "do something great." When it came to defending this faith, my mother had always been as unflappable as a beer vendor at Memorial Stadium, keeping an eye on her audience, ready to haggle or meet any rudeness face-to-face, insisting on exact change. But there had been, if I'd heard right, something other than joy in her scream when my father had pulled those scissors out of his pocket, followed by the house's keys. I would return from school to find her wandering in its upper reaches, the rooms unfurnished—with no prospect of furniture arriving—carrying some magazine rack from the old apartment with a lost look as if she'd come to the stadium on the wrong day and was trying to sell her wares to empty seats. "So what's the problem here?" I asked when, for the second straight day, she spent an entire evening balanced on a stepladder in the kitchen, arranging the cabinets.

"Problem? There's no problem, ho-ney. Whatever do you mean?"

The problem was that she'd spent two days assembling a pyramidal display of my father's coffee cups behind the glass-fronted cupboards, like exhibits in a museum case, while upstairs we were still sleeping in sleeping bags. Plus, there were open copies of *Sunset* magazine and *Better Homes and Gardens* fanned about her ladder, magazines I'd never known her to look at before but which I'd started finding all over the house. "It's weird," I told her, indicating the cabinets. "This. Whatever it is you're doing."

"Well, thank you. Very much. There's nothing like"—she was breathless with going up and down the ladder—"working all day to create a bright and relaxing environment, so that the people walking in and out of this place won't be completely embarrassed for us, and then to be told it's weird by someone who hasn't done anything to help. I'd settle for a thank-you."

"What people walking in and out, Ma? There's nobody around here except you and me. Dad's been out with Elmore for two days."

"And you don't think we might have company?"

"Like who? There aren't very many surprise dinner parties in Bowenville. People who just drive around and drop in strangers' houses, asking to eat."

"Will you hand me the pussy willow, please?"

"Pussy what?"

"Wil-low. Don't be nasty with me, young man."

"Do you mean these sticks?" I asked. There were bundles of them on the counter, tied up with ribbon. "Mom, I'm telling you, this is a kitchen, not a greenhouse. Do you think if the Garaciellos came over, they'd notice sticks?"

"Good decorating," my mother said, moving to the next cabinet, "is like good lingerie. It's less about being seen than it is about knowing that it's there." A phrase I would've bet money she'd filched from one of these magazines.

We went on like this. My father was aware of my mother's confusion, though he refused to say anything about it. At night, I'd catch him staring into the empty refrigerator (my mother had also stopped shopping) with an expression of both wonder and fear, like a man whose house was being eaten by insects no one else could see. Or stumbling from the bathroom to search for the roll of toilet paper that my mother had always previously re-filled. Two weeks passed before my mother gave me at least a partial expla-nation for their standoff. "You understand, Nugget, don't you, that your father has a problem with money?" This was said grim-lipped, her hair still done up in a rag, as she took a paint chisel to the woodwork of our carriage house—a building that had been used by the previous tenants as a storage space, with old balloon-style tires and ancient batteries stashed away. But in the silence that followed this comment, when our eyes met, we both burst out laughing. "I'm not saying he doesn't provide," she protested. "Or that your father's not a genius. He's the smartest man I've ever known. But after all these years he's been denied and denied by the idiots who do business around here, you see, and after all this waiting and all this holding back and having to skimp, now that he's got his break, he can't hardly control him-self, I don't think. Do you understand? He just has to grab and grab. Imag-ine how you'd act if all at once you got something you'd always wanted."

I was tangled up trying to decode a pile of rotting carriage tack, and she paused with her scraping to watch me. "How *would* you act?" she asked, a sweaty smear of hair lopped across her forehead. It was the most candid look I'd seen from her in some time. "If I said that you could have anything in the world, what would you pick?"

I heard this question only in terms of Geanie. Ever since our conversa-tion in her mother's dressing room, she'd been more and more distant and difficult to pin down; when summer had arrived, she had (unlike the sum-mer before) disappeared again into her "practices" and her studying. So I gave my mother the response that I held on to against the sick feeling I'd made a mistake. "I'd want to be right," I said.

"Oh, no, ho-ney—that's a terrible answer. I mean anything—anything you could dream of. Nobody dreams that way."

Naturally, this was the last thing I wanted to hear. "Why not?" I asked. "Maybe if people around here cared about being right, we wouldn't have money trouble."

My mother reacted as if I'd kicked her. "What is that supposed to mean?" she asked, as I clanked the tack down the loft's steps. "So if you do something wrong, I should cut you off, is that it? I should stop cooking?"

"You *did* stop cooking," I pointed out.

Hearing this, my mother stomped her tiny tennis shoes in a way that would've been funny had I not heard the real anger in her voice. "Tell me once," she said, "just once when your father has gone against you that gives you the right to talk that way!"

It was a cheap shot, but I couldn't imagine telling my mother exactly what had happened with Geanie, or what I really meant. I'm sure she would have agreed had I explained that, when it came to my father, I was less concerned about his decisions being "right" than I was about them being astute, correct. I was ready to believe in his success, wanted to be convinced that he'd made the *right* bets, and that the whole growing web of his activities—the Alomar Company, the charred fields out in Kings County, these signings of mortgages for Elmore Haywood's blacks—would finally, now that we'd moved into this new house, work out safely in the end. Which was also how I felt when my father told me that he'd decided to borrow money from Bobby Ansi.

I had first heard Bobby Ansi's name the previous summer. Lonnie had gotten me a job at Municipal Auditorium on Twelfth and Wyandotte, installing and tearing down convention booths on Wednesdays and Sundays. The auditorium was beautiful. No matter the temperature outside, there remained a leftover coolness to its lower halls and auditorium floor set deep down in the city's bedrock, beneath tons and tons of concrete that Tom Pendergast had poured into an art deco cube overhead, and I remember watching them open that place up on Wednesday afternoons, after it had been dark during the week, standing down on the floor as they switched on the floodlights that dangled from the roof. And how the hum of the bulbs would often disturb a sparrow or a pigeon that had snuck in, and we would watch it fly alone and calling against the creamy tile dome, dodging among the caged lights and satin banners for the American Royal. It looked like an inversion of the quarry, a scoop of sky captured under concrete.

Lonnie and I had been assigned to draw up the layout of the booths for whatever convention or sales show was coming in—house alarms, windows and siding, medical equipment—choosing from among the names on the shipping manifest who would, and who would not, receive the most-traveled space for their display. "Hold it!" Lonnie would shout from a folding table just inside the loading dock. "Somebody here tell me since when eleven came before three? So if we're *on* display three, what's Marsucci doing dragging number eleven in? Jack, go grab his jive ass and bring him here."

The jive ass that I'd grabbed in this case looked like he had marbles sewed under his skin, glistening knobs of cheek and jaw and temple, wine-colored slacks, a matching jacket with white stitching. "If you're going to tell me to turn around," he'd said when I stopped him, "you should've done it at the bottom of the ramp, not up here."

He said this despite the fact that I had caught him halfway up this same ramp and had followed him up the rest of the way, telling him to quit.

"I'm just the messenger," I said. "It's not my fault that this ramp is here, or that if you take the displays to the floor out of order, they'll set them up the wrong way."

"Who put a greenhorn like you on this detail?" he asked without listening.

"I've been on this detail three weeks," I said. I did not know yet that greenhorn meant a civilian, a non-Italian. "All I know is that Bobby said it has to go in order."

"Bobby? What the fuck do you know about Bobby?"

"I don't," I confessed. "I'm just saying there's a system—"

"Who the fuck are you to tell *me* what Bobby thinks?" the man said. "You think Bobby Ansi cares about some aftershave? I don't know. Maybe Bobby ought to send you over to my house tonight and explain to me how I should fuck my wife."

"What did Marsucci say, that stupid cunt?" Lonnie asked when I came back, and when I mumbled, "Nothing, it's fine, forget it," to smooth over things, he cursed and pulled his lips back from his teeth.

"So where's that display?" he shouted at Marsucci when he showed up again a few minutes later. "We're still on number eight here, so I know for a fact that you wouldn't have pulled any jive-assed shit and taken that one up anyway."

"Don't you talk that nigger talk to me," Marsucci said. He cut his eyes at the other men working to unload the displays on the open dock. Several of them were dressed as he was, in suits and thin-soled dress shoes, though when they'd arrived, they'd handed the crew chief union cards.

"Who am I going to talk it to, then?" Lonnie said. He was waving the cargo manifest in Marsucci's face. "See, here's the order, Frank. One through forty-eight displays. And at the bottom here's a signature. Maybe, though I can't say for sure, *maybe* Bobby signs this list because certain contributions and adjustments have been paid to get displays high up on that list. So what I hope, Frank, is that what didn't happen was that you didn't meet one of these same salesmen in the hotel bar across the street and that he didn't offer to slip you a twenty to put his display in a better spot. . . ."

Until that day, Lonnie had always ducked my questions about who Bobby Ansi was, exactly. However, after his argument with Marsucci—who'd finally broken down and slipped Lonnie a twenty, begging him to "fix things up with Bobby"—he'd stepped outside during one of our breaks, his hands shaking so badly he couldn't light his cigarette. "You want to know what Bobby Ansi does?" he said to me. "He takes a cut. That's it. He doesn't make anything, he doesn't build anything, he doesn't invent. All he does is take a cut. You sell a pack of cigarettes down here from a vending machine, five cents of that goes to Bobby. You buy a drink, that's a dime. You want to run a restaurant? Park a car? Bet on a baseball game? That's fine, so long as Bobby gets to take a little bit. He's just as bad as any of those guys in Mission Hills sitting on top of somebody else's money. And my father . . . shit." He shook his head with pursed lips. "Do you realize that I came home one day and my father had opened up my calculus book and done a problem set? It wasn't perfect. There were mistakes. But for a guy who never finished high school? And what's he do? He spends his life sitting around and keeping track of who owes Bobby what, for how long, and in what way."

"Why?" I had asked.

"Fuck if I know," Lonnie had said. "'Cause Bobby helped him out when he was in trouble as a kid. 'Cause it's good pay." He had finally steadied himself enough to get the cigarette lit—a new habit for him—and squinted at me through the haze.

"No, I mean, why does Bobby get to take a cut?"

"Because the one guarantee is *somebody's* going to take a cut. There was a guy who did this before Bobby, and then Bobby took his place."

It would have been one thing if this Bobby Ansi had posed merely a theoretical threat—trouble, perhaps, for a man like Marsucci or for the Teamsters Union chiefs (whom he paid off) or for any of those other men who swarmed in and out of those convention trucks—but of no consequence to a kid like me, I certainly never imagined my father would plan to go into business with him, though when I look back, all the signs were there. My mother had been only partially right; the Alomar Company had offered a taste of what my father wanted, not the whole thing. The whole thing was Royce MacVess's ranch. Because it straddled the highway, MacVess's property would be the logical place for access roads and the shopping centers and services that accompanied them. If it wasn't developed, the value of the other properties that my father had bought in Kings County would be significantly reduced. But more than that, I think he saw MacVess's ranch as his best chance to finally make it big, the equivalent of the pig farms that Prudential Bowen had acquired to found the Campanile. If the Bowens couldn't buy it themselves, then he certainly wasn't going to purchase it *for* them, only to turn around and sell it back at cost plus 50 percent. And so in one sense it was natural that my father would pursue other investors to help him make an offer on the place.

But I failed to understand the risk that this might entail. No matter how my mother acted, no matter what she said about money—though it concerned me on the surface—I simply didn't see any signs of financial trouble, not in the way I'd seen them in the early days of the Alomar Company, when my father had bummed trolley fare from me. If it had taken six years to get us from that point to Briarcliff Drive, I figured it would require at least that long for the process to be reversed. Plus, I was completely blind to the mysterious intricacies of the bank ledger, of debt and equity, or of compound interest. Nobody explained to me that the Alomar Company had assumed significant mortgage obligations when purchasing its new properties, which, together with property taxes, had eaten up all of the company's original investment. Or that, in order to cover expenses, my father had already sold the Bowen Company portions of the land he'd bought at the 50 percent profit that his contract required—a return that kept him in business but was many hundreds of times less than what he'd expected to receive.

It was a death spiral, really. But I refused to see it. We had this enormous house, didn't we? And so when my father told me that we would be having Bobby Ansi to Thanksgiving dinner, along with the Garaciellos and Joey Ramola, I was prepared to accept his explanation that this was a completely rational decision, one that any businessman would have made in his place. After all, Bobby Ansi owned a respectable construction firm, which had already—as I'd noticed on our trips to Kings County—done work on the highway. He'd already invested in the Alomar Company through Joey Ramola, who managed some of his money. "I figured we'd check the guy out," my father said. "Nick says he's got good money. Why not take a peek?"

"What about the Bowens?" I asked.

"I already tried that," he pointed out. "I don't want to buy this property just so I can sell it back to Prudential Bowen. And I can't go to any of the usual real estate guys in town for money because they're afraid to compete with him. This guy Ansi isn't a pushover. I'm not going to lie about that. But you've got to consider what these Italians want. They don't know anything about suburban development. You think any of those boys down on the docks could survey a piece of property? No, what they want is to look like you and me. That's why Nick sends his kids to your school. I don't know what you think, but Nick was a guy *I* like working with, at least."

"Sure," I admitted. "He seems all right to me."

"The point of this is that every man wants to be redeemed," my father said, though it wasn't clear whether he meant himself or Nick. "That's what Kings County and the suburbs are going to be—redemption, purity. You start off and maybe your father was a stonecutter or a farmer or an asshole lawyer, but out there you're just Mr. and Mrs. Garaciello, living on a clean American street. Prudential Bowen understood this. Why do you think, back in the thirties, he did business with a gangster like Tom Pendergast, hired him to line his creek with concrete? Because we *are* where they're *going,* guys like Garaciello and Ansi, and so they have to treat us with respect."

We had this discussion in his bedroom. We were going out to eat that night, and my father stood up stiffly in his fresh wingtips and his creased pants and paced gingerly across the room, like a knight who'd just put on armor and was checking it for squeaks. Then he came over, adjusted my tie, and laid his palm gently on my cheek.

"It's just a family dinner," he said. "No more, no less. So you'll go out there and have fun for me, won't you? And won't sit around and overthink?"

"Sure," I said. "I can do that."

"Good," he said. He reached into his jacket and held out a pair of cuff links to me, palm up. "Try these on," he said.

On Thanksgiving night I was lighting the tiki torches my father had planted along our drive when the Garaciellos' car whooshed up. It was an Oldsmobile sedan that Nick had bought to replace the Impala and it cornered through our gate so fast that its fender clipped the first line of stakes. Two torches crashed into the grass and as I ran to stamp them out, the car bridled to a stop under the side stone portico of our house, released its passengers, and then jerked forward again. After that I heard the slap of dress soles on pavement and looked up to find Lonnie running toward me.

"Hey, what's the rush?" I said, holding up a fistful of wicker. "These things are for decoration, not target practice."

"Just forget them and come up," he said.

"I tried that already. My dad said I was supposed to light all these things."

Instead of returning to the house himself, Lonnie sprinted past me to our stone gate, jumped out into the street to hail a second car and, when it turned in to our driveway, leaned in the window and waved his arm at the remaining torches as if giving directions, though it was twilight and the house could not have been more than thirty yards away. This wasn't the only greeting the car received. First Nick, then Joey Ramola (whom I was also surprised to see) sidled down the drive, each of them stopping to bend into the back passenger window to say hello to the occupants, to shake hands and exchange stories, to point out the way to our house—or in Nick's case to point out Joey, another ten steps on. I'd never seen anything quite like it. The car itself never accelerated much past walking speed—a leisurely stroll, the windows down, as if participating in a presidential cavalcade. Through the window on my side, I saw a woman holding a yellow puppy wearing a red collar about its neck, a sight that you were certainly unlikely to see when Prudential Bowen showed up at a party.

Up at the carport, I finally got a look at Bobby. He reminded me of a pharmacist, a birdy man in his fifties with a strong beaked nose and a receding chin. I would not have picked him out as a leader, except perhaps for the deeply tanned, nut-brown color of his skin, as if, at this time of year, he'd recently been out of state. He wore heavy glasses that he removed in order to be kissed, no tie, a striped oxford buttoned to the neck, and a ratty tan overcoat with the belt flopping loose about his waist. You could see control, though, in his dark brown fingers, which, when he was kissed in greeting, delicately touched his greeter's face. Also, he made absolutely no effort to appear interested in the talk that went on around him—even Nick, whom I had never before seen put himself out, seemed eager and coarse-grained by comparison—but instead gazed dreamily over everybody's heads at the house, the portico roof, our lit windows, taking things in.

Meanwhile, my father was preparing for his first appearance as lord and master of his own Bowen-built mansion, which had put him so deeply in debt. I could see him waiting behind our glass side door—to go outside and speak to the men would have meant abandoning his position of authority—with his wife at his side, luminously dressed in a matching lavender suit and ribboned flats, her hair limp from the steam of the kitchen, but otherwise as beautiful as she'd ever be. I saw, too, how my mother's weeks of decorating work had finally paid off. The house glittered and loomed behind them like a cruise ship, impressive in its size and weight; there was the clatter of silverware from the kitchen, distantly; there were candles lit and glowing on the radiator, dried Thanksgiving gourds and corn tied beneath the hall light sconces, put there by my mother's hand. The glow from a fire in the living room licked out on the parquet floor behind them, and my mother, in some emotion that went unnamed, reached out very lightly to touch my father's hand. Unfortunately, the first person to greet them in this state was the woman with the dog, who'd introduced herself and taken my arm, as if expecting me to escort her in. "Mom, Dad, this is Tracy," I explained. "She's Bobby Ansi's *friend.*"

"That's fine, that's fine," my father said, grandly. There was a glazed look in his eyes. "I'm Alton Acheson, and this is my wife—"

"I'm sorry, just a second," Tracy said. The dog, either excited or frightened by the house, had started scrambling in her arms, and she set it down, speaking to it angrily, "Okay, Bobby Junior, you behave," and then straightened and offered her hand, palm-down, to my father. "Wow, I'm sorry. He gets a little excited in a new place. Now, could you go over that again—I didn't catch your names?"

"Acheson, Alton Acheson—and my wife, Allie," my father said. But by then both my parents were looking sorrowfully over her shoulder at the dog, who'd squatted down behind Tracy's high heels and begun silently to pee.

At dinner my mother arranged the seating specifically to help my father make his pitch, installing him at the head of the table and Bobby to his right hand, facing a long bank of windows that reflected the glow of her candles and her silverware, thus doubling their effect. My mother sat facing Bobby and contrived to insulate him by placing Lonnie and his mother next, followed by Nick and Joey, with myself, Nikki, and Tracy at the far end. I will give credit to my father for making it sound as if he—and by extension myself and my mother—had decided, due to our appreciation for his original investment in the Alomar Company, to offer Bobby this opportunity ahead of a large number of "big guns" who were currently beating down our doors to get involved. It was the King of Kings County at his finest, speaking of the *dream* of land and its development, of its "trapped wealth" as he had back in the old days, when he and I had lounged together on our Gramercy apartment porch. And I have to say that as I watched him, from my position at the far end of the table, I believed in him as I had then—pretending to listen as Tracy and Nikki spoke of James Dean, but actually turning my ear so that I could hear my father's words drifting to me through the candelabras, across the banded dessert spoons of my parents' wedding silver. He hit Bobby with the whole routine, starting off with Tom Durant, the similarities between the railroad and the highway, the fact that the true value of the land would always be, as I heard him say, "unlocked by some great change in transportation, in the movement of things." And explaining how these changes were rare, historic moments, things that came along once a century—the railroad in the 1860s and now the interstate highway.

Before the salad was collected, he'd spread out his maps—pointing to the land that he and Nick had already surveyed and purchased for the Alomar Company. With a fork, he traced the borders of MacVess's ranch, explaining where the positions of the access roads would be and why it, and not the lands he'd already purchased, would be the prime developmental property. From my post at the foot of the table, I could see each and every face—Lonnie sneaking sips from his mother's wineglass when her attention was turned, Nick wrinkling his nose at something Joey Ramola said, his hair back in its usual stiff V, though with gray along the temple that I didn't remember noticing previously. The Italian-style menu that my father had first suggested had apparently been rejected by the kitchen staff (composed of volunteers from the Pemberton cafeteria, all of whom had been my father's clients, plus Elmore, who'd agreed to tend bar). Instead they delivered a roast turkey garnished with plums and apples, no tomato sauce visible anyplace, accompanied by au gratin potatoes, whose taste I recognized from school. As the plates piled up, as my father in his excitement lit his first cigarette—to be followed immediately by Joey and Nick— and as the pewter mists of smoke rose up in the air and I heard my father's voice booming out terms like "quitclaim" and "compound appreciation," it was hard not to imagine that perhaps this *was* his great and historic moment, one that we would all look back on someday, from worlds of wealth and comfort, as our beginning. Hard not to imagine that the St. Nicholas Hotel, where Andrew Carnegie used to stay, or Henry Ford's Fair Lane on the River Rouge had not themselves witnessed similar scenes.

"You do understand that, don't you, Bobby?" my father was saying. "This was all a dream. You get that, don't you? The walls of this house, that road out there, every single damn building on the Campanile. It was all Prudential Bowen's imagination—nobody thought the city should come out south this way. But because this guy understood that the automobile was more important than the streetcar—*just* like what's happening with the highway—he built the place with garages, free parking, a drive-in shopping area. And because he thought it up, we all have to live in it. Nobody has that kind of power, to affect a city's *memory*—and the money?" He riffled through the deed for our house, pulling out a worn yellow sheet. "He bought this entire area for a hundred dollars an acre originally and sells this house in 1918 for twenty grand. Do you realize the kind of return that offers, not to mention what it's worth today? It's like stealing, with the very great advantage that it's perfectly respectable. And those same kinds of returns are going to be available on this MacVess property, I promise you. Better, probably."

"Of course, your view is that I am not respectable," Bobby said when my father finished. The room went silent—except for Joey Ramola, who'd been whispering to Tracy about a singer that he knew, his voice trailing off gradually.

"When did I say that?" my father protested. "I would never suggest such a thing."

"But you imply it," Bobby said. "That is why, for instance, you feel comfortable in telling me this great secret. Now that I know it, why wouldn't I just go out and buy this land myself?"

"It was my impression that you were looking for a vehicle, Mr. Ansi. A . . . representative. I thought"—my father gave one agonized look down the table at me—"I was under the impression that you had money that you would prefer to invest under someone else's name."

"A respectable name, I suppose. Like yours or Mr. Bowen's."

"If you want to put it that way."

"But you are not yourself actually a respectable man," Bobby said. He laid this out in the manner of a riddle, his fish eyes widening behind his glasses, though in a manner that made it impossible to guess what the right answer might be.

"No," my father said finally. "No, I'm not."

"Good," Bobby Ansi said. "Because I have certain questions that I want to ask, certain things in all your fine history—in all the dreams you have about this property—that have not yet been answered. And in asking about them, I would not want to offend your respectability—or actually I'd want to make sure your respectability is capable of understanding these crucial things." His eyelids fluttered. "The first being what our friend Henry Bowen calls the 'Negro Question,' when he's in the mood to be funny."

"Does anybody want dessert?" my mother asked in a strong distracting voice, though even she could not prevent a quiver of anxiety at the end. She edged out along the bank of windows, her tan back reflected in them.

"Absolutely," Bobby said. "That and black coffee. And send out Mr. Elmore, please—he works with you, doesn't he? When you're not using him as kitchen boy?"

"He's a friend," my father said angrily, through his teeth.

"You're not also afraid of words, are you, Mr. Acheson?" Bobby asked. "Because I can't imagine anyone being successful doing this job who is afraid to call things by their proper name."

My father watched as Elmore pushed uncertainly through the kitchen door. "Put me down for a no on that, too," he said.

"I do not myself, as a rule, choose to work with Negroes so intimately," Bobby continued in a casual tone, "though I do have quite a few who perform functions for me in their neighborhood, as well as a large number who are tenants—as I'm sure Mr. Elmore is aware. But since Mr. Elmore will be playing such a critical role in this process, it seems shameful to leave him out there in the kitchen. Besides, I'd like to hear his opinion on a few things. Does anyone object to that?"

In response, the three women who'd come with Bobby's party—Nikki, Mrs. Garaciello, and Tracy—rose from the table and withdrew into the parlor. Of the men who remained behind, no one, including Elmore, had anything to say.

Bobby picked up my father's copy of the deed abstract for our house— a thick sheaf of yellowed papers held together by metal fasteners—and thumbed through to the back. "Are you familiar with the 'racial covenant,' Mr. Elmore?" he said.

"It's Haywood, Mr. Haywood," Elmore said. "The other's my first name. And no, I never heard of that."

"Let me put it another way. You have, I understand, been helping other Negroes buy homes along Paseo and Standard avenues, east of Troost, in neighborhoods that are otherwise white. Am I correct in that?"

"That's right," Elmore said.

"And do you know why you have been selected to do this?"

"'Cause white agents don't want to sell black folks anything?"

"That's true, that's true," Bobby said, chuckling. "And why is it that you have attempted to buy and sell property for your Negro clients only in neighborhoods that aren't owned by the Bowen Company—away from the Campanile?"

Elmore laughed at this. "Because I don't want an ass-kicking?"

"That's right," Bobby said. "That sounds absolutely rational to me, though there is also a legal reason for this, which Mr. Acheson has so far failed to mention." He passed the abstract down the table, first to Nick, who handed it to me, then I to Elmore, who sat at the corner of the table on my right, as far away from Bobby as he could possibly be. To my surprise, confronted with the document, Elmore reached down into the pocket of his pants and produced a pair of bifocals, complete with neck chain, which he balanced on the end of his football-flattened nose. I could still remember Elmore in his rotting parka, cursing at Pemberton football games, and so it was strange to see him strike such a professorial pose, his jaw jutting out underneath the glasses, as he read the legal text. But what I noticed most, looking over his shoulder, were his hands, their joints swollen and crooked from, I supposed, his playing days, but his cuticles and nails perfectly clean and clipped. Their blackness also could not be avoided, the purplish hardness of the knuckle ridges, the graying skin between thumb and forefinger as he gripped the page; even then I had the sense that this piece of paper had never before been handled by hands the color of his. The top of the page that Bobby had given him read:

The Bowen Investment Company DECLARATION OF RESTRICTIONS
To AND COVENANTS
Briarcliff Developments

Dated June 18, 1918
Filed June 21, 1918
At 2:20 o'clock P.M.
#21535
Book 20 Misc., page 602

DECLARATION OF RESTRICTIONS AND COVENANTS
AFFECTING BLOCKS 26, 27, 28, 29, and 30 of
BRIARCLIFF DEVELOPMENT

This heading was followed by several thick, single-spaced paragraphs of text, beginning with the words "Whereas the Bowen Company, a corporation, and certain other individuals have heretofore executed a plat of Blocks 26 to 30, both inclusive, of Briarcliff Development . . ."

"I think you'll find the relevant lines in section ten," Bobby said.

Then Elmore flipped ahead, through paragraphs titled, in capital letters, SETBACK OF RESIDENCES FROM STREETS and WINDOW PROJECTIONS, to a short, two-line paragraph just after OUTBUILDINGS, FREE SPACE REQUIRED. This read, in full:

SECTION 10: OWNERSHIP BY NEGROES PROHIBITED:
None of the lots hereby restricted may be conveyed to, used,
owned, or occupied by Negroes as owners or tenants.

When he finished reading, Elmore flipped the page, but there was no more explanation. The next section, Section 11, began BILLBOARDS PRO-HIBITED, and he closed the book, blinking at its cover quietly, and then at my father, who at first met, then turned away from, his gaze.

"This is no small point, as I'm sure Elmore would agree," Bobby said. "When I was growing up, it didn't used to be only Italians who lived in the northeast. It was as you say—fancy houses, WASPs, business owners, lawyers all over the place. And during my entire life, they have been moving out this way, the whites, the Italians who have money, anybody who could afford to leave. But the question is why? Because Mr. Bowen advertised these new areas as all-white. He said that if you're in an all-white neighborhood—a neighborhood that can never change, because he owns all the property from the beginning—then of course your property values will be protected. Was this true? Who knew? Nobody had ever thought of it before, much less advertised it in the paper—'Are you concerned about change?'—that's how Mr. Bowen's advertisements read when I was growing up. Do you remember this, Mr. Acheson?"

"No," my father admitted. "That might have been a little early for me."

"But where did you live, growing up?" Bobby asked. "Since we are now saying that where we grow up affects our dreams."

"Greenway Terrace," my father said.

"A Bowen property," Bobby said, tapping a spot behind the Campanile on the outspread city map. "And before that, where did your father live?"

"Sixteenth and Harrison," my father said.

Bobby pointed east of downtown, to what was now in fact a black neighborhood near the Italian north end.

"So he was a lawyer, one who left my district and moved permanently into Prudential Bowen's territory. How many people are there like this? From 1918 to today? Lawyers, doctors, businessmen, the owners of factories? And after them the smaller people, the schoolteachers, the shop owners, the salesmen. Ten thousand people? Twenty thousand? Sixty thousand? It would be interesting to count, wouldn't it, how many people live today in Mr. Bowen's houses and how many of them came from our part of the city. Everybody moved, except for those who couldn't afford it, the ones whose parents were newcomers, like Joey, Nick, and me. What could we do? The Negroes were already living there. They were living in our apartment buildings and in our alleys. One street was white, the next for Negroes—it had always been that way; no one had thought differently until, of course, Mr. Bowen started his development, and by then it was too late. By then no one person owned things, so it was impossible to write in these covenants, because somebody always defected, because the Negroes owned property themselves—for all these reasons, we were surprised by it.

"I am saying this only as a matter of history, Mr. Acheson, so we are clear on what exactly made Mr. Bowen a success."

"A success?" My father had finally burst free of his chair and was pacing up and down the bank of windows across from Bobby, as if, after a long time of puzzlement at the conversation's direction, he'd finally figured out where it was heading. "What made Prudential Bowen a success was that he purchased good land early and cheap. You don't have to go through all this crap to know that."

"But you have to have a reason to get people moving, don't you?" Bobby said. "The car is nice, the highway is nice, but none of them is quite so good as fear—then, of course, you already know that, or why else would you and the Bowens be financing mortgages for Elmore, if not to scare whites out of those neighborhoods and into your new properties in Kings County? Not that I oppose this, by the way."

"You don't have to listen to this, Elmore," my father said, grabbing the deed abstract from Elmore's place. "What Elmore and I do in our business is simply fill a need. We became aware of a population that was interested in our services, one that nobody else was paying attention to, and we met that demand. It was an interim business for me, something to do while I waited for those Kings County properties to mature."

"And all *I* want you to do is make sure you keep at it," Bobby said. "You, Elmore, the kid there"—he nodded at me—"but mostly Elmore. Mr. Haywood. Without his end of the business, nobody is moving to Kings County."

He said this in a much lighter tone than anything he'd come up with previously and then stood from his chair as if some agreement had been sealed. With a smile at my father, he attempted to pick up the slice of sweet potato pie that my mother had delivered (the kitchen staff's variation on my father's request for Italian candied yams) and his coffee, an action that caused Nick to jump up and help him.

"But the two aren't joined," my father protested. I noticed, however, that he, too, was aware of the change in Bobby's tone of voice and had moderated his anger accordingly. There might have been, though I could not be sure, the flicker of a smile beneath his mustache as he snuck a peek at Elmore.

"I know my limitations, Mr. Acheson," Bobby said. He lingered in the entryway between the dining room and the parlor, his thumb tucked delicately over the dessert spoon on his pie plate. "When you ask me to go up against someone like Prudential Bowen, you're asking me to go up against the biggest boss in the city. Our only hope is that whatever *we* are doing, he stands to profit by it, too—and, more important, will not change his policy. If he wants to move Negroes into the east side, I'm all for it. I only want to make sure that he will continue to support such work if we buy the MacVess property. And, equally, that Mr. Haywood will resume his activities. If necessary"—he nodded to Nick—"I can help him with security."

"So what you're saying," Elmore responded, "is that my clients get houses and the white people go run away and live in the country on your place?"

"Now, there's a man who speaks directly," Bobby said.

"So you're in?" my father said.

Bobby Ansi did not answer this. Instead he took a bite of pie, gazing benignly at my father over the plate. Then he said to my mother, "Mrs. Acheson, this is lovely. I don't think I've ever had yam pie."

"It's an experiment," my mother said.

"Well, what are we waiting for?" Bobby said, heading to the parlor. "I thought we'd come here to see the lights."

When he left, the other men went with him into the parlor, leaving behind my family and Elmore—who had not moved from the spot where he'd been sitting when he read the deed. I was aware, of course, of a profound ugliness to the scene, the kind of ugliness that we in Kansas City would not develop calming words for until later in the decade, when the neighborhoods in which Elmore sold his homes would erupt in riot and when Prudential Bowen, in order to protect his properties, would call in tanks to guard the Campanile's streets. I do know that my father, mother, and I would rarely speak of that dinner ever again, especially of those few minutes that we stood in silence with Elmore around that looted dinner table, its silver forks and knives now dirtied by the diners' mouths, the linen napkins stained. But it would be false to pretend that something so simple as my father's deception of Elmore Haywood was the only thing that caused this feeling. I would say this even if, after Martin Luther King Jr. had spoken on the Mall, telling the country about his "dream," every white in the country, my father included, had accepted his correction and behaved differently. No, because just then we were outside any dream at all, or rather the room that we inhabited was filled with agreements about which Dr. King had not allowed himself to speak. I remember my father leaning his hands atop a chair back and bending his neck so that what Elmore and I saw—we were still sitting together—was the crown of his blond hair as he shook his head back and forth, and the white-knuckled grip of his big hands. It was a gesture that could have been one of sadness, of laughter, of fury (and likely was a combination of all three), and when he looked up, his face was flushed in the cheeks and around the corners of his mustache, and his eyes were watery—though again not with sadness but more like wonderment and relief. "Elmore, I'm sorry," he said. "All of that"—he gestured into the other room—"was unnecessary. I didn't mean to get you involved in this like that."

Elmore was sitting in what had been Tracy's seat. He reached for her wineglass, wiped a print of lipstick off the rim with his thumb, and took a drink, swirling the liquid in his mouth thoughtfully. "I am now, though, aren't I?" he said.

My father nodded; he examined Elmore with some approximation of his old teasing squint. "Sounds like maybe he'd rather hire you than me. What do you think, Nugget? Maybe we ought to put Elmore in charge of this damn company."

But this comment missed its mark; the joking tone had come too quickly, too easily, and Elmore could not match it. He looked down at his feet.

"Elmore," my mother said, "let me get you your own plate. Or at the very least a clean glass—there's plenty of wine left yet."

"No, no," Elmore said. This time he did lean back in his seat and returned my father's gaze directly, twirling the stem of his wineglass. "Why leave all this stuff behind?" he said gesturing to the table. "The scraps are good enough for me."

It was an insult, of course, but the insult itself was a form of capitulation, a return to normalcy. And as my mother went to get Elmore a clean glass and a new plate, despite his protests, my father and I moved quickly on to the next thing.

The lighting ceremony was easier, quicker. Our party watched it from my father's second-floor bedroom, as he'd planned originally. We had to hurry to get there, since by the time my father and I made it into the parlor, it was already ten minutes to eight. Lonnie was missing; during the long conversation with Bobby Ansi, he'd slipped off someplace. But everyone else trooped upstairs eagerly, the only odd thing being that my father, somehow in the transfer from the first floor to the second, seemed to have become drunk almost immediately. Whether this was simply the result of a release from stress, or some other reason, I can't say, since I didn't see him drink anything more since we'd finished our conversation with Elmore, but his hands appeared numb and lifeless when he tried to pull the cord to open the window shade. And his words, as he introduced the spectacle, were slurred and incoherent, so much so that he gave up on a speech and said, "Well, there it is anyway," before stepping back from the group and sitting on the bed.

But the Bowen Company lights needed no introduction; we were used to them, even those of us—like Nick, like Bobby or Joey—whose parents had themselves been born in Italy. Somebody had tuned in a transistor radio on my parents' dresser, and we heard Prudential Bowen's voice, the boss of bosses, counting down to us across the airwaves and then, out on the black Missouri horizon where we were staring, across an old dirty creek that had once run through pig farms, the buildings lit up suddenly—the tower of the Palazzo Vecchio, with its castellated battlements outlined in red; the green curl of Brunelleschi's dome, above Santori's Seafood, the façade of the Uffizi Palace, which housed Harzfeld's department store, and the spire of San Lorenzo, all lit up for us across the creek. The fireworks went off, and over the radio we heard the crowd roaring. I did not know then nor do I know today, when I see those lights go on, what to say about them other than the fact that it was American. You couldn't tell whether it was real or fake, but you knew that it made money.

"Goddamn it," I heard Joey Ramola say. "Do you know what I'd give to see that many people standing around *my* restaurant today?"

"Is that a saw?" another voice said. It was Tracy, whom I noticed off to my right, holding her forgotten puppy. She was pointing at the foreground of the scene where an oak limb hovered before my parents' bedroom window, breaking up our view of the Campanile. "It *is* a saw," she said. "Who would ever leave a saw up in a tree?"

"There's a story behind that," my father said from the bed. His voice sounded strange and distant, as if he spoke with his hands cupped about his face. "It's historic."

In fact, my father and I had left the saw there after it became pinched in the underside of the limb, which we'd been trying to cut down for this party. The group waited for him to finish the story, the puppy squirming in Tracy's arms. "Al, you're not going to leave us hanging on this historic saw, are you?" Joey Ramola said finally.

"Oh, I'm sorry," my father said. He had his back to the window. "Jack will tell it to you. He knows better than me."

"The saw is left there from a famous Civil War battle that was fought here, Mr. Ramola," I said. "The Confederates hung a Union prisoner in that tree, and when the Union forces retook this hill, they tried to cut down the branch where their comrade was hanging. The saw stuck—so they left it as a monument."

"Jee-sus," Joey said under his breath. "He's almost up there with his old man."

"The saw you see is a replica, of course," I continued. "Hung there by the landmarks commission when the original rusted away." As I spoke, I felt Nikki Garaciello's hand take mine and the points of her breasts brush my shoulder blade.

"You know where Lonnie is, don't you?" she said. "He went to meet Geanie down by the creek. He said I was supposed to bring you with me."

According to Nikki, Lonnie had left word that we should meet him down by the Wornall Bridge, and so, once the fireworks display ended, I hustled her downstairs and walked that way. The Campanile on Thanksgiving night was as crowded as Times Square on New Year's Eve. The crowds were so great that the police blocked off the intersections and people milled about, gawking at the lighted buildings overhead. Partygoers hung over the balconies of Prudential's hotels, toasting the pedestrians below them in the streets, and the bars and restaurants stayed open late. It was an amusement park and a huge block party all rolled into one, only it didn't feel that way to me. Bobby Ansi's story was still there, mixed up in my head, about how all these buildings had come to be; I saw my father, seated on his bed, refusing to look out at the ceremony. And though Nikki and I spent an hour wandering through the crowds, past the mechanized statues of Santa's elves in Harzfeld's windows, past the statues of Bacchus, Zeus, and Iphigenia, we never once caught a glimpse of either Lonnie or Geanie.

Sales

G eanie seemed genuinely apologetic when I finally talked to her—
though for two days after Thanksgiving, the calls I made went
unanswered. It wasn't a big deal, she claimed; she'd told Lonnie
that it would be fun to go out once the lights came on and Lonnie had left
this message with Nikki because I'd been too busy to leave. Though these
were perfectly good answers, they did nothing to dispel the sick feeling in
my stomach and so, in my frustration, I went after her as I'd gone after my
mother. If it wasn't such a big deal, why not pick out a place for us to meet?
I asked. Why not mention it to me? She'd answered with a hitch in her
throat, a sound that I recognized as both worry and pity, but I'd pushed
right on, my voice buzzing so I hardly recognized it, until I heard her saying, "What do you want me to say? Do you want me to tell you you're
right? Okay, Jack, you're always right. But have you ever considered that
sometimes people just do things? That it's okay to have fun without everything being *explained*?"

We were barely on speaking terms when, the following Saturday, I borrowed my father's car and drove her to the Garaciellos' house at Fifth and
Troost. The Garaciellos had two residences—one farther out in the nicer
neighborhoods of the "northeast" and this house, in the old Italian North
End. I'd only ever visited this second house. The wood shingles that covered it had gone mossy from all the shade, and the front yard consisted of
two concrete slabs, painted green, which Lonnie's grandmother sometimes
swept in a black shawl. Inside, you were so smothered in contradictory as-
pirations that you felt as if Norman Rockwell and Stan Lee together had
slathered you with paint. There was the piano with lesson books for Nikki
and Lonnie, and gold stars and red pencil marks above the lesson plans. A

flutter of report cards tied off to an oil painting of Christ. Actual Whitman samplers, a *Last Supper* carved in relief. But there were also copies of *Popular Mechanics* beside the sofa, a stack of Elvis records on the phonograph stand, signed LP covers of Ritchie Valens and Frank Sinatra with palm fronds stuck behind them, their tips fluttering with the pivoting front-room fan. "Uncle Bobby put the concert on," Nikki said to us, nodding at the albums. She was posed on the sofa in her saddle shoes reading a copy of *16*. "We've got tickets to go backstage, okay? I give one to Tommy Thompson and what does he do?" She rustled her magazine haughtily. "He *sells* it, if you can halfway believe."

The "children's" room upstairs had been divided neatly in half. Nikki's side was all pink and ruffles, a phone set on a doily, a little journal at her bedside along with its tiny key, while Lonnie's side smelled of aquariums and model glue. But while Lonnie sat working on a model airplane at a folding table covered with newsprint, I could see also that there was a chair pulled up beside him and a pair of Nikki's sneakers underneath. "She's good at it," Lonnie said when he saw me looking. "I used to think that she'd just gotten a lot of small-brush practice from painting her nails, but it's better than that."

"LONNIE!" Nikki howled this from her bed, where she'd gotten on the phone already. "I do *not* work on plane models—Jack, don't listen to him!" She'd covered the receiver, supposedly to block out this conversation, but her fingers were widely splayed. She rolled over to talk, wiggling the points of her shoulder blades.

"Better than what?' I said, trying at the same time to follow the teakettle hiss of Nikki's conversation from the bed.

"Better than anything I've ever seen—the striping, the decals, even the dope work. She talks all the time, but if you can put up with it, you're home free."

"*That's* nice, Lonnie," Geanie said. "Real complimentary."

Lonnie was now showing her the finished Spitfires and Camelbacks that hung above his bed on strings, tapping them one by one with a scalpel—a gesture that reminded me of his first day on the Pemberton kickball court, when he'd shouted, "Pick me!" Only his face had grown gaunter and more serious since then, his skin had lost the slight gloss of what my classmates had called "garbage grease." The fact that he now stood six foot two had changed things as well, balancing out the awkward size of his feet, wearing away baby fat so that his body, in his usual tank-top undershirt, looked impressively muscled. I also had the feeling, as he palmed the small of Geanie's back, that the two of them had been here before and that this "tour" was designed to hide that fact from me. "The experiment I'm working on now is to build a plane that can carry a camera—it's primarily an issue of airfoil and lift," he was saying in a voice meant, I think, to sound tolerant. "Geanie says there's a certain level of mathematic skill you have to be born with, and if you don't have that to start, then it's not even worth trying." He stretched out his hands as if his math skills were contained there.

I picked up his Messerschmitt wing. "An experiment, Lonnie? Really? So I guess you and Geanie are working back and forth on this?"

"I'm the writer," Geanie said anxiously. "For any serious science-fair project, you've got to turn in a twenty-page paper on your hypothesis."

"I guess that's probably what you guys were doing when Nikki and I were looking for you on Thanksgiving," I said. "Working on papers, I guess."

"Hey, she's not *my* girlfriend," Lonnie said to me. He grabbed the balsawood wing from me in a manner that broke it somehow, internally—the skin intact but the skeleton drooping.

"Who said anything about girlfriends?"

"Did somebody say something about girlfriends?" Nikki asked. She had removed the phone from her ear and held it up like a microphone between Lonnie and me.

"Cut it out, you guys," Geanie said. When Nikki swung the phone to her, she yelled into the mouthpiece, "I don't want to be ANYBODY'S girlfriend."

"You want to comment?" Nikki said to me.

"I didn't start this," I said. "Talk to Lonnie."

"Geanie and I have an intellectual partnership, Acheson," Lonnie said, peeling back the doped skin of the model's wing. "A meeting of the minds. Although, being a guy who's spent his whole life at Pemberton, you probably don't respect that kind of thing."

"Jack has respect," Nikki said. She had again covered the phone's mouthpiece with her palm. "Jack's your friend."

"Yeah?" I said. "Well, tell your brother that I thought the whole idea behind us being friends, the whole idea behind this stupid Surveyors' Club thing—"

"Idiots' Club," Nikki said. "I told you we should call it that."

"—was that we do stuff together. Was that one person, or two people, don't sneak off and do things without telling anybody." I completed this sentence despite the furious glare that Geanie was giving me.

"'Sneak off?'" Lonnie said. He leveled his scalpel at me. "How 'bout 'fuck off,' man? How often do you just walk over to Geanie's house without calling me? Or Nikki? How many times have you and her 'snuck off' in the woods? Do you see me interfering in that kind of stuff? Do I stand around and keep track?"

Geanie whistled. It was her full, length-of-the-field hockey whistle, and it vibrated the paintbrushes and scalpels on Lonnie's model table. Still whistling, Geanie took the phone from Nikki, blew directly into the mouthpiece, and then handed it back.

"Now, then," she said in a calm voice. "Can we bring this meeting to order?"

"Hello?" Nikki said into the phone. She banged the earpiece against her palm, but when Geanie licked her lips, she hung it up quickly.

"It's my understanding," Geanie continued, "that the agenda for today is to watch a test flight of Lonnie's plane, which he and I have worked on and which he's going to enter in the city science fair. Does anybody else have anything?"

"I do," I said. "After Lonnie's done, I've got something to say."

It is easy for me to remember the emotions of the boy who made that pitch, with the streetlights coming on brown around Garrison Park, a few blocks from the Garaciellos' house. I can even *see* myself there, though the view is from above, as if Lonnie's model plane—boxed up in the Buick's rear end, having failed (thankfully) on this cold night to start—had in fact gotten off the ground. I can see the beaten roof of the Garaciellos' Roadmaster, old-fashioned even by the early sixties. I see the liver-colored bricks of Fourth Street, set down at the founding of the city, the pale dead grass tufted in their seams beneath our feet, the cone of the streetlamp shining down atop our heads, and there, in the center of the picture, unrolled between my gloved hands, the beautiful green and lavender of my father's map. My friends laughed at me as I pointed to it, scarves of steam whispering from their lips—not unkind laughter, but laughter nonetheless. I was not surprised by their laughter; I'd been gripped, ever since I picked up Geanie, by the utter conviction that my idea was ludicrous and would never be believed. But once I unrolled the map, the words poured out naturally. "What's so funny?" I asked with a mock-confused grin on my face, one that suggested I was willing to endure this embarrassment because I knew the merits of my case. "Why can't we buy a piece of land, the four of us? Come on, Lonnie—you're the guy who goes around bitching about other people's houses. So why not buy something for yourself?"

"Because it's a pipe dream, man," Lonnie said. He'd stepped away from the trunk's hood and pulled his coat tight, shaking his head. "It's just not realistic."

"You mean, 'realistic' like trying to take pictures with a toy plane?"

"I mean, 'realistic' like why would I want to spend money on a bunch of rocks? Especially when I can go there now anyway?"

"What about an investment? Come on! You know how this works! You and Nikki were there with me, driving around in those fields, in this car, getting ready to buy this land with her father's money"—I pointed at Geanie—"and put houses on it. Tell me you don't know this. Or that the land value will go up five hundred, six hundred, maybe a thousand percent once the houses go in? So what's stopping us?" This I addressed to both Lonnie and Geanie, who I knew would respond to a logical argument. "Lonnie, you tell me that you couldn't figure out the boundaries for an acre property that included the quarry. Or, Geanie, that you couldn't write up a contract to buy it."

"Yeah?" Lonnie said. "That's nice and everything, but who's going to pay for it? Where are you going to get the dough?"

"How much did that plane cost?"

"A couple hundred," Lonnie said.

"Two? Was it more than two?"

"Not much."

"And how did you pay for that?"

"I got a job, I saved money. You know—you worked with me."

"So we're talking an acre of this property goes for a thousand bucks—less, maybe, if we're talking about a place up on a hill with a rock quarry that would be difficult for building. So say eight hundred. We've got four people. Are you saying we each couldn't find two hundred bucks?"

"She could, maybe," Lonnie said, tilting his head at Geanie.

"Maybe that's right," I said. But I wanted to avoid having Geanie feel like she was in this only for her money. "And maybe as a last resort, we could take a loan out from Geanie and agree to pay her back. The point is that it's not that much. We could raise the money ourselves. It's not a joke—it's a real possibility."

"But what's the rush?" Nikki asked. "If your father's buying it, or Geanie's dad"—I noticed, in Geanie's presence, that she left out Bobby Ansi—"why can't we just ask them to let us use that one piece? And what would we do with it anyway?"

There were a dozen other questions like this, each coming at me from a different person and thus with a different unspoken spin that needed answering, so that I felt like a tennis player with three different balls in play. The funny thing, though, was that the answers came easily—and that I enjoyed giving them. I'd been watching all these years, hadn't I, just like Nick said? I knew where and how to flatter; I knew what to avoid so as not to offend. I knew, for instance, that Geanie would be interested only if the idea were presented to her as a challenge, as a way to prove to her father and her grandfather that a girl, too, could apply the tricks of their trade. I knew that for Lonnie it needed to be practical, a gesture of resistance to Bobby Ansi, and how to answer Nikki when she said, "So if Lonnie's doing the surveying and Geanie's drawing up the contracts, what's the point of including me? I'm not even any good for money."

"Are you kidding?" I said. "Who's the only one of us in this group who actually knows anybody at school or might be able to help raise funds there? Besides, you're the only other person besides me who's talked directly to MacVess."

"Even if I hit him in the nuts?"

"Who's to say? That was six years ago—and besides, an old man like that? A high-school beauty like you? He might like you better for it."

It was in the end a contest, you understand. I'd never won a contest before. And in this case (so I imagined) the stakes weren't just shabby blue field-day ribbons but Geanie Bowen's attention, which actually meant something to me.

And so, if you pull back again to a position overhead, just above the streetlights—far enough away that my actual words ("Come on, all of you, what's the one thing we have in common? What's the one thing we know how to do?") begin to fade—I can tell you from that distance what I see.

The boy below is wearing a too-thin pea coat and jeans instead of a fedora and a yellow suit. His head is covered with a stocking cap, so it is impossible to see the color of his hair; his face is lost in shadow. But watch his gestures there as he jabs his finger at the map, as he removes his gloves to hold down the curls on either end, as he smooths, very softly, the knitted brim of his cap between his fingers as if to make a crease—a gesture designed to give the impression that he is listening to the arguments of his customers with attention and respect. And note that finally, when he makes his reply, he doffs this hat, not so much in a gesture of passion but one of revelation, not tossing it away or stuffing it messily in his pocket but placing it in a smooth and upright dome atop the car hood, as if to suggest the orderliness of his argument. These, you can be sure, are the gestures of his father, selling, selling, selling. And you know that, deep in his bones, he has felt a powerful flash of joyfulness at this—of selling for selling's sake, of taking an idea and installing it in others' minds so that they, too, come to believe in its reality. A joyful feeling of recognition, whether or not he feels later, as I did, a dark foreboding about the consequences that his own idea might unleash.

MacVess

"I guess I don't see any harm in talking," Royce MacVess said to me. The four of us—Nikki, Lonnie, Geanie, and I—were sitting in his kitchen while he beat a dozen raw eggs in a mixing bowl with a whisk. He was dressed in a blue satin robe, a pair of pale blue pajamas on whose cuff hems, down by his ankles, I could see the initials *RM* and what looked suspiciously like a tied-off woman's black stocking, the heavier leg band gripped tight about his forehead. Behind him an empty frying pan warmed atop the kitchen's small electric range. "I'm not saying it's for sale, mind you—you don't have any idea of the sort of pressure that's been going on out here. Do you know that I've already had offers on the whole place? These are men who claim to speak for me in my own interest—'Mr. MacVess, our goal is to see that you are compensated fairly for your property.' But their affiliations, when I look into them . . ." He bent over the table, whispering. "I am fairly certain that at least one of them is a Catholic."

"Our interests are . . . um, primarily historical," I said. "That is to say, we understand your family's importance to the county—"

"How?" It was hard to know exactly how to take this. MacVess had the mixing bowl cradled in the crook of his arm, going at it vigorously, and he cast little thin-lipped grins of expectation our way.

"I'm sorry . . . how?" I looked at the others; they were jammed together on a red tartan window seat. The three of them shifted their eyes at MacVess, urging me to respond. "I dropped the *sheet*," I whispered.

"Whispering is impolite," MacVess said.

"What he means is, we're interested in how farms work," Nikki said. With her foot she slid my cheat sheet on Royce MacVess's past back to me, under the table.

"So you're from an agricultural school, then?" He sniffed; his stirring slowed noticeably. "I suppose I could get one of the boys to take you through the shop, but I have to say that my relations with the last group from Kansas State were highly disappointing. Imagine a legitimate college program in America that not just enrolls but offers scholarships to Mexicans. . . . I don't mean Spaniards, or somebody with a foreign-exchange visa. *Señor,* one of them called me—"

"What she meant to say was that we're interested in *this* farm, specifically for its connection to the MacVess family history," I said quickly.

"For preservation," Geanie put in.

"Exactly," I said. I had the cheat sheet cupped once more against my thigh. "For example, we understand that your father was one of the first settlers in the area, that at one point he owned the largest ranch in four states, that the Flatrock Ranch is still the largest ranch in Kings County. And that the quarry that you have on your property—please correct me on any of this, if you think I'm wrong—is not only one of the first quarries in Kings County but was also a meeting place for the Shawnee."

During this speech MacVess had sunk slowly into his chair facing the window seat. The kitchen was sunny, eastern facing, its table newly laid with pewter fruit bowls, breakfast plates, water glasses, and a book in a cellophane cover, titled *I Saw Poland Betrayed.* On MacVess's chair there was a heavily worn needlepoint seat cover of the now-dead President Kennedy, whose chin jutted between the V of his pajamas. The rancher stared at a pair of finches feeding outside the window, apparently having forgotten us and the frying pan, from which a pencil line of smoke coiled into the air.

"I'm sorry, sir," I said after a while. "If now's not the right time, perhaps . . ."

MacVess fluttered his fingers at me. "Just thinking."

"My apologies," I said. Behind him on the stove, the frying pan had begun a faint, high-pitched rattling.

"From the mouths of babes," MacVess said finally, lowering his gaze, and in silence he examined all four of us, one by one, his knuckle now pressed hard against the fold of his upper lip. The last in line was Lonnie, his hair slicked back from his forehead and—at my insistence—a thin black tie and his wide starched Christmas collar clamped around his neck. "The mouths of babes," MacVess repeated.

"Why's he looking at me when he says that?" Lonnie asked.

"I'm sorry, sir. Mr. MacVess," I said. "My friend Larry here was wondering if this means you might be interested in our project?"

"I don't like the word 'preservation' too much," MacVess said. "You *preserve* something when it's dead. That's what we did to the Shawnee in my museum, of course, was to preserve them, their customs, their little moccasins, their necklaces, these very precious leather shirts they used to make—all wiped out completely by us, you understand. The whole business destroyed. You've visited the museum?"

"Sure," I said, though I could tell my partners weren't too happy with this lie. "As officers in our school's historical society, it's one of our duties."

"But the idea of a living preservation," MacVess said. "That's something different again. That's an idea that works." He consulted the finches again thoughtfully. "This *is* what you said, isn't it?"

"I think you might have heard those words," Geanie said. "Living and preservation. I'm pretty sure they were both in there."

"Maybe not exactly in that order," I said.

"But a living preservation is your idea?" MacVess said.

"Absolutely."

"In so many words."

"The idea is to have something that's both living and preserved."

Lonnie made a horse-fart sound, but when MacVess narrowed his eyes, he straightened up and said, "Oh, yeah—I'm in. Preserve me."

"A living preservation, *not* a reservation," MacVess said. "A working ranch where students could come to study and work. A repository of American values, of the way that we can still live, instead of . . . instead of . . ."

"Instead of those developers, sir?" I suggested. "You see, we figured that by purchasing one small part of the ranch, we could make sure that it was preserved—"

"Don't worry about the developers," MacVess said. "Prudential Bowen will have to build a highway over me before I sell this place. What I'm talking about is a word that's even better than preservation: 'resistance.' Mmmm? How do you like the sound of that? An outpost of resistance." He was up now, out of his chair, pacing excitedly. "I had thought there weren't any young people anymore who cared about such things. That their interests were limited to rock music and to television—but of course that's what you'd get from newspapers, isn't it? And yet, if you are interested enough to come out here, on your own accord, to try to find out the truth—well then, how many other young people like you do you suppose there might be?"

"Sir, I'm not sure we'd have the money for the whole ranch," I said. "We were really only talking about an acre."

"If you're interested, wouldn't there be others?" MacVess said. "I admit I'm losing money right now. There are these despicable debts. Nobody cares if *I* resist anything. If I resist, I'm just an old man, out of step, getting in the way. But what if we did have young people out here, working, cutting calves, putting in man-hours? If there were others like yourselves who wanted to know the truth . . . well then, we wouldn't be so easy to dismiss, would we? We would—"

In his excitement, the old man swung around and grabbed the handle of the cast-iron frying pan. His voice stopped with a slight uptick in pitch. And he froze for a moment, the pan quivering in his grasp, an unfortunate gap remaining in the fly of his pajamas, left over by the wrinkling that had happened while he sat. "Sweet Jesus, Mother," he said in a small voice. "I'm being singed."

Lonnie shoved the table back to get around to him. I was up, too, though both of us stopped when it looked as if MacVess wanted to hand the pan to us.

"My floor," he said.

"Jesus Christ, let go of it!" Lonnie cried. And then MacVess did. The pan slipped from his hand not with a clatter but with a hiss and a plume of yellowish smoke as it hit the linoleum sideways, where it stuck, melted in.

By this time it was already clear that my plan to purchase Royce MacVess's quarry was not going to win Geanie back for me overnight. This is not to say she didn't play along with it, that she did not pretend to be interested in its strategies or did not, along with the rest of us, spend several afternoons that spring out talking to Royce MacVess—who, with his burned hand wrapped up in a bandage the size of a softball, seemed eager for the attention, at least. But now, when we drove out to Kings County, Lonnie handed me the keys to the Impala and then climbed with Geanie into the backseat. When I caught Geanie's eye at such moments—with the wind whipping her hair as she cuddled with Lonnie in the backseat or making tea in Royce MacVess's kitchen while Lonnie covered the burned spot in the linoleum with a shopping bag and tape—she gave me a blank, apologetic gaze. It said (as best I could interpret) that we might have once been meant for each other, but unfortunately, sadly, it wasn't possible just right now, because she had some other place that she needed to be.

A few weeks later, Lonnie's plane made its first successful flight in Garrison Park. The plane was gas-powered, with a gleaming red fuselage and double, biplane wings. Lonnie had constructed the frame out of aluminum and wood, had rigged a taut cat's cradle of wires to stabilize the wings, and had installed electromagnetic switches to control the wing flaps and the tail, so that the whole thing could be flown from a remote-control box he unloaded from the back end of the Roadmaster and filled with batteries. "This is the throttle," Geanie explained to me, touching an oiled metal bar alongside the engine. "And the guy wires for the flaps run through these pegs."

"So he made it from a kit?" I asked. I was still hoping to downplay Lonnie's accomplishment in some way.

"The engine is," Geanie said. "He just bought that. But the whole body he built himself out of wood instead of steel, so it could carry extra weight." She waved her hand above her head at Lonnie, over at his control box, and the prop began to spin.

"What for?" I said as we backed away.

"That's the experiment," Geanie said. "Anyone can fly a model plane. Lonnie's idea is to put a camera in it, to take pictures from overhead, but cheap."

There was a poverty around Garrison Park that you did not feel in Prudential Bowen's neighborhoods. The clouds above were winter clouds, gray and reefed; a cold wind blew in across the river from the north and flattened cardboard boxes against the ball-field fence. You could see the smoke curl up from the paper plants along the levee, and the raw brown towers of downtown just off to the west. Not surprisingly, the mayor had also chosen the north end as the perfect route for the highway to take through the city. "Welcome to I-35, ladies and gentlemen," Lonnie had said earlier, pointing to a wall of earth that cut off Fourth Street, clods of dirt rolling out along the bricks. "The same road we drive to MacVess's place? This is where it's gonna end up—heading out across the river, all the way to Iowa." But what I felt in this neighborhood, seeing the completion of my father's dream, was nothing; it was the opposite of his stories of his own, my own, and great men like Henry Ford's and Tom Durant's inevitable success.

I was more than impressed, however, by Lonnie's plane. Children filtered out of the projects to watch it, and the insults that they shouted at each other—"Watch out, suckah, or Mr. Lonnie's gonna bomb you with that thing"—explained where he'd picked up his lingo for our football games. One, about eleven, wearing a green satin warm-up jacket and socks on his hands, confronted Geanie, Nikki, and me, saying, "Y'all got to move, okay? You crowding up the landing strip." Then Lonnie guided the plane out for one last pass toward the river. You couldn't see the water from here, exactly, only the wired neck of a crane and trucks that read ANSI CONSTRUCTION scurrying atop the highway's berm. For a moment the plane was a dark speck above the spires of the Paseo Bridge, where the interstate would cross the Missouri, and all at once I understood how, with a camera, Lonnie would be able to see everything, how the course of the highway would be laid out clearly, and that from above we would know the map that all our parents had hidden from us, the future that we had been too young and dumb to see. "He did it," Geanie was saying. "Isn't it beautiful? See, I told you he had something. He's your friend, Jack. It's really something you ought to be willing to believe."

Nikki came up with the best description of what spending time with Royce MacVess *felt* like. "It's like getting to know somebody inside out," she said, capping her pen and stowing away her social journal as we pulled onto the Flatrock Ranch one day. "Most people seem normal in the beginning, and then, the longer you get to know them, the weirder they get. But with him, he's so crazy from the start of things, when you first see him, that he doesn't have anywhere to go except to seem more normal from there."

In fairness, there were normal things about Royce MacVess. He ran his ranch efficiently—even Lonnie had to admit that. He had two barns, a steel-fenced culling pen, a machine shop, a squat metal grain silo, a concrete-floored garage, three winter ranch hands, and four collies that patrolled a wide gravel-and-mud clearing at the end of his property's main entrance from the west. Seeing him there in boots and jeans, a straw hat on his head, I often mistook him for one of the hands. In fact, you rarely saw the Royce that I've described except in the privacy of his own house, which was set off down a flagstone path from the working areas of the ranch. It was a redecorated version of the ranch's original bunkhouse, white clapboard outside, blond tongue-and-groove paneling within, and Royce kept it in pristinely ordered condition, as clean and dusted as the bauble-filled apartments of widows that lined the north bank of the Campanile. He had signs, done in needlepoint (sewing being a habit he cultivated openly and one that, if you asked around, was hardly looked down on by cattlemen on the Kansas plains) for nearly everything that could be turned on or off, opened or closed. COFFEE'S ON! THE BAR IS OPEN! Plus, there was a seemingly endless number of glass cases and shelves filled with buttons, leaflets, or windup toys related to his "political forays" and which seemed to come from some strange parallel universe, an alternative American history:

Agricultural Act of 1961
Say NO to Socialism in Our Fields

This is a republic
Not a democracy—
Let's keep it that way.

Give 'em Hell, Joe!

An Old West–style poster:

WANTED!
A reward of $5.00 to anyone who can point to the
Word "democracy" anywhere in the Constitution,
in the Declaration of Independence, or in the
separate constitutions of any one of the fifty states.

I had no familiarity with the Agricultural Act of 1961; nor did I know much about Joe McCarthy. What I did recognize when Royce stepped into his bathroom, automatically changing the needlepointed message that hung against its door from THE W.C. IS OPEN TO HOLD IT, PLEASE! was lone-liness. Membership in the last heat.

It was this recognition that made us think we could convince Royce to hold a "farm party" as a way to raise money to buy the quarry. These had been a tradition at Pemberton and Briarcliff for years—basically drunken events that took place far enough out in the country to be safe from the police. We had all heard stories about cow tipping, about how the foreign transfer student had gotten so drunk he fell asleep in a tree, deeds that would have been unimaginable within the city limits but were somehow allowed and encouraged out in the country, for a single night, once a year. Naturally, none of us had actually been invited to this kind of party, and so it had never occurred to me that we might have it out at the quarry until Nikki proposed the idea.

"It's pretty much the last decent chance that any of us have of doing something cool before our senior year," she had said matter-of-factly. "And guys, I hate to break it to you, but if we haven't done anything by then, it's usually too late."

I made our pitch to Royce on a spring afternoon; the sun still set early, and the room had just crossed the pivot point from daylight into dusk, the yellow light from the single lamp at Royce's elbow emphasizing the shad-ows rather than actually brightening things. Outside, down the flagstone path, I caught a glimpse of a pickup leaving Royce's barn, loaded up with hay, its headlights flashing once through the window before it rumbled off. "So what do you think?" I said. "We charge five dollars a head, put that toward a preservation fund for the quarry. Plus, you'll have a hundred kids or so who'll get a chance to come out and see the ranch."

"If it's successful," Nikki said, "we could have a fund-raiser"—this was the term we'd chosen to replace farm party—"for every school in the city."

"I'm listening," Royce said. He kept three good cabinet televisions in the house, and just now his eyes were focused on *The Andy Griffith Show* playing with the sound off. When the commercial came on, he said, "Now, what school is this you said would be coming? Or did you say?"

I glanced at the others. Since my father and Nick Garaciello were also spending time in this same living room, trying to convince Royce to sell *them* his ranch, we'd already decided to lie about our names. This hadn't so far been too much of a problem, since the rancher had seemed, during most visits, far more interested in talking about himself than in who we were. But it would be tough to lie about the school where the partygoers would be coming from, even though we were worried that MacVess might not view a private school like Pemberton favorably.

"Pemberton Academy, sir," I said. "I thought we'd already mentioned that."

"Because they have all the money," Nikki put in.

I glared at her. "Well, that and also because we go there," I said. "Larry and I do. Harriet, here, and Helen go to Briarcliff."

"You do?" MacVess said, sitting forward quickly. He was wearing a satin robe of peacock blue and had a plush maroon towel wrapped around his neck. His eyes roved among the four of us. "I thought you said you went to some Christian place."

"There are Christians there," I said. "It's mostly Christians, really— wouldn't you agree with that, Larry?"

"Only two Jews I know of," Lonnie said.

"You're not kidding about this, are you?" MacVess asked. "I don't like jokes, practical or otherwise. They detract from conversation."

"There might be some Jews who don't admit it," Lonnie said, but MacVess had already hurried out of the room. When he returned, after some loud closet noises and hanger scrapings, he was carrying a leather-covered album as thick as a phone book and wore a sweater that was the same color and texture as a wicker doormat. The sleeves rode high on his forearms, and the armpits pinched so that his elbows levered out from his hips. In the center of this sweater was a felt letter *H*. MacVess spread his arms as if we were supposed to recognize something. We watched him silently.

"What?" he said. "You don't know what this is? And you call yourselves a historical society? It's an original Hill School sweater. That's what Pemberton used to be before they moved the campus and made up that fake name. The Hill School. I'm an alumnus. I can't believe you didn't know that."

Judging from the pictures Royce showed me, the Hill School had been located in a stone house with dark canvas awnings, somewhere around Thirty-sixth Street. About fifteen students from age six to eighteen posed in knickers on its steps. "You can imagine, a country boy coming into that environment—no graces. I was better off trying to shoe a horse than speaking French." The curly-headed boy he singled out, with a small black ribbon looped around the starched collar of his shirt, looked to me like he would have done fine in French class. I was more surprised by an older boy in the back, his hand wrapped around the chain of a porch swing like a trolley rider hanging from his strap. "And there's our ugly friend," Royce said, almost fondly. "He'd skipped classes that year all semester; the teachers were against it, but I remember he paid the photographer a dollar to let him stand in."

He was right; the boy was ugly. He had a crushed-looking face, the interval too small between his sharp black eyes and his shallow chin, and his hair—an indeterminate gray in the photo—tufted wildly out from underneath the brim of his porkpie hat, as if in defiance of the straight haircuts of the other boys nearby. I felt a strange lightness in my stomach as the others leaned in to see the photo—except Geanie, who was staring out the front window with a concerted expression of disinterest on her face.

"These were the days before cars, you understand," Royce said, reversing the album to allow the others to see. "So he offered my father a deal to drive me into town on his buckboard, provided my father paid his tuition, too. My father agreed—local boy, his father clerked at our feed store, seemed a hardworking kid. But when our friend gave me that ride, what did he do? He dropped me off, then spent the day buying fruit and vegetables down at the market on Fifth Street, picked me up at three o'clock, and then he had a whole route to work on the way home, selling the produce back to fifteen or twenty farmers along the way—then used the profits to pay the teachers for his grades."

Nikki and then finally Geanie had glanced casually at the picture, but Lonnie, during this whole discussion, had kept squinting at it. After a while he'd taken the book from Royce and studied it under the light. "That's Prudential Bowen," he said.

"You mean, you recognize him?" Royce asked. He seemed genuinely mystified at this at first, but as his gaze passed from face to face—our eyes slightly averted from him now—his expression seemed to contract, the wrinkles around his mouth tightening. "Well, I guess that his face is a pretty common thing to recognize—or would be for a group of historians like yourselves."

"Oh, no, *Helen's* fascinated by the Bowens, aren't you, Helen?" Lonnie said. "She thinks they're the greatest family this city has ever produced. Isn't that right, *Helen*? Wouldn't you be interested in how Royce knows Prudential Bowen?"

"How'd you know him?" Geanie asked. Despite her clear irritation with Lonnie for having forced the subject into the open, she now seemed interested in the story.

"He lived in this very house," Royce said. "This was the bunkhouse. You had about ten men in here at any given time—a foreman, five or six cowboys, a skinner, occasionally a blacksmith who did the shoeing."

"That must have been pretty tough for a kid," Geanie said.

"But he chose it, right?" Lonnie said. "It was his decision. He figured if he was going to make it, he had to get away from his family."

"Really what he did was switch families," Royce said. "He adopted ours, or at least my father hired him to do our books. He slept in the bunkhouse, but he ate at our table in the big house—which is gone now."

"And you didn't mind?" Lonnie asked.

"Did I mind?" Royce gave a queer, regretful smile at this. "My father liked to work, raise cattle, build roads—he never cared that much about what he called 'sitting around and counting money.' So when Prudential said he was looking for investors to buy a pig farm and some other land in Jackson County, my father allowed the kid to use his name. He took up a collection from the farmers on his produce route, made them partners in the deal. The land was purchased, the money paid. He moved out to the city to look after it. A few years later, people started noticing advertisements for something called the Bowen Company in the paper, so my father rode the train into the city and asked Prudential what the hell he was doing." MacVess bleakly chuckled. "He'd already built some houses by then, which he showed my father, along with the contract he'd written on that pig farm. It said that the land belonged to Prudential Bowen, not the farmers who'd bought in, so long as the Bowen Company returned their original investment with interest—which is how he built the Campanile."

The room was silent then, all of us watching Royce in his weird, crimped sweater and his waxy hair. "So that's why—" I said, then stopped myself.

"Do you mean that's why I don't want to sell this ranch back to Prudential Bowen?" Royce said. "Is that what you meant to say?"

"Nossir," I said, though he was right.

"Or why I am suspicious of any other developers who might come sniffing around here asking me to buy this property? Or even four supposed members of a historical society, who also just happen to want to buy my quarry?"

Lonnie had leaned back in his chair with his arms behind his head. He glanced over at Geanie, who was staring furiously straight ahead, then slapped his hands on his thighs as he stood up, walked over to MacVess, and threw an arm around his neck. The gesture seemed to be half a headlock and half a hug, with Lonnie bending down to peer into the shorter man's face. "Royce, Royce, Royce," he said. "Now, that was a hell of a story—come on, guys, don't you agree? I am so pleased to have heard that."

"Do you think so?" Royce said uncertainly. Under the pressure of Lonnie's embrace, his neck had sunk into his shoulders like a turtle's.

"Do I think so? I *know* so," Lonnie said. "Come on, that guy Prudential Bowen is practically a king back in the city. But you . . . well, I think I can speak for the entire Surveyors' Club when I say we appreciate a man who calls a spade a spade."

"Well, it's just a . . . it's just personal experience." Royce blinked at all of us, as if he'd just awakened from a deep sleep. "So you're not with the Bowens?"

"Wish I was," Lonnie said. "Wish I had that kind of money." He smirked as Geanie bolted angrily toward the door. "But I tell you what—as long as I don't, anytime you want to bitch about Prudential Bowen, all you gotta do is call on me."

The bad feeling lingered with us during the drive home. We rode in silence, this time with Lonnie back at the wheel, humming aggressively as he drove, and Geanie glowering beside him in the front seat. "Well, Lonnie, thanks for totally messing up our party," Nikki said once we'd left Royce's driveway.

"The last time anybody at school invited me to a party, Smiley and Wilson puked in my car," Lonnie said.

"The difference is that this time it would have been *our* party," Nikki said.

"Yeah, and it was my car that they puked in," Lonnie said. "All I'm saying is, why would we let a bunch of rich kids come and trash this place?"

"Do you notice how whenever he says 'rich kids,' he sneers at me?" Geanie asked.

Lonnie spit out the Impala's window, between his front teeth. "Who else am I supposed to look at, old crazy man MacVess? I guess he used to be rich until your granddad swiped his inheritance money away."

"My grandfather did not swipe his inheritance," Geanie responded. "We're sitting in the middle of his inheritance, for chrissakes. My grandfather borrowed money from some of Manual MacVess's friends—"

"So you *did* know the story." Lonnie smiled broadly. "How come you think she didn't mention that when we first went to the quarry?"

"And they all made a profit on that investment, too, which is a lot more than they ever got from Manual MacVess, I bet. So do you really want to talk about rich people trashing things, Lonnie? Or do you want to talk about somebody who started out poor but didn't sit around and complain about everything?"

"Poor old complainer," Lonnie said. "That's me."

"Screw you," Geanie said. I'd never seen her this angry—nor had any of us ever crossed her so directly—and her skin had broken into a splotchy crimson, from breastbone to forehead, as if she'd been stung by bees. She knelt sideways in the Impala's front seat, facing Lonnie, so that her cheeks vibrated with the wheels. "Everything my granddad had, he earned on his own—and legally. It was a deal, an investment deal, and he paid back every penny."

Lonnie winked at me in the mirror. "That must be how come it's your grandpa who runs the Campanile and not old Royce back there."

"It was his idea," Geanie said.

"And it must also be how come you never told him your real name."

"I was suggesting that we have a party," Nikki said. "Not argue."

"That would be doing something, at least," Geanie said. "And I still think we could convince Royce to do it. Lonnie didn't give everything away."

"That's the Bowen spirit," Lonnie said. "Maybe while we're at it, we could hang some Christmas lights around the quarry."

A week later we all met for a movie at the Campanile Theater, whose marble staircase was modeled on the library in the Church of San Lorenzo in Florence. According to the words on a brass plaque beside the ticket window, the pillars on the walls represented "a new form of ornament, invented by the world-renowned artist Michelangelo." But Lonnie and Geanie arrived in the middle of what sounded like an old argument. "My point is that if we're all the same, if we're really *friends*," Lonnie was saying as I joined them in line, "then maybe we should divide everything up. What do you think, Jack?"

"Don't answer that," Geanie said to me. "It's a kick he's been on lately, and it's all bad. I wouldn't want to divide it with anybody."

"I think five or six million would improve Jack's life significantly." Lonnie slid his elbow across the marble ledge of the box-office window, pushing himself between Geanie, who was trying to ignore him, and the cashier behind the glass.

"Four tickets to what? What do you guys want to see?" Geanie asked, her eyes lifted to the marquee.

"You see, notice this reaction, Jack," Lonnie said. He peered intently at Geanie's neck as she leaned back, studying the movie titles. "It's the famous Bowen stare. If you get too close to certain subjects, she can make you disappear."

"How about *To Kill a Mockingbird*?" Nikki said. "I was supposed to read that for class."

I stepped out of line and grabbed Lonnie's jacket. "That's it," I said. "You're done."

"Cool it," he whispered, knocking my arm away. "This is an experiment. We're going to find out if Geanie can actually see *through* me."

"Four tickets," Geanie said to the cashier. She did seem to stare directly through Lonnie's intervening face, exactly as Prudential had with my father out on the street, though I noticed that her cheeks were white and her hands shook as she reached into her bag. "Three for *Mockingbird* and one for whatever my friend wants."

"Sounds like maybe I should see *Dr. No*," Lonnie said.

"Please stop it," Geanie whispered quickly.

"Twenty million is the figure I hear," Lonnie said. As he spoke, I set my back and hauled him away from the window so Geanie could pay.

"But these tickets are only two-seventy-five," Nikki said.

"—for Geanie's part of the company," Lonnie said over his shoulder. "Which she'll get this summer when she turns eighteen—so I was just thinking if we were true friends, we could split it up four ways. What do you think, Geanie?"

I was shocked at the bitterness of these words, the suggestion that Geanie, by virtue of her wealth, somehow *owed* us money. In all my years at Pemberton, I'd never heard that one before. Lonnie had broken from my grip and stalked over to the staircase, whose Florentine lines had been muffled by red carpeting. "Hey," I said, following him. "You gonna kick in for these tickets? Or are you just going to whine *and* let Geanie pay your way?" Lonnie sneered down from the landing, an outraged twin of Sean Connery, whose cardboard likeness posed beside him. Then he turned his pockets inside out.

To her credit, Geanie confronted our argument head-on. She paid, visited the concession stand, bought herself and Nikki a Coke, and then strolled over to the bottom of the stairs. "We have a question for you boys," she said coolly. "If Nikki and I convince Royce to have this party, what are you going to do—fight or help out?"

Which was how I ended up at the Garaciellos' house, down on Fifth Street, packing up Lonnie's airplane, two kegs of beer, and a sack of fireworks into the back end of the old Roadmaster station wagon. Booze had been Lonnie's one responsibility for the party, largely because, having already turned eighteen, he was the only one of us who could buy it, and I saw when he opened the woodshed that served as the Garaciellos' garage that he had gone overboard with this. The two kegs of beer were impressive enough, more than satisfactory to obliterate the entire junior and senior classes, but Lonnie had also come up with "the hard stuff." When Pemberton boys used this term, huddled in the corner of the lunchroom, they generally meant a half-pint flask of Old Crow, shared by two or three, but Lonnie had assembled two full cases of fifths, whose cardboard tops he peeled away to show me, there in the murk of his garage. There was row after row of sealed bottles—vodka, gin, whiskey, peppermint schnapps—together with a grocery bag of mismatched packages of cigarettes, each lacking its tax tag. "Jesus Christ, Lonnie," I said, stepping back. "What are you trying to do, kill everybody?"

"Would that be such a bad thing?" Lonnie said as he picked up one of the kegs and heaved it into the Buick's rear end, its springs rocking.

The last thing we loaded up was the box that contained his airplane, along with its control gear, which Lonnie slid into the backseat, saying, "All right now, this one's a secret, bud, okay? I'm thinking about giving a little demonstration—you know, see how she does out in the open air. But the one thing you've got to do for me is, you can't tell Geanie that I brought it, okay?"

"Why not?" I asked. "It's your plane, you built it. I can't imagine why she wouldn't let you fly it."

"Well then maybe you don't know Geanie."

We were tucking a blanket around the plane's box to conceal it, both of us leaning in from opposite sides of the car, but when Lonnie said this, I quit and slammed my door. "What the hell does that mean?"

"I don't know, man, what do you think it means?"

"If it means you've got something to tell me about Geanie, then tell me, all right? Because I'm done trying to guess about this crap. You want to tell me why you've been pissing on her for the last month?"

"Pissing on her?" Lonnie said. "Think again."

"What would you call it, then?"

"Educated resistance," Lonnie said. "Just like our pal Royce." Then he hopped into the front seat of the Roadmaster, fired the engine, and screeched off down the alley before I could get in. This was, I knew, his usual way of leaving his garage, since the "driveway" beside his house was too narrow to accommodate a car. Still, it irritated me, because I was forced to walk that mossy slab of concrete between Lonnie's house and the gray brick one to the west, an area that was dotted with the dried turds of a chow his grandmother kept. When I got to the top, his grandmother was standing up there, sweeping the green pavement of the yard. She lifted a single, bony finger to me and, shuffling through the ten feet that were required to cross the Garaciellos' painted lawn, went inside and returned holding a bottle of wine. "*Festa*," she said, offering it.

"No, no." I raised my hands, palms out. By then the Buick had rounded the block and was rattling up before the house.

"*Festa*," the old woman repeated. She shook the bottle at Lonnie. "*Prendi questa. La porterai alla festa con te.*"

"Now, there's a woman you don't have to resist," he said as I carried the wine out to the Roadmaster.

"Resist what?" I said. "She's your grandma."

"Resist being developed," Lonnie said.

"See, now that's what I don't get," I said.

"Why do you think Geanie wouldn't want me to fly that plane?"

"Tonight? I don't know—maybe because she'd be afraid that you'd screw things up and wreck it." It seemed a reasonable concern to me.

"And then I wouldn't be able to use it in the science fair."

"So what's wrong with that?" I asked.

Lonnie shook his head grimly. "That's what you don't get about Geanie."

"That she likes you?" This was a painful thing to say. I'd worked up to it, intending the words as a challenge, only to have Lonnie ignore me completely.

"She's trying to develop *all* of us, brother," Lonnie said. "We're on the Bowen improvement plan—you, me, even Nikki. She doesn't want me to win that science fair or get a scholarship because she's really concerned about me. It's because she likes results—they tie things up real simply. I'm supposed to be just peachy-keen thankful that she even bothered. 'Oh, thank you, Miss Bowen, for being so kind to me. I'll do exactly what you say.' And then she moves on to some other project. Well, I'm not going to take that. A woman tries to treat you that way, you got to show some balls."

Though I recognized most of these characteristics in Geanie, Lonnie's description warped them in a nightmare way. "Why don't you just quit seeing her?" I suggested.

Lonnie groaned, as if I'd missed his point completely. "Do you want me to tell you what your part is?" he asked. By this time he'd driven us straight down Fifth Street to the sloping dirt hill that bordered the highway's construction site. It was the wrong direction to leave his neighborhood in the first place, and beyond that, he'd hopped the curb and was now driving on a makeshift track up the berm.

"How about you just tell me where we're going," I said.

But it was too late by then. It was generally too late when Lonnie was driving. Having followed the path to the top of the berm, he aimed the Buick straight down the back side of the hill. The grade was even steeper there, and down below, where the slope leveled out into the trough of the highway, the flats were littered with heavy equipment, trucks, trailers, and the same immense, house-size crane whose neck I'd seen two months earlier, when we'd driven out to Garfield Park to fly Lonnie's plane.

"Say, 'Lonnie is a genius,'" Lonnie said, smiling wolfishly.

"Lonnie is a stupid moron if he runs us down this hill," I said.

"'Lonnie . . . is . . . a . . . genius,'" Lonnie repeated, drawing the words out for emphasis. He pumped the brake and the Buick slid a foot.

"Lonnie is not right now providing me with a good example of that," I said.

"How about 'Lonnie is my friend'?"

"Come on, man, that's bullshit," I said. I opened the door, but Lonnie released the brake, and the car lurched forward another ten feet, then swerved into a skid.

"It's just a question," Lonnie said.

By then I had recognized the pattern of his questions—they were the same as the ones that we used to feed him in middle school, at the end of a Garbage Hunt, after Lonnie had been caught and pinned. *I am garbage. Say it! Say it! Lonnie is garbage. Say it! Say it! Say, I'm the Garbage Man, and I love grease!*

"All right, Lonnie, I'm your friend," I said finally. Once I said it, the anger that I felt toward him lifted. "Jack Acheson is Lonnie Garaciello's friend."

Lonnie shrugged nonchalantly as if he'd expected this, then released the brake, and we careened down to a cluttered expanse of dirt, which, after a hundred yards, deepened fairly quickly into a trench—its walls lined with limestone and rough clay, its upper reaches pocked with sawed-off pipes, jutting from the mud, and in some places what looked like open sewers, dribbling water down a rock face. Road workers had spread gravel atop the muddy bottom of this pit, but even this was completely uneven, marred by holes and deep puddles that Lonnie had to dodge. I'd read about the trench in the papers and, with my father, examined newsprint photos of it—a loop that was to surround the entire eighteen square blocks of downtown and make it "accessible to the car and ready to join the twenty-first century" in a way that the trolley lines "would have never been able to achieve." I was no city planner, but it was hard for me to understand how driving on a highway sixty feet below the surface of the street would be better than riding the streetcar, which had stopped at every block and trolled slowly through the middle of town. From down here in the ditch with Lonnie, I could make out the upper floors and spires of the city—the Power & Light Building, the Warburton Building, where my grandfather's law offices were—but only distantly. I was also completely mystified at how one was supposed to get off this highway. "There'll be ramps," Lonnie explained.

"Do they have them now?" I asked.

"Later," Lonnie said, waving his hand at the Buick's roof. "Overhead. And there'll be bridges, too, supposedly—at least there better be, since my dad says Bobby's company is getting paid a ton to put them in."

But I was most surprised by the view that confronted us as we rounded the northwest corner of downtown. It was normally a picturesque spot; the city stood high on old limestone ramparts to our left, and to our right we could see the stockyards and the bottoms of the Kansas River laid out below us, from our position midway up the downtown bluff. There the road (or in this case a winding gravel service track) lifted up out of its trench, and I saw before me what had been Fourteenth Street. Or at least I found out later that it had once been Fourteenth Street—and Twelfth Street, Thirteenth Street, and Fifteenth Street. Because at the time, I didn't recognize anything; what I saw before us was nothing more than a plain of rubble, apartment after apartment reduced to its foundations, twisted heaps of scrap metal, piles of uprooted trees. I remember glimpsing a bathtub, set out like a cartoon atop a heap of bricks, but most of the rest of what I saw, of what was there, looked like the movie reels of bombing campaigns or cities in England that had sustained the Blitz. And it was here, in the wreckage of what would be the highway, that Lonnie finally told me his secret.

"Do you know why I asked you those questions earlier?" he said. "I asked you because, if you're my friend, I've got to be honest with you. You probably think that I wanted you to answer that way, that it wasn't really a question—but the fact of the matter is, pal, that it would have been a lot easier if you'd said you *weren't* my friend."

"Why don't you ask me again?" I said.

Lonnie laughed. As much as I'd liked, or at least understood, his earlier plea for friendship, I disliked his laugh. It reminded me of the laugh that scientists in the movies gave to people who failed to understand the power of their death ray or their poisoned gas. "You know, I appreciate your sense of humor, man. I do, I really do. I think maybe that's what muffed it up with you and Geanie—I don't think she believes that somebody who's funny can also be serious. Or get her where she wants to be."

"I thought you said you were avoiding her development."

"I wish I could," Lonnie said. "I really do, brother. But I'm afraid she's sort of the key to this whole thing. To what I need to tell you."

"What's that?" I said.

"She's in love with me," Lonnie said seriously. "As soon as she gets her money this summer, we're going to bolt, together. Get her away from her family."

I ought to have been happy to hear this. It was a delusion, and I knew it— based on my own instinct and the fact that Geanie would never leave her family. I also figured that if things were going well, her love wouldn't be something that Lonnie needed to boast about. And yet as we continued south through the scar that would in three years be the highway—the highway my father had asked me for so many years to believe in—it was hard not to wonder if delusion wasn't a sensible response to the world. The highway certainly stank of it, and I felt the same dizzying sickness looking out my window as I did listening to Lonnie. Here we passed, on my right, as the trough of the dig plowed across Southwest Boulevard and headed up Union Hill, a row of apartments that had been shaved somehow in half, and in one of the upper-story rooms was a solitary blue sofa and a mirror hung above it, winking out through the missing wall. Here a bicycle wheel half buried in the mud. A pair of glasses. A slanting table leg. A row of twenty houses with their roofs caved in. The smell of sewer gases polluted the air and a banner draped along the cab of a wrecking crane read YOUR TAX DOLLARS WORKING.

In the same way that you expect champagne at a wedding or silver flasks of bourbon at a football game, there were certain bare-minimum require-ments for a farm party—hay bales, a good-size bonfire, a roughly mown field for parking the parents' cars (and later making out in their backseats), and a body of water for the single boys to throw each other into while everybody else was in the backseats. We'd considered holding the party without Royce's permission; the spot we'd chosen, where Royce MacVess's creek cupped and curved against the hillside of the quarry, was far enough away from his house to do it. But when we arrived, I saw that Nikki and Geanie had been right to get him involved. A football field's worth of prairie grass, previously waist high, had been cut down to yellow, ankle-high knobs, creating a wide clearing for the party. Rings of hay bales had been set up around a fire pit with what looked like at least two pickups' worth of cordwood stacked nearby, and just beyond this idled a John Deere tractor hitched up to a flatbed, itself stacked with bales of hay. MacVess himself was lifting Sally Jenkins, a friend of Geanie's, into the saddle of the same white horse he'd ridden to the highway opening— though when he saw me, he cut his eyes away.

"The thing about a horse is, they recognize honesty," he said loudly. He was dressed in what looked like a Texas Ranger's costume, with long white suede gloves, a pair of baggy blue pants, and a bandolier strung across his chest. "If you act like yourself on a horse, he'll respect you for it. On the other hand, if you're a *fake,* you can yell and beat on him all you want, but he'll have you off in no time—"

"Is he going to do this all night?" I asked Geanie. Lonnie and I had by then carried in the alcohol and I was kneeling beside her, helping to unfold the table that was going to be the bar. As we clicked the legs into place, I could hear her laughing at me.

"Anybody else here think I'm funny?" I asked. I glanced around. Lonnie had stalked back to the car, but four or five girls, hockey players, were giggling as they covered tables with calico cloth. "Let's get it over with. Take your best shot."

"Shhhh." Geanie reached across the table and covered my mouth. She was wearing a pair of faded jeans and plain boots and a light checked shirt that the wind pressed tight against her chest. It was a fairly small chest but one you saw a lot more of in this shirt than in the sweatshirts and team jerseys that she usually wore. I poked my tongue against her palm until she drew her hand away, and for a moment the weird solemnity of Lonnie's confession evaporated. "You should have seen your expression when you saw Royce," she said. "It really was too perfect."

"How am I supposed to look?"

"Do you remember when you and your father broke into my house? When he was arguing with my father in the backyard? You looked like that."

"It didn't seem to bother you then."

"What I mean is, you don't have a liar's face," Geanie said. "A good liar might've come in here and walked right up to Royce and shook his hand, but you looked horrified. Like you wanted to run away."

"I don't even know what you told that guy."

"The truth," Geanie said.

"And what," I asked, "is that, exactly?"

We were then watching Royce teach Sally Jenkins to ride. Sally's glasses had fallen off, and without them she'd clutched simultaneously onto the stallion's mane and Royce's bandolier, grips that the rancher was gently trying to loosen. *Now, child,* he was saying as the horse nickered. *The one thing you don't want to do is make any of those quick kinds of movements near Goldwater's eye. . . .* "I told him that we weren't trying to steal his land," Geanie said. "I told him that we really did like the quarry, that you and Nikki had first found it with your parents—or actually, Nikki told him that—and I told him that we'd been there a bunch of times without his permission. I also told him that your dad really was a developer and that you'd heard about the property from him, and so it had been your idea that we try to buy a piece."

"Did you tell him who *you* were?" I asked.

"He didn't ask."

"So you've got it, then," I said.

"Got what?" Geanie asked.

"The liar's face," I said.

"I do tell people the truth," Geanie said. "I tell all of you the truth, all the time. The problem is, you don't listen to me."

The party was itself a testament to the organizational abilities of both Geanie and Nikki, who, fortunately, were each interested in organizing different things. Nikki had shown up in a pair of white patent-leather go-go boots along with her usual short schoolgirl's skirt as well as a bikini top, which gave her the excuse to unbutton her blouse farther than usual over her brown chest. It was a shocking outfit, especially compared with the long jeans and high-necked sweaters that even the school's most popular girls chose to wear (even this was slightly risqué given that Briarcliff's dress code still required skirts). She was without a doubt the public face of our whole team, in charge of invitations, decorations, matching paper plates, the tablecloths that covered the party's folding tables, plus anything that required the slightest sense of cool—including the turntable Tommy Thompson had brought to the party and wired to his car battery so that Nikki's record collection could be played.

By contrast, Geanie handled the logistics, assigning jobs, organizing hay rides, making sure that everything worked smoothly behind the scenes. I was anointed bartender, a position I welcomed, since it allowed me to do something other than stand around and look foolish. As for Lonnie, she gave him the responsibility (through me, notably, so as to avoid talking to him directly) of greeting the guests as they came in and taking their keys—an unpleasant job but one that Lonnie seemed suited to, since once we'd unloaded his alcohol, he'd shown no interest in coming into the party. Once people started to arrive, I forgot about him and the blanket-covered plane he'd stowed in the Roadmaster's backseat, not to mention the rambling confession he'd offered me out on the highway. It was easy to forget things at the bar. Even in a hayfield, it was important for seventeen- and eighteen-year-old Pemberton students to act like they knew what they were doing when they ordered a drink. The easiest way to do this was to pretend you knew the bartender and address him by name, which meant that for the first few hours of the party I shook hands with and was affectionately teased by a whole rank of boys who previously had never paid much attention to me. Women, I was pleased to discover, tended to order drinks by leaning toward me across the bar, so that their necklines opened up. I'd just poured a whiskey and soda (which at this party was a whiskey and ice, since Lonnie hadn't thought to bring mixers) for a senior girl named Maggie Dorritt—famed among my classmates as "Maggie Two-D's" for the same sweatered breasts that now grazed my bar—when I heard a familiar, stuffed-up voice say, "If you got to have tits to get a drink at this place, maybe we should go get Belcher."

When I turned around, I saw Freddy Prudhomme standing behind me, his right hand stuck up in the left sleeve of his T-shirt, which he was using to wipe his nose. In a semicircle around him, in a rough approximation of our old Trojans huddle, clustered the boys from the last heat—Larry Stark (aka, "the Stork"), the Jewish quarterback Billy Eckstein, Ozzie Tubman, and even Elton Bunglehoff, whose crippled arm had become famous as the arm that carried crates of water bottles out to the varsity football team during Friday-night games. It was now caddying a six-pack of Schaeffer beer. "Why's Freddy making you drink that stuff?" I said as I released Freddy's slightly slimy hand. "Let me get you something real."

"I don't drink, I just carry," Elton said. "Freddy says drinking makes me confused."

"I said it makes you further confused," Freddy said. "Besides, we didn't come to drink, we came for the fringe benefits, right?"

"Maggie *Four*-D's," Elton said.

"Plus your girl Geanie—"

"No-D's," Elton said, making a face.

"It's all right," I said to Freddy, who had flattened his hand against Elton's chest and, arm stiffened, was leaning soundlessly against the smaller boy, causing him to stumble slowly back. "She's not my girl anyway."

"Whoever she is, she said you might want a little help," Billy Eckstein said. "And that you might not mind seeing some old friends."

I was glad to see them, honestly. Somehow the futility that I'd once associated with their faces—summed up for me in the sight of Freddy writhing on the Pemberton football field, his broken wrist between his knees—seemed more comforting than the success of our party. Plus, Freddy and Larry had, somewhere along the line, picked up a lot more familiarity with liquor than I had, and they showed me how to "depth-charge" glasses of beer with shots of whiskey, to be passed out to girls like Maggie Two-D's. They also took care to doctor any drinks requested by former members of the Crusaders or Marauders football teams. Billy Eckstein carried with him a vial of Spanish fly that he dissolved in certain "special" beers. And when George Belcher, by then a varsity lineman, bellied up to the bar and said, "Well, if it ain't the goddamn Trojan reunion. What are you guys doing back there—waiting for Coach Lewis to show up and pray?" Freddy knelt quickly behind the bar table, pinched his thumb and forefinger at the bridge of his nose, and, sliding them downward, drew out a long skein of mucus that he dropped straight into George's beer. Having stirred this with his finger, he offered it to Belcher, saying, "No hard feelings, George. In fact, I and every lousy football player at this bar would like to offer you a toast on the success of next year's team."

Whenever I left the bar to take a leak, I went back to being anonymous. These walks took me through the hay bales that circled the fire, around a crowded patch of grass that served as the dance floor, lit by Tommy Thompson's headlights, and past the flatbed for the hayride (where some of the couples who'd gone out on the last ride could still be seen rolling among the bales) into shadows of the trees along the creek. I made the trip twice without anybody talking to me (unless you counted Sally Jenkins, who said, "Hot dog?" forlornly as I passed the buffet), and, pissing in the darkness—gazing out across the same field where I'd watched my father sprint off to his "getaway" car—I realized that I would have liked to tell Royce that none of these people here were the slightest bit interested in his ranch's history. This was true of Maggie Two-D's, whom I could see dancing in the firelight with a letterman's jacket draped around her shoulders. It was true of George Belcher, who was standing on the hood of Tommy Thompson's car, snot-filled beer in hand, rocking the shocks so that the record skipped. It was true of Dorian Straithwaite, who'd spent the last two hours talking to Royce MacVess about the evils of Earl Warren, and whose poetry on the subject of black people—

> The politicians send us the checks to provide all our goods,
> So we raise little pickaninnies back in the woods.
> They help us keep track of our facts and our figures,
> But what do we care, 'cause we're damn lucky niggers?

—had been circulated widely on the Pemberton playground in seventh and eighth grades.

Which explains something of my state of mind when, during my third trip, I heard a strange buzzing overhead. As I tilted my head back to look at the sky, someone called out, "Hey, Jack!" Glancing down, I saw Nikki, her blouse now unbuttoned completely and tied in a knot over her belly button, waving to me from the top of a hay bale. "Quit stargazing and get over here!" she said. "You owe me a dance."

"Did you hear something?" I asked as I pushed through the crowd. Instead of listening to my question, Nikki leaped from the hay bale into my embrace, her bare knees grabbing my hips, and her white boots crossed behind my back.

"Hear something?" she said. "What I hear is a party—isn't it great? Just listen to it."

"I *was* listening," I pointed out. This time, however, all I heard was

Tommy Thompson shouting and brief, unsynchronized snatches of the song "Little Deuce Coupe" interrupted by the ripping sound of a needle sliding across vinyl.

"Do you know what that sound means?" Nikki asked me.

"It means George is jumping on the car," I said.

"That sound means we're in. No more last heat. Do you remember what happened when we found the quarry?"

"You almost killed yourself," I said.

"What else?" Nikki asked. In order to even her face with mine, she'd loosened the grip of her knees about my waist and slid down so that her crotch clamped against mine. Even I was capable of recognizing an invitation like that, and I'd been about ready to accept it (after all, Geanie wasn't offering anything) when the buzzing sound returned, several degrees higher in pitch. The shouted conversations around us trailed off for a moment, and then all at once the sound was directly overhead, a gnawing shudder of noise, and—not more than a few feet above the ducking guests—I saw two fiery streaks of sparks swoop past, leaving behind a glowing neon line that wobbled in my vision. The music from Tommy's stereo had cut out, and the faces in the crowded circle of the party pivoted in unison to watch as this mysterious double trail of sparks banked out into the night, above Freddy and Elton at the bar. "Wow," I heard someone say, "they've even got fireworks!" But Nikki's reaction was somewhat different. "Oh, shit," she said, scrambling up from the grass where I'd dropped her. "Shit, shit, shit! Don't be such an idiot—please don't be such an idiot, Lonnie. What did I ever do to you?"

Except for the pain that it caused Nikki, for once I was in agreement with Lonnie's decision to be an idiot. It went against every instinct I had—particularly in the embarrassment department—but to me the sight of his plane zooming down over the guests, low enough that on a second pass I could see its silhouette in the light of the sparklers he'd affixed to its wings, was more impressive to me than all the notoriety of the party. I knew how hard it had been for Lonnie to fly that plane in Garfield Park in the daylight, but here, guided only by moonlight and sparklers, he handled it magnificently. As I crouched beside Nikki, the plane made three or four more passes, so perfectly controlled that Lonnie seemed to be dangling it from a string. Aided by the light of the bonfire, he was even able to dive-bomb certain targets specifically, dropping down suddenly over Shaun Lambert's head and buzzing Bobby Jackman and George Belcher and Preston Petersen with such accuracy that the guests around them began to back away, as if they were diseased. Preston Petersen became so unnerved by the attacks that he bolted for the parking lot with Lonnie's plane trailing him like an oversize wasp, until Marcia Oldberg's Cadillac cut his knees out and he somersaulted over its grille.

Other than this, Lonnie's stunt was not, I realized, designed to hurt anybody. The only real danger came when Royce MacVess, several beers into his conversation with Dorian Straithwaite, mounted up on his horse, drew his Texas Rangers revolver from his belt, and fired a few potshots at Lonnie's plane—an event that rightly caused nearly all of the women and more than a few men at the party to scream. But Lonnie was pretty much finished by then; his sparklers were guttering out, and besides, the stunt had been conceptual, an attack whose coolness—if I understood him right—was in its control, its distant and Olympian mastery. I began to worry about where he was going to land the thing when the plane took one last bank and then came in low and hard—enough so that I finally tackled Nikki and held her down on the ground with me—straight into the roaring bull's-eye of the bonfire, which in turn exploded with a sustained volley of reports. These were firecrackers, of course, and it was hardly Lonnie's fault that, thanks to MacVess, nearly everybody else believed that they were gunfire instead.

Which was why, as the frame of the plane wilted and twisted in the bonfire, my first thought was not for our frightened guests but for Lonnie.

I figured that I knew where he would be. And I figured, too, that there would be one other person—besides Nikki—who would have realized that Lonnie had been trying to send a message by burning up his plane. And so, in the confusion of the moment, as Nikki climbed back up on her hay bale and pleaded with the guests not to leave, saying, "It's nothing! What are you, chicken? It's just a toy plane!" I left the party and worked my way through the tree line to the clear ground along the creek, reversing the path that Nikki and I had followed when we'd run from Royce MacVess on that first day. It took only a few minutes to reach the shallow stone crossing downstream and then perhaps another ten to climb the hill, feeling my way through the darkness from tree to tree, until I reached the edge of the open meadow that surrounded the quarry. That was when I saw Geanie. She'd beaten me up there—she'd always been, and still was, faster than me—and I could see her clearly in the middle of the meadow, hands on her knees. "What the hell are you doing?" she demanded breathlessly. I almost stepped out of the trees to answer, because I couldn't actually see anybody else there for her to be talking to. Then she continued, "Well, go on—say something for yourself." And I realized then that she was talking to Lonnie, whose back I could just make out now, barely above the camber of the curving meadow grass.

I have often heard the witnesses to accidents say—years later, when I put them on the stand—that "everything happened so fast." But during this accident, during *my* accident, things happened more slowly than I would like to admit. It is true that it was long past sunset—too dark, really, for me to see the expressions on either of their faces. But neither was I blind to what was happening, or confused at any point. There was a moon out and the meadow welled with a pale glow—caused, as I knew from previous nighttime trips, by the reflection off the quarry's limestone cliffs, which they must have been close to. And so things actually happened quite slowly, enough so that I had to *choose* not to step out from the trees and instead reverted back to my old trusted habit of watching, as if this was the only sure way to keep safe. "Stand up," Geanie was saying. "Stand up. If you're going to ruin an entire party—do you have any idea how your sister feels, by the way?—the least you can do is explain it to me like a man."

"You sure you don't have anything to explain to me?" Lonnie said.

"Stand up," Geanie repeated. "I refuse to have this conversation with you sitting there wallowing like that."

"I heard you were leaving town." Lonnie did stand up then, a hulking dark shadow, its edges tinged with the silk of the red Hawaiian shirt he'd donned for the party. "So I figured that you probably didn't really give a shit about the stupid plane. Which also made me figure I could do whatever I wanted with it."

"Listen, Lonnie, now, there are a couple things—" But then Geanie seemed to catch herself, to see that Lonnie had closed in on her by a step.

"Your father told me that you were going to school in St. Louis next year," Lonnie said. "It was a nice conversation."

"He talked to you?" Geanie said.

"I called him to discuss some things," Lonnie said. The calm, offhand manner—his scientist's sneer—in which he made this claim, as if he called Henry Bowen regularly to talk, caused my stomach to cramp. "But I also figured that, if you really were going to leave without me, I'd give you the chance to say it to my face—or at least make you, since that's a hell of a lot more than Jack and Nikki will do."

"Let go of me, Lonnie," Geanie said.

"So the first thing I'd like to start with"—it looked as though Lonnie had grabbed one of Geanie's wrists and then, using this as a fulcrum, was trying to catch hold of the other, a game I'd seen him play in fun with Nikki—"is, why don't you say, 'When it comes to Lonnie, I couldn't give a shit'?"

"Why would I want to say that?" Geanie asked.

"I don't know, why would you?" Lonnie said. "But if you don't like that, how about another one? How about, 'I don't care who I fuck? It's just for fun'?"

"Fuck you," Geanie said. And then, with a lurch, I saw Lonnie twist her wrists so that her body disappeared and his torso slanted, kneeling down above—the same position that we used to pin Lonnie on the playground.

"Well, go on and say it," he said. " 'I fucked Lonnie because I thought it would be an interesting experiment.' "

"I'm going to call someone, Lonnie."

"How about 'I'm garbage'?"

"Oh, *come* on," Geanie said.

"Try it out. Here, I'll put the whole thing together for you: 'I fucked Lonnie because I'm garbage.' "

Geanie was silent then.

" 'I'm garbage,' " Lonnie said. His voice now was sweet and leering—the voice that Shaun Lambert and Preston Petersen had used with him. The voice that I had used. "Say it: 'I . . . ammm . . . gar . . . bage. . . .' "

I was already running by the time I heard Geanie's whistle. It was a loud, full-blast screech and I angled toward it through the meadow grass. I stumbled, the whistle quit, and by the time I'd picked myself up and sprinted the final ten yards, bringing the pale vault of the quarry into view, Geanie was perched alone at its edge. When I took another step, the noise caused her to whip around and look at me. "It was an accident," she said, though I couldn't tell whether she was addressing me or Lonnie, who seemed to have disappeared totally. And then, as if I, too, had disappeared, she stood and headed off to my right, at first walking, then jogging, quickly down into the trees.

Success

My father and I were, of course, the ones who ended up handling the details of Lonnie's death, both on that night and on many other nights until the litigation surrounding the accident had been settled. I say "of course" because it strikes me now that our approaches to handling trouble that involved the Bowen family were, despite our many personal differences, remarkably similar. If Lonnie was—or had been—about confrontation or resistance to the force of what I'd once heard Royce MacVess call "Bowenism," my instinct had always been to protect Geanie from unpleasant facts. I can't explain this instinct fully, logically; certainly there were times when I felt as resentful as Lonnie did of her protected status, the "innocence" that her parents' money was able to provide, particularly of the consequences of the Bowen Company's policies. Even "innocence" isn't the right word, really, since Geanie was and always had been, in certain ways, more experienced than any of us—otherwise I doubt that we would have found her quite so interesting. And yet, still, it remains a fact that I did protect her, that no matter how many stories I told her about my father's business, I never once mentioned how her father and grandfather had screwed him on their contract to fund the Alomar Company. And it had never occurred to me to repeat Bobby Ansi's story of how the Bowen Company had excluded blacks from all its properties.

This same attitude—unquestioned and, in fact, unasked for—also governed my actions regarding Lonnie's "accident." I'd been the one who climbed down into the quarry to examine Lonnie's body where it had landed, one arm pinned awkwardly behind his back, his jaw broken and twisted sideways by the rock that had interrupted his fall, so that his lower row of teeth pointed toward his ear. He was so altered that I had difficulty getting close enough to listen for his breath. But I *did* do it. I did kneel on the quarry floor next to Lonnie. I did touch him, and I did climb out again, scrabbling on gravel, skinning my hands and knees—the farther I went, the more strongly I felt the illusion that something down in that quarry was chasing me—waiting until I got to the top to retch. While Geanie, in contrast, wandered back to the party. In shock, perhaps. Probably dazed. But also without alerting anybody, other than to sit down on a hay bale beside the fire, dry-eyed, repeating to the occasional passerby, "It was an accident."

I'd been the one who drove Sally Jenkins's car through the washboard roads of the Flatrock Ranch to Royce's house, where I called my father, who instructed me to wait thirty minutes and then call the sheriff. And it was my father, not Prudential Bowen or Henry Bowen, who roared up in his blue LeSabre a record thirty-five minutes later, his collar and shirt uncharacteristically wrinkled, his suspenders still hanging down about his legs. I was waiting for him outside the light of the bonfire, which had fortunately quit exploding. As he pulled up, he said only, "Where's Geanie?" and then waded into the party and returned with her, his linen suit jacket draped over her shoulders. Seating her on the LeSabre's rear bumper, he climbed back into the car with me.

"So did you have permission?" he asked.

"What do you mean, did I have permission?" I asked.

"I mean, did old Royce know you were going to have a party?" my father said patiently. He gazed out at the confusion of the party serenely, no more outraged or concerned than if we'd been at Winstead's drive-in. The only suggestion of seriousness I could find was that, having lifted a cigarette from his pocket, he seemed to have forgotten about smoking it and instead tapped its unlit end against his nose.

"Yeah, he knew about it," I said. "Geanie told him. And Nikki. He even came down and mowed the grass."

My father raised his eyebrows, as if this were a piece of information of some significance. "How'd you get him to do that?" he asked.

"I didn't," I said. "Geanie and Nikki went to talk to him."

My father breathed deeply and affectedly of the clotted, early-dew air.

"It was my idea originally," I said. "But Nikki and Geanie put the party together. They went out and talked to him, told him who we were—or Geanie told him who *I* was anyway—and I guess . . . I don't know. I guess they talked him into it. He was lonely, plus Geanie told him we were going to get five dollars a head."

"You paid him," my father said.

"We were going to split the gate, if that's what you mean."

"So there was an actual verbal agreement, a for-profit arrangement to use the property," my father said. Though these charges sounded like an accusation, I was still glad to hear him talk. The familiarity of his tone (slightly husky, as if coming down with something) created the illusion that what had happened would not affect us terribly in the day-to-day, or, rather, simply that the day-to-day would continue, uninterrupted—a feeling that I'd lost, for the first time, down in the quarry. Unfortunately, I also had the sneaking suspicion that he was negotiating something.

"He also brought down some wood," I said.

"What about booze?"

"What booze?" I said, glancing at the bar table. I had told Freddy and Elton that the cops were coming, and they were now trying to drag one of the kegs off to the trees.

My father clicked the car's ignition, then powered down his window, finger on a bank of switches in the LeSabre's door. "Drop it, Freddy," he said calmly. "You won't want it tomorrow anyway." He powered the window up. "Well?"

"Lonnie brought it," I said.

"And how many people know that?"

"I don't know," I said. "Mostly me and Lonnie—and whoever he got the stuff from. We drove it out from his place. And some of Geanie's friends."

"So Royce could have provided it."

"What are you doing?" I asked.

"I'm trying to figure out what happened," he said.

"No, that's not what you're doing," I said. "If you were just worried about what happened, you would've asked me about Lonnie first."

"Would you have been ready to answer that question first?"

This was when I began to cry—less for Lonnie than for the fact that my father's tone had shifted enough to signal that things weren't matter-of-fact, that even he would not be able to return me to the day-to-day.

"I told you over the phone," I said. "I just went up there and found him. He must have fallen in accidentally—it's like a sixty-foot drop."

"Was he drunk?"

"How should I know? He could have been."

"They can test for that," my father pointed out.

I thought of Lonnie's plane, its perfect control, its banking.

"No," I said. "I doubt it."

"And he was familiar with the place," my father said. "You all had been there before, which is why you started visiting MacVess originally."

I nodded.

"Did Royce know that?"

"He knew we were interested in the quarry."

"So which of these things do you plan on telling the police?" my father said. "That Lonnie accidentally fell into a quarry that he'd never seen or that he fell into one that he knew pretty well, while dead sober—pardon the expression—and while a party filled with all his high-school buddies was going on someplace else."

"They weren't his buddies," I said.

"Not even Geanie?" my father asked, glancing toward the back window of the LeSabre. "Not to sound critical, but it seems funny that you hiked all the way up that mountain by yourself and just happened to see Lonnie fall into a quarry—without warning him, even." My father had cupped his mouth between his thumb and forefinger, which left his cigarette smoking slightly off center, against his cheek.

"I said I found him there."

"While if, on the other hand, you'd gone up there with a girl—like Geanie, say—whom you had a crush on, maybe then that would make more sense. There were a couple of her friends in there, when I got her from the party, who said they'd seen her come running out of the trees." My father's eyes were the same fierce, bloodshot blue as I remembered from the day we'd sat waiting for my grandfather in the Grotto Restaurant. Back then he'd leaned across to me and said, "Whatever happens, don't say anything." Now he offered no such suggestion, at least not directly.

"We can't *use* this, Dad," I said.

Patiently, he readjusted his cigarette, and smoke fanned from his nose in a flat, downward sheet. "What I'm saying is that I like your story, Jack. I think it makes sense that our friend Royce was negligent—certainly it would be easy to show that he conducted himself with a pattern of negligence, from taking money to provide an unchaperoned party to supplying booze for kids who are underage." He nodded out toward the glow of the bonfire. Since his deal with Bobby Ansi, he'd shortened his hair in back, though the front parts, the blondest, were still long and had been combed back, and I could see the line where they ended along the back of his head, as if he wore a gilded cap. "All of which led to his negligent responsibility for Lonnie's death," he said. "Since I would be willing to bet that the quarry he fell into, *accidentally*, isn't marked in any way. It's a story that I'm sure Geanie, if it was explained to her properly, would understand and appreciate. But *you* have to understand that any story is a choice, and that once your make that choice, you have to stick to it, permanently." Both our windows burped down an inch, then up again. "*Do* you understand that?"

I didn't answer right away. There really wasn't anything to wait for, but I did it anyway for Royce's sake, staring out my side window at the field he'd mown for our parking lot—and the clean, washed ranks of our new Buicks and Cadillacs, their chrome gleaming beneath the moonlight. "All right, I'm in," I said to my father.

"Fine," he said. "Now bring me Geanie, please."

I know what you're thinking; it's one thing to say that *I* was a protector of Geanie Bowen and perhaps by proxy the Bowen family. It might make sense, due to my feelings for Geanie, that I would choose not to mention the (at the very least) ambiguous scene that I had witnessed along the edge of the quarry. That I would not mention, when the Kings County DA called the house, or even later in any of the sworn depositions that would be required to make a case of "wrongful death" against Royce MacVess, any of the things I knew or could have at least surmised about the relationship between Geanie and Lonnie—all as a way to protect Geanie, a protection that I may have hoped to be rewarded for, eventually. But my father regarded the Bowens as an enemy. He was in the process of trying to trick them out of this very piece of property by replacing their investment with money from Bobby Ansi. Yes, that's true, but I would also argue that my father had learned that there was a profit to be made in protecting the Bowens far earlier than I had. After all, hadn't the Alomar Company itself come into existence to protect Henry and Prudential Bowen from the unpleasant business of confronting Royce MacVess? Or swindling poor farmers like the Wilcoxes, who didn't know that the highway was coming? We both knew that there was a profit to be made by protection, in standing between wealthy people and the transactions that they chose to make.

And so, as it turned out, my father was not afraid of words, as Bobby Ansi had claimed. Because when a story is created to give its owners protection—as most business stories are—from having to hear certain words or consider certain concepts, somebody must at some point commit to being its author. This job, if the story fails or is rejected, can be as dangerous as telling the truth. In order to explain why the story must be changed, the author must be willing to say what really did happen, often to people who expect to be protected from these kinds of things. This was what my father did with Geanie Bowen as they sat together in the front seat of his LeSabre, my father's white linen jacket so oversize as it draped her shoulders that it gave the impression—though she wore a red-checked ranch shirt underneath and had at one point in the evening possessed a straw cowboy hat, which would later be found up in the meadow grass along the quarry—that she was wearing a choir girl's surplice. Her wrists and elbows were pressed together, vertically, in front of her chest, and though it was not cold, her fists pinched the jacket's lapels together tightly at her neck.

If you watched this procedure, as I did, from a position just off the LeSabre's bumper, you would have noticed that Geanie listened to the first part of this opening speech without much response, frozen bolt upright in her seat, as if my father terrified her. Gradually this posture, broken only by the brief jerks of her chin against the lapels of my father's jacket, began to change as the unpleasant part of the exchange ended and my father began to explain the new story, the story I had helped to give him, that would take its place. Then her fists dropped from where they'd clutched my father's lapels; her shoulders relaxed. At one point, listening and nodding more intently now, she swept her hand through her hair, which was unbraided and lay like a dark coil of copper against my father's jacket, and she removed a stick that had been tangled in it. Finally, when my father laid his arm across the seat and patted her shoulder, in a gesture of encouragement and sympathy, she actually laughed. When she did this, it was hard not to notice, from my vantage point, that the braces had in fact corrected her overbite and that her jaw and profile were, right then, as firm and beautiful as they had ever been.

I am sure that my father had some version of this conversation with *all* of the interested parties—with the Bowens, with Nick and Marcy, with the lawyers that were supplied to him by Bobby Ansi. My father entered these conversations as prepared as he could possibly be, having stayed out at the ranch until the end, making sure the alcohol was fully inventoried and listed in the sheriff's notes, making sure he took every guest's name, and waiting there with Nikki until her brother's body had been recovered and examined. After which my father had driven Nikki home, not to their grandmother's residence apparently but to a second house that the Garaciellos owned in a nicer neighborhood out on Gladstone Drive, east of the old Italian quarter. And he sat there another two hours, telling the new story to Nick and Marcy—though of course I wasn't there, and so don't know exactly what he said.

As far as the rest of the party went, it wasn't a pretty scene; by the time the Kings County sheriff arrived, somebody had already broken the side windows of the Garaciello's Roadmaster and pried open the glove box, convinced that Lonnie had hidden the guests' car keys there (these were later found in a paper bag near the quarry). A crowd had gathered and, pushing through, the sheriff found Nikki Garaciello, still quite drunk, fingering the broken glass in the Buick's front seat and bawling, disconsolately.

The last detail was Royce, whose actions on this night, perhaps more than anything, put the final grace notes on my father's story. Apparently he, along with a smaller group of the more impressionable Pemberton boys—mostly those, like Shaun Lambert, who'd been singled out personally by Lonnie's plane—had come to believe, if I understood the sheriff's report properly, that they were under attack in some way. And so while Geanie and I drove home along the highway in my father's car, they had been busy dousing the bonfire with water from the creek, had organized patrols to "sweep" the surrounding fields (an activity so similar to our old Garbage Hunts that the parallel hardly seems worth mentioning), and had begun to build what the sheriff termed a "defensive perimeter" of hay bales around the party. It was a last stand for Royce, in a way. The sight of the sheriff's flashing lights—appearing first, if he had looked for them, as blue and red beads along the highway's berm and then again on his own property—had unhinged him, apparently. And when the sheriff plowed in through the hay bales, he found Royce there on horseback, gun drawn, the smell of woodsmoke in the air, his Texas bandolier across his chest—no more perfect a self-portrait in terms of what my father hoped the sheriff, and later on the court, in the sheriff's depositions, would see.

In the end, however, my father's story was a business story. And though I had not understood—and would, quite frankly, have been unable to predict—what he intended to do with it, I had known perfectly well when we had spoken together in the car that he'd addressed me like a business-man, not as a son. Having agreed on what I'd say, we did not again discuss its veracity. Two days later Nick's car pulled up in our driveway, and my father met him in the backyard and led him into the carriage house to keep him away from the lawyers that were already working inside the house. It was a bright spring day, the wisteria in bloom along the carriage house's window, and I smelled this as I listened to their voices down below me. "What I want to know is one simple thing," Nick said. "I know what your kid says happened, and that's fine. But I would like to know, before I sign off on anything, whether or not there's someone specific to blame."

"Why would you think there would be?" my father asked.

"This is my wife's kid, you understand—not mine. He was a baby when we got married. I told her I don't think there's anything that Jack would do against him."

"Jack was his friend," my father said.

"As far as I can tell, he was his only friend," Nick said. "He was a queer kid, fine, all right—don't think I didn't notice that myself. But you've got to understand, as a mother, Marcy doesn't see it that way. And there's Nikki, too."

"What does Nikki say?"

"She says she was with your boy right before this goddamn thing. That Lonnie was flying his plane around scaring people, and that she doesn't think there's any way Lonnie falls in there on his own. He knows the place."

"Was she sober?"

"Don't ask me that."

"Do you really want to know this, Nick?"

"Would it be something I could do something about?"

"No," my father said. "But if you don't believe me, ask Bobby."

I don't know if Nick ever spoke to Bobby Ansi, but I do know that this conversation was the beginning of my realization that there would be other consequences for the story my father and I had created, ones that I had not expected. I had called Geanie several times by then. My calls had gone unreturned, and when I'd stopped by Mr. Maslin's office at school, I was told that she'd withdrawn from her labs. And so, when my father, my mother, and I stood in the pews of St. John's Cathedral, down on Fifth Street, and watched as Marcy Garaciello, gorgeous in her widow's weeds, threw herself down on her dead son to weep—dressed as he was in one of those over-starched, chalk-stripe suits and folded silk handkerchief that had gotten him off wrong at Pemberton in the first place—I felt ashamed. I knew by then that the reward I'd imagined for keeping Geanie's secrets had been illusory and that, by making such an agreement, I had disfigured myself instead. When the ceremony ended and the casket was carried down the church steps, we filed past the family, who waited on the sidewalk, as if taking attendance. And I was not surprised that when I took a step toward Nikki, her face covered with lace, two men in black suits suddenly blocked my way.

The suit itself took six months to settle. There wasn't much drama to it, in the sense that (to borrow a phrase I heard my grandfather say once, back when he and my father were still speaking) the lies on the record were too good to dispute. The strategy played out nearly exactly along the lines that I'd heard my father and his lawyers discuss already, several hundred times over, in our living room. It was the contention of the plaintiff, Mr. and Mrs. Nick Garaciello, that Royce MacVess had been responsible, in civil terms, for their son's wrongful death. And, like any good story, it became acceptable because in the end it had something in it for everybody. For the Bowens it had the benefit of being settled out of court, which meant that their daughter (already on vacation at their ranch in Wyoming and scheduled, though I did not know this yet, to begin the fall semester at the Mary Institute in St. Louis, known for its excellent field-hockey team) would not in any way need to be involved with the case. For Royce MacVess the settlement included the provision that any criminal charges—such as criminally negligent homicide (a charge that I remember hearing our lawyers pronounce with a snicker) or serving alcohol to minors would be dropped. And in return Nick Garaciello and his wife and daughter would be compensated monetarily for the pain and suffering of Lonnie's death.

This, of course, left out my father and Bobby Ansi, who had himself been present at several of my father's homegrown legal meetings, arriving with driver and entourage, only to spend most of his time off in the corner drinking tea. However, even before "the accident," my father had done his homework on MacVess. He knew perfectly well that the rancher barely had the money to service his own debts, much less pay out a court settlement in cash. And so, one might say that he found it expedient to downplay his involvement in the case—particularly in his dealings with the Bowens, for whom he played the part of a dutiful employee, trying to help his boss's daughter.

This made his high spirits all the more noticeable when we arrived at the Campanile Steak House for our usual Thanksgiving reservations in the fall of that year. We had interrupted our long string of Thanksgivings there with the party that my father had given for Bobby Ansi, and so to a certain extent the ritual of our appearance was made new—my father's bulk rustling ahead of us in the small, tile-floored anteroom that held the maître d's stand, the quiet alcoves just beyond, filled with the clink of silverware and the wing tips and pearled necks of, on this day of all days, the city's best families. We sat in the grill, which on Prudential's orders had been decorated in the memory of the city's western past, replicas of Remington's cowboys, hardened in bronze, and photos of old horse shows in Municipal Auditorium, the cindered light of Tom Pendergast's monument hazy in the background—sights that would have done Royce MacVess proud, I expect. "Well, here's to the golden spike," my father said once dinner was over and our dishes cleared away. "Here's to the tin lizzie, to the Keystone Ironworks, to Lake Erie Railroad and Amalgamated Steel—"

He'd been at this long enough that the patrons at the other tables had begun to deliberately look away. There were bread crumbs spilled on the linen beneath his elbows, and a piece of gristle that he'd chewed and spit out sat on the corner of his plate. The maître d' came by with his hands behind his back. "Perhaps if the gentleman would like to continue shouting," he said, "he'd be more comfortable at another place."

"Waiter!" my father called, clapping his hands and craning his neck. "It's been a half hour since I ordered that champagne," he said to my mother. "Now, what kind of idiot do you suppose must be in charge of the service at this place?"

My mother folded her napkin. "Thank you, sir," she said to the maître d'. "The food was lovely, but there seems to be a draft at this table that makes me sick."

She stood up and, taking me by the hand, left the restaurant without another word. It had snowed earlier in the day but then the temperature had dropped and the dry granules of the flakes seethed around the feet of Bacchus and Poseidon, their fountain basins empty, their spotlights and wires rusting. I felt my mother's tiny fingers shiver in my own. My father found us at a hot-chocolate stand that overlooked the humped darkness of Brush Creek. He was wearing a cashmere overcoat that did not belong to him and from beneath its folds he produced a bottle of champagne. "Waiter!" he said, striding toward the vendor. "What do you have in the way of stemware?"

He returned with two paper cups. When he poured champagne into the first, the glue moistened and the liquor leaked out the bottom in a steady stream.

"A toast," he said.

"I don't want it," my mother said, pushing the cup away. On most days, I knew, my mother would have found champagne in hot-chocolate cups funny.

"But you have to," my father said. A strange confusion played across his face, and he continued to offer the empty cup. "This is it, isn't it? This is what we came for. This is what I promised. Now, I know it's taken a long time, and I'm sorry for that, Allie, I truly am. But now we've made it, haven't we, Nugget?"

"I don't want it, I don't want it, I don't want it," my mother said, staring out at the blackness of the creek. She was dry-eyed, though my father's champagne had dribbled on her shoes. "It's happened, all right, Owl-ton. I've very happy for you. I'm so glad, really, that it ended up this way." She turned and gave him a pretty smile. "But if our ship's come in, all I can think of is that we have to get off on land, don't you see? And things change then, don't they? I know if you read your books clear through—which you don't do, honey, I know that—it doesn't turn out all that well for Mr. Gould and Dr. Durant in the end. So even though right now you're happy, even though I'm happy for you . . . oh, I'm sorry. Don't listen to me. I'm just confused. I've never met any other man I wanted to be married to even for a second. But can't we just be quiet about what we did? Can't we? We did it, I'm not sorry we did it, but can't we maybe just not shout about it right away? Now *don't touch me.*" She said this as my father reached his hand out to her, pulling her elbow violently to her side. "Don't touch me. Don't touch me. Tomorrow I'll be different. Tomorrow we'll turn over a new leaf and I won't say these things, but tonight you go out and celebrate and Nugget will escort me home and everything will be okay. I just can't watch it. I just can't watch it, please."

But we did watch it, of course. Because this was the year, as I told you in the beginning, that my father stepped into the full incarnation of his success, the moment when, arguably, he made his closest bid to greatness, even according to the terms of Tom Durant or Prudential Bowen. The celebration looked the same as every other year: The grandstand was there on the Wornall Bridge, holding the freezing members of the Bowen family, including Geanie, who'd returned from St. Louis for the holidays. The mayor was there, flanked by Prudential and Henry on the stage. But this is the year when, as the crowd counts down from twenty, Prudential Bowen wobbles to the edge of this stage, his hair like a half-blown dandelion, and says to my father, "I need to talk to you, *please,*" and the crowd parts suddenly, all respectful-like, around my father's yellow suit. It is the year when, as fireworks explode overhead, the great Prudential Bowen shouts angrily in my father's ear, and despite his anger my father listens cheerfully, his eyes gazing off into the distance, filled with the colored beads of the electrified Campanile. There is an explanation, naturally, for why this happens on this particular Thanksgiving—the last Thanksgiving of my high-school career. Prudential Bowen is shouting at my father because he has just learned that my father has made an agreement with Royce MacVess to buy his property. And my father is smiling and looking off into the distance because, having negotiated this deal himself, he is already aware (as my mother and I are, roughly) of its details. He knows that in return for an agreement to drop all charges and any claims to future suits—as well as private assurances in regard to his safety, delivered by Bobby Ansi—Royce MacVess has agreed to sell all five thousand acres of the Flatrock Ranch to the Alomar Company. He knows that this sale will be completed at the price my father offered Royce originally, a thousand dollars per acre, minus two hundred grand in damages, to be paid to the Garaciellos over a period of five years. And he knows, as Prudential now knows, that he has done this without using a cent of Bowen money.

This is why, when the cheering stops and the crowd's attention returns to Prudential, his smile has an unconvincing list. It is why the Bowen executives in the front row—none of whom bothered to greet my father when we came in—now follow his progress with envious curiosity. And it is why I have no idea how to react when I look up on the stage to find Geanie Bowen's mossy eyes gazing through me.

Return

The next time I spoke to Geanie Bowen, I was thirty-five. In typical Bowen style, the invitation arrived via the front page of the *Kansas City Star*—along with the obituary pages of the *New York Times* and the *Washington Post,* which my father had apparently hurried out to buy not long after seeing the headline himself. But the Kansas City headline mattered most, a full banner above the fold, which I saw when I dragged myself down into my parents' kitchen in August of 1983, after a night of fitful sleep:

REAL ESTATE PIONEER PRUDENTIAL BOWEN DIES

His development of the Campanile residential and shopping districts stands as national model in the real estate and city planning fields; earned him title "The Michelangelo of the Midwest."

Prudential Bowen, for 75 years a driving force in the development of commerce and culture of Kansas City and its environs, died at 3:15 p.m. yesterday at his home, 1214 W. 55th Street. The Bowen name, today, has been associated with more than 60 residential subdivisions, more than 30 apartment complexes, more than 20 shopping centers, and four hotels. But the story of Prudential Bowen has been a narrative interwoven with that of the Campanile District and marks his greatest creative effort.

His was a dollar-conscious genius. At the birth of the Cam-

panile District in 1907, the initial area was out of the city limits and in part occupied by dairy barns, hog lots, rubbish
dumps, quarries, corn land, and truck gardens. But its undeveloped quality made it affordable for the young Prudential
Bowen, who purchased his first lot, a 10-acre tract at 51st and
Grand, with capital borrowed from the ranchers whose cows
he'd tended in what was then rural Kings County. By 1909, the
early plans attracted syndicate aid from two cattle barons,
Frank O. Crowell and Manual MacVess.

It has been said, accurately, that the measure of Prudential
Bowen's achievement wasn't the dreaming of such an altered
area so much as keeping it always a going venture, carrying, as
his biographer put it, "the marriage of Miss Beauty to Mr. Dollar into something more than a gay honeymoon." What became the multimillion-dollar Campanile development was,
from the first, watched closely by architects and Realtors in the
larger cities. They still come here to study the Campanile in detail, and interest goes beyond the charm of the weather-stained
stucco walls, iron balconies, tiled roofs, arcades, and lofty towers that made the district unique, even outside the holiday period, when it becomes a lighted fairyland.

Proceeding often by trial-and-error methods, Bowen became surer in his touch as one expansion of his districts succeeded the other; by as late as the 1960s and 1970s, he was still
innovating, leading the way for the explosive growth in com-
muter suburban districts in his former boyhood home of Kings
County.

Bowen acknowledged the proprietary interest that many
Kansas Citians claimed in the Campanile and his other developments, but he defended the company's right to manage them
as he saw fit.

"Everybody wants control over their everyday life," Bowen
said. "But we ultimately believe it is ours. They are not the
people who are putting up the money or taking the obligations;
we are the ones doing that."

He is survived by his son, Henry, his daughter, Elizabeth
Walters, and three grandchildren.

"What do you think of that?" my father asked when I looked up from the article long enough to turn to its second page. We were sitting in my parents' kitchen in the house on Briarcliff Drive, one of the few places in the city—along with its surrounding Campanile District—that hadn't changed during the twelve years I'd been away.

"'Dollar-conscious genius' is nice," I said. "And this thing where he says that he believes the everyday life of Kansas City people ultimately belongs to the Bowen Company—funny how the truth slips out, isn't it?"

"What?" My father snatched the paper away from me and ran his finger down the story's column, his lips moving slightly. His plate of eggs and bacon had long since been demolished, and his unlit first cigarette of the morning waited in the ashtray beside his coffee cup, out of respect for me, though the way his fingers jumped and trembled over Prudential's obituary, I figured it wouldn't stay unlit much longer.

"It says here he 'ultimately believes' that the Bowen Company is his company," he said. "What's so funny about that?"

"Not technically," I said.

"If a guy says something, that's what he says."

I pointed to the quote with my butter knife. "The 'it' there in the second sentence—'But we ultimately believe it is ours'—that refers back to 'everyday life,' not the Bowen Company. Or it would if this were a contract."

My father wrinkled his eyes at this. The sentence represented for him a triple whammy of things he didn't like—any mention of "Bowen" and "contract" in a sentence, along with a reminder that his son was a lawyer. Unfortunately for him, I particularly enjoyed *being* a lawyer when I got to be one around my father.

"If I said, 'My son is a lawyer. It's a crying shame,' what does the 'it' mean?" My father addressed this question to my mother, who'd arrived at the table, as always, last with her own breakfast.

"That the two of you have been bickering?" my mother said.

"Only technically," my father said.

"I don't see what the big deal is," I said. "You don't need a lawyer to know that half the time people say what they mean only by accident. Take away that idea, and half the English departments in America would have to fold." This was a fourth whammy for my father—that his son, having been offered the kind of college education that he'd always had to fake, had chosen to major in what he always referred to as "reading." I could already feel whammy number five on the way.

"I'm waiting for somebody to be quiet by accident," my mother said.

"Besides," I said, "Dad himself said that we were all just walking around in Prudential Bowen's dream. In this very house."

This fifth whammy referred to my father's famed dinner with Bobby Ansi, which had led to the purchase of the MacVess property, but I avoided making the reference too direct. In my father's letters, particularly over the last five years, the usual allusions to Bobby Ansi and the MacVess property had dropped away. I no longer knew what he owned of Royce MacVess's ranch, if anything (or if not, what had happened to it), and the questions I'd asked about it on this and other trips had received answers so vague and deliberately misleading that I couldn't penetrate them using either of my degrees. Nor could I put a finger on his mood, the reason he'd made a special trip out that morning to buy the *Times* and *Post* obituaries of a man who'd cost him, by his own estimate, tens of millions of dollars, or why, when I'd come downstairs, he'd made a feeble effort to cover up these other papers with the *Star*'s sports section. The only help for this came from my first degree, a line from sophomore English about "clinging to those we hate," but it had been so long I couldn't remember the whole thing. Plus, I wasn't sure that it applied, given the way my father was smiling at me.

"Do you know what Carnegie said at his funeral?" he asked.

"Not very much, I bet," I said.

My mother, who was between us, eating a bowl of cereal, chortled at this, and my father looked at her sternly. "He's being literal, at least," she said.

"Sometime not long *before* his funeral," my father continued, "Andrew Carnegie said, 'When I go for a trial for the things done on earth, I think I'll get a verdict of "Not Guilty" through my efforts to make the earth a little better than I found it.' So before I suggest this for Prudential's epitaph, I guess you'd better tell me what it really means."

"To me," I said, "the fact that he imagines that there might *need* to be a trial means he's pretty sure he did something wrong."

"So people say the opposite of what they mean?"

"Something like that," I said. "They protest too much."

"What happens if you protest too little?" my mother asked.

But my father, uncharacteristically, let the matter rest. He took his first drag of the day, a scarlet flush rising to his cheeks.

"So we'll be picking you up for the funeral tomorrow around— What time do you think we need to get there, honey?" he said to my mother.

"Noon, if we want a seat," my mother said.

"It's going to be a madhouse for parking, all up and down Ward Parkway. Which means, Nugget"—my father was standing then, cigarette lit, preparing to leave—"that my advice to you is, wear comfortable shoes."

"What are you talking about?" I asked.

"You're going to the funeral with us, aren't you?"

"Why in the hell would I do that?" I asked. "Why in the hell would *you*, for that matter? Since when did Prudential Bowen do any good for you?"

"It says right here he was the Michelangelo of the Midwest." My father pointed to the paper. "Unless they don't really mean that."

"I wouldn't mean it," I said.

"Geanie's probably going to be there."

I slammed the table with my hand and got up, carrying my plate away to the kitchen (something my father refused to do). "I'd rather shoot myself, thanks," I said.

But this was where my father caught me. Behind me I could feel him grinning, and when I glanced back, the sunburned crow's-feet around his eyes were creased.

"According to his theory," he asked my mother, "what's he really think?"

When I'd left Kansas City after high school, I'd wanted out, quite simply—to go someplace where I didn't know who built the highway, where I didn't know who owned the property, who screwed whom to make the money, or who any of the "great men" of the community (or their children) might be. It might not seem that Syracuse University, in upstate New York, would be the place for such a readjustment program, but it worked for me. I knew no famous people at Syracuse, visited no shopping centers modeled after European cities, nor saw, outside of student housing, much in the way of a market for its real estate. In my first freshman English class, the professor—a Jew named Steinberg with a legitimate Brooklyn accent, both new experiences for me—held up an oversize map of the nation's highways, state roads in red, tollways in green, and the vast vascular system of the interstates marked in the aortic blue. "In this class we'll be reading about visions of the American frontier, okay? We'll start with Turrow"—a new author for me, until I read the syllabus and saw Thoreau's name—"who says, 'I turn my mind west when I go dreaming.' But before we get started, I gotta tell you one sad thing about that. The West is dead, no offense to Mr. Kerouac. It's paved. We ran it over. We got no place left to go exploring." He was touching, with his fingers, the far ends of the highway, 95 up in Maine, 80 out in San Francisco, which he traced clear back to Syracuse, even Kings County's 35 where it hit the Mexican border down in Nuevo León. "So if you want to talk about frontiers, if you want these guys to make any sense today, forget the West and imagine they mean exploring *your* frontiers, inside."

I didn't know if I agreed with him. There was plenty of the West, the real West, that I hadn't seen—the Bowens' ranch in Wyoming, for instance, where Geanie had retreated the summer after Lonnie's death. But any class that instructed me to forget her, and everything that had passed between us, was the right place for me.

I had money in those days, too. This came, as had the money for my tuition at Pemberton, via my grandfather, Big Alton, to whom I had drawn closer during my senior year of high school. Any movement toward my grandfather was, by necessity, a movement away from my father—who had over the years limited our contact with Big Alton and my grandmother, Elaine, to very brief and generally unpleasant major holiday meals, visits that usually began with my grandfather's hearty greeting to his son: "Who bailed you out?" My first Christmas home from college, my grandfather invited me to his offices in the Warburton Building at Tenth and Grand with its two-story cutaway atrium, its oak banisters, and its metal spiral stairs. "This young man needs a place to study," he told the head clerk, a man in his seventies, who led me down a burgundy-carpeted corridor to a door, its name tag recently pried away, and behind that a mahogany desk, a lamp, a phone, and windows overlooking the bustling shops on Grand Avenue, where I'd once ridden streetcars with my dad. I studied for my finals there. I was also assigned a secretary, a Swede named Ulma Lofgren, who typed up my final papers for me. I found it hard to imagine my grandfather sleeping with her (according to my mother, secretaries had been the source of Big Alton's affairs). But once, as Ulma swayed away from us, one high-heeled foot placed directly in front of the other, he'd nudged me and said, "Don't worry. By the time you graduate, we'll have her daughter here."

All money comes with obligations, though. During my senior year, I returned from a weekend camping trip to find that a telegram informing me of my grandfather's death, via heart attack, had arrived the day I'd left. A letter followed, typed up by Ulma, explaining that, according to my grandfather's express instructions, my allowance would continue only if I enrolled in law school upon graduation and "avoided any volunteer military service." My father appended a note that read, *"Listen to the fucker this time, kid. This war isn't one you want to see."*

It was the only time in my life that I'd ever seen my father and my grandfather agree on anything, and I listened to them, thankfully. In 1971, with help from my freshman English teacher, who had friends there, I enrolled in New York University's Law School, graduated in 1974, and by 1975 was practicing contract law with a small firm in midtown Manhattan and living in a fourth-floor walk-up on Thirty-second Street. I had a job, no need for allowance, no ties to home—I was finally, completely free.

I had stayed that way for eight years. As with religion, or real estate, it is possible to become a zealot on the subject of *belonging* in New York City. And, like any convert, you have moments of grace—clear, windless Saturdays in October when you, along with two young associates from your firm, have traveled up to Baker Field to watch the Columbia-Yale football game; the discovery that the piano player in a bar on Abingdon Square knew people from your high school. Even the simple act of buying a toothbrush at the drugstore outside your office and then walking down Sixth Avenue with a briefcase full of papers, a suit on your back, an apartment key in your pocket, can feel like communion—the sacrament of belonging in your chosen paradise, at least as much as anyone you can see. There are moments, too, when you will realize that these aren't the only sacraments you'll be asked to take. Moments from late-night cab rides on the FDR, still thick with traffic. There is the Williamsburg Bridge, its pilings greasy black. There is the lurid sign of the Domino Sugar factory and beyond it, Brooklyn's glass office towers, brick stacks of apartments whose inhabitants, lives, and customs are no more familiar to you than if you were staring across the Yangtze into Shanghai.

In more concrete terms, however, two things had brought me back to my parents' kitchen that morning, where I read Prudential Bowen's obituary. The first was a dinner that I'd had with the senior partner of my firm, Michael Callaghan, the man who'd hired me—in part, as he'd confessed, because he'd also been a Syracuse grad. "Irish reticence" is not a common phrase, but Michael Callaghan had it; short, bull-chested, in his middle fifties, though the crisp black line of his part and his trim waist made him seem younger than that, Callaghan communicated, when he did communicate, primarily by nudging you in the ribs when he thought you'd said the right thing. I liked him; he was fair, specific in his passions (the Rangers and the Mets), the sort of New Yorker who lived his city life inside three or four pubs that were within walking distance of our offices, then returned home to his wife and family in Westchester, faithfully. Our dinner had been outside his normal range, a Brazilian place near the Public Theater, one that must have been chosen by his secretary, because Callaghan hadn't liked it himself. When our first dish arrived, skewered on a shoot of bamboo, he'd shook his head and laughed; fifteen minutes later we were in a narrow bar called the Pyramid, just down the street.

It was supposed to be a celebration, I think. But Callaghan had failed to mention this. Instead we sat shoulder to shoulder, a pair of televisions silently reeling off the Mets game, one to the left of the bottle display that I looked at and another to the right for him (his preferred position for conversation). As a steady stream of strangers grazed our backs, he asked, "So how are things at home, Jackie?"

I suppose he might have been asking about my love life, or how things were at my apartment, but I never even considered this. Instead, slowly at first and then—with the help of a few Callaghan elbows—for the stupifying length of an extra-inning, West Coast game against the Dodgers, I told him about Kansas City. I told him about my father and my mother and the Alomar Company, from their first meeting at that golf club in North Carolina through our picnics, about old Royce MacVess on horseback, the mobsters that my father had done business with (though I left Lonnie's death an accident, as in my father's story), and the way my father had stood there amid the electric outlines of a mock-Florentine village while the city's richest man shouted in his face. I had not told the story once, not in that full form, in the years since I'd gone away, and the more I told it, the better and funnier it sounded to me. I told him of the statue of Bacchus without his dick, of Elmore Haywood's accent, and of my run around the end of the Crusaders' line, and by the time the game was over, I realized that Callaghan hadn't said a thing.

He waited until we were outside on the street. "So, Jack," he said, "why don't you go back home and see those people? A real vacation—not just a weekend. You've got more than enough hours built up for that."

"I don't think I can do that," I said. "We've got briefs filed on the McPherson account, and I just started on this Williams deal."

Callaghan was laughing as I ran through my client list. He opened the door of his cab. "I know what you do," he said. "That's why I'm inviting you in."

"I'm fine—I'll walk," I said. "I just don't think this vacation . . ."

"I mean we want to make you *partner*, Jack," Callaghan said. "It's a serious commitment. You don't go take this time now, who knows when you'll get another chance. One month minimum. And talk it over with that father of yours."

"Why?" Shocked, I wasn't sure myself whether I was asking why I should talk to my father or why he'd made the offer.

"I don't know," he'd said, nudging me. "You tell me."

The other cause for my return had been a letter I'd received from my mother, a few months earlier in June. My father had sent me letters on the Alomar Company's progress throughout my college years—though if he was looking for any editing, or even a response, he was sorely disappointed. The early versions of these letters, particularly the ones that I'd received in school, had been relentlessly upbeat, as if he intended to compete, in words and images, with the cash Big Alton was sending me:

> Dear Jack,
> I am too old to be a prodigy anymore (though yr not) but these days I feel like young Rockefeller after he quit keeping books for old man Hewitt and hung up his own shingle there in Cleveland. He used to tell himself, "Look out, or you will lose your head—go steady." And so I do the same. If my head swells any, it's for having to make room for all these goddamn feasibility studies, erosion entrapment, and flood control that have

to go in before any of the shopping centers, movie theaters and houses that I've been picturing for the past fifteen years get to get built.

Or, more practically:

> Dear Jack,
> Sewers, sewers, sewers. Currently I am spending ten hours a day looking at runoff studies and discussing the advantages of septic tanks. Do you have any idea how much those things cost? No wonder Prudential got the city to put in his own sewers, back when he was building Mission Hills.

The letters had stopped not long after I'd taken my job in Manhattan—a fact I had attributed to my father's final realization that I would not be coming back. And then, in June, a few months before my meeting with Callaghan, I received one final missive, this one in my mother's sharply printed hand:

> Dear Jack,
> Your father needs you.
> Allie

Which was, at least technically, how I ended up standing at the corner of Sixty-first Terrace and Ward Parkway in Kansas City, as Prudential Bowen's mourners filed out of the Campanile Christian Church across the street. "The great architect Sir Christopher Wren had inscribed as his epitaph *Si monumentum requiris, circumspice*—'If you seek his monument, look about you,'" the pastor had said during his eulogy. "And I say to you now, if you want to see Prudential Bowen's monument, look about you as you go out the doors of this church. We who live and work in this city will be eternally indebted to him." A statement that certainly applied to the pastor, since Prudential himself had paid for the rough-hewn, Gothic walls of the Campanile Christian Church. I supposed that it also applied to most of the mourners who now trooped en masse down the tree-lined sidewalks of Ward Parkway, toward the Bowen mansion on Fifty-fifth Street. I recognized most of them and knew, from Lonnie's tours back in our freshman

year, that nearly all had signed, at one time or another, Bowen contracts—
all except the dapper, gray-suited apparition that I saw coming directly at
me, walking slowly enough to hold up three lanes of oncoming traffic, one
hand on a gold-headed cane, the other mopping a purple silk handkerchief
across his face.

"I've been looking around for monuments," I said to Elmore Haywood
as he finally reached the curbing. "You're the first I've seen."

"Screw monuments," Elmore said. He had stopped at the edge of the
curb so that the traffic he'd held up was now speeding by perilously close
to his back. "It's the eternal indebtedness that gets you turnout. Half the
people here showed up because if they don't, they're afraid Henry'll call
their mortgages in."

"So why're you here?" I asked.

"Same reason you are," Elmore said calmly.

"Great. Maybe you can tell me what that is."

"'Cause you don't got no place else to be," Elmore said.

It was true enough, and I grinned at this, sticking out my hand as if
to shake—and, if necessary, help him up onto the sidewalk. But Elmore
waved me off. "I don't do any more steps than I have to these days," he
said, pointing down to the legs of his suit pants. "Bad knees."

"You can't just stand there in the street."

"I can until you get that car and pick me up," Elmore said. "Then we'll
go get Rockefeller." He gestured over his shoulder, where, across the grassy
median of Ward Parkway, my father could be seen shaking hands in the
front yard of the church, his hair only slightly darker than the yellow tulips
in the flower beds.

"He's supposed to meet me over here," I said.

"And you believed that?" Now Elmore was grinning. "I guess it's true,
then."

"What's true?'

"He said you hadn't changed."

It was to be the theme of the night—change, or the lack thereof. Or
whether or not change made any difference anyway. By the time I picked
everyone up and drove to the reception, cars were parked bumper to
bumper all along Fifty-fifth Street, while the other side was marked with

red-lettered signs reading EMERGENCY—NO PARKING, BY ORDER OF POLICE. At the Bowens' electric gate, a Mission Hills cop waved us away.

"Excuse me, Officer," my mother said. "We have a passenger in this car who needs assistance, so I'm sure you wouldn't mind if we dropped him off?" My mother's accent had gone into such high gear that this last word sounded like *aw-uff*.

The cop flapped a white postcard. "You got to be on the list."

"Try Colonel Pickering," my father said.

The cop checked the list and then, looking disappointed, stuck his head in my window and said, "Which one of you is that?"

My father pointed at Elmore, who had not moved a muscle during this exchange.

"Bull," the cop said.

"He's a colonel *and* a former right tackle for the Boston Yanks," my father said. "If you don't believe me, I suggest you take it up with him."

Elmore still looked as imposing as ever when sitting down, an effect increased by his anger at my father, and the cop evidently decided it would be easier to let us through. "But you're just dropping him off, okay?" he warned me sternly. "This car's got to come back out—and if it doesn't, I'll come looking."

Just beyond the Bowens' gate, my father had directed me right, toward Henry Bowen's house, instead of toward Prudential's twin mansion to the left. I parked the car in front and got out, refusing to do any more than that. But when I handed my father the keys, he climbed into the driver's seat and, with a jaunty wave, drove himself, Elmore, and my mother up onto Henry's perfectly tended grass and, skirting the flower beds, disappeared through the side yard, around the far corner of the house. Standing there alone before Geanie's house, I felt no older and no wiser than when I'd dragged my father's golf bag across the long green swale of lawn before me, at the age of thirteen.

If alcohol was one of the things that I was supposed to rescue my father from, I did a very poor job that night. After a half hour of wandering around Prudential's terrace alone, shaking hands with well-meaning people whose names I'd forgotten—or whose faces I'd forgotten while recognizing, once they said them, their names—I found my father and Elmore on the edge of the crowd, holding drinks in both their hands. At first I had thought they were examining a spotlit statue in the center of Prudential's backyard. It featured a naked young man riding piggyback on another older man and was identified by a brass plaque as representing *The Genius of Victory*. But when I closed in on them, I realized that they were staring off to the right of the statue where three bird feeders dangled from a metal wire. "Lookit, we got an expert," Elmore said, eyeing me. "You ever see a squirrel run on a power line up there in New York City?"

"I've seen plenty of pigeons sit on them," I said.

"And what happens when they do that?"

"Nothing," I admitted.

"That's what I've been *saying*," Elmore said, though whatever it was he'd been saying, it hadn't been to me. "I don't care how much voltage you put in that wire, when a squirrel gets up there, he's got to be grounded or he won't feel a thing."

"Why don't you touch it, then?" my father said.

"Because I *am* grounded," Elmore said. "Unlike some people I could name."

My father relinquished one of his drinks and traced the length of the feeder's wire with his finger, pausing at either end where the wire was joined to the statue's neck and to a metal pole by small, white ceramic disks. I noticed that the feeders also hung by these. "So," he said when he'd finished. "What's that look like to you?"

"An electric wire," I said

"I heard it from Prudential Bowen's own lips," my father said. "I was sitting right in his office, and he said to me, 'Don't worry, Acheson, it's only the squirrels I electrocute.' Now, why would he say that if that's not what this is?"

"It's a family secret," a voice said, and, suddenly, I found myself face-to-face with Geanie Bowen, dressed in a navy skirt and blazer—perhaps in homage to her grandfather—her hair pulled back in a bun. I noticed that she, too, was drinking two-fisted. "The squirrel community and my grandfather have a long and violent history. I could tell you more, but we're trying to keep it out of the press."

"You could have that whole wire charged up with every volt in New York City," Elmore said, starting in again. "But if nothing's grounded—"

"Never mind him," my father said, indicating Elmore.

"The first feeders were on poles," Geanie went on. "He put creosote on them to keep the squirrels from climbing up."

"That never works," Elmore said sympathetically.

"Neither did tin collars, barbed wire, or trapping the squirrels alive, painting a yellow dot on their fur, and deporting them to the country." Geanie's breathing was a little shallow, I noticed, and she rushed through the more morbid, deadpan parts—or at least the parts I figured she intended to be morbid and deadpan—so that they were hard to catch (not that my father or Elmore would have caught them anyway). "Which brings us down to electricity," she was saying. "The thing is, you're right, it doesn't work without a ground, so he figured out that he needed two wires, one with a charge, the other without, with a layer of insulation in between, so that when the squirrel climbs out on the line, he has to grab both wires. That's what's up there now."

This high-end explanation caused my father to grab Geanie's shoulder. "Wait a second," he said. "Have you been in touch with my boy, Jack?"

The timing of this question was a minor piece of art. The fact that Geanie and I were *out* of touch had remained the primary characteristic of our relationship ever since I'd dropped her off next door, the night of Lonnie Garaciello's death—a long silence that could not have felt more visible and grotesque to me if I'd been carrying it on my shoulders, like *The Genius of Victory*. But then I'd forgotten that it was part of my father's own genius to stumble directly onto such grotesqueries and discuss them.

Geanie's rush of words dried up immediately, and I heard the click of plastic against her teeth as she drained one of her wines and then tottered off to set the empty in a planter. "No," she admitted, returning. "I'm a terrible correspondent, I'm afraid."

"So no communication at all?"

Geanie shook her head.

"Dad—lay off," I said. I would have liked to hear Geanie explain why she hadn't written me, but I didn't want my father do the asking.

"It's all right," Geanie told me. To my father she said, "I didn't write your son once during college. Or phone. And if you want the truth, there's no good excuse for it. Except to say it's something I regret."

"Why would you?" my father asked. "He never answers letters anyway."

"Is this thing on?" Elmore said to me, waving his hand around the bird feeder.

"Why don't you test it?" my father said. "Please. I'm trying to set up an intellectual conversation here. This is an experiment."

"I'll say," Elmore said.

"So," my father said to Geanie, "you went to college . . . where?"

"Yale," Geanie said.

"And you studied . . . ?"

"I'm in graduate school right now, for sociology."

"So let me ask you this," my father said. "At Yale, did you learn that if some guy says something in a book, he really means the opposite?"

"You mean, like when people at this party tell me what a great man my grandfather was, even though they're glad he's dead?" Geanie asked.

"I'm glad we cleared *that* up," Elmore said.

But this was the kind of answer my father liked. He smiled beneath his mustache, the wrinkles beside his eyes making long white gulleys in his summer sunburn, as if to wince at getting hit. Then he raised his glass. "I guess that saves me from having to say anything to you about your grandpa, then, doesn't it?" he said.

Spontaneously, the rest of us followed suit, our plastic rims touching in the middle and lifting, at my father's direction, up toward Prudential's electric bird feeders overhead—a wordless toast that somehow seemed appropriate. After we all drank, Elmore said in forceful Cockney, "The king is dead, long live the king!" and hunched his shoulders with an absorbed expression, as if we'd been discussing something else.

Two hours later I was shouting this same phrase from the backseat of my father's Cadillac, sailing downtown along Main Street, with Geanie Bowen's cool, grieving palm in my lap. My mother had left the party ahead of us, hitching a ride home with one of her friends from the Children's Hospital Auxiliary—her charitable activities appeared only to have expanded while I'd been away—but not before giving me an appraising look, one eyebrow cocked on her pretty face, as if to suggest that this, right here, was a good example of why she'd written to say my father needed me. But it was not much of a night for responsibility, or worry of any sort. Even I had been able to relax enough to put on a brave front when, after two or three trips down the bar line, we actually pushed through Prudential Bowen's side hedge and found my father's Cadillac parked dead center in Henry Bowen's backyard, a summons on the windshield along with a note—*"Hope you had fun, Colonel. I'll be looking for you on your ride home"*—left apparently by our cop friend.

Nor had things gotten much better from there. As on most drunken nights, nothing could quite compete with the high of *deciding* to get drunk in the first place—not that my father and Elmore Haywood didn't try. They shuttled us from bar to bar, working steadily northward from the Campanile, bouncing between Broadway and Main, with a professional judgment that, had I been more sober, would have worried me severely. We visited Irish bars tucked away at the tops of marble staircases, a blues bar with posters peeling from the walls, a bar shaped like a ship, complete with brass-encircled windows, and a bar with sawdust on the floor and men in checkered shirts and cowboy hats—always bursting out again with fresh hope into the cool summer night, the moon blaring overhead. As for Geanie and me, we started out fresh in each bar, but there were so many things we didn't know how to talk about that our conversations often lapsed into vague smiles and a good deal of staring into the air—at least at the beginning.

I didn't acquit myself particularly well in this initial meeting, nor was I sure that I wanted to in the first place. My pulse quickened like a kid's each time we slid into a booth or bellied up to a bar and Geanie's hip brushed against mine. I had never seen her wearing makeup before—much less a tailored navy suit or pale white hose and flats instead of her usual hockey shirt and tube socks—and these things pleased me more than I would have guessed, especially the purse, which she opened frequently, since I had no money for drinks. Her face was rounder, higher in the cheekbones, and the few deft lines that added parentheses around her lips seemed the product more of experience than age. At the same time, those years of silence still rode my shoulders, offering commentary. I knew Geanie could sense them, and when *their* voices whispered in my ear, they didn't sound much like genius or victory: "Terrible correspondent? Are you kidding? Are you going to let it go at that?" I felt angry when, driving between one bar and the next, Geanie held my hand, and then angry later when she let go of it. I felt angry when she asked if I had a girlfriend and angry when I turned the question around and she responded, "Yes. Though I'm wondering if that's a good thing." Mostly, I think, for lack of a better target, I got angry with her impassive Bowen stare. It never meant anything, I told myself. It never said whether you were in or out; it was always just watching, trying to decode what you were going to think. Which led, perhaps not surprisingly, to an argument that I manufactured from nothing, or what I thought was nothing since, once I got it started, I couldn't remember what it was about. This happened in the bar at the Grotto, our last stop for the night.

"So which is it, then?" I asked, interrupting another, different conversation—one I'd begun myself—during which Geanie was explaining to me what her dissertation was going to be about.

"That's what I'm trying to decide," she said, looking surprised at my tone. "I'm not sure I know enough to write about the subject I've got now. But if I pick something else, that means I have to do even more research."

"Let's not try to dodge the question," I said. "Pretend we're speaking honestly."

"I *am* speaking honestly."

"Then answer me: Which . . . is . . . it?" I had leaned across the table then and invested my words with a drunkard's significance, attaching to them all that remained between us that had been left unsaid, Lonnie included. "That's what I'm asking you. All you do is watch, watch, watch. Well, I'm saying you have to pick."

"Pick what?" Geanie said. As she glanced over my shoulder, as if for help, toward my father and Elmore, who were playing dice with Joey Ramola's son at the bar, I finally saw something that gratified me—a flinch of fear. "I was the one who came up to you, Jack. I was glad to see you. It's lonely here, the funeral was weird. We were friends, Jack. If you didn't want to have a drink, why didn't you say so?"

"So that's it," I said. "That's what you pick—old friends out for a drink."

"It's not like you called me either," Geanie pointed out.

"So are we *just* old friends?" I continued. I was not about to be deterred by logic at this point. "Is that what you pick? Because, see, this time around I'd like some answers. Did you ever think that old friends might not cut it for me?"

I had staggered off to the john after that, having delivered what I believed to be an indisputable parting line to great effect—though what effect I hoped for would have been impossible for me to explain. When I came back out, Geanie had gone away.

Some undefined time later, a hand shook my shoulder, and I sat up to find my father's bloodshot eyes peering into the Cadillac's backseat. "You want to hit?" he said.

"A hit?" I said. Having spoken the phrase aloud, I was able to run it through my memory banks, producing first the improbable idea that he was offering me marijuana, and then secondly that he was offering me a drink, neither of which I wanted currently. "Thanks," I said. "I think I'm okay."

"Come on, you made it this far," my father said, shaking me again. "You at least owe it to yourself personally to have a try."

I can't say which was stranger, climbing out of the Cadillac to find my father driving golf balls down the center of Grand Avenue—a street that had been, within my memory, the busiest in the city—or the fact that he and Elmore Haywood seemed to regard this as a perfectly reasonable conclusion to the night's activities. There was no question that they had a routine. Elmore had procured a sleeve of Styrofoam coffee cups that he inverted on the asphalt to serve as a slightly higher-than-normal tee. They hit from a high spot, just shy of Ninth Street, not far from the plywood-covered doors of the Warburton Building, where my grandfather's offices used to be. It was close to dawn by then. The sky had brightened to a pinkish green off to the east. Behind us I could see where Grand Avenue fell away steeply toward the same concrete trench of highway that Lonnie Garaciello and I had driven on our way to the farm party. The occasional pair of headlights drifted soundlessly through its shadows.

But the real action was to the south. There, down the vaulted corridor of Grand Avenue, my father and Elmore Haywood launched balls that lifted quickly above the double braid of streetlights and landed with an amazingly high, two-story bounce around Eleventh—followed by seemingly endless, trickling runs past what once had been Baker's Shoes, Emery, Byrd, Thayer's Department Store, the Tower Movie Theater, Rothschild's Clothes, and other shops and offices that I remembered from the old days. These buildings were now dark, uniformly, both the storefronts and the windows overhead. There were no movies listed on the Tower's marquee, no window displays in Simpson's Tailors, no newsboy opening his stand outside the Palace Clothing Company, where these balls finally tended to trickle to the curb. No crowd of Saturday-morning drunks outside Connie's Deli. In fact, as dawn broke and my father and Elmore Haywood continued, betting a dollar on the length and straightness of each pair of shots, the only signs that I could see were the real estate signs mounted on the upper floors of these buildings, which they peppered with their occasional hook or slice:

COHEN & ESREY
Real Estate Ventures
FOR INFORMATION
913-555-4545

For Lease
Swinger Realtors
Prime office space

Richard Ellis
Partners
FOR SALE NOW

"Where is everybody?" I asked when, after a half hour, it became clear that neither of them saw any reason to explain this ritual to me.

"What? Elmore and I aren't good enough for you?" my father asked. He'd worked up a sweat by then, his dress shirt damp against his back.

"If you're going to talk, talk," Elmore said. "If you want to play, play."

"It's a simple question," I said. "You can't tell me that this is normal, hitting golf balls down what's supposed to be a busy street."

"It's normal now," Elmore said.

"Since when?"

My father grinned. The sweat had lifted the smell of booze onto his skin—no worse, I suspected, than the smell that came off me—and his hand, as he tendered me the driver, trembled visibly. "Since everybody moved out to Prudential Bowen's new developments in Kings County," he said. "Where the hell you been?"

"I thought that was *your* development," I said. "Along with the idea that the people there would be driving downtown on the highway."

My father probed the upper folds of his ear with his finger and then examined its tip. In the daylight I could see that the stubble on his cheek and chin, which had grown in overnight, was peppered with white. "This kid's so curious about what I'm doing, maybe we should let him run the office a couple days."

Elmore considered this skeptically. "You want to do that?" he asked me.

"I already *did* my time," I said. "I spent half of grade school surveying cornfields for this guy. All I want to know is what happened to them."

Elmore shook his head, clicking his tongue inside his mouth. "The way it works in this town, son, is once you in, you in. Once you out, you out."

I rifled my pockets but found only pennies. "All right." I held my hand out for the driver, which my father tossed to me. "But if I work, I play for free."

Elmore popped a cup off his stack, set it down on the pavement with a ball on its butt end. The sun must have broken the horizon by then, because when I stepped into the hitting area, I could see, down the full length of Grand Avenue, bright strips of orange that had seeped in between the buildings and along the through streets to the east, so that it seemed as if I were going to tee off through tongues of flame. I wound up and swung as hard as I could, delivering a skittering ground ball that caromed off the brass gate in front of the Federal Reserve and then rattled like a pinball in the doorway of the old Sayers Drug building across the street, where it died unceremoniously.

My father and Elmore both watched this in silence, chins in their respective hands. "Now, that kind of pitiful shit," Elmore said, "is *exactly* what you'd expect from some poor fool's been rotting away in New York City the last ten years."

I swung the club again, for rhythm, listening to its swish. I could imagine the exact shot I wanted to make, a high, arcing fade that got up quickly over the streetlights on the left. It would flirt with the tan brick front of the empty Rialto building before taking a magical turn back toward the yellow centerline of Grand—where, once it touched down, it could run forever. Or until Twentieth Street, at least.

"I want to go again," I said.

Elmore glanced over at my father, his chin still in hand. My father reached down into his slacks and pulled out a wad of ones, most of which he'd won from Elmore, and tossed them the black man's way.

"My, my, my," Elmore said as he counted the cash. "Well, all righty, then. Looks like we got a young man who's finally come to play."

A&E Realty

The new company that my father and Elmore had founded, A&E Realty, was located on the third floor of the Gramercy Apartments on Thirty-sixth and Paseo, in the same apartment where my father had first dreamed of owning land around the highway. At seven-thirty in the morning, there would already be a line of men—painters, carpenters, wallboard men—squatting on the front-porch stoop, looking for work. When I opened the door, they followed me upstairs single file and then sat quietly on the two ratty sofas in what had been our living room, maintaining the same order that I'd found them in outside. After so many years of subway riding, I enjoyed these quiet mornings, even the smell of the workers' cigarettes after I opened the porch doors to let some air in. Once I'd found a clipboard and written down their names, I'd go check the company message machine for news of any broken toilets, leaky roofs, or misbehaving tenants that had come in overnight. This was in my parents' bedroom, where my father and Elmore now kept their desks amid a fluttering collage of yellowed city maps, lists of numbers for contractors, city code inspectors, and policemen, as well as a large, framed quotation:

The public deserves exactly what it gets. No more, no less.
—Tom Ponzi

Nobody bothered to explain why I needed to get there at seven-thirty instead of eight, when the offices opened, according to the sign outside. Then one morning I slept in and arrived to find Elmore (who lived in the first-floor apartment) standing on the front porch in his bathrobe, holding two younger, and fortunately smaller, men apart by their shirtfronts. "I was taking a piss. I couldn't hold it," said one man, waving a spackle blade. "Then this motherfucking cocksucker here tries to take my place."

"'S all right," Elmore said, giving me the evil eye. "We got a well-rested lawyer showing up here right now. I'm *sure* he knows how to resolve this kind of thing."

The foreman was another surprise, one that even my father thought worth explaining. Namely that he was Toby Wilcox, the same kid whose mother had owned the first farm my father had purchased in Kings County and that he'd lived for five years in the second-floor apartment just underneath the A&E Realty company offices. "He's a good kid," my father had said to me, as if this were a reasonable answer to my astonishment that anybody from the Wilcox family would even agree to talk to him in the first place. "What you have to understand is that Toby himself, you know, he never had a dad. Now, you might not think it's any great shakes to be related to this old man, but Toby here . . . well, I guess the best way to put it is, he's gotten protective. Of me."

"Protective?" I had said. "What is he, some kind of masochist? I'm surprised he didn't shoot you on sight."

"You know, he and his mom bought a little place up on Virginia Avenue, a couple blocks east of Troost, in some territory that Elmore and I were working—"

"You can't tell me you bought his house."

"No, no—not exactly anyway." My father had given a small, tight grin, whether of pride or embarrassment it was hard to say. "This was the early seventies, okay? There'd been a big thunderstorm the previous night, knocked a lot of trees down, which is sometimes a good time to ask people about moving out. I'm going up to this little bungalow that had its roof ripped off, and all of a sudden, big as life, there's Toby Wilcox on the rafters, trying to tack down a shower curtain over this thing."

"So he didn't *have* a gun," I said.

"I offered him a job before he could get one," my father said. "I had about twenty houses that needed their roofs replaced. Plus, the Wilcoxes weren't going to be able to fix the roof they had. They'd taken that money from the farm sale and bought this same bungalow, along with an apartment building over on Troost. Nice building. Eight rental units. Only problem is that rents and property values were going down since people had started moving out to Kings County."

"Which is what you convinced them to do," I pointed out.

"Say what you want," my father said. "The kid's there. He does his work. He's *been* doing it for over five years. And don't be surprised if the person he's mad at is you, not me, for being so lucky as to walk into an office job on your first day."

I was thankful for the warning about Toby, since I would not have recognized him in his current state. Though close to my age, he'd gone bald on top and had chosen to compensate for this by wearing the rest of his hair as long and as thick as possible, including deep sideburns and a heavy, ginger-colored tail that curled down behind his ears. His work uniform consisted of concert T-shirts with the sleeves cut off, ranging in taste from ELO's fluorescent spaceships to Black Sabbath's pentagrams; his pants were uniformly jean cutoffs, the linings of his pockets visible beneath the fringe, and he wore bandannas to cover his bald spot, making it look like he had a full head of hair, at least. The only remnants of his country life were a slight twang in his diction and the circle of a Copenhagen tobacco can that had been worn into the back pocket of every pair of shorts he had. "Well, look who's back," he'd said when I handed him my clipboard on the first day. "Man, things must really be fucked up in New York City when the lawyers start moving here."

"I'm on vacation," I assured him. "But even lawyers were kids once, you know. This apartment's where I grew up."

"Yeah, well, at least you can find it," Toby said. He had his head down, flipping through my notes on the jobs for that day, though I recognized this as a reference to his mother's farm. "On the other hand, the way some of these neighborhoods get trashed, I don't know but what I'd burn my old place down, just so I didn't have to imagine what was going on inside it since I'd moved away."

I stopped short of pointing out to Toby that if *I* burned *this* place down, he wouldn't have anyplace to live. Instead I said, "It's still got some memories for me."

"No it doesn't," Toby said. He jabbed a finger at the day's first job applicant, a sixteen-year-old black kid in a pair of dirty Toughskin jeans with patches on the knees. "Hey, Tito, this guy look familiar to you?"

I was unfamiliar, at that time, with Toby's habit of calling his persistently rotating crew of extras by the first names of the Jackson Five, though apparently the boy wasn't, because he answered right away. "Why, is he a cop?"

"No. I mean, he grew up here, right in this apartment," Toby said.

"Not in any world I ever seen," the kid said.

"No, probably not." Toby handed the clipboard back to me. "Ghetto's ghetto, lawyer man. Once it starts, that's the end of memory."

I could hardly blame Toby for feeling suspicious about me. And he was right about my old neighborhood—provided you accepted the Bowen Company definition of a ghetto as "a place where black people lived." In the years that I'd been away, the line between the neighborhoods that had been protected by Prudential Bowen's contracts and those that hadn't (a line that fell exactly at Troost Avenue) had become in essence the city's new color line. To the west the residents were all white. To the east they were black. It was as if the white residents of every single bungalow, house, apartment building, and mansion, through streets too numerous to name—Forest, Virginia, Tracy, the Paseo, Indiana, Brooklyn, Euclid, Bellefontaine—had been replaced by a black resident via some massive and secret governmental experiment, of the sort that Lonnie would have enjoyed in his science-fiction movies.

However, I had been in plenty of places that had no memories for me, and the Paseo wasn't one of them. Though we'd lost the great elm that had once shaded the Gramercy, a victim of Dutch elm disease, I was amazed on those cool, gray spring mornings, after a night's rain, by the lushness of things. The entire length of the Paseo seemed choked with vegetation, beds of wild daylilies in empty lots, its medians abstract fields of dandelions, to say nothing of trees—lindens, pines, mulberries, oaks, sycamores, magnolias whose rounded tops seemed by far to outnumber the rooftops and threatened to overtake the city. My old room, rarely used, had been turned into something of a conference center for the entertaining of "larger" clients, of which we had few. There was a scrap of orange rug, a large fakewood table with its veneer chipping from the corners, and against one wall, in the same place where I remembered it, my father's childhood desk had been returned. The drawers were filled with rubber bands and paper clips, but when I cleared this away, I found the same carving—PROPERTY OF MR. ALTON ACHESON II, ESQ.—that I'd stared at in my own childhood days.

The properties that A&E Realty managed also had plenty of memories for me. They were the buildings of my youth, a hodgepodge of apartments, duplexes, and single-family rental units on the old east side, all of which my father and Elmore had purchased on the cheap, after the great white migration out to Kings County. It was Toby's job to keep these acquisitions in shape. In the mornings he led his crew out to the heavily padlocked ice cream truck where he stored his tools (*Jermaine, backseat—no, I know your name's not Jermaine; that's what I'm calling you. Come back ten days in a row, on time, and you'll get your own name*) and headed out, his loudspeakers trailing a flute solo from Jethro Tull, while I hung around taking phone calls and opening the previous day's mail. If any rent checks came in, I entered these transactions into ledger books that already contained row after row and year after year of similar notations in my mother's consistent hand. Sometimes, if the A&E checking balance was precariously thin, I drove to the Bank of Missouri on Sixty-third and Troost Avenue and deposited them right away.

My father also had a second job doing "consulting" work for the Bowen Company—a development that, like the loss of the Alomar Company, he refused to explain—so I partnered with Elmore most of the day. I would hear him at the bottom of the Gramercy's staircase around nine-thirty, cursing my father as he struggled up the stairs. (My father was fond of pointing out that if the office and Elmore's apartment had traded places, he would've been walking those stairs much more frequently.) Once upstairs, he signed checks for various paint- and hardware-store bills, answered phone calls, and then around noon we proceeded, in Elmore's slowly rolling Lincoln, to visit people who owed A&E money or who'd filed complaints that could not be solved through maintenance (*Mrs. Wilmott in 2B is a "dirty heifer"; the residents at 4225 Euclid have a dog that barked last night until three*). My role, though I'd explained to Elmore that I'd never passed the bar in Missouri, was to take over when Elmore lost patience with his interviewee and said, "All right, talk to my lawyer about it, then."

At which point I would invoke the relevant statute—or make up what sounded like the relevant statute—piling on what Elmore called the "whereases and wherefores" until the tenant was sufficiently impressed to pay up or drop his complaint.

Only once during my first week did we vary this routine. This happened on a Friday, when instead of climbing the stairs, Elmore called me down to his Lincoln early. When I opened the door, I found my father in the backseat. "You get any calls for Roscoe this morning?" he asked me as Elmore put the car in gear.

The strange thing was that I had received three such phone calls, in fact, each from what sounded like an old woman. "Yeah," I said. "I told them I didn't know anybody named Roscoe. Why, was that the wrong thing to say?"

"To my mother?" Elmore chuckled and shook his head. "The problem with Miss Hattie is that it doesn't matter *what* you say."

We pulled up a few minutes later at a tidy, olive-painted bungalow that had clearly been tended with a more personal hand than most A&E properties. There was a small, still-bright chain-link fence around the yard, beds of roses along the foundation, and a little birdbath overhung by a magnolia tree. I climbed in back while Elmore rang the doorbell and then, bowing slightly, kissed the hand of a frail, elderly woman and escorted her in formal fashion, arm in arm, down the house's short concrete walk and through the gate. "You know how to handle a pistol?" my father asked me.

"What, you mean Miss Hattie?" I said. It was hard not to smile at this woman's deeply serious and stern expression, chin up, her whithered cheeks sucked in—as if daring her audience to notice the slight unsteadiness of her gait or the fact that her dress had slipped off one shoulder, revealing grayish, wrinkled skin.

"No, I mean a pistol," my father said, and then, before I could answer, he climbed out to help Elmore lift Miss Hattie into her seat.

Our lunch provided an ideal climate for my father's favorite conversational game, in which bizarre or inexplicable behaviors were treated as if they made perfect sense—except, of course, to the outsider, who was in this case me. We ate at Niecie's, a diner on Standard Avenue, which Miss Hattie seemed to think was a much fancier, evening place. "I'll have a martini," she said decisively, having perused a menu that did not, as far as I could tell, offer anything stronger than root beer.

"That sounds lovely," Elmore said, winking at the waitress. "But if you're going to drink that way, you better get something to eat."

"Filet mignon," Miss Hattie said decisively, without a second look.

"Excellent choice," Elmore said, snapping his menu closed and handing it to the waitress. "Why don't we make it two?"

This was finally too much for the waitress, a young girl who seemed no more familiar than I with Hattie's routine. "Two of what?" she said. "You ain't picked even one thing yet that we actually got to eat!"

"That's all right, honey," Elmore said. "You just go on back and tell Miss Niecie that Miss Hattie's here and wants her special. She'll know what you mean."

It was hard for me to figure out why, exactly, my father and I were even there, given that we overheard this exchange from a separate booth. Our only interaction with Elmore and Hattie came halfway through the lunch, when Elmore reached cautiously around the side of the booth and slipped Hattie's red purse into my father's hand. A few minutes later, my father just as surreptitiously returned it. This exchange still remained unexplained after lunch, when we arrived at Miss Hattie's house. As my father and I watched from the backseat, Elmore stopped the car and then stiffened suddenly. "Now, Miss Hattie," he said, "why in the world would you go do that?"

"You can't leave," the old woman said. "I'm not going back to that horrible place. You leave this time, you're gonna take me with you."

Elmore had turned around by now, very gingerly, and reached toward Miss Hattie. The two of them struggled for a moment against the seat, and then I saw Elmore come away with a small, nickel-plated pistol that he tucked into the pocket of his jacket. In response, his mother began to cry, quietly, balling up her fists, and she continued crying as Elmore walked slowly around the car, opened the door, and led her away.

Later on that evening, at the Grotto, my father explained the whole context of the story for me—that Miss Hattie had been the proprietress of a famous speakeasy down on Eighteenth Street, back in the thirties. (Where, according to my father, she recollected doing business with Big Alton, who'd apparently frequented her place.) And that Roscoe's full name was Roscoe Willoughby, a musician and semipro baseball player who'd been the love of her life—and who might also have been Elmore's father, since Elmore looked enough like him that Hattie had begun to confuse the two. Or, in my father's interpretation, she allowed herself to pretend that Elmore was Roscoe for the purposes of enjoying a "date" once a week.

"And the gun?" I asked. "Does she also pretend with that once a week?"

"What do you think we were there for?" my father asked.

"I don't know, since nobody ever tells me," I said.

My father reached into his pocket and opened his palm to display the .22 slug that he'd removed from the chamber of Hattie's pistol when Elmore had passed her purse to him alongside the booth. "You should've been paying better attention," he said, tossing the little bullet at me so it rattled on the bar. "You hang around this town too long and you'll be doing this yourself someday."

"What's that supposed to mean?" I asked.

"It means," my father said, "that if you're giving up your dream because your mother's worried about me, you'd be making a big mistake."

"Don't listen to him," Little Joey said from behind the bar. "Taking care of your father if he's in trouble—that's an honorable thing."

It was well known around the bar that Little Joey had begun making plans to run the Grotto as soon as his father, Joey Sr., had been indicted in a racketeering investigation a few years back. Unfortunately for him, while this investigation had apparently landed Bobby Ansi and Nick Garaciello in jail, his father had gone free.

"I didn't say he should hope his father *makes* a mistake," my father said.

"He wouldn't have to hope long for that," said Elmore Haywood, who'd just walked in. "All he'd have to do is wake up in the morning."

"Gratitude among friends," my father said, "now there's an honorable thing."

This conversation was clearly my father's attempt to prepare me for a dinner my mother had arranged for that night, celebrating the partnership that Callaghan had offered me. If Little Joey's Lounge, which had replaced the old Reserve Room in back, was depressing in its attempts at newness—a mirrored disco ball and empty dance floor in one corner, faux Roman columns that the patrons kept running into as they went to take a leak—then the comforting thing about the restaurant itself was that it looked exactly the same. We sat at the same window table where my father and I had been sitting with Horace Cogle on the day Prudential Bowen offered to invest in the Alomar Company. We unfolded our silverware from the same white paper napkins atop the same red-checked tablecloth, and asked Joey Sr. to bring up one of the same old baskets of peanuts whose shells we cracked as we looked over the same menu, trying to choose what to eat.

"Nice crowd," my father said, surveying the seven or eight couples that were scattered in the booths behind us.

"You're joking, right?" I said. "I remember when you couldn't get a table at this place. You can't tell me that *everyone* moved to Kings County."

"It was the busing," my father said to me. "Up until '77 we had three white schools in Missouri, all in Bowen neighborhoods, and three black ones. Then the Court finally came in and ordered the city to mix them up." He waved his hand.

"Only about twenty years too late," Elmore pointed out.

"For me," my father said glumly. "If the Court had done that back when I still owned the MacVess property, we'd all be millionaires today."

"Are there a *lot* of white people who think that *Brown* was decided just to help them sell real estate?" Elmore asked me. "Or is it just him?"

"All I'm saying is, you couldn't have imagined a better advertisement for Kings County," my father said. "No black people to bus out there."

"Well, I think it's kind of nice to live in a city where you can get a table on Friday night," my mother said. She was still intently reading her menu—a habit of hers, no matter how often she'd seen Joey's fare, as if she might have missed something. "Of course, I'm not as sophisticated as the people Jack knows in New York City."

My father had been right: my mother may have been a bit more subtle than Miss Hattie, but her goal that evening was basically the same. Her approach involved congratulating me on Callaghan's offer and then, in the guise of motherly concern, discussing the "ramifications" of my decision—nearly all of which ended up as talking points for the ruinous dangers of accepting. "Ho-ney, I'm no expert," she said as our entrées arrived, "But I just happened to see this article about two young lawyers who'd been made partner in a New York firm that went bankrupt six months later?" Opening her purse, she removed a neatly stapled clipping from nothing less than the *National Law Journal*—a periodical that I felt certain my family didn't normally subscribe to. "These poor boys lost everything, even though the event that caused the firm to go bankrupt happened before they even signed on. Now, I don't want to say anything against Mr. Callaghan, who I'm sure is a wonderful man . . ."

Most of the evening followed this script. My father and Elmore abstained from the discussion, their heads quietly bowed over their pasta, eyes safely averted from any appeals I might direct their way. The only time they became involved was when my mother forced me to admit what a partnership would actually cost, a figure I'd deliberately avoided mentioning. "Okay," I said, relenting. "It's complicated giving some round figure, since you don't have to pay it all up front. But a full partnership at a New York law firm these days will run you about a hundred grand."

At which point my father crooked a finger at Joey Ramola, who glided over, still dark-haired, the owner of a brand-new toupee. "What do you need, Al?" he asked. "Everything okay?"

"The bill goes to the kid," my father said, pointing at me. "And while you're at it, why don't you bring me back the wine list."

I could hardly get angry at my mother for quizzing me. Up until that summer, she'd never made me feel guilty for the years I'd been away—after all, she herself had left home at an early age. This time, however, she had sensed that the offer from Callaghan was a more serious and permanent threat, and the more she questioned me, the more I found myself exaggerating the qualities of this job—and not just the job but my entire life in New York City. It was a *perfect* job, a job that I'd be a fool not to take, and the social life that I described to her, though invented from the *New York Times* society page, began to sound exciting even to me. "Nearly everybody I know from college is there," I explained. "And not just kids from Syracuse, but imagine how many colleges are in the area. You've got Columbia, Yale, Princeton, some of the brightest young minds in the country, all gathered in one place." I did not mention, in this discussion, that very few of these minds, particularly the female ones, had much interest in meeting a Syracuse graduate from Kansas City. Nor did I explain that I wouldn't have had time to talk to them anyway, since at Callaghan, Metzger & Lyme, I generally worked between eighty and ninety hours a week. I even lied about Mr. Callaghan, stretching the three hours we'd spent together watching a Mets game—the longest time we'd spent together since my hiring—into what I described as "a real solid relationship."

"So you have a whole new family out there," my mother said, smiling sadly. "I'm very glad to hear that."

"Gimme a break, Ma," I said. "It's not like I'm trading in this family. Consider it an addition. Hell, if you want, I'll have you and Dad out to visit, and we'll go to dinner with Mr. Callaghan." Though this image, as I glanced at my father and Elmore, their napkins tucked into their necks, was one that even I found impossible to believe.

The one reason that my mother *didn't* give me for staying in Kansas City was Geanie Bowen, whom I'd made an appointment to meet later on that night. She'd left a message the day before, inviting me over for a swim at her parents' "old place," which my mother had delivered to me, along with several explanations that apparently she felt she'd waited long enough to give me. One was that Henry Bowen had left the big house on Fifty-fifth Street after Geanie's mother died a few years back (I had at least heard the news about her death). Another was that Henry had moved to a brand-new housing development out in Kings County, in order to "set an example" for the city's elite. And, furthermore, that his new house was part of a larger development named "Fairhaven Estates" that was going up on a section of Royce MacVess's ranch—land that the Bowen Company now controlled, instead of my father—though how and why the land had been lost, my mother either could not or would not explain.

She did explain, however, why my meeting with Geanie should not under any circumstances be mistaken for a date. Geanie was engaged. According to my mother (who generally knew her local gossip), her fiancé was in London, doing research. And though Geanie had come home to be with her family, she would be returning to Connecticut in the fall and would furthermore—without question—be married by the spring. This was also what Geanie seemed to be working up to telling me as we sat out beside her father's concrete pool, later on that night. I suppose that in another situation, on a different day, her stalling would have irritated me. But instead I found that I enjoyed watching her delay. I had learned, during this period of small talk, that Nikki Garaciello was now a grade-school teacher in Emporia, Kansas. I had learned that though nobody lived in Geanie's old house, the Bowens still owned it—and Geanie still had a key. Engaged or not, certain details also suggested that Geanie wanted to look good for me. The tennis skirt she'd been wearing when I arrived showed the full length of her legs, her strong white hamstrings and the faint, bacon-colored freckles above her knees. Halfway through our conversation, she'd stripped down to a swimsuit and dove into the greenish water of Tom Pendergast's swimming pool, where she now stood, talking to me. But the main thing that I found interesting about our conversation was the quick glances she cast in my direction, filled with the same flicker of fear she'd shown when I'd yelled at her the night of her grandfather's funeral.

"The thing about time, Jack," she was saying to me. "Do you ever think about that, about how fast things are always going? Doesn't it seem like it could have been just a couple of years ago that we were still all fifteen?"

"I wouldn't mind *feeling* fifteen," I said.

"That's exactly the point I'm trying to make," Geanie said. "I was lying there on the lounge chair before you came over, staring up at those trees"—she grabbed the pool's edge and floated onto her back as an example—"which is something that I remember doing all the time when I was fifteen. Or ten, or eleven, say. So when I'm lying there, just looking up at the trees—you do it, too—that's all I can see. I can't see my body. I don't *feel* any older than I did at fifteen."

"Well, there is a little headache that I don't remember," I said.

"Even the house looks the same," Geanie said, ignoring me. "My point is, before you came, I realized that there was nothing here at all to prove I wasn't fifteen. Not in my sensory environment. It could have been, for all I could see, that absolutely no time had passed, nothing had changed."

I had followed Geanie's gaze up into the trees by then. Their uppermost branches rose high and deep, the leaves with faint purple shadows underneath. Dry clouds bolted overhead, moving rather quickly from west to east, and they alternately dimmed and then suddenly uncovered the moon, this cycle of dimming and opening, dimming and opening, proceeding at a rhythm I could not trace.

"Then what happened?" I asked. Though I'd brought swim trunks, I'd chosen to sit in my lounger instead, my feet splayed on either side of the woven bed, back straight, and my neck had begun to cramp from looking up.

"Then you came," Geanie said. We both laughed at this.

"So that's why I was invited," I said while we were still laughing. "My mother was a little worried about me hanging around with a woman who was already engaged."

"I was hoping she'd told you that," Geanie said.

"So the better question," I said, "would be whether or not married people still feel like they're fifteen when they stare into the trees."

Geanie stroked down to the far end of the pool, a predictable response, and one that I therefore also enjoyed. "God, I hope they do," she said.

"You can send me a report on it, then," I said. "From wherever you'll be living—probably someplace out east, right?"

"Andrew's from Boston," Geanie said. "It's a little bit of an issue, though, since, as you can see, he doesn't really like coming back to Kansas City."

"That's only because he doesn't know the trees," I said.

"And what about you?" Geanie asked. Realizing that I wasn't going to get angry—seeing that, in fact, I had now peeled off my T-shirt—she turned around to watch me, elbows propped on the gutter. "Where are you going to end up, Jack? I heard that you were supposed to be a partner in New York City by the end of the month."

I dove in then. The pool's green color, as Geanie had many times explained to me, came from the fact that the water wasn't chlorinated—though it was otherwise supposed to be clean. "Natural," was how she put it. But I was surprised, when I opened my eyes, at how dark it was, how murky; I'd swum nearly to the deep end, my eyes burning, before I made out Geanie's feet, kicking along the wall, and when I surfaced, I was so close to her that her hand rose up instinctively to my chest—though not hard enough to push me away. "Do you know what I've been thinking?" I said. I ducked beneath the water and surfaced again inside her arm, so it angled across my shoulder. "Crazy as it sounds, I've been wondering what it might be like to stay."

The following Monday I answered the phone at my father's desk in the A&E Realty offices and heard Henry Bowen's foghorn voice on the other end of the line.

"I'd like to speak to Alton Acheson, please," he said.

"I'm sorry, sir," I said, putting my feet up on the desk. "He's not in."

"Well, when is he going to be?"

I was surprised, hearing the impatience in Henry's voice, at how vividly my father's struggles with the Bowen Company's secretaries came back to me.

"I don't know. Let me check his schedule," I said, whisking through the pages of the *Time* magazine I'd been reading before the call came. "Mm . . . mm . . . mm. He looks pretty busy today, sir. May I tell him who's calling?"

"This is Henry Bowen."

"All right, Mr. Bowen—are you an A&E tenant?"

When frustrated, Henry Bowen made a harrumphing noise, similar to the sound a buffalo might have made after taking a long drink. "I'm with a company," he said.

"Very good, sir," I said. "Could you tell me the company's name? Not to be impolite, but we do business with a lot of *different* companies here at A&E."

"The *Bowen* Company."

"B-O-W-E-N," I said, sounding it out. "Now, sir, I'm not familiar with your company specifically, but I can tell you that if you're looking for any subcontracting work, Mr. Acheson already has his own team—"

"I want you to *do* work," Henry said. "You do *do* work, don't you?"

"Of course, sir," I said, picking up a pencil. "You just tell me the address of the property in question and the work that you need done, and I'll have the foreman out there to make a bid by the end of the day."

"This is my daughter's idea, not mine," Henry said. "She's got two houses she wants to renovate. You familiar with Fifty-fifth and State Line?"

Summertime

From a distance the Bowen houses looked as impressive as ever, with their whitewashed phalanxes of windows and their stern expanses of roofing tile and brick. Even from the ground, standing right up next to the house, as Toby, Geanie, and I did on that first day, things seemed to be in relatively good shape. The paint on the ground-floor trim was a bit thick, perhaps, and beginning to crack from multiple applications; perhaps a few lines of rust showed around the shutter hinges. But the problem was that in an effort to save money, Henry had been painting *only* the ground floor of the mansion during the years since he'd moved away. Consequently, when I shakily mounted Toby Wilcox's extension ladder clear up under the eaves of the great house and, on his instruction, reached up to test the guttering, the bottom of its trough crumbled away at the touch of my fingertips, leaving me with a handful of rotting leaves.

There were other problems with the place. Apparently the Bowens had lived in these houses long enough—and had had enough pull over the years with the city—that they'd never been properly inspected. Their guts—the electricity, the heating vents, the pipes—hadn't been updated since the 1930s. Or as Toby put it, shouting over the shoulder of his Blue Öyster Cult T-shirt as he led us through the basement, "Little lady, I'm gonna tell you one thing. You see that knob-and-tube wiring? You see that asbestos lining around the furnace vents? You bring a city inspector in here to look at this stuff, and he's gonna have a hard-on for weeks."

Back at the office, we had argued over whether to take the work, a drama that pitted Toby against me, with my father and Elmore presiding uneasily. Ulterior motives aside, I thought it made sense to go ahead. It would be profitable, good, steady pay. Toby could hire extra guys. Plus, if we wanted to, we could steal a page out of the Bowen playbook and charge eight dollars an hour for the labor instead of the usual six and still undercut Bowen's own workers, who got twelve generally. But the issue was decided by something that Toby said in his own defense. Removing his kerchief and running a deeply tanned hand over his bald patch, he said, "Boss, you've asked me to fix up some pretty crappy places over the years, okay? Never once did I bitch. But this place is more jacked up than any property this company has ever *thought* of owning." At which point, seeing the gleam in my father's eye, I knew that we would make a bid.

Geanie and I spent the final weeks of June together in this way. Up in the Bowen attic, which we reached by climbing over mountains of steamer trunks and an actual raccoon coat on a coatrack, I learned of Geanie's concern that her fiancé, Andrew, was—to use her words—"something of a depressive." In the twelve Bowen bathrooms with their marble floors and porcelain-and-brass fixtures (where, in every floor above the first, the water pressure had been reduced to a trickle, due to corroded lead pipes), I learned that her father, Henry, had, at the age of sixty-nine, recently begun to date. In the basement, searching for a leaky sewer pipe amid cobwebbed racks of wine bottles, I learned that Geanie did not feel particularly confident about her dissertation topic—"A Statistical Analysis of Population Patterns in South Soweto, 1972–1978"—a topic I couldn't offer much advice on, except to suggest that it be changed.

We began to hang around together at the house, after the workers left, driving to pick up take-out pizza and a six-pack, and then returning to lounge around the pool. Sometimes, around ten o'clock, we would walk through the warm summer evening down to the Mission Hills Country Club, crossing the famed Indian Creek and wandering in the fuzzy darkness of the fairways. The qualities I'd loved in Geanie hadn't changed. A week into the project, she'd managed to convince A&E Realty's ragtag squad of workers that they represented not a cheaper alternative to the Bowen Company's employees but a crack restoration team, charged with one of the most historically sensitive projects in the city. She'd also uncovered the source of Toby Wilcox's loyalty to my father. Apparently, the apartment building that Toby and his mother owned had been in such bad shape that, when my father ran into him, the city had been about to shut it down. "Toby says that he'd improvised all the wiring in the building along with most of the plumbing," she told me. "When a tenant finally complained, the inspectors showed up and had a field day. It was your father who taught him how to file all the paperwork, get things up to code. He saved the place from being condemned."

This was the Geanie Bowen that I remembered from high school and the Surveyors' Club—the girl who'd possessed the rare ability to make you feel as if you were in the center of things. Of course, things were not the same. This time I wasn't asking her to go out with me; this time I had no high-school scruples about "doing the right thing," and, most important, I owned a return ticket to New York City. I was safe; I could look but always escape. Besides, when I listened to Geanie compare her father's old house unfavorably with his new one out in Fairhaven Estates, which she called "the land with no trees," those missing years still whispered in my ear. Then I felt as if, however fairly or unfairly, I ought to steal something from her as coolly and efficiently as her father and grandfather had stolen the Alomar Company from my family.

However, there were other emotions that I didn't admit to. Such as the fact that when Geanie laughed at an observation of mine that no one else would have noticed, I felt the giddiness of freshman year. And thoughts that flickered through my mind like ghosts. That I didn't *have* to go back. That, engagement be damned, I desired nothing more than to hear her admit she'd made a mistake to leave me in the first place.

One thing that I knew I didn't want to do, as June drew to a close, was end up being "friends." By then time was getting scarce. I called in some extra vacation days, promising to get back to Callaghan after the holiday. And so when, on the Fourth of July, Geanie had called up to ask if I could help her move a few pieces of furniture that afternoon, I'd agreed—but only because I had another plan. The first problem with my plan became apparent when Geanie showed up an hour late, leaving me to feel like a fool for having agreed to work on a holiday in the first place. Second, the piece of furniture that we wrestled down the steps—an oak bureau in her old room—wouldn't fit in her car anyway. This finally sent me steaming into the kitchen for the cooler of beer that I'd brought with me, three cans of which I'd already finished during my wait.

When Geanie came back to find me, I noticed that she'd changed into a lime green cotton skirt and a pair of white sandals. "So where are you off to tonight?" I asked.

"I don't know," Geanie said.

"Must be a nice place," I said. "I feel like I've been there a lot recently."

"I'm supposed to go to the Fourth of July picnic at the country club, with my dad," Geanie said. "And before you start getting mad at me again, I'd like to point out that I didn't get any other invitations. Present company included."

"Do you want to go?" I asked.

"Do you have any idea what a country-club Fourth of July party is like?"

"No," I said honestly.

"It's pretty much like a funeral, only with sparklers," Geanie said. "Plus, *she'll* be there." This was her coded reference to her father's new date.

"Good," I said. "Then you won't be missing anything."

"Why?" Geanie said, looking at me curiously.

In response I tossed her a beer. "Because," I said, picking up the cooler and draining my own beer. "Tonight you're going out with me."

At midnight of that same evening, I nosed my father's old Ford Fairlane up the hill to Ninth and Grand Avenue, in the heart of the old downtown. Behind me lay every bar that my father had introduced me to since I'd returned to town, nearly all of which Geanie and I had visited—including several I bet the old man himself hadn't seen.

"Where are we going, Jack?" Geanie said as she lit a cigarette, a habit I'd not known that she'd acquired until that night. "Are you okay to drive?"

"Rock solid," I said.

"I'm only asking because you've got a green light."

I did have a green light. I hadn't noticed because I'd been looking farther on down the hill, toward the dark trenches where Grand Avenue crossed the highway. "Much obliged," I said, toasting her with the beer I had tucked between my legs. "Gotta watch the traffic around here."

"Andrew has a theory on drunk driving," Geanie said. "I think it applies even more in Kansas City than in Boston."

"Let's hear it," I said. "Andrew, by all means."

"You don't have to be sarcastic about it. If there's one thing I can't stand, it's when you meet someone and they have to pretend like they've never, ever even considered sleeping with somebody in the past."

"You and Andrew have *slept* together?" I said. I lifted my foot off the brake, and without my even touching the gas, the old Fairlane idled through the intersection and began rolling down the hill. The light had turned red by then, unfortunately.

"Which is more than you've ever told me," Geanie pointed out. "Do you realize that you've never even so much as mentioned another girl's name to me?"

"Susi," I said, making one up.

"And then most guys, if they do mention an old girlfriend's name, the only thing they'll say about her is something negative. Which always makes me wonder why they went out with her in the first place, if she was so universally a bitch."

"That's ol' Susi for you," I said. I was engaged, just then, in an experiment with the Fairlane's steering, trying to see if the car would roll clear down to the highway without my touching the wheel. At the moment, it seemed to be pulling to the left.

"Andrew's theory on drunk driving is that you have to practice," Geanie said.

"That's it?" I had noticed that without my foot on the gas, the Fairlane rolled so quietly that I could hear the tires clicking over the asphalt's seams— an effect that I'd stuck my head out the window to investigate.

"It makes sense, at least," Geanie said. "I mean, you wouldn't go jump in an eighteen-wheeler and start driving it without any practice, would you? And if that's true, then why would some drunk person, without the slightest bit of practice, think he could jump in his car in the middle of the night and drive straight down the hi—" Her voice stopped there. During this speech the Fairlane had finally reached the bridge above the highway, and, taking control of it again, I'd nipped neatly around the concrete median, crossed the bridge, and hit my turn signal as we pulled up to a blue-and-red shield that marked the entrance to Interstate 35 South.

"What are you doing?" Geanie said uncertainly.

"Practicing," I said as I made the turn, flawlessly. Dropping down into the nightmare darkness of the on-ramp, I hit the gas.

As we swung around the downtown loop, Geanie rode in silence— what I guess amounted to a formal protest, in hopes that I would come to my senses. But my senses were fine. A blast of muggy air surged in through our windows as I brought the Fairlane up to speed and, cutting off the high beams of an approaching pickup, settled in behind the chrome back of a Freightliner, his rubber mud flaps bearded with grit. This stretch of road had become familiar to me as an adult; it was the route home from the airport, north of the river. More recently it served as a shortcut for my father and me after drinking at the Grotto. And so, at just the right moment, as we shuddered underneath the Broadway overpass, I shifted into the left lane and joined a sprinkling of mergers as I-35 came out of its trench and lifted onto a short, elevated section that bisected the city's west side. "You know, Lonnie once drove me through this before it was built," I said.

"What's the point here, Jack?" Geanie said. She'd rolled the Fairlane's window up, leaving a small crack at the top, and now slouched against her door, the smoke from her cigarette rising in a pale line to the window's crease, where the wind snatched at it.

"The point is that it scared the shit out of me at the time. We were, like, driving around on nothing but dirt—dodging these huge cranes and these road graders." I myself ducked and dodged, swerving the car from lane to lane in an effort to imitate the feeling of that ride. But the huge, bombed-out field of rubble that Lonnie and I had driven through had disappeared. Now it was a cloverleaf, its maze of curving on- and off-ramps lit by three halogen lights on fifty-foot poles, a bluish glaze that caused the surrounding grass hills and small copse of pines to look as if they'd been cut out of construction paper. "I thought we were going to die," I said. "It was nuts, completely nuts, but the funny thing about it is that if he hadn't taken me on that drive, I would've never remembered what actually used to be here. Like there." I pointed to a series of billboards, one for Dolgin's Jewelers, another for the Bank of Missouri, mounted on rooftops that were lower than the highway. "There was this whole block of apartments there, just cut in half. You could see everything inside—all the plumbing, all the wires, everything. It looked like a bomb went off in the middle of the city. And do you know what the funny thing was? The funny and perverted and very Lonnie reason that he gave me for driving through all this crap?" I leered at Geanie, but she was still refusing to look at me. "He said he wanted to show me my father's beautiful highway. It's like a gift, huh, always being able to say the one thing that you least want to hear?"

"You mean, like now?" Geanie said. We were just then passing the last two exits—for Broadway and then Southwest Trafficway—that would have led us back to the Campanile. But instead I veered west, heading toward Kings County.

"What's wrong with talking about Lonnie?" I asked. "I figured since we were complimenting people we used to sleep with, you might want to say something nice."

"Did I mention the other half of that equation?" Geanie asked. "Which is that if you do tell a guy you slept with somebody, he's not supposed to be jealous about it—especially seventeen years after the fact?"

"Somebody skipped the telling part, it seems to me."

"What do you want me to say?" Geanie had rallied some of her confidence and was now leaning in close. "Is that what all these fucking moods are about? You treat this like it's some big secret, like it's supposed to mean something?"

"It means something to me," I said.

"But what?" Geanie asked. "We were in *high school.* High school. Have you looked at yourself lately, Jack?" She waved her hand in front of my face, and I knocked it away. "You're thirty-five years old. Thirty-five. My God, if you're still pissed off about something that happened to both of us when we were seventeen—"

"I still feel fifteen inside," I said, quoting her unpleasantly.

"Then look at the fucking world," Geanie said. "It's gone, whatever it is you're remembering. They built the highway. You're driving on the goddamn thing. People moved—I mean, just look at all this crap."

She was right about that. We'd hit Kings County by then, the same stretch of highway we'd used to drive out to the quarry, and the farmland that had once surrounded it was completely unrecognizable—or rather it was recognizable only in the sense that it looked exactly like the kind of highway roughage that you could find outside any city. The fields were now pockmarked with frontage roads and parking lots, with lit signs that advertised the TIRE WAREHOUSE and on the right, a huge square box of a building whose sign read KOPP'S CARPET OUTLET, with a small caricature of a British policeman holding a billy club, a garish lampoon of my father's dream.

"And anyway, even if I did sleep with Lonnie, what's wrong with that?" Geanie demanded. "You and I weren't dating, as if that should make any difference. We did it. It happened. We did it a few times, Jack. I'd never had sex before. I wanted to see what it was like. For chrissakes, it was just an experiment."

"Did Lonnie think of it as an experiment?" I asked.

"Why is that my responsibility?" Geanie asked. She was crying then; she'd turned her head to the window, but I could hear her sniffling.

Not long after that, we approached a high, spotlit billboard that rose some thirty feet above the highway. It showed a turreted brick house with a new wood-shingled roof and, in the lower corner, an unmistakable photo of Henry Bowen's watering-can head, enlarged to five feet in width. The legend read IF YOU LIVED IN FAIRHAVEN ESTATES LIKE ME, YOU'D BE FIVE MINUTES FROM YOUR TV. I reached out to nudge Geanie, but she was already looking at it, our eyes rotating together as this apparition approached and passed. The highway was dark then for a moment. The blue letters of a Goodyear Tires sign floated by on the right, behind the grid of a chain-link fence. Then we hit a second Fairhaven billboard just the same as the first, Henry's face and house growing out in front us, except this time the legend informed us that we were ONLY THREE MINUTES FROM YOUR TV. At some point during this, I'd begun laughing. I lifted my shirtsleeve to wipe my face, and when I brought my arm down again, Geanie caught my hand. "The family's great, aren't they?" she said. "You got to love the family. Let's go home, Jack, huh? Come home with me. It's just three minutes—we'll have the place to ourselves, I guarantee."

"I was there," I said. "Up at the quarry. I heard you and Lonnie arguing—the whole thing."

"I knew you were there, Jack," Geanie said. "Or I thought you would be. I thought you'd come and find us. That's what I kept thinking. I kept thinking and thinking that any minute Jack's going to save me. But that's not your responsibility."

"How was I supposed to know what was going to happen?"

"I don't know, Jack. You grew up with him. Now, slow down a little. Here's the exit, and when you get to the top, go right, and I'll show you the way."

From the highway Geanie gave me directions to Fairhaven Estates, pointing out its familiar-looking wrought-iron gates after a long drive east on 119th Street—now a sleek, six-lane road whose curbing shone like porcelain under new streetlamps, instead of the gravel track the members of the Surveyors' Club used to drive. Inside, I think I first truly understood what my father meant when he said the Bowens had been, all along, constructing dreams. Geanie and I wove through curving repetitions of what always seemed to be the *same* street, past buildings that seemed like rearranged combinations of the same parts—two front doors on each structure, two taupe garages on either end, a lower story made of brick, and a smaller stucco upper floor, painted to match. You did not own the yards, or trees, or even your exterior walls in Fairhaven Estates, Geanie explained to me; you owned only the floor inside, then paid a monthly fee to gardeners provided by the Bowen Company, which perhaps was why the seedlings, trussed up with wires, were in exactly the same spot in every yard and no one's grass was balding.

We did find her father's house eventually; it was the building that had been pictured in the sign. Geanie pointed out a lighted turret over a field of lower split-shingle rooftops and followed this like a star, her finger rotating through her side window, across my windshield, and then back again as I wove among the lawns of a neighborhood called Kensington Court, trying to find the street that would lead us there.

I don't remember much about how we got inside. At some point I was standing in a room with a vaulted ceiling that resembled, in its lack of ornamentation and its pure white walls, nothing so much as a giant version of the squash courts I remembered from Pemberton Academy. There was a single leather couch in the middle of the white carpet, a single coffee table, and a portable black-and-white TV flickering and playing commercials from the mantel of a stone fireplace. "Do *not* laugh," Geanie said. She had disappeared somewhere and returned with two iced drinks on a tray, carrying her sandals in her free hand. "I know it looks terrible, and I know you don't like my dad, but when Mom died, he just abandoned the old place and *everything* she'd decorated. That whole place was hers—now, except for work, it's like he doesn't want to see anything."

"Maybe *she'll* help out," I said, meaning her father's new girlfriend.

"Why do you think I'm trying to sneak Mom's old stuff in?" Geanie asked. "I figure if he doesn't notice there's no furniture in the living room, then maybe he won't notice if I bring the old stuff back bit by bit."

"I think a TV counts as furniture," I said.

"I said no laughing."

"It's not at you," I said. "I was just trying to imagine what Lonnie would've said about Fairhaven Estates."

"*I* think he would have loved it." In the television light, she was giving me a mischievous smile. "I think he would have lived here."

I leaned across and kissed her; her lips tasted like scotch. And though she did not respond, neither did she push me away.

"Don't you want to hear the end of my brilliant thought?" she asked.

"No, not really," I said. "So hurry up."

"You take a kid who always got picked on, who's *desperate* to fit in, give him some money, and you've got the kind of person who lives in Fairhaven Estates."

"Or who builds it," I said.

"How do you think I know this?"

"And what about me?"

"You'd never make it in Fairhaven Estates, Jack," she said. "But the difference between you and Lonnie is that you don't give a shit."

This time she kissed me. I didn't care by that point that she seemed to be wrong in her estimation of my feelings. What I liked was the feeling of her body as she rolled over into my lap, and the way her hair fell down on either side of our faces. It was too dark to really see her eyes, or whether or not there was something there other than her usual blank gaze, but her hands, unbuttoning my shirt, undoing the buckle of my pants, moving my own hands to the zipper of her dress, seemed committed enough to me.

I woke up later in a different room. This one had a tented ceiling with an exposed blond rafter running through its peak and two skylights that informed me it was still dark outside. When I rolled over onto my side, I saw the coal of Geanie's cigarette glowing against the bedsheets and she was sitting up naked, ashing into a tray she held just below her breasts. "You know what he did, don't you? The thing that got me sent away to boarding school?" she said, as if she'd been waiting for me to wake.

"I thought he called your father," I said. I hadn't minded talking about Lonnie earlier, but here, in Geanie's bed—or in somebody's bed—I was starting to feel sorry I'd brought him up.

"Well, first what he wanted to do was go away. That's it. It was his opinion that he and I were only going to make anything out of ourselves if we left our families completely. Can you imagine asking a girl to do that at age seventeen? And then actually expecting that she'd follow along?"

"Did you want to?" I asked.

"Would you have done it?"

It surprised me to realize that, despite my frequent embarrassment on my father's behalf as well as my dislike of the last heat, I had never considered running away. "I guess I always figured college was coming up quick enough. Plus, it was never a realistic option. If I left, I wouldn't have had the money to go to college, much less finish high school. Not to mention paying rent."

"Yeah, well . . . that wouldn't have been a problem for me."

I sat up suddenly and stared at Geanie as she put out her cigarette. Despite the air-conditioning, she had kicked her sheets down around her ankles and seemed completely unembarrassed by her nakedness, her pelvis and her ribs making beautiful white and gray lines beside me. There was a pair of framed glass doors at the foot of the bed that looked out over the lighted roofs of Fairhaven, and Geanie stared out at them, reached over to scratch my chest backhanded. "So you got that money, didn't you?" I said. "All that money that Lonnie was talking about?"

"That's another thing different about you, Jack," she said. "You have never once thought of me in terms of money."

"Was it really twenty million bucks?"

"It was enough," Geanie said. "The point is that I did get it, or I was going to get it—access to the trust my grandfather set up for me—sometime after junior year. So it was Lonnie's idea that we take that money and go away. Go to college when we wanted to. Make our own decisions. Live however and wherever we wanted to, so long as it was someplace else. It was one of those ideas that sound both crazy and perfectly realistic. Sort of like building a copy of Florence in Kansas City."

"So . . . what? He just wanted you to leave all your friends and family, all the people you knew, and give him money?" I said. "Doesn't sound like a good deal to me."

"It was more complicated than that," Geanie said. "We'd be living on interest only, no spending of the capital. He'd keep strict records of the amount he used for school and pay me back—which I believe he would've done, honestly. Plus, it was so much goddamn money . . . Lonnie used to say that if I didn't ever leave Kansas City, I'd only ever be the girl who inherited her life from the Bowen Company. That if there wasn't ever any real fear in an experience, then it wasn't worth anything."

"I'm sure he had plenty of theories," I said. I was thinking then of Lonnie's voice, speaking to me over the phone from the Bowens' kitchen, telling me that Geanie was the kind of bossy woman he couldn't stand.

"*Oh,* yes," Geanie said. "You know Lonnie and theories. And not all of my reactions were completely practical either. I thought that having sex was going to be an experiment, but it wasn't. Not the first time. The first time you do it with somebody, I wasn't prepared for the way it made me feel."

I was curious to know how doing it with me the first time had made her feel, a question I'd learned never to ask in bed. "So you were almost going to go."

"I didn't go *because* I was almost going to go, if that makes any sense," Geanie said. "I kept trying to put him off. I said we were too young, I said that we should wait, but you know how Lonnie is. Arguing just made him angrier. I think he could feel it, Jack. Like he almost had me; like he was almost free. He kept saying for both of us it was 'an issue of life and death,' and then—well, you saw it."

"I didn't see it," I said.

"I got my leg up." Geanie cocked her right leg in the air, the knee bent, her toes pulled back, as if Lonnie were balanced over us just then. "That's what I remember: I was trying to scratch his face and I was whistling, really whistling, and then I got my leg up under him and pushed." Her calf thumped against the mattress but together we kept staring at the ceiling. "We shouldn't have been near enough to the edge of the quarry for him to fall in just from that. I've always thought that maybe he couldn't see. Or maybe he forgot it was there, or maybe I *did* push him in—I've gone over it a million times, but there's no sure way I could've changed it. Unless I didn't fight."

"It sounds like you didn't have a choice," I said.

"If I had told you that, would you have thought I was any less guilty?"

"I never said you were."

Geanie sighed. "Nobody makes up stories for innocent people," she said. She rolled over on her side away from me. "The funny thing is, Lonnie ended up being right about almost everything. I went away, I did my own thing, but I was always waiting around for my father to ask me to come back and work for the company."

"Here?" I had lifted my head, looking over her shoulder at her profile. It was true that I'd thought her guilty. "I figured you hated real estate."

"Hating something and being good at it are two different things," Geanie said. "I'm a shitty academic—"

"Oh, come on."

"All right, I'm an average academic, which is the same thing. Nobody really will ever care about what I'm writing in my dissertation. But this— this place, this company . . . I don't know how to explain it. It's not just that I could do it. I know I could do it. It's just that . . ."

"You would have been as good at it as your father," I said.

"Do you think that's true?" Geanie reached for the covers, pulling them up tightly around her shoulders. "God, I hope it isn't, because then I really ruined everything."

When I woke, Geanie was still asleep, snoring lightly into her pillow, another habit I hadn't known she'd acquired until that night. I found my jeans and socks downstairs by the solitary couch, along with our two drinks, the ice long melted, a tray of cigarette butts, and the three pieces of clothing—bra, panties, one-piece dress—that Geanie had been wearing last night. I was tugging on my zipper, Geanie's lingerie still clutched in my fist, when Henry Bowen walked past me in a swimsuit and a pair of penny loafers, a copy of the morning paper in his hands. Never before had I been so appreciative of the Bowen talent for causing unpleasant or inconvenient sights to disappear. Not until he had his back to me did Henry even acknowledge my presence. "Well," he said, opening the glass door to the pool deck. "At the very minimum, you had a more successful night than your father—though that's not saying much."

On any other day I would've been willing to play along with Henry and disappear; now I followed him outside. He was sitting in a lounge chair, the paper undisturbed in his lap, staring at the wooden skeletons that I'd mistaken for tepees the night before and which, I could now see, were in fact the bare two-by-four frames of a new row of houses, going in about fifty yards from his back porch. "Going to mess up the view a little," I said, tossing Geanie's bra and panties onto the table between us.

Henry shaded his eyes. The sun was fierce already, its glare exaggerated by the fact that nowhere on Henry's property, or amid the hamlet of shingle roofs below us, could you see a shade tree. In this heat, workmen had already begun revving saws and battering hammers against the frames—a din that, when I'd awakened in Geanie's room, had caused me to imagine I was back in New York.

"How often do you get to look at three hundred thousand dollars in capital getting nailed together outside your back window?" Henry asked.

I whistled. "For all or one of them?" I asked.

"For half of one," Henry said.

"You ever think about using that extra money to buy some trees?" I asked. "Or do you figure that just keeps the squirrels away?"

Henry had lifted his straw hat and was waving it vigorously over his head, a gesture that I first thought was simply celebratory, urging his workers on. Then a man carrying a clipboard noticed him and came jogging toward us across the grass. "Sam, tell this young man about our development," Henry said, taking the clipboard.

Sam was in his mid-forties, clean-shaven, wore a tie under his jumpsuit, and began his pitch in a confident, autopilot voice. "We've got seventy-five units in the ground, with the capacity to expand to one twenty-five," he said. "They're custom-built, with a choice of five basic floor plans, starting in the low two hundreds and going clear up to the high threes. But the greatest amenity here at Fairhaven is that we provide a controlled-maintenance environment"—around this point he noticed the bra and panties that sat on the table between Henry and me, a sight that so flustered him that he stammered through the rest of his pitch—"that allows residents to enjoy the pleasure of lawn and garden dwelling without actually having to worry about the upkeep."

"Never mind about the upkeep, Sam," Henry said, looking up over the edge of the clipboard. "This kid's not a buyer. He's just trying to figure out how much money his father lost when he got rid of this property."

"Lost?" Sam said to his shoes.

"His father used to own this property," Henry explained. "Before he decided very generously to give it back to me."

"Give?" Sam said. This last piece of information caused him to forget about the panties, at least. He scraped a chair over the concrete and sat down before us, running his fingers through his hair. "I guess it would depend on what he paid for it originally," he said.

"Now, there's a good question," Henry said.

I had realized by now where Henry was leading me, and the cockiness that I'd felt at presenting him with his daughter's panties vanished immediately. "A thousand dollars an acre," I said, trying not to flinch or lose my grin.

Sam stared at me as if the panties on the table might as well have been mine. "But we're getting seventy-five dollars a *foot*," he said.

"Well, it gets me visiting privileges at least," I said.

Henry by then had signed the papers on Sam's clipboard and handed it back, dismissing him. Sam paced quickly across the deck, then broke into a half jog across the lawn, as if eager to escape before any further violence was done to me. "If it was up to me, you'd have more privileges than that," Henry said to my surprise.

"How do you mean?" I asked. I was standing up then, though somewhat unsteadily. It had occurred to me that this very scene would have represented for my father the height of his great dream—sitting out on his pool deck, signing purchase orders, while his city of the future was being constructed at his feet. However, as I looked down on Henry's long, bare legs, his shirt unbuttoned to allow a small white pooch of belly to droop over his plaid swim trunks, it also struck me that he didn't seem to be enjoying himself particularly. His complexion looked a lot worse than it did on his billboard. His hand shook when he signed the papers. And I noticed an empty glass on the far side of his chair, rimed with the telltale grit of Alka-Seltzer. "Let me put it to you this way," Henry said. "What do you think would posses a young woman from this city, with all the opportunities that she might have, to move to Connecticut and study Africa?"

"Soweto," I corrected him. "'A Statistical Analysis of Population Patterns in South Soweto.'"

Henry gave me a look from under his hat, as if to ask why I thought this bit of information did anything but prove his case. "You know she's supposed to go there," Henry said. "To study. A school will actually pay money for this."

"It's probably a requirement," I said.

"A requirement?" Henry said searchingly.

"You ever give her a better reason to stay?" I said.

"That's your department, isn't it?"

"So . . . what? You're saying the only reason you can think of for her to come back to Kansas City is to get married? Of what possible practical use is that?"

"Can I offer you a piece of advice?" Henry said. We were in the kitchen then. A slab of wood hung above the stove with the words MYRNA'S PLACE burned into it as if by a branding iron. "If you ever propose to a woman, find a better argument than that."

"Why don't you hire her?" I asked.

"Don't own anything in South Africa," Henry said. He'd removed mayonnaise, a carton of bread, and some bologna from the icebox and was attempting to put together a sandwich whose construction made a good argument for the practicality of a wife.

"Who the hell else is going to run it when you're done?" I asked.

Henry made a gesture that seemed to suggest that whoever it was, they wouldn't prepare for it by studying South Africa.

"But why not Geanie?" I said. "She could do it, and you'd be a fool not to give her a chance. All you'd have to do is ask."

"And how do you know what it takes to run a real estate company?" Henry asked. "Are you basing this on your father? If so, let me give you *two* pieces of advice."

Henry had finished making his sandwich and, carrying it on a plate, opened a door that led onto a back staircase.

"First, I'd suggest you call home before you leave. Your father might need a ride. Second, could you pick up Geanie's underthings? I'm sure even a great future CEO wouldn't want those lying around for her workers to see."

I phoned my mother from a filling station at 103rd and State Line. This was due east of Fairhaven Estates, in the opposite direction of the highway, which I'd felt too shaky to handle. My mother answered before the second ring. "Well, it's so nice of you to call," she said, in a voice that suggested she felt the opposite.

"Look, I'm sorry, Ma. I went out with friends, lost track of time. By the time I got everybody home, I wasn't in good shape to drive."

"You're not the only one in this family."

"I'm not the only one to do what?" I asked. "Is there a problem?"

"Would you mind telling me where you are, Jack?" my mother said. "How about if we just start trying to be honest about that?"

"I'm at 103rd and State Line," I admitted.

"Oh, really—and what friends do you have out there?"

"I took Geanie home."

My mother did not answer this right away. It sounded to me like she'd covered the phone's receiver with her palm.

"Jack, I'm going to put Elmore on right now, to give you directions to get your father. We haven't been able to get him ourselves, because we've been sitting around here trying to find you—"

"I'm glad I come first, I guess," I said.

"But I do have one other thing to say, Jack, about you and your father's interest in the Bowen family."

"Is Dad all right?" I asked.

"Which is, goddamn it, Jack."

"Hold on, Ma. Look, I'm sorry—"

"Goddamn, goddamn it, goddamn it, to both of you," my mother said. "You'll deliver that message for me, won't you, please?"

According to Elmore Haywood, my father had been arrested for his third DUI the night before—leaving the same country-club party that Geanie had been scheduled to attend—and so, following Elmore's instructions, I drove out to pick him up at the Kings County Courthouse in downtown Olathe. Though it was the seat of Kings County, Olathe remained far enough south of the city that it still resembled the small, sleepy country town that it had been when Prudential Bowen had grown up there. The prime difference, however, was that it appeared to be abandoned. The main street ran due west between high oak trees whose acorns crumbled under my tires, and as I rolled past what must have been, in Prudential's day, the shaded and resolutely modest clapboard homes of the town merchants, I saw that they were now shuttered, their lawns grown knee-high. I'd had plenty of idle daydreams about coming back to Kansas City during my lazy mornings driving down the Paseo, or out drinking with my father and Elmore. But the night before, when Geanie had braced her palms against my shoulders and offered me the reverse of her blank green stare, holding my gaze directly as I entered her, I'd sworn that I would never leave this town so long as she was in it. It had seemed like the obvious decision at the time, but if I ever felt fear and the touch of death at putting it into practice, it happened now. Part of this was simply physical; the Fairlane had no air-conditioning, and my body, hungover and dehydrated, had broken into a feverish dry chill. With it, the fluid inside my brain had apparently dried up, too.

I made a left along the small, awning-shaded law offices of the town square and then pulled up before the courthouse, a big, art deco limestone building that likely dated from the Fairlane's younger days. My father wasn't there, and I sat outside trying to sweat and, failing, listening to the locusts already humming in the evergreens along the courthouse lawn and smelling my own alcoholic stink. The yarn I'd spun for Michael Callaghan about the doings of Prudential Bowen, and my father's involvement in them, had sounded exciting in the distant harbor of a bar in New York City, but in the broad daylight of Kings County, Kansas, it seemed a terrifying and lonely thing. I was also thinking of certain stories that Royce MacVess had told me on the day he'd shown us Prudential Bowen's photo in his picture book. How clerks in Manual MacVess's grain store would order Prudential to pick up boxes they had nailed down to the floor. How the boys of this town had once abandoned Prudential Bowen in the hayloft of a barn, curling a dead rattlesnake at his feet. These stories blended in with the stories that I knew of Lonnie, and the buildings of the Campanile, and the billboard of Henry Bowen's face inviting me to watch my television in Fairhaven Estates, until what ought to have been the normal streets of a normal small town began to warp and snake, the heat waves curling up from the sidewalks as if at any minute their surfaces might boil away.

I found my father in a bar two blocks down from the courthouse, eating a pickled egg and smoking a cigarette. "Welcome to the big city," he said when he saw me. "I thought lawyers were supposed to show up before the trial, not after it."

"Most lawyers try not to go to trial in the first place," I said.

"You talk to your mother?" he asked.

"Yeah," I said. "She says goddamn it."

"To you or me?" my father asked, eyeing my rumpled shirt.

"Both of us," I said. "I was out a little late."

My father reached across to touch a red mark that Geanie had left along my neck. His finger smelled like brine, and as he turned, I saw that his right eye was swollen into a squint, the skin beneath it turning green. "I always thought you had a little bit of your grandfather in you, fooling around with the married women."

"I wouldn't have done it if she was married," I said.

"That's because you don't have *too* much of him in you," my father said. "If you did, you wouldn't be here."

"Good, then maybe you can tell me why I *am* here," I said. I sat down next to him. My father's face, as I adjusted to the bar's gloom, seemed to have a black line around it; so, too, his beer bottle and the napkin holder next to it.

"Are you talking about going back to New York?" he asked.

"I'm talking about anything," I said. The sickness that had begun in the parking lot had now caused the bar's contents to appear uncomfortably distant. I felt like I was on the wrong end of a telescope. "I'm thirty-five. I ought to take that job, but when I try to imagine myself like Mr. Callaghan, it's all wrong. The whole bit, house in Westchester, squash-club membership . . . it's like I'd be impersonating somebody. Do you think it's strange that I can't imagine dying in New York?"

"Bartender—get my lawyer a beer and a tomato juice," my father said.

"I *also* don't want to die in Olathe," I said.

"And ice," my father said, as if this would help any. He then looked at me appraisingly. "Talking to Henry sometimes makes me feel the same way."

"But you always used to know what you wanted," I said, and then flinched at my use of the past tense. "Or do know, I mean."

"Used to's fine," my father said. "Go ahead."

"So how did you pick? I mean, I like working for Callaghan, but it also always felt temporary. It was a thing to do. But it's different if I have to make a totally permanent decision. It seems like you shouldn't have a single doubt."

"Real estate was the one thing that I knew I'd do differently than anybody else." My father handed me the tomato juice and waited until I drank. "That's it," he said. "That's all. I figured that was how you felt about this lawyer thing."

"I did the lawyer thing to get away from here," I said. "Like taking the bus."

"Then stay this time," my father said. "Spend the summer with Geanie."

"What if she leaves *and* I quit the job?" I said. "How do you wake up every morning and go to work feeling like you've fucked something up completely?"

"How or why?" my father asked.

"Either one."

"*How* is patience, patience, patience," my father said.

I laughed. "Is this advice you take or just give?"

"And *why*," my father said, "is that you always know you're going to lose to somebody in the long run. What matters is who you lose *with*."

We left the bar around noon. As we walked down that blazing Olathe street back toward the Fairlane, my father kept wrinkling his eyes at the courthouse—an expression that usually meant I was about to be shown something I would not understand. "Come on," he said, heading back up the courthouse steps. "I got something funny you can think about the next time Henry makes you feel sick."

I followed him in through the main hallway and down a heavily air-conditioned flight of steps to a door that read COUNTY RECORDER in grooved plastic. The room beyond was dominated by eight massive wooden cabinets that held perhaps a thousand cream-colored books—or maybe "tomes" would be more accurate. They were bound in canvas that reminded me of basketball shoes and were marked along the spines by sets of three numbers, an entirely mysterious system with no card catalog that I could see, and yet my father strolled among them humming, touching his thumb against one spine and then the next, as if he were browsing in the local library. He slid one book out on oiled brass rollers. "Section, township, range," he said, pointing to the numbers:

$$16\text{—}14\text{—}25$$
$$18\text{—}14\text{—}25$$

"That's nice," I said. "I always like a range."

"Not *a* range," my father said. "*The* range. That's the last number. But you do have more than one section in here. This is the index for sixteen through eighteen."

We regarded the book in silence. As usual, my father had stopped at this point, refusing to proceed unless I asked a question. "An index to what?" I said finally.

"To all the people who owned your quarry," my father said. He opened the first page of the book. It was a ledger whose top margin repeated the numbers for section, township, and range in blue ink: 16, 14, 25. The first entry read, in cursive, "Kings County." "That's the first grantee," my father said. "Which means that what you don't have on here are the Shawnee, whom you'd call the original screwees."

I cleared my throat. "Where's your entry?" I said.

"First you check the list, see who sold what to whom."

I put my finger next to my father's at the top of a double-columned list, mine on the "grantor" column, his on the "grantee," and together we ran them down the names, as one might feel a tombstone in place of the body underneath. It looked like this:

GRANTOR	GRANTEE	USE	BK	PG	COMMENT
United States	Kings Co.	G	25	227	
Kings Co.	Wm Bluejacket	WD	32	240	
Kings Co.	Geo. Hubbard	R/W	33	18	
Bluejacket	Man. McVess	WD	36	689	

"These guys *all* bought land?" I said. "Or had it given to them, huh? Hubbard, Bluejacket, MacVess."

"Depends on the use column," my father said. "*WD*, that's for warrant deed and that means an outright sale. *M* is a mortgage. *R* slash *W*, that's for a right-of-way."

I glanced up at my father, surprised by this burst of eloquence. He looked a mess. His collar was yellowed around his neck, his hair greasy, and I realized that the sharp stench of urinal, which I'd attributed earlier to the bar, was in fact coming from him.

"Well, don't look so goddamned shocked," my father said. "You didn't think I've been in this business all these years without learning anything, did you?"

This time *I* was just grinning at him, an expression that caused him to look so uncomfortable I was sorry I hadn't tried it before.

"Anyway, the point is that every rip-off, con job, and scam that's ever been run on a piece of land in Kings County is all right here in the open." He indicated the shelves surrounding us. "The question is knowing how to read it. On this page my bet is George Hubbard got the right-of-way grant because he was contracted to build some roads. You look in a county deeds office up in Iowa and you'll see a helluva lot of right-of-way grants for Tom Durant. That's how he got all his land around the railroad. Of course, if you wanted to find out exactly how big this right-of-way was, you'd have to look up the deed—that's what these book and page numbers are for."

"So this last entry is where Royce's dad bought the quarry."

My father nodded. He flipped through several more of the ledger pages, skimming as he went, until he reached an entry that read:

MacVess   Alomar Co.   WD   36   689

"And there's ours," he said, "when we bought the property."

I reached out to touch the entry. It was strange to imagine so many years and lives, as well as one death, summed up in a single line of print.

"So what's funny?" I asked.

"I don't know," my father said. "You notice anything?"

I skimmed through the few remaining ledger entries. "There's no warrant deed here for the Bowen Company," I said.

"Really?" my father said. He'd turned his back to lean against the counter without looking at the book. "Now, that would be funny."

We were back in the car before I got my father to explain anything more than this to me. Fortunately or unfortunately, depending on how you saw it (I wasn't sure which applied to me), the fact that the quarry's title was still in the Alomar Company name didn't mean that we still owned it, a paradox that my father took pleasure in developing at great length. Apparently Prudential had decided it would be in his interest to simply take control of the Alomar Company as a whole, originally, and then gradually sell the land back to the Bowen Company as he developed it over the years—a procedure that had allowed him to save on taxes in some way. "It's a long shot," my father said. Though he'd just lost his license, he'd insisted on driving, having claimed that, speaking of titles, the Fairlane was *technically* his. "I wouldn't want to get your hopes up or anything."

"What hopes?" I said.

"I put a little extra language in the deed that Royce and I signed when I bought that quarry land, specifically—about eighty acres. The kind of thing that Prudential might not take the time to look up, considering that, compared to the rest of the ranch, it's hardly what you'd call prime property."

The car had crested a slight rise, and I could see, out ahead, the green, still-forested mound of the quarry. "What's that?" I asked.

"Well, it just says that if that land ever gets built on by anybody, then the title reverts back to me. Or to someone related to me."

The call to Callaghan was not as difficult as I imagined. I made it from my mother's living room, holding a newfangled cordless phone that my father had given her for her birthday. At some point my mother had thrown away her *Sunset* magazines and decorated to suit her own tastes, the result being that every object, other than the phone, in that room—and indeed in all the rooms I strolled into, as my former boss's voice fed into my ear—was deeply familiar to me. The entire downtown could empty out of people; some two hundred thousand whites could stampede from the east side out to Kings County; presidents could be elected, the Vietnam War fought and lost; my father could become a drunk and a slumlord; but this would not affect the pyramid of coffee cups that filled the upper reaches of my mother's glass-fronted kitchen cabinets. It would not affect the fact that the yellow-and-white trim of our breakfast nook looked good with daisies from the yard, nor the fact that dining rooms should be done in olive, nor that the silver sideboard belonged beneath the Jack O'Hara seascape, nor that the three small brown squares of soap, stamped with quotations from Voltaire, should occupy a porcelain dish in the downstairs half bath, as they had done for a decade.

Still, once I hung up on New York, the silence that greeted me in my parents' house chilled me. I pulled my father's old Fairlane out of the carriage house and cruised randomly through the city, down Broadway and back up Main, out on Fifth Street through the north end, until the chill went away. I wouldn't call this feeling regret, necessarily. But I would say that it is possible to make the right choice on a subject—to make a decision that you are sure is the one you want to make—and still be afraid.

Closing Costs

I'd made one clear promise to Geanie the first night we'd had sex at Fairhaven Estates. I had stopped her, ever cautious Jack, to ask if she had a condom. She did not, neither of us did, but the question had interrupted the flow of things enough for her to sit up straight—while still, perhaps unfairly, holding me in her hand.

"You do understand," she had said, "that I am one hundred percent going back to school in the fall. I don't want to lie to you about that."

"Do we have to discuss this now?" I'd asked.

"And second of all, whatever happens stays between us."

"You mean, like an experiment?" I'd said unkindly.

"I mean, like I am going back and I am going to get married. I don't want to bullshit you about that."

I had agreed to this. I had figured she would need this kind of arrangement to absolve herself of any responsibility for our affair. So I accepted and kept my gaze blank. Nor was it my responsibility to worry about condoms (which, it turned out, Geanie did not like) or her diaphragm. Some nights when I entered her, it was there. And on other nights, like that first night, I accepted Geanie's explanation, whispered in my ear. "It's all right. We're safe. It's never once gone wrong for me this way."

If I was going to lose, it didn't seem a bad way for me to go. And the truth was that no matter what mixed emotions I might have had about that promise, I didn't feel like I was losing in those days. We found a king-size mattress and an old brass four-poster bed in a guest room at her father's house and set this up at one end of what had formerly been a third-floor ballroom, a feature of the house that I'd noticed during the repairs. It had been converted into a storage area, with a thicket of floor lamps and old velvet love seats blocking the entry. But beyond this was a hockey rink of varnished oak, and rank on rank of windows down either side, roughly even with the lower branches of the backyard's trees. I loved to lie there with her in the early evening, before we went out, when we had us a copy of the newspaper to thumb through and a cold beer to share. Then the city felt alive to me, as it did when I was a kid. Despite all the people who'd moved out to Kings County, it was still there, the grand old buildings on Main Street, the Mexican cantinas on the west side, the steak houses, the long sweeping boulevards, the murmur of the crowds at the baseball game. After we made love, Geanie and I would go to one of these places, but I liked it best when we were still trying to choose. Then we were discussing the city of our imaginations—the people who'd be at the symphony that night, the restaurants on Southwest Boulevard—which we'd both carried out to Connecticut and New York, respectively, but had never really left.

In the mornings, Geanie lugged her books to the Campanile public library and wrote while I got up and made coffee for the A&E Realty team. Unlike Toby, I knew that the paint scraping and the window painting (which I graduated to after strict supervision) that I was doing on the Bowens' houses *wouldn't* be my permanent occupation and that made it easy to enjoy. I liked the sun, the heat, and the private view I had across the sprawling lawns and rooftops of Fifty-fifth Street from a ladder three stories in the air. This was far better than the view, say, into the air shaft outside my bathroom window in New York, where the window ledges, air-conditioner butts, and even the screens were covered by a mysterious black fur that, when you touched it, disintegrated into grease. Or the view from my office at Callagahn, Metzger & Lyme, a side-angle shot of the pure glass front of something called the Etruscan State Bank, which on sunny days, at certain hours, turned a screaming Windex blue.

Geanie liked the work, too. She and Toby got along famously. In the years that he'd spent working on A&E Realty's rental properties, Toby had become an expert in what my father called "urban design" and what Toby called jerry-rigging. He knew how to fix a furnace, how to replace a fuse box, repair a leaky gas line, patch an asphalt roof, and even in one case—

thanks to a broken water pipe—how to remodel an entire room, stripping everything down to the studs and starting over from scratch. In the afternoons, when she returned from the library, Geanie tended to follow him everyplace, asking questions, discussing materials, going over purchase and expense orders with far more confidence than she ever exhibited with her dissertation work during the day. These houses were no small project either. Toby had put the word out that he was hiring for two dollars an hour over his usual pay, and very often by the time I woke up, there were twenty or so men swarming around the properties. There were paint cans, Skil saws, electrical wires, scaffolding strewn about the back porch and filling up the interior hallways. From my post atop my ladder, I would see Geanie, as relaxed and composed as she could possibly be, checking over the purchase orders with Toby in the garden, her red hair flashing, her eyes bright—a scene that reminded me of nothing so much as her old man sitting out by his pool overseeing the construction of Fairhaven Estates.

One reason I did not feel immediately concerned about Geanie's plan to leave was that for the first time since I'd known her, she seemed more lost than I did. The self-confidence she'd shown at her grandfather's funeral, the assurance with which she'd taken on the responsibility of fixing up her father's house—these seemed to be less actual reflections of the way she felt than reflex responses, cases where she seemed to be playing up to the memory of how she used to be. Clearly something about going back to Connecticut had frightened her. She constructed a desk out of an old door set across two sawhorses up in our bedroom and sat there working in the evenings, her books piled up around her like bricks—imposing-looking stuff in maroon or green library bindings that she'd brought with her from Yale. "Could you please tell me why I'm doing this?" she asked me. "Can you give me one good reason why in God's name I am trying to write about people in a place I've never been?"

"I thought you were interested in it because of your father," I said.

"As if he would care what I write!" In such cases she would get white-faced, flipping through the pages she had written too rapidly to read them.

"Well, wasn't that part of the idea?" I said. "I just assumed you picked the topic because he split the races up here."

"If that was why I'd chosen it, then it would be a good idea, wouldn't it?" she said. "It's the reason *you* would've chosen it, maybe, which is what makes you a better person than me. Do you know why I picked this subject?"

"Whatever it is, it can't be as bad as you think."

"I picked this subject because I knew it would make people happy. It's popular to study this goddamn crap. But the fact of the matter is, it isn't real to me."

One afternoon in mid-July we met Henry Bowen for lunch at Giotto Square. This new project was the Campanile's answer to the huge indoor malls that Henry himself had been building in the cornfields of Kings County—you entered through a replica of Ghiberti's famous doors, past McDonald's, into a fully controlled "vertical" shopping environment, five floors of it, with a glass-lined atrium in front. We ate on the second story, a roofless, tile-floored restaurant overlooking the escalators. The service, at least, was excellent. It was an example of power and security, the whispering flurry of the maître d', the three waiters who materialized to pull back our chairs so we could sit, the craned necks of the other diners as we passed—a feeling that I assumed Geanie shared with her dad. And yet, to my surprise, she ran through her long list of accomplishments on the house in a meek tone, leaving words in the back of her throat, as if she, too, were part of the waitstaff. Henry buttered a piece of toast as I'd seen his father do at the Grotto, and when Geanie had finished, he said, "Good. What're you having?"

Geanie hadn't even opened her menu yet. She'd brought with her a new leather-bound clipboard that contained an alphabetical file of her invoices, together with a summary of repairs. She closed this and picked up her menu.

"Notice anything interesting?" Henry asked.

The menu was constructed out of woven bamboo. On the laminated cards inside, cartoons of flowers twined in and out among the dishes.

"Seems like there's a lot of salads?" Geanie said.

"*Only* salads," Henry said triumphantly, leaning in. "Do you know how long this one's been after me to eat more healthy food?"

"No," I said—though I did remember Geanie telling me about her father's eat-it-or-wear-it policy in her childhood.

"Forever," Henry said. "And what did I always say? Go ahead, Geanie, and tell him what I always said."

"I don't know, Dad," Geanie said. "I recall telling you that you might want to try eating something besides meat. Since Mom died anyway."

"I always said this was a steak town," Henry said. "Who in Kansas City cares about salads? Barbecue, maybe. Some pasta, fried chicken. But this company calls me up." He brandished the menu. The name of the restaurant was Lemongrass. "They say they've got twelve of these things open on the West Coast. Twelve! Well, all right, I'm listening. Putting up twelve profitable restaurants anyplace is no easy feat. But when they tell me they want to open one that serves only salads, I'm ready to laugh them off the line—until I get a little information from the female perspective."

"I think this might have been a conversation you had with Rose, Dad," Geanie said. This was the name of Henry's new girlfriend.

"Take credit where credit is due," Henry told her, patting her arm. "And so I made one request. I said, 'I've got a new building going up, Giotto Square, and I'll put one of your restaurants in there under one condition. And that is that you name an entrée after my daughter, without whom I would've never considered this.'"

I glanced down at the menu. It was true; under the entrées in the menu, there was one called "The Genie."

"You've got to be kidding," I said.

"Seventy percent of eating-out decisions are made by women," Henry said. His eyebrows were the color of dead pine needles. "You better watch what you say. Now that Geanie knows about this place, you might be visiting here more frequently."

"You've got to at least look at what she brought you," I said. I picked up Geanie's clipboard and shoved it at him. "She's doing a great job on this house."

"Invoices?" Henry said, thumbing the clipboard's papers. "Now, why would I want to look at these?" He glanced between Geanie and me, grinning. "I already know the two of you can spend money. I can tell that when I sign the checks."

Geanie and I had argued in the Giotto Square parking lot about this encounter, our voices and the clack of her heels ricocheting between the grease-stained concrete floor and the low ceiling overhead. "I'm just saying you deserve some credit," I told her. "You've done great work—work he wasn't willing to do. You wouldn't have brought all that stuff if you didn't want him to look at it."

"Can I worry about getting my own credit from my own father in my own way?" Geanie asked me.

"But I'm on your side in this one."

"Do there *have* to be different sides?" she asked.

One night I woke in the middle of a thunderstorm and found Geanie down on the second floor, in the room-size closet that held her mother's dresses. I hadn't been in this room since we'd started working on the house and so was surprised to find the dresses there—and that Geanie was methodically stuffing them into plastic trash bags. "Help me out," she said in a determined voice. "This'll go a lot faster if you hold the bag."

She handed me a trash bag, and as I held it open, she sorted roughly through the dresses, shucking the dry-cleaning cover, tossing the wire hanger into one corner of the room, then balling up the dress and dumping it into my bag. I'd had enough experience with my father's unexplained projects that I held off on the questions. Instead I just worked with her, grabbing dresses on my own. We must have pitched thousands of dollars of dresses this way—red, gold, satin, blue, tulle, knee-length, floor-length, beaded tops, padded jackets, every fabric and style you could imagine. They were only partly visible, thanks to the fairly regular flashes of lightning but even these began to dim, and as the storm moved away and we began to work in near-total darkness, I said, "You want to try turning on a light, maybe? Might speed things up a little bit."

"I'm afraid if I turn on a light, I won't be able to do it," Geanie said.

"And what exactly *are* we doing?" I asked.

"We're sending my mother's clothes to the thrift store," Geanie said. "I've been putting this off all summer. I know I have to do it. I know somebody has to do it. And so I just decided if I did it right now, in the middle of the night, when I woke up in the morning it would be over, like a dream."

"We're not going to have to worry about waking up," I said. We'd been working half an hour, and the racks were still three-quarters full, to say nothing of the shoes.

"I can't do it during the day," Geanie said. "I don't want to have to see it."

"Then why not let somebody else do it? For chrissakes, you're rebuilding this entire house. That's more than enough, don't you think? I don't see anyone else in your family stepping up to help." (Except, I thought, me.)

"But they're my *mother's* dresses," Geanie said. She increased her shucking to a frantic pace. "They've been here five years."

"You're right," I said. "Of course you're right. And you're right to be upset. Who wouldn't be upset?" The fact that Geanie was conducting this operation in her bra and panties made it more distressing; I wished I could give her an old hockey jersey and a pair of shin guards for protection. Instead I circled my fingers around her wrist, slowing her down gently. "But can't we think about this logically? Would your mother, for instance, want you to do this? Would it have been important to her?"

"She would hate it," she said. "She never wanted anybody touching any of these things."

"So you need to do it for yourself more than her, maybe?" I said.

In response Geanie shucked one more dress, a pearl evening gown that had been crammed into its sheath of plastic as tightly as a sausage; it opened like a parachute. Instead of struggling to ball the dress up, she let it engulf her, the upper edge of its tulle fabric whispering just underneath her chin. "Who else is going to put them away?"

I nodded for Geanie, encouraging her, running my finger along her cheek to pull a strand of hair back behind her ear. "But isn't there a way that we could let you get rid of this stuff, and not have to do it at three A.M. What about a blindfold in the afternoon?"

This, at least, got an approving snort from Geanie.

"I happen to know about twenty guys who could relieve you of a bunch of expensive dresses in . . . what? Maybe half an hour?" I said. "Just nod, give me a sign, and this room is clean, understand? Perfectly clean?"

I led her back to bed this way. She crawled into it on her side, her knees pressed up to her chest, and I lay down chastely beside her, ever the good lover, caressing her cheek, ignoring my erection. The rain had quit, the room grown deliciously cool. I could hear a secondary shower of droplets whispering down when the wind moved the branches of the Bowens' trees. I could sense Geanie awake beside me, but, feeling in charge, decisive, and fairly responsible—more responsible than any other man in her life, anyway—I felt confident enough not to say anything. I listened to Geanie breathe.

"If your mother died," she asked, "what would your father do with all her things?"

I couldn't figure out how to answer without sounding like I was criticizing Henry, so I let the question fade. And the next day, I had Toby's crew pack up all of Mrs. Bowen's dresses and her shoes so that the room was entirely clean.

Toward the end of August, we took a ride in my father's Fairlane out to visit Nikki Garaciello. She was living in Emporia, a decent-size town that was in the next county south of Kings County, about an hour down I-35. The blacktop road off the highway exit wound along the Neosho River, and just as it turned to gravel, we arrived at Nikki's place, a newly built though modest two-story house with an asphalt-shingle roof and a corrugated shed for a garage. It was still early, despite the fact that Geanie had to stop twice to use the restroom on the way—due, she said, to an overdose of coffee—and we sat out on a back deck made of treated two-by-sixes, drinking lemonade, watching Nikki's two boys play down at the far end of her backyard, which ended in a cornfield.

The visit had been long delayed, the victim of many schedule changes, last-minute cancellations, all of them, as far as I could tell, entirely innocent. The only real qualms I felt about seeing Nikki had less to do with her brother's now-distant death than with the subject of her father's incarceration. I'd heard a good deal about the trial from my father and the regulars at the Grotto: portraits of the lawyers involved, reviews of evidence, condemnations of the Teamster witnesses whose testimony had finally sunk both Nick and Bobby. What I didn't expect was Nikki's frankness on the subject.

"So," she said, sitting down across from me in a one-piece swimsuit, a towel wrapped around her waist, "I suppose you heard that my dad got put away."

I had no idea how to react to this. Nor did I get any help from Geanie, who'd been quiet on the drive out and was now distractedly watching the kids play hide-and-seek. "Oh, come on, Jack," Nikki said. "That's the first thing everybody thinks of, whether they admit it or not—how my dad got put in jail. My theory on the subject is to get the facts out right away, so I don't have to watch people wonder about it."

I glanced back toward the house, but her husband—also a teacher—had already said good-bye to us as we pulled into the driveway, heading out to referee a soccer game. "How long is he in for?" I asked.

"Fifteen years—from when he went in. Which means he gets out in about '95, if he behaves. And you don't have to whisper—I've told the kids. They all know that Papa Nick's in jail. I even took them out once to visit him with me."

"What did they charge him with?" I asked.

"Tax evasion," Nikki said. "Among other things. But they never really get you for the big stuff, do they?"

"And what's so bad about that?" I said.

"Well, Bobby, as you may or may not know, is a famous man," Nikki said. "He convinced the Teamsters to invest their pension money in some casinos run by his friends. I know the *Times* did a story on it. You ought to have been in New York by then."

"Around what year?" I asked.

"In '79."

I shrugged. "Sorry, I was only reading briefs."

"And your father?" Nikki said, teasing. "I'm surprised he didn't mention it. Out of all those families in both our classes—and all those people who sent condolence cards after Lonnie's accident—he's been the only person to go visit him."

I studied Nikki, worried that this might be some veiled reference to the role my father had played in the suit that followed Lonnie's death, but I saw by her expression that she was offering a compliment.

"Yeah, well, he doesn't like to admit it much when he does nice things," I said. "Which reminds me of certain other people I could mention around here." I nodded at Geanie, trying to include her in the conversation. "She's been trying to fix up the old Bowen homesteads, thirty rooms each, not one of them inspected since they laid the last brick. Plus her father isn't helping any, so Geanie's been left holding the bag."

"So how does your husband handle it?" Geanie asked. Her voice had a strangely metallic tone and, though addressing Nikki, she stared straight at me.

"Handle what?" Nikki said.

"Having a father-in-law in jail," Geanie said. "Does he feel the need to remind you of this every day? Does he get upset that Grandpa Nick isn't around to help with the babysitting? Or that he might not be perfect in every way?"

Even Nikki seemed taken aback by this question, and we sat in silence until we were distracted by the kids. Down in the yard below, Nikki's younger son, Lonnie, had tripped during a chase, his laughter cut off suddenly when the older one smashed a dirt clod over his rear end. "Hey—what are the rules around here?" Nikki shouted to them.

The older boy, Nick, froze, his hands lifted in a "who, me?" gesture, as if he hadn't done anything. "The rules are, you never hit a man when he's down," Nikki said. "So what that means is you stand still and give your brother a free shot."

"Aw, Mom!" Nick said.

"Do you want me to come down there and do it for him?" Nikki asked.

Apparently this was a legitimate threat because Nick hung his head and kicked the ground while Lonnie scrambled up and trotted into the cornfield, returning with his own dirt clod. It was so big that he could barely carry it, and when he tried to throw it at his brother, it simply grazed his hip and broke against the ground.

When our attention returned to the table, Geanie tilted her lemonade to her lips and said, "Maybe a simpler question would be to ask how you like having kids."

"How it works is that your life is over," Nikki said. "Whatever plans you have, you can forget them for at least five years. I was teaching sixth grade when I had Nick, right? And by the time I got into class, after waking up to feed, change diapers, and talk goo-goo talk, I felt like the kids were probably smarter than me."

Geanie rose unsteadily during this. She swayed a little once she reached her feet, her hand grabbing tightly on the deck's railing.

"Could I use your bathroom for a second?" she asked. "I've had so much coffee on the way up, I feel like I'm about to spring a leak."

I have often thought, over the years—particularly as I have assembled this manuscript—about what happened after that trip and whether or not things could have turned out differently. On the way home, Geanie had said she didn't feel like driving into the city, and so we'd stopped at her fa-

ther's place in Fairhaven Estates and I ordered take-out. I was still frightened by the way she'd spoken to me there on Nikki's deck, by the anger in
her voice (which might well not have been directed exclusively at me); I
was also angry that she would choose to defend her father against me—
who I thought, by comparison, had acted like an ass that summer. I could
smell fall in the cooler evening air, and with it, Geanie's departure to Connecticut. And so, as I sat there on her father's deck, eating pizza from a
cardboard box, I had prodded her into an argument. "I'm sorry for the
crack I made about your dad," I said, without any apology being intended.
"Maybe I shouldn't have said that in front of Nikki—but still, facts are
facts. Your dad should be helping you. It isn't right the way he acts and
eventually, Geanie, at some point, you're going to have to stand up and tell
him that."

It was the last in a line of several similar comments, delivered to pro-
voke a response. This one finally worked. "Of course you're right, Jack,"
she said, "You're always right. Do you know the only other person who in-
sists on being right as much as you do? The only other person I've met like
that? That person is my dad."

After she said this, I stood up and carried the pizza box and my paper
plate out into the kitchen, trying to collect myself before I said something
rash. I had often imagined the arguments I wanted to make to Geanie before she left, though I had planned to wait a couple more weeks. But my
emotions—my desire to know—had me by the throat; I turned on the
cold water from Henry's tap and twisted my head sideways to drink from
it, as I had done in my mother's kitchen when I was a kid, then I stared out
a bay window at a row of stuccoed, finished walls. These belonged, I realized, to the same houses whose frames I'd studied jealously with Henry at
the beginning of the summer. When I went outside, Geanie was lying on
a lounger with a sweatshirt balled behind her neck. I remember in particular her hair. In the evening light, its colors shimmered from a dark pheas-
ant brown around her scalp out to a glowing, almost whitish-copper
toward the ends. Squatting beside her, I tucked a strand behind her ear, a
familiar gesture that she suffered reluctantly.

"Look," I said. "I've got to ask you to do something for me. I didn't
want to do this now—and especially not necessarily out here in the middle of no-man's-land."

"Why not?" Geanie said. "We have all our best arguments here."

It was a sarcastic remark but one that was meant to include me, so I laughed with her. "Yeah, well, we've had some doozies, haven't we?"

"Have you ever thought about the word 'doozy'?" Geanie said. She rolled her head in my direction. "What's the root, do you think?"

The question was a dodge. She could sense something bad coming from me, but at the same time, the gesture summed up what I liked best about her—feeling the trouble coming on, she'd tried to find *something* to appreciate.

"You know that I'm in love with you," I said. This was the hardest part, looking straight into her green eyes and seeing the awkward nod and swallow that these words caused her to make. But once I'd gotten started, I plunged straight ahead. "I love you, I've been in love with you. I know I'm not supposed to talk about this"—she had turned away from me now, looking glumly at the house's west wing—"but the truth of it is, I want you to stay. I want you to stay here in Kansas City with me. I think it would work. We could just keep living like we're living, only permanently."

"I'm in school, Jack," Geanie said.

"You're teaching," I said. "Most people who are finishing dissertations do that to make money. But we both know you don't have to worry about that."

"And there's the small matter that I'm engaged."

"Maybe that's what you're supposed to do," I said. "Maybe you should go back and get married. But if you are going to do that, then I've got to quit."

"What you mean is that you want *me* to quit," Geanie said. "Isn't that really it? Do you know how long my father's been waiting for me to come home?"

"Would that be so bad?" I said.

"And do what? Be a wife?" Geanie asked. "It would be funny if it worked out that way, wouldn't it? Since that's all he's ever expected out of me."

"Who cares what he expects?" I said. "If you want to go back to school, work something out, that's fine. I'm a patient man. I chose to come back here. I'm glad I came back here. I'll wait—but you've got to make a commitment to me. You can't go try to 'work things out' with Andrew and then call me if that falls through."

I'd spoken calmly, but even so, Geanie rubbed the heels of her palms against her eyes as if they ached. "God, I wish you wouldn't do this now," she said with a bitter laugh. "You have no idea what . . . this is the wrong, wrong time to ask."

I gambled then; I admit it. I thought that I recognized the same fear that I'd seen in her when I'd first returned to the city—a fear that I hoped I could use to my advantage. It wasn't the right way to do things, but I believed that if I could just swing her, if I could just get her to agree, that everything would turn out okay. And so I bet the pot, I put all my chips in play. "There's never been a right time with you, Geanie," I said. "But I need to know. If not now, then let's say next week."

I suggested we spend the weekend apart—hoping that some time alone would allow both of us to cool off. Driving home through Royce MacVess's old fields, I pulled over at a stop sign beside a weathered and abandoned old country school, a white clapboard building whose lintel read P.S. 136. Beyond it, though, I could see the head of a sewer main sticking up in the middle of a bean field and, farther on, the I-beam frame of a new Hy-Vee. It was a sight whose deep weirdness only Geanie would have been able to fully appreciate and I chose to take it as an omen that she would stay. I survived the weekend. On Monday morning, I found a message from her on the A&E machine, a good sign. And I was still planning to tell her about the schoolhouse when I pulled into her father's drive and found her sitting on the front steps of the stone porch—the same steps where she'd appeared holding my father's golf ball the summer before freshman year—with two suitcases and a traveling trunk at her back.

"I'm sorry, Jack," she said. She winced as if she expected me to yell at her, but the whole situation seemed so monstrously wrong, I was speechless.

"I know that I shouldn't *feel* like I need to apologize," she said. "I know that I was honest with you about leaving, even though we haven't talked about a date—and I appreciate your not talking about a date, Jack. I can't tell you how much I do."

"The work's not finished," I said. It was a pathetic response.

Geanie glanced back at the house. "I talked to Toby," she said. "He said he could finish up in a week, both this and Grandpa's place, if he worked full crews. I told him that all he had to do was phone, and I'd mail a check."

The idea that I would be concerned about money in such a situation was, for me, the final monstrosity. I couldn't imagine anything worse. "Looks like you've got it all figured out," I managed to say, and I started the Fairlane's engine.

"Jack," Geanie said. She *did* look miserable. Her hair was pulled back in an unwashed ponytail whose tightness added to the drawn quality of her face, and her business suit was covered with a faint speckle of white paint, having been left accidentally in a room where our workers had been rolling the ceiling. I waited a long time for her to speak, happy that she looked this way and thinking perhaps at the last moment that she might give in and stay. "What do you want?" I said finally.

"Well, I just thought . . ." Geanie's supposedly expressionless green eyes were bloodshot, I realized, from crying. "I just thought if I was leaving, you'd want to drive out to the airport so I didn't have to go alone. My flight's not until three."

Instead of taking her straight out to the airport, I drove Geanie silently due east on Fifty-fifth Street, reversing a trip I'd often made from the A&E Realty offices. We crossed Ward Parkway and passed Loose Park, beyond whose trees could be seen the towers of the Campanile. We crossed Main, Oak, and Rockhill Road, all of them lined with houses that had been built by the Bowen Company, their residents universally white, and then finally we crossed Troost Avenue, where the faces of all the drivers and all the people in the streets turned black. "Where are you going?" Geanie said to me.

"I just thought, you know, before you go back to Connecticut to study black people, you might want to see some of ours," I said.

"You think they don't have black people in New Haven?" Geanie asked.

"I've never been to New Haven," I said. "But I bet none of the black people there helped pay your tuition."

"I pay my tuition," Geanie said.

"Come on, now," I jeered. "If you're going to be a sociologist, you're going to have to do better than that. Where do you think your father and your grandfather got the money that they're using to pay your tuition?" We were at the Paseo then, and I took a left toward the Gramercy Apartments. "To move out to places like Fairhaven Estates? It was all because they promised people that if they built a Bowen house, they'd never have to see a black face, right? Isn't that true? You know about those racial covenants, don't you, Geanie? So I just figured, before you left, that you might want to see our little Soweto, the one your family created there."

"You think this is the same as Soweto?" Geanie asked me.

"Why not?" I said. "It's apartheid, isn't it? You've got one nice, wealthy, all-white part of the city—which also happens to be where all the jobs and shops are, not to mention the place where banks are interested in giving people mortgages. And then you've got the east side, where all the black people are forced to stay."

"Where are the guns, then?" Geanie asked.

"You think black people don't do anything but walk around and shoot each other? I drive down this street every day and no one shoots me."

"I mean, white people with guns," Geanie said. "I didn't see any white people back there at Troost preventing people from crossing the line."

"That's terrific!" I said. "That's perfect! You're telling me that the great thing about the Bowen Company is that they pulled this off without shooting anybody? That's genius, I guess. A perverted form of genius, but genius nevertheless."

"What do *you* care, Jack?" Geanie shouted. We both were shouting now. "Since when did you become such a big patron of the blacks?"

The truth was that other than Elmore and Hattie and Miss Niecie, whose restaurant I liked, and Tito—along with a few other guys on the A&E maintenance team that I'd grown fond of working with—I didn't sit around all day and worry about blacks. I didn't even really care that my old neighborhood was now all black. The trees were mostly the same, the porch of the Gramercy as pleasant as it had ever been. It still looked and felt a lot more like the city that I'd grown up in than did the house out at Fairhaven Estates. The only real change was that things were less valuable, that more houses were boarded up or needed paint, that the St. Regis Hotel down the street was now a fleabag, lived in by bums and drug addicts who were on Section 8—which in a paradoxical way made it less likely that someone like Prudential Bowen would want to buy it and turn it into another Fairhaven Estates. I should have told Geanie this; I should have told her that I didn't care what she studied, or what her father had done, I only cared that she was leaving.

By then it was too late. In my anger I'd already driven straight past the Gramercy and continued into the really tough neighborhoods of the city, north of Twenty-seventh Street, where people actually did carry guns, both white and black. Shoddy brick apartments lined the street, their porches hung with laundry, their windows replaced with plywood. Groups of young black men, wearing ribbed undershirts and bandannas around their heads, glared at us from the corners. It was the worst neighborhood in the city, the most glaring example of what Prudential Bowen's new developments had left behind. And I used it as an opportunity to grandstand. "I just thought," I said, "you might be curious to know the effect your father and your grandfather had on the city."

"Whose father are we are talking about, Jack?" Geanie said.

"Ours, both of ours," I admitted. "Though I guess the difference is that yours made all the money."

"And which matters to you more? The people on this street or me?"

"The people on this street aren't leaving," I said.

She got out of the car then. It was the last thing I'd expected. We were idling on the corner of Truman Road and the Paseo, next to a gas station, with the overpass to I-70 looming up ahead. Geanie walked deliberately to the gas station entrance; following her, I pulled over to the curb.

"What are you doing?" I said.

"Leaving," Geanie said. She backtracked to my trunk and heaved on it, though it was still locked. "I've got to get to the airport, Jack. I'm going to call a cab."

"You can't just stand around here on the street with all your things," I said.

"Why can't I?" Geanie said. "Isn't that what you want? You want me to experience the east side of the city? Fine, just let me get my bags."

The Defense

The eight years that my father, mother, and I spent together, after Geanie Bowen's departure, were the calmest that we'd ever enjoyed as a family. I passed the Missouri bar and then signed up with Jackson County to do public defender's work. It was a poor way to make a living but a good way—for a former contracts lawyer—to get trial-room experience. The courthouse was on Twelfth and Oak. I kept an office in the old Warburton Building around the corner, where my grandfather's offices had been, and also bought a house in Hyde Park. Things had changed; the Warburton's primary tenant was a nail salon, the white stucco mansion that my father and I had spied on had been relaced by duplexes. But my office rent and mortgage *combined* was only a few dollars more than what I'd paid for my apartment in New York City. Downtown still breathed, too, no matter how dead it seemed in comparison to the old days; the politicians, the beat reporters, the cops on police plaza were all there; the descendants of Bobby Ansi still ran fruit stands down on Fifth Street. And I spent my evening hours, in all seasons, at one of the two downtown establishments that stayed open late. The first was called simply the Thirteenth Street Bar, where other defense attorneys and prosecutors gathered after work. The second was the Grotto, in Little Joey's Roman-decorated back bar, where my father and Elmore Haywood could reliably be tracked down after 6:00 P.M.

"You put any killers out on the street today?" my father asked me one night when I entered the Grotto. He usually kept track of the cases I was handling and, on this particular evening, he'd found a mention of one in the *Star*.

"Only the innocent ones," I said.

"'Jackson County prosecutors will try a Kansas City man charged with four area robberies, including one at a pet store, in which an alleged accomplice was shot dead.'"

"The operative words are 'charged' and 'alleged,'" I said.

"Did he say why he was robbing the pet store?"

"Joey, what part of 'charged' doesn't he understand?" I asked.

"The part that involves a credit card," Joey said.

My father also had the infuriating habit of asking, "White or black?" once I'd listed the charges in a case, a comment that invariably elicited an eye roll from Elmore, if he was there.

"What difference does it make to you?" I asked one day.

"It doesn't make any difference to me at all, except Elmore and I have a bet."

"I have an argument," Elmore said. "Your father has a bet."

"I bet I'd rather hear your argument," I said.

"My argument is that there aren't any more black killers or robbers than there are white ones. The difference is, the black ones get caught at it."

"Now, there's where Elmore and I disagree," my father said. "Because I happen to think that black criminals are as smart as anybody."

"*They're* smart enough. It's their lawyers who are dumb," Elmore said.

"Hey, take it easy," I said.

"So your guy *is* black," my father said.

"I'm saying if you can afford a good lawyer, he's going to stop things before you ever get to trial," Elmore said. Then he mumbled something into his beer, his eyes following Little Joey at the far end of the bar.

"What?" I asked.

"He's saying that a good example of how it helps to have an expensive lawyer owns this restaurant," my father said loudly. "Along with Nick and Bobby." It had come out in the papers that Nick Garaciello had twice been charged for murder in his twenties, before my father had met him. Both times the witnesses had recanted. As for Bobby Ansi, he'd been described as "the leader of Kansas City's most prominent crime family," which was why Elmore didn't like to talk about him when Little Joey was around.

"What's that got to do with any bet?" I asked.

"What your father claims," Elmore said, "is that it makes sense for all the black people to live in one part of the city, because all they do is steal things."

"I never said that!" my father exclaimed. It did seem an unlikely thing for him to say; he was a fairly popular character in the neighborhoods where he owned property. One of the few whites, in certain neighborhoods, whom people spoke to openly.

"All right, then," Elmore said, relenting. "What did you say?"

"I'm just saying that right now I'd be willing to bet you that there are more black people committing crimes in this city than white people," my father said. "It's just a fact. I'm not blaming anybody. I'm not in favor of it. But Elmore's got bars over his window and sleeps with a shotgun under his bed—now, you tell me, son, how come when we were living there, we never had to do that?"

These conversations took place maybe three years after I'd passed the bar, right around when I began to get cases good enough to show up in the paper. About two months later, I was trying one on the twelfth floor of the courthouse. The defendant, a girl named Toshayna Jackson, had been charged as an accomplice in the robbery of a liquor store up on Fifty-fifth and Paseo—the same store that had once been the Tiller grocery, whose phone I'd used to call Geanie Bowen when I was fifteen. I believed that she was genuinely innocent; her only real crime seemed to be that when her boyfriend had flashed a gun before entering the store, she'd stayed inside his car instead of running away. Still, frightened by the prosecutor's demands for jail time, Toshayna had asked me to plead her out—which I'd done, but not without the usual, terrible feeling that I'd failed. Having collected my briefcase and my papers, I straightened up from the defense bench to find my father and Elmore Haywood lounging in the front row of the gallery. I ignored them and walked straight out into the hallway, still angry at the result.

"If it's any consolation, you *look* like a good lawyer," I heard my father say behind me. "But that's about all I'm qualified to judge."

I continued without pause to the elevator bank, which was where he caught up to me, standing just within my peripheral vision, leaning slightly forward as if daring me to look at him—as he did when he was up to something.

"So I guess this means you won your bet," I said angrily.

"What bet?" my father asked, as if he genuinely didn't know what I meant. "I was just coming to see my son the lawyer save somebody."

"Yeah, well you saw him lose," I said.

"Elmore seemed pretty happy with how things went."

"Why should Elmore care?" I asked.

My father's comment had achieved its desired effect, which was to force me to look at him. "It's Latin, right?" he said, changing the subject. "The nolo contendere business? Do you know who it made me think of? Horace Cogle. Remember him?'

I did; he'd been a player in one of my most vivid childhood memories, the man who'd led my father into the Reserve Room of the Grotto, where Prudential Bowen had offered him funding for the Alomar Company. "Is he still alive?" I asked.

"Dead. Kid runs his business." He was still grinning, despite this report of his friend's death. "That was the other thing I was thinking about in there, seeing another Acheson practice law in this building."

"The more things change, the more they stay the same," I said wearily.

"Some things change," my father said.

"How's that?" I asked. The elevator had arrived then, and when I stepped onto it, my father followed me. It was crowded, so he stood in front of me, his broad shoulders looming before my face. He spoke staring up at the numbers on the front of the car.

"For instance, you're the first lawyer in this family that I've ever seen keep somebody innocent out of jail," my father said. "All your grandfather did was help rich people like the Bowens keep their money."

"How do you know Toshayna was innocent?" I said. "I thought I was representing nothing but killers these days."

"Elmore told me," my father said. The elevator had opened into the courthouse lobby, and my father filed out with the rest of the crowd, so that once again he'd reversed the situation and I was following him.

"What the hell would he know about it?"

"She's his niece," my father said.

"Why didn't he tell me?" I said, stopping.

"Didn't want to lie to you," my father said. "I think it's Elmore's opinion that she knew a lot more about that robbery than she was willing to say."

It meant a lot to me to be complimented by my father, even if that compliment included a very cloudy definition of innocence; it was equally

gratifying to have helped Elmore's family, especially since after the trial Elmore wouldn't let me buy a drink for a month. In fact, it would be easy to
argue that during the middle and late eighties my father and I finally came
to terms. I stopped being embarrassed by him, or at least learned to enjoy
his embarrassing behavior, while I think he finally accepted the idea that
my chosen profession—though lacking the grand ambition he'd had for
me, as heir to the Alomar Company—was of some use. So much so that I
received a steady stream of referrals from A&E Realty, both employees and
tenants, some of whom remembered me from the rounds that I'd made
during my first summer back in Kansas City, when I'd served as Elmore's
"legal representative." Besides these strangers, I also handled my father
twice for drunk-driving arrests; both times he invoked the "lawyer-client
privilege" to prevent me from telling my mother about it. I also took a pro
bono case for Elmore's mother, Hattie. She'd been booked on a federal
charge when, during her regular trip to the post office, she'd accidentally
spilled the contents of her purse across the counter, sending her nickel-
plated pistol into the postal worker's lap. On Elmore's advice I'd changed
venue until I drew a certain Judge Walker, in his mid-eighties, who remembered Hattie's speakeasy and let her off.

Despite the arrests, my mother claimed that since my return to the city,
my father's drinking had decreased. "He's settling down," was how she put
it. "Or at the very least, he's not trying to kill himself quite as quickly as he
was before. Having you back in town helped him take his mind off that
other thing."

That other thing was, of course, the loss of the Alomar Company and
Royce MacVess's property—a story that, every weekend, my father spent
an hour or two memorializing in his third-floor office. As my mother and
I spoke, seated in the side yard, I could hear his typewriter clicking away.
"Why would he be unhappy now?" I asked. "It seems like A&E Realty is
bringing in enough money to keep you two afloat. He's got the house, a
bunch of employees—why not call that a success?"

"It isn't the same," my mother said. "You set your sights your whole
life on one thing, give it every bit of energy you have, every talent you
possess—and your father wasn't without talents. And then to have it come
so close and then slip away . . ."

"But that's life," I said. "Sometimes you want one thing, you aim for it,
and if you miss, you've got to take what you can get. If you're paying at-

tention, a lot of times it can be better than what you wanted in the first place."

"Is that how you feel about Geanie?" my mother asked. "Because I don't see you, at least in terms of women, taking a lot of what you could get."

"That's a cheap shot," I said. "People and business aren't the same."

"Well, you and she definitely missed," my mother said. "How many kids does she have now?"

"Just the one," I said.

My mother smiled as a typewriter's bell rang above our heads. "If she'd been the right one, ho-ney," she said, "you wouldn't have had to ask her to stay."

As for me, I had my own theories about the development of Kings County. Indeed, if you were a defense lawyer working in the Jackson County Courthouse in downtown Kansas City, it was impossible not to notice the implications of my father's story. They were my clients. From 1950 to 1980 the population of Kings County had ballooned from 60,000 to 270,000, the vast majority of these new arrivals being upper-middle-class white refugees from the city. The tax bases of the two rival areas rose and fell respectively. Kings County constructed four new high schools during the decade, while Kansas City closed two. By 1985 the few white students who'd remained in the Kansas City, Missouri, school district after busing began (belatedly, as Elmore had pointed out, in 1977) had fled, leaving our classrooms 90 percent black, while those in the Kings County school district were correspondingly 90 percent white.

Everybody knew this story; everybody knew that something epochal, bizarre, and fantastic had happened to the city, particularly those who were my age or older and could remember how it used to be. They knew what had happened but not why, and this story became something of an obsession for me—as if I was carrying on with these strangers the final argument that I'd botched with Geanie. I honed and rehearsed it at innumerable bars and dinner parties. I told it to clients, many of whom, given the crime wave that hit the east side in those years, were young, black residents of neighborhoods where my father and Elmore Haywood had started selling houses back in the late fifties. I explained, as Bobby Ansi had done in our dining room, the Bowens' historical use of racial covenants. I went on to how they had deliberately moved black families into the east side in an effort to scare whites into Kings County. I explained that the mortgages they offered to these families had been arranged and approved by the Bowen Company, who also had an interest in getting whites to leave the city. I gave glorious denunciations of the effects of this process—and if I met any opposition, working myself into a towering rage—how the segregation of the city and the destruction of its tax base, its rotten schools, its newly armed black youth, had not happened merely by accident. These explanations changed nothing at all, but what mattered to me was getting the story out, making the pieces fit. I felt this way even though people like my father and Elmore Haywood (both of whom I otherwise cared about deeply) and the Bowens came off as villains. They'd attempted, and in the Bowens' case succeeded, to get rich by ruining the city. And anybody who refused to recognize these facts was living a dream.

For years, in the interest of keeping the peace, my father and I had engaged in an unspoken détente on the subject, my father holding forth on his version of reality at Little Joey's bar in the Grotto, while I made my arguments in the lawyers' bar on Thirteenth Street. One night in the early nineties, however, I started talking real estate with an attorney named Mallory O'Neal, who handled land acquisition for the city. We'd been on a few dates—she was an Irish brunette, sharp-chinned, pale, with a beautiful expanse of collarbone—and she'd heard enough of my story to challenge me. "What I don't get is, if your dad was so smart," she said, "then where's all your money?"

I lifted both hands in the air. "When you accept investment capital from a guy like Bobby Ansi, what do you expect?"

"I still think you would have taken it," Mallory said. Being from Arizona, she had significantly less aversion to profiting from the suburbs than I did.

"Taken what?" I said.

"The land," Mallory said. "Come on, if your father had held on to that property, you'd be sitting on a yacht in Greece right now, instead of talking about it with me."

"You think that's what I should have done?"

"I don't know about 'should have.' Let's say 'would have.'"

"Well, do you know what I think you should have done—or should do?" I said. "What somebody should do? Prosecute the Bowen Company."

Mallory laughed at this. "Yeah, that's always a good move for a prosecutor—file charges against the biggest taxpayer in the county."

"How do you think he became the biggest taxpayer?" I said. "He did it by sucking all the other businesses out of the city, out of downtown, out of the east side—" And I was off again into my standard denunciations. Mallory was usually a good audience for these, listening with a skeptical cock of her chin, throwing out challenges to my self-contained story—arguments were what I liked. But this time, before I'd gotten completely revved up, she plucked my sleeve.

"Your dad," she said. "Is he a big guy? Likes to wear old-fashioned hats?"

I nodded. "That's him. Why?" But Mallory had already gestured over my shoulder, and when I turned, I saw my father sitting on a barstool, spun around to face our booth, a yellow motoring cap tipped back on his forehead.

"Came by to see if you wanted to get some dinner with Elmore and me," he said. "But it's against my principles to interrupt a good story."

Fortunately, Mallory had the good manners to stand up and introduce herself while I recovered from my surprise, as well as to invite my father to sit down—which he did with a wry smile, saying, "Well so long as you don't think it'll hurt your reputation, associating with a rapacious developer like me."

"I don't know," Mallory said, reaching under the table to touch my hand. "What do you think, Jack? Developers are fine by me, so long as they're buying drinks."

"I thought he just told you I didn't have any money?" my father said.

"He did," Mallory said. "But I've also known your son long enough not to believe everything he tells me—at least until I've heard the other side."

I should've allowed the pall of my story to pass—it was the past, after all. As my father pretended to ransack his pockets for cash, his hair curling from beneath his cap, his attention straying to Mallory's cleavage (she was exactly his type, a brunette with an attitude), I felt entirely pleased to see him. But I'd had a few drinks myself and so when he silenced my anticipated protests—"Don't listen to grumpy here"—and launched into an explanation for why Mallory should *immediately* abandon her loft down on Eighth Street and buy a "decent place" out in Kings County, I couldn't resist a dig.

"Do you know what the funniest thing is," I said to Mallory. "This guy has spent his whole life selling Kings County and the fact is, he hates the place."

"Well, if you ever decide to live someplace civilized," he said, "Let me know. I've got a couple of great deals on the market right now."

"So what are you doing drinking downtown every night?" I said. "Do you know what I bet? I bet the great King of Kings County here doesn't even know a single decent restaurant west of the state line. Besides McDonald's, maybe."

Which was how, at ten o'clock that night, Mallory, my father, and I ended up retracing my family's old surveying route through the city, following State Line past the old Bowen mansions. Mallory could not have known that, as we turned west along Seventy-fifth Street, we were also passing through the graveyard of the Alomar Company. In fact, it had taken me several years before I'd managed to piece together the whole story. Apparently, my father's great miscalculation had been that, back in the 1960s, the suburbs hadn't sprung up fully formed around the highway as he'd imagined they would. Instead, they'd slowly worked their way south and west, piggybacking on neighborhoods the Bowens already had in place. In the process, county taxes went up. There were sewer assessments, road assessments, school assessments. Meanwhile, my father had sunk most of Bobby Ansi's money into buying Royce's ranch and, as the Bowens built out toward him, the expense of owning the MacVess land steadily increased. He'd landed a few loans, built a few cheap houses (my father had, out of embarrassment, never told me where), but by 1980, Bobby Ansi was under indictment; he needed money. Even my father couldn't blame him when he accepted Prudential's buyout offer, along with the title to a two-hundred-acre parcel of land north of the river, where Bobby had built his wife a house. My father had received nothing—other than a job offer to sell the houses that Prudential would be building on his former property.

But I wasn't thinking of this story that night. The drinks had flowed freely at the bar, Mallory looked great, and though I'd enjoyed teasing my father about Kings County restaurants, I had done it in part to show him off. We pulled over at a Texaco station so that my father could use the restroom—an increasingly frequent habit with him in those days—and while Mallory and I waited in the car, I described the cornfields and pastures that had once occupied the corner. "It's hard to imagine," she said, as we stared out at a Bowen Company real estate office, an immense Hy-Vee grocery, and a handful of smaller "local" mall tenants that had replaced this farmland. "When you don't know the history of something, you just figure it always looked that way."

"Yeah, well you could say the same for my father," I said. He'd just opened the door, slinging a six-pack of beer to Mallory. "Dinner," I said. "I guess I lose the bet."

"Very funny," my father said, eyeing me.

"Mallory wants to know the history of this lovely mall."

"I thought you weren't interested in the details of the business," my father said, "on account of its corrupting influence."

"It was corrupt," I said, laughing. "You know that."

But my father did not seem amused. We were on Mission Road now, heading south past fluorescent acres of car dealerships. "You know who he sounds like when he talks like that?" he said to Mallory. "He reminds me of myself, when I used to talk to people about Tom Durant. In a way, I've learned to take it as a compliment."

This observation surprised me, though I recognized some truth in it. "The difference is, when I talk about it, I'm not trying to be Tom Durant," I said.

"Who's Tom Durant?" Mallory said, looking back at me.

"My dad's childhood hero," I said.

"It never hurts to have one," my father said. "My question for you is— who are *you* trying to be? And how long are you going to stay mad at me for not being it?"

"I am what I'm going to be," I said. "I'm a defense lawyer."

"Trying to fix my mistakes?" my father said.

"Is *that* what you think I'm doing?" I asked.

My father shrugged. At first it seemed as if he was going to accept this answer, and then, to my surprise, he suddenly jerked the convertible's steering wheel hard to the right, cutting through a lane of traffic and jouncing into the parking lot of the Ranch Mart shopping mall. The lot was almost completely empty at this time of night and we screeched to a stop in the middle of an open pool of asphalt, crosswise to the spaces.

Without shutting off the engine, he got out, circled the hood, and opened Mallory's door. His Bowen Company outfit—blue blazer, gray slacks—was livened only by his yellow motoring cap, and he regarded her with an expression of regret.

"Could you excuse my son and I for a moment?" he asked Mallory.

"Why?" Mallory asked, climbing out. It seemed a sensible question to me.

"Because I want him to take a shot at me."

It was a response that, given the situation, and the curious, almost formal reluctance in my father's expression, caused me to burst out laughing. Until, to my surprise, he suddenly lunged down and grabbed my shirt, as if to wrench me from my seat—a difficult task, since I still had my safety belt on.

"Oh, for chrissakes," my father said, noticing this. He walked in a quick circle, grabbing both sides of his cap and pulling it down on his head.

I unbuckled and climbed out.

"Why would I want to take a shot at you?" I asked.

"How should *I* know," my father said. "But I'd sure as hell like to figure out some reason, because it's killing me to watch you like this."

"But I didn't do anything," I said.

"That's the point! What's the first lesson of Tom Durant?"

"It's rigged," I said.

"Hell, yes, it's rigged," my father said. "You want to blame me for that? Fine. You want to blame me for this shopping mall? Fine. But the one thing that I'm not going to do is watch my son waste his life worrying about what I did. I'm sorry if I screwed it up, but forget me. Forget it. Forget the whole thing happened. Don't make it part of your life. I saw how you ran Geanie off—"

"I didn't run her off," I said. "She left."

"And I would, too, if I had some guy telling me that I should feel guilty for the rest of my life for something my dad did. The times I've heard you talk about her, you make it sound like she was born into something that was permanently fucked up."

"Maybe she was," I said. I looked around for Mallory, but she was gone.

"So's everybody." My father had been kneading his cap as he spoke and he tapped me on the shoulder with it and sat down on the Cadillac's hood.

"I thought if there was one thing I got across, you would've picked up at least a little bit on that."

I climbed back in the passenger's seat and we sat for a while like that, me in the seat, my father on the Cadillac's grille. Mallory had disappeared on foot, which was a real achievement in this part of Kings County. There was no hint of a sidewalk anywhere at the intersection of Ninety-fifth Street and Mission Road, which I could see just past my father's head; no balconied porches, or hotel awnings, or lush elm trees that had made, say, the intersection of Thirty-sixth and Paseo Avenue down by the Gramercy Apartments so walkable in its day. Instead, parking lots the size of airfields dominated all four corners of this intersection. Some of them had small brick planters of stubby evergreen bushes dividing them—a salient feature of Kings County gardening—and the lots were dotted by smaller, freestanding businesses surrounded by more evergreens and planters filled with rocks. From where I sat, I could see a McDonald's, a Hardee's, a Fotomat, a Hooter's, and a branch of the old Winstead's drive-through, a copy of the building where Lonnie, Geanie, Nikki, and I had eaten burgers down by the Campanile. My father was right, I had always woven Geanie into my explanation of this landscape, making her departure a part of it. On my first date with Mallory I'd described Geanie in almost unrecognizable terms, a cartoon of a rich girl who'd known nothing of what her family had done to the city and who had studied, of all comic things, racial resettlement in South Africa. In the process, I had paved over most of our real history.

The choking sensation that I always felt out here wasn't just caused by my envy for its tax base, or the fact that I knew there were other intersections as ugly as this one between Seventy-fifth and 135th streets. I had also used Kings County to flatten Geanie into a somebody whom I could never have loved in the first place.

"Speaking of running people off," I said, "where's Mallory?"

"She's right over there," my father said. And then, following his gaze, I panned over a sea of asphalt until I saw Mallory picking her way amid a few scattered cars in the lot across the street. We watched in silence as she disappeared into the Hooter's.

"What's that place like?" my father asked.

"It's the best, Dad," I said. "The class of all Kings County."

My father nodded and thumbed his nose. "Well, maybe we better try it then," he said, standing up. "Because I think she stole my keys."

That weekend, in a gesture of truce, I accepted my father's invitation to play golf and drove with him again into Kings County, some twenty blocks past the Ranch Mart mall to a modest neighborhood of ranch homes, plotted along a curving street. We pulled up beside a yellow one with black shutters, its front decorated by a stone birdbath, an ornamental plum tree, and a for-sale sign that bore my father's name in a small slot underneath. The neighborhood had a more broken-in feel than others that we'd passed; the oak trees that lined the front yards had thickened overhead, there was an actual sidewalk along one side of the street, and the houses, though small, had been constructed sturdily of brick or clapboard—rather than the beige stucco and wallboard of the newer developments. The owner had seen some use, too. A thin and hawk-faced woman in what appeared to be her late seventies, she answered the door wearing a pair of house slippers and turquoise stretch pants, pushing a walker with punctured tennis balls on its front legs. "I was starting to think you got lost, I really did," she said. She led us into the kitchen, where cloudy plastic cups had been arranged on a blond, "country-style" kitchen table, along with a pitcher of lemonade. "Either that or you were dead."

"That's me," my father answered. "The late Alton Acheson."

"You and my son," the woman said. "What if I ever really needed you?"

"It's more my tee time that worries me," my father said.

"Ha!" the woman said. Though we'd not been introduced—a favorite habit of my father's—she elbowed me in the side familiarly. "For two years he's been claiming he wants to sell my house, all so he can drink lemonade with me."

My father widened his eyes in shock. "You're not selling?"

The woman pursed her lips, turned, and threw away an invisible key.

"It's a fair question," my father protested. "I am your agent."

"Doesn't that mean you work for me?" the woman asked.

"It means I don't get paid for drinking lemonade."

"Him and God," the woman said to me.

"What about them?" I asked.

"They both work in mysterious ways."

My father applauded this, great popping claps from his meaty palms. "Irma," he said, wiping his eyes, "this is my son, Jack—Jack, Irma Wilcox. Toby's mom."

"Of course I remember," the woman said. Her hand in mine felt brittle, like a cluster of dried leaves. "Little Lord Fauntleroy. Toby's told me all about you coming back to town—but of course nobody brings you out to visit, did he?"

"He's been busy," my father said.

It seems obvious that this trip, along with his revelation of his friendship with Mrs. Wilcox, was an attempt by my father to answer my story about his destruction of the city—though at the time it didn't seem like much of an argument to me. After we'd finished our drinks, he walked me down to a small gate in a chain-link fence along the back border of the yard. Beyond it was a short, terraced hill, then a swath of tightly mown grass that looked unmistakably like a fairway. My father gestured to the yard next door—and beyond it to a whole series of ranch homes and fenced backyards, each the size of a double tennis court, with differing incarnations of decks, spilled child's toys, the occasional aboveground pool. "I had all these built in 1975, about thirty of these houses, and not a soul in them," he said. "Nothing around here but range land."

"So you sold her back her own farm," I said.

"In a manner of speaking," my father said. "Although her old place was a little bit farther west, as I'm sure you'll remember. By the quarry. What we did was take over the little house that she and Toby had bought back in the city—"

"The one with the bad roof?" I asked.

"That's right. Gave her a hell of a deal, too—straight trade, that house for this one. That's how desperate I was to get some people moved out here."

"Unbelievable," I said.

"I'll say," my father responded. "Do you have any idea what these little houses are worth today? If Elmore ever buys this damn thing, she's going to make more money on this house than I ever made with the Alomar Company."

By then Toby and Elmore had shown up to round out our foursome—Toby in a pair of hemmed denim shorts, a wad of Copenhagen in his cheek, Elmore sporting black golfing slacks and trundling his clubs behind him on a handcart. They'd overheard the last of this conversation and clearly enjoyed watching me struggle with the idea that Elmore would be buying Mrs. Wilcox's house, right in the middle of all-white Kings County.

"Ask him how *long* Elmore's been trying to buy it," Toby prompted me.

Our party had fanned across the fairway by then, each of us casually dropping balls as if we'd driven them there from the tee. When I glanced at my father, he said, "Oh, I don't know—last couple of summers, I'd say he makes about an offer a week."

"All right," I said. "What's the scam?"

"There's no scam," my father said. "Henry Bowen has a rule—anyone selling a house along the course can play golf with his agent *and* the buyer for free."

I could have thought up several good reasons for why my father played so poorly on that day. It was natural for him to seem old, I suppose, while walking across land that I'd watched him survey as a much younger man. His son had only a few weeks earlier called him a crook. Additionally, as we worked our way around to the front side of the course (the hole where we'd started turned out to be number fifteen) the shake-shingle roofs of Fairhaven Estates hove into view, a sight he might well have found humiliating. Golf, however, was a game that had always come to my father naturally, a gift, a beautiful thing to see, even on a bad day. And so I was shocked and surprised to discover, as he and I squared off against Toby and Elmore, that something seemed fatally wrong with his swing. He duffed a shot, something I'd never seen him do; his drives, instead of ballooning high into the air, came off instead as low line drives, stopping twenty yards short of where they'd normally be. Every three holes, he stepped shyly into the trees to take a leak. "Why don't you try pissing in the fairway," Elmore called as we waited for him at the tee. "I doubt Henry would mind."

"I thought about it," my father said as he returned and surveyed our drives, which had all landed in the rough. "But I wanted to be somewhere you could find me."

I hadn't bought my father's suggestion that Mrs. Wilcox's house was a fair trade for her farm. But if there *was* a defense for what he'd done, an explanation for why the Wilcoxes, or Elmore, or I had loved him—even if he'd screwed each of us in his own way—I felt it as I watched him play.

There was more to it than just golf. The course that Henry had built out on Royce MacVess's farm was luxurious, too expensive for any of us to join; the houses of Fairhaven Estates had been built by forces that none of us could hope to compete with. In our group, my father had been the only one of us who'd even managed to try. As the round wore on and he continued to hack up the course, I began to notice that Elmore, Toby, and I followed his shots expectantly, then looked away in sorrow when they failed. And I realized, as we finished the round in silence, that we were all waiting, as we always had, for my father to do something spectacular, to attempt some shot we'd never imagined possible, even if it meant our own defeat.

It was dusk by the time we'd played our way around the course back to fourteen, the last hole we had left. As my father hit a wedge from 150 yards out and dropped it short into a bunker, I saw Elmore—clear across the fairway—turn and with sudden violence heave his club into the rough. "I ought to be able to hit that shot," my father said to me. "I'm sorry—no excuse for missing it."

"Who cares, Dad?" I said. "At least we're getting a free round off Henry, right? And besides, if we are losing, it's not like you got any help from me."

"It's not the losing that bothers me," my father said, looking down at his hands. "It's like, when I used to play, I could imagine these shots and then make them real. Now it's just imagining."

"Well, you've got a good setup, at least," I said. "Free golf, a couple of willing partners. Seems like it beats working."

"For now it does," my father said.

"What's that supposed to mean?" I asked.

But my father had wandered off into the trees along the fairway, unzipping his pants with his back to me. "This pissing thing isn't just getting old," he said over his shoulder. "It's cancer. I'm supposed to have an operation at the end of the week."

In August, just a few months before the long-ago first Gulf War (which, it seems strange to say, you are probably too young to remember) my father had an operation to remove his prostate and then, a month later, another to remove what I suspect, not being a doctor, were his testicles—though neither he nor my mother would ever discuss the specifics of this procedure with me. "Whatever they did take out," my father would tell me, "you can be sure I've used it enough already."

But they couldn't take out his pelvis, which was where the cancer had spread, and—after a brief, phoenixlike rise to health during the holidays—he was back in the hospital by January, so that the doctors could administer morphine. My mother by then had put in enough time with the St. Luke's Hospital Auxiliary that he was allowed to have a private room for less than its normal cost. Once it became clear that my father would be staying more than a few days, she also took it upon herself to furnish the place, replacing the normal, sallow hospital chairs with dark-varnished Stickley chairs from our breakfast room; replacing the sheets and blankets with those brought from home; installing a coffee table from the dayroom and several pots of daisies along the windowsill. These were, as I'd always suspected, her primary antidote to the changes in my father's life, her one assertion that somehow things would stay the same.

One of the reasons my father had waited so long to get his prostate checked was that he'd hated listening to his doctor's lectures on how smoking would kill him. Now that he was clearly going to be killed by something else, he considered the hospital's ban on smoking inhumane—a position that led him to spend a good deal of time sitting on the radiator bench beside the window smoking and exhaling through the open crack, then asking my mother to smuggle the used butts outside in a sealed plastic bag. The other thing he didn't like about hospital life was his reliance on the television. As long as I'd known him, my father had believed that television was merely a mechanism for keeping people inside "the dream" and preventing them from learning anything useful—like, say, to read a quitclaim document at the Kings County deeds office. He still felt this way, but the morphine that he took made him too drowsy to read, and so, very often when I came to visit him for lunch, carrying up a foil-wrapped plate of lasagna from the Grotto, I would find him lying in bed with the curtains drawn and the war on the screen. It was, seemingly, on every channel in those days—greenish, night-vision photos of missiles falling on Baghdad, of Patriot missile batteries outside Tel Aviv, of American bombers bouncing off the decks of carriers out at sea—and it frightened me to find my father in its presence, his hair long and lank against his pillow, my mother's cluttered furniture lit with the glow of bombs and missiles going off half a world away. For once I was glad that my father and I still had our own battles to fight, whose *casus belli* by now felt like familiar territory.

"How come they never talk about Rockefeller or Carnegie when we have a war?" he asked me one day when I'd thought he was asleep.

"Well, it's a war, Dad," I said. We were, at that moment, listening to Bernard Shaw report from his famous hotel room in Baghdad. "Other than the fact that it's partly over oil, I don't see what Rockefeller would have to do with it. Or Gould, or Carnegie, even if they weren't already dead."

"That's the point," my father said. "They wouldn't have had anything to do with it. They paid their way out, each one of them. Three hundred bucks was what it cost for another man to go to the Civil War in your place. I think Rockefeller paid for eight of them. Best investment any of them ever made."

"What about the Union Pacific?" I said, half in jest. "Or the time Jay Gould and Jim Fiske locked up ten million dollars of currency and in the process ruined the stock market and made wheat drop by twenty-five cents a pound. Or when Leland Stanford bought a bunch of Chinamen to build his train tracks over the Sierras—"

"Do you know who one of the earliest investors in Durant's rail line was?" my father asked. "Abraham Lincoln."

"Here's the thing that I still don't get," I said. "Warnings aside, how did you think teaching me all that stuff would make my life better?"

My father was still smiling in the light, now of the CNN studios in Atlanta. I saw his eyes move underneath his closed lids, but it was the smile that kept my attention, his whole expression—it was strangely beatific, as if he really were, even now, enjoying himself, and I wondered what had caused it. Whether it was the morphine, or my recitation from his favorite pantheon of men who'd "done something"—or if, just possibly, it was that he simply enjoyed arguing with me.

"You know, it's funny," he said, "when I was a kid, I used to ask your grandfather the exact opposite questions. Or wish I did. I was always wondering how come he *didn't* tell me something."

"He went to war," I pointed out.

"The great hero," my father said, drawing the word out until it rang falsely.

"What do you wish he'd talked to you about?" I asked.

"Do you know that your grandfather changed his name?" my father said. On the television, just beyond his voice, I could hear Christiane Amanpour saying that the Iraqi army was the fifth largest in the world. "Went in the army Private Billy Atwater of Hays, Kansas, and came out Alton Acheson, a captain. Completely obliterated any trace of *his* father, you understand? Sam Atwater. Gone. Never mentioned him. Said he'd died before I was born. When in fact he died when I was about ten. My father said he was going on a business trip, took a train down to Hays, buried him, and came back."

"Didn't Grandma say anything?"

"She knew better than that," my father said. "Besides, it was bad for business. Sam Atwater was a drunk, kind of a con man. Ran all sorts of scams. Used to claim he was an optometrist, even though he never finished high school. Used to sell oil futures."

I had heard pieces of this story before—how my great-grandfather, the drunken scalawag of Hays, Kansas, had been denied by his own son. How my father would never have known he had a grandfather if one of Sam Atwater's friends, a man named Munson, hadn't shown up at Pemberton Academy the day my father turned eighteen and driven him down to Hays to show him Sam Atwater's grave. But I had never seen the story as quite so convincing an indictment of Big Alton's integrity. After all, his attempt to reinvent himself wasn't so different from what I had done when I'd left Kansas City for New York, or what my father had attempted to do by starting the Alomar Company instead of joining Acheson & Ketch—each of us, moving like a sine curve, had chosen our course as a correction for what had come before. The difference was that at the time it seemed likely that the Acheson line was going to end with me.

"What else didn't he tell you?"

"Do you know how I found out about his affairs? Every other weekend he'd pack up and say that he was out of town on a business trip; then he'd check into a hotel downtown. One day I cut school to go to a movie and saw him in the street."

"And you would rather have had him announce this publicly?"

"But I found out anyway! Why hide? What good does that do anybody? And his clients! The cream of Kansas City society. You say you don't like Kings County? You don't like walling black people off into one part of the city? Who thought it up, do you guess? Who wrote those contracts? Your grandfather did. Did he warn me? Did he tell me, 'This is how business really goes on in Kansas City'? The Campanile's not Florence, it's a bunch of shops built next to a river of shit—that's the American way."

"What about the Wilcoxes? What about Lonnie? Are you telling me that we didn't hide what really happened to them?"

"Do you ever lie to protect your clients?" my father asked.

"Not under oath," I said.

"So with Elmore's niece—if you'd known that she had robbed that grocery store intentionally, would you have defended her?"

"But that's my job. It's how the system works."

My father raised his eyebrows. "Ah," he said. "The *system*."

"Don't try to tell me the Alomar Company was part of any system," I said.

"Without it, would you ever even have gotten to know Geanie?" my father asked. "Much less spend all those nights over at Henry's house when she was living here?"

I did not answer this.

"And as for me, I have no complaints," my father said. "It's nice to get paid. If I live long enough, I still might get paid. And in the meantime I imagined something, I spent my life on it – and now there it is. It might not be perfect. You might even say that's it's ugly, but what you can't say is that it does not exist."

By spring he was home again, back under my mother's care. Radiation treatment had failed; he'd decided against chemotherapy, the cancer having spread too far into his bones for it to succeed, and instead he'd had a small machine, the size of a door alarm, implanted beside his spine, which delivered him morphine at regular intervals and allowed him to leave the hospital. This was a death sentence, in essence, though curiously enough it didn't feel that way. The machine's insertion had left a long pink scar along the side of my father's spine, which he was fond of showing off—together with a small plastic port, through which could be added refills of morphine. Other than this, however, the trappings of sickness receded—the IV bags, the hospital beds, the plastic bracelets, the glowing TV. My father lived and slept at home again, rose in the morning and, with my mother's help, put on a fresh suit, smoked at the breakfast table, and sat outside in the yard to read the paper, while she did her gardening.

During this time he also continued to keep tabs on the inner workings of the Bowen Company. In particular he was suspicious of the uptick in Henry's charitable giving since his wedding to Rose Bennett, the woman he'd been "dating" around the time that Geanie left. My father had established a clip file of the Bowen Company's donations to local institutions, including the art gallery, the hospital, a battered women's shelter, a fund to repair the city's World War I memorial. "Five hundred thousand dollars to the zoo, for chrissake," he said during this period, reading from the paper. "The money is for a nature center that will teach urban youth to appreciate the environment—dear God Almighty, can you imagine Henry Bowen even saying that? 'Urban youth'?"

"Maybe he's teaching them how to get rid of squirrels," I suggested.

"Or maybe Rose Bennett is a good woman," my mother said.

"She'd better be," he said, "because I know damn well that charity is not a Bowen emotion. You can't sit around feeling charitable in real estate."

"It's not much of an Alton Acheson emotion," I pointed out.

"At least I'll talk to you about it," my father said. "At least I'll admit that such a thing exists. But when Henry Bowen writes a check to 'urban youth,' it can only mean two things—either he's sick or he's figured out a way for *that* to make money."

One day he insisted that we have lunch up the street at Loose Park, where he carefully chose a bench under a concrete pavilion, giving us a clear view of the park's north end, as well as the Briarcliff School across the street. Along with the sandwiches my mother packed, he brought the paper, his cigarettes, and a pair of binoculars that he wore on a strap around his neck—the same pair he'd used back in our surveying days. My father had never been much of a parkgoer, but when I expressed surprise at this choice, he said, "Why shouldn't I go to the park? It's a public place the last time I looked." Then, fifteen minutes later, he checked his watch, aimed his binoculars over my shoulder, and said, "Well, there he is. Right on time."

Even without the binoculars, I could recognize the tall, stooped figure of Henry Bowen, angling up the park's sidewalk from Fifty-first Street. His hair had gone white in the years since we'd spoken beside his pool in Fairhaven Estates, but the more remarkable transformation was in his gait.

He shuffled instead of striding, his chin tucked like that of a runner going over rough ground—though he followed the pavement the whole way. "What is this all about?" I said. "I thought he lived out in Kings County these days."

"They moved back into town, he and Rose," my father said. "They've got a place in the Fortezza Towers."

He pointed off to a severe black-windowed tower just behind the Briarcliff campus to the north, completed within the past year.

"I figure he walks up here from his apartment," my father said. "The noon constitutional. Like he and his father used to do on the Campanile."

"And you just sit here and watch him?" I said.

"Oh, no—we talk," my father said. "He's busy now, but he'll usually come by. You've got to be careful not to scare him away." It was a strange thing to say, but not nearly so strange as Henry's tiny steps, the forward cant to his body that gave him the look of someone running in place. We followed his progress clear along the loop of sidewalk that ran around the northern end of the park. On the one hand, he acted as you'd expect Henry to act; instead of just walking, he seemed to be engaged in a thorough inspection of the grounds, stopping every few steps to pick up a scrap of trash, which he stuffed into the pocket of his tweed blazer, until both pockets were bulging and his arms were filled. There were trash cans along the path, and he stopped at each to unburden himself, then immediately continued forward to repeat the same routine, diverging from the path to inspect picnic benches, tables, swings.

However, it did seem unusual, as he approached our pavilion, that he was dragging a tree limb he'd found in the center of the park. There was a trash can just outside the pavilion to our left, and, having reached it, Henry stopped and seemed to totter in place, as if consumed by doubt. The branch was clearly too heavy for him to pick up and put into the trash can, and yet at the same time he seemed unwilling simply to leave it on the ground. When I stood up to help him, my father reached across the table to grab my arm. "Henry," he said in a soft voice. "It's Al. What are you doing today?"

At no time did Henry's face reveal any sign that he was listening. But when my father finished speaking, he gave one of his familiar, hollow coughs, as if this comment were the most foolish thing he'd ever heard.

"Doing?" he said in a sarcastic voice. "Oh, I'm not doing anything. I'm just standing here. What're you doing?"

"We're not doing anything, Henry," my father said.

Henry coughed again at this. The sound was exasperated, as if the whole problem with this park—or even this city—were that nobody ever did anything, particularly help clean up. "Well, don't mind me," he said.

He bent over to go to work on the branch again, trying to lift it, and my father then nodded at me to go help him. When I did, Henry widened his eyes at me in shock. "Thought you weren't doing anything," he said.

"I'm going to give you some help," I said.

"By talking?" Henry asked testily.

"No, by lifting," I said.

Henry pointed to my father. "All that one does is the talking."

It was hard to tell whether he recognized me. After we'd lifted the branch and stuffed it into the trash container, Henry had continued, with meticulous focus, to break off every portion of the branch that poked over the container's edge. This seemed to mollify him, enough that when he'd finished, he actually looked me in the face.

"I'm Jack Acheson, Henry," I said, holding out my hand. "I used to go to school with your daughter, Geanie."

"Who?" Henry said uncertainly.

"Your daughter, Geanie," I said.

"I know her," Henry said. His tone implied that the problem was he did not know *me*.

"All right," I said. "I'll let you go, then. Just wanted to say hello. I guess you're cleaning up the park?"

"My father built this park," Henry said proudly.

"I know he did, sir. I've heard that."

Then Henry shuffled toward me. His eyes were the leached-out hazel of watered-down tea, and he spoke secretively, holding up one hand to shield his face. "Whoever he gave it to," he said, "they've done a terrible job of keeping this place up."

I escorted my father home after that, holding his arm because he'd grown unsteady on his feet. It was a beautiful park, Loose Park, even if Henry's father hadn't really built it (the land had in fact been donated to the city by Mrs. Loose after Prudential had convinced its tenant, a country club golf course, to move into Mission Hills) and together my father and I strolled past beds of tulips and into a garden with roses planted in circular beds, surrounded by limestone pillars. Freed of the Bowen Company's sartorial restraints, he wore on that spring day a nailhead jacket, a pink silk tie, and a pair of robin's-egg-blue pants, and there were tears streaming down his face. As if unfamiliar with the process of crying, he did not seem interested in wiping them away, and after a while, they bled down into his mustache, now all-white, until it, too, was wet.

"That's the one thing that gets me," he said, glancing back at Henry. "Every so often, if you watch him close, you can tell that he remembers what he used to be."

The Senior Tour

For three days after my father's death, my mother and I ransacked every attic closet, desk drawer, abandoned cedar trunk, and cobwebbed basement cabinet for the unnecessary treasures he'd squirreled away: A pair of worn, two-tone golf shoes whose white polish had begun to flake. A secondhand driver. Ten or eleven extra putters, in various stages of repair. Boxes and boxes of tasseled loafers, wingtips, brogans; sport jackets in plaid, in herringbone, in mauve, in bright red check. And when we had finished and the last box had been loaded onto the Junior League's Thrift Store truck (the clothes still smelling painfully of his skin), we stuffed his papers in endless manila folders, neutralizing his clippings behind the glued plastic of the album page. It was a curatorial mugging, our form of grief. Toward the end she hung his pictures on the walls in silver frames, a hagiographic gallery of the king, favoring his prime years before he'd begun to drink. Her favorite portrait, hung on the stairs, showed him down in Carolina, thirty pounds lighter than I'd ever seen him. He was captured at the height of a backswing, his driver bowed like a windshield wiper around his shoulder line—aiming for the fences every time. "My God, that man had a beautiful golf swing," my mother said, although, behind the picture's glass, the danger that had once accompanied it had vanished entirely.

When there was nothing left to clean, my mother closed herself off in a small study by the living room and spent three days watching a weekend broadcast of the U.S. Senior Open on my parents' one TV. I tried to be as practical about the situation as possible—buying the groceries, sorting out the legal details of my father's estate at the kitchen table—while my mother mourned in the darkness with the television and the drawn shades. Every so often I'd go in and visit her, running my hands along the thin bones of her shoulder blades, which felt no more substantial than a cat's, as she described to me Jack Nicklaus's amazing charge to the lead. But my practicality didn't help, that I could certainly see—especially not when she bought a second, smaller television and installed it in the kitchen, as if somehow the sounds from its little speaker did a better job of replacing my father's voice than I did.

On Sunday night I leaned a ladder against the house and climbed up to replace one of the security lights. My father had wired the whole property, light by light, over the years so that the yard looked like a car lot, and as I unscrewed the burned-out flood lamp and tucked it inside my shirt, I found myself imagining my own photograph of my old man. It was from a day when we'd walked to play tennis at the courts along Brush Creek. But I saw him now down on the floodlit grass—his usual pear-shaped 260—wearing his favorite yellow suit, white oxfords, and carrying an ancient, gut-strung Don Budge racket that looked like a soup ladle in his mitts and waving to an imaginary crowd as he stepped arrogantly to the baseline to face my first serve.

"Will you stop agreeing with me, please?" my mother said. She had wandered outside and sat down below me in the grass, the bob of her black hair and the outline of her shoulders visible through the branches of a magnolia tree.

"About Dad or about the golf tournament?" I said, removing the new flood lamp from my mouth and screwing it in, so that I could speak.

"Either one," my mother said. "*Anything.*"

"What if I told you that senior golf was a stupid thing to watch?" I said.

"I don't know. Let's give it a try."

"All right, say your pal Jack Nicklaus wins this thing," I said. "Does it make any sense to you at all that a man should get paid half a million for rolling a white ball into a cup instead of . . . I don't know, something that *helps* somebody."

"You mean like lawyering?" She coyly invoked my father's phrase.

"I mean like *anything,*" I said. "Like sewing a patch on a pair of jeans."

We were by now walking together through the side yard and beneath the carport, myself with the extension ladder over my shoulder, my mother sipping a cocktail, her tan features and very small upturned nose illuminated by a generalized white glare, similar to what one might find on a New York avenue.

"It wouldn't really be five hundred grand for one putt," my mother said. "You have to divide it up by total strokes, since each one counts the same."

"Or teaching kids to read."

"That's the one thing I do wish you'd appreciated about your father," my mother said, stopping in the fairy-tale light of the driveway and putting her hands on her hips.

"What is," I said over my shoulder, "counting putts?"

"His moral sense," my mother said.

This comment caused me to stumble, which I then exaggerated, dropping the ladder, into a bogus faint. I had verbena about my ankles, the dried-out stems of daylilies scratching against my calves, and I hooted up into the starless, white-crowned heights of my mother's trees, as if my father's soul might be floating there someplace.

"He cheated," my mother said complacently. "But he never demagogued."

"That's kind of a big word," I said. "You got a definition for me?"

"It means trying to hurt people by always being right," my mother said.

I had no doubt that my mother believed I had hurt my father on several occasions in just this way, but instead of arguing her point, she dug a cedar chip from the flower bed along the drive and tossed it playfully at me. At sixty-one, she still had slender arms and shoulders, and with her face tucked into shadow, you could have mistaken her for a girl of thirteen—not much older than Geanie Bowen when she'd thrown apples with me. "Not everything in this world is business," she said. "You might also consider the possibility that he took a lot of time to make friends."

"Oh, really?" I said. "I never noticed that."

"Like the Wilcoxes?" my mother said, tossing another chip at me. "Like Elmore Haywood? All his clients? If your father had wanted to have a funeral, we would have had to turn people away from this place."

"Why don't we have a party, then?" I said. "What's he going to do about it?"

My mother didn't answer this. The next chip she tossed was not at but rather to me, a short, underhand delivery that I was able to catch.

"Unless, of course, you think you're too old to handle it," I said.

My mother made a farting sound.

"Pardon me," she said. "I have a loose tooth."

It had been my father's wish that he be cremated (and thus *not* buried in Union Cemetery beside Big Alton and my grandmother) and his ashes remain portable, a request that my mother had fulfilled by storing them inside the silver bell of his Texas State Amateur golf trophy from 1952. His second instruction had been that there be no service and no pastors—nothing *boring*—associated with his death. And so by noon the following Thursday, the Texas State Amateur golf trophy from 1952 could be found in the center of our dining room table surrounded by a groaning banquet of ribs, of brisket, of deviled eggs, of cannelloni, fried chicken, actual real candied yams, and a dozen other dishes, all laid out on my mother's best silver—the greatest display that room had seen since my father's dinner with Bobby Ansi nearly thirty years before.

In her invitations my mother had written, "*Come play a final nine with my husband, Alton Acheson. Best ball, beginners welcome, forget about your handicap. Shotgun is at 3:00 P.M.* But I had answered the door at 10:00 A.M. to find my father's first mourners—Dr. Stephen Randle and his wife, Ellen, to whom my father had sold a house on the end of our block—holding a huge glass bowl of chicken salad, explaining that Elmore had told them to show up early. The visitors had been fairly steady after that, and by noon people had begun to spill out into the side yard, between the portico and carriage house, where my mother had set up tables and chairs. It seemed as if everyone my father had ever known was there, some of whom I recognized, others I'd never seen before in my life. By eleven Joey Ramola and his son had arrived with the Grotto's entire kitchen staff, and they began carrying tubs of lasagna in from a catering van while Little Joey set up a portable bar and his father, in his maître d's tuxedo, took over the job of answering the door. But the rarest and most interesting sight was my father's clients, the old-line Pemberton graduates who'd driven in from Fairhaven Estates mixing somewhat uncertainly with their former cooks, mechanics, and doormen who now lived in the properties managed by A&E Realty. None of them seemed particularly aware of what I'd seen as my father's attempts to divide the city—though I couldn't help but wonder what would have happened if they'd compared the sales pitches he'd given them.

Toby Wilcox and his mother arrived in his ice cream truck. Mrs.

Wilcox, clacking up the driveway in her walker, had baked an apple pie, for which she began almost immediately to apologize. While Toby, accompanied by a crew of A&E Realty employees—I saw Tito there—heaved their ladders up against the side of the old stone house and, unrolling bales of Christmas lights from the back end of the truck, began to string them up, Bowen-style, between my father's security lights.

Mallory showed up, too, having forgiven me for our disastrous trip into Kings County. She was taller than my mother, lacked her tan, but they shared a preference for directness over grief—"I only met your husband once," I heard her say sympathetically to my mother, "and just *that* nearly killed me"—and ten minutes after their introduction, the two of them adjourned to the kitchen, their sleeves rolled up, serving cake. Even Henry Bowen made an appearance, step-shuffling up the driveway on Rose Bennett's arm. I knew that my mother was going to be okay when she met them politely in the drive and then guided Henry to a seat next to Hattie, casting a sly glance at me.

However, it was Nikki Garaciello—or Nikki Herman, as she was now called—whose appearance meant the most to me. She arrived late, around four o'clock, having had to wait for her husband to return from his classes before she left him with the kids. I'd snuck upstairs to my parents' bedroom by then. Very little about the room had changed since the night my father and I had stood here watching the Campanile lights come on with Bobby Ansi. My mother had left my father's newest suits in the closet (all except the yellow one, which we'd dressed him in when we'd burned his body); his tie tacks and his cuff links were arranged neatly on his dresser, his shoes hung on their shoe trees, his ties covered the inside of his closet door in a spangled mass. A saw blade still dangled in the tree branch outside his window. My father had so enjoyed my lie about how it had gotten there that he'd glued a new saw in when the old one rusted and had, in imitation of the Bowens, erected a brass plaque in the garden, memorializing my story. I heard Nikki enter and step up behind me, the points of her breasts brushing my back as they'd done when she told me that Lonnie had left to meet Geanie. "I've got bad news for you," she said into my ear. "There's a saw stuck up in your tree."

"Memorial to the Union dead," I said when we finished our embrace. "And to the only story I ever told that my father thought was worth a shit."

I was surprised at the bitterness of my own voice. Before Nikki had arrived, I'd been watching Rose Bennett read the plaque of my story, and I'd laughed at how pleased my father would have been to see such a thing.

"That's a good start," Nikki said, handing me her plastic glass of wine. "Drink a couple more of these and we might actually get someplace."

"Where are we trying to get?" I said.

"Out of here," Nikki said. As she led me down the steps to the front hall, she pulled off the high-heeled pumps she was wearing and tossed them behind my mother's umbrella stand. "Your dad went through this process twice with me, you know. Once with Lonnie and then again when my dad got sent away."

"The one thing I've been looking forward to in this whole funeral was never having to be involved in any of his processes again."

"Cursing the dead is part of it," Nikki said. "So is drinking, screaming, crying—none of them things we can do here."

From the house we followed Briarcliff Drive and then a side street that led down the bluff to the swing sets along Brush Creek, just down the hill from my parents' house. On the way Nikki had stopped at her car and retrieved a pint of whiskey from her glove compartment, a bottle I now cradled between my thighs.

"When all that stuff happened," Nikki said, "your father was the one person who didn't make me feel like I should be experiencing some picturesque grief."

"Picturesque grief," I said, "is something that I do not have."

"Well, what do you have, then?" Nikki asked.

"Did you know that my dad was going to use Lonnie's death to get that piece of land? That he was thinking of it from the very beginning?"

"At least it wasn't completely a big waste."

"But it was wrong, don't you think?"

"Let me tell you something about wrong, Jack," Nikki said. She'd started swinging back and forth next to me, so I couldn't clearly see her face. "Wrong are the things you do that you can't tell anybody except your lawyer. My father had a lot more of those than yours did, I'm afraid."

"I *was* my father's lawyer," I pointed out.

"Do you remember where the highway is in our old neighborhood?" Nikki asked. "Down by Garfield Park? There used to be a real steep ravine there. Lonnie and I were playing in the park, and we heard these tires squeal and a huge crash, and when we ran over, we saw a car had gone down in that ravine. It was late afternoon, the light was flat, and for a second—just a second—I thought the car was my father's car, and I remember thinking right away that I hoped he was dead. Because it would make my life easier at school, of all things. Then the light changed, and I saw it wasn't his car."

"Whose was it?" I asked.

"When they opened the trunk up, they found Joe John Tocci, one of our neighbors," Nikki said. "That's what I mean by not very picturesque."

I couldn't figure out anything to do with this story but to laugh at it; it seemed another tale that would have been good for Callaghan—humorous and colorful so long as you were far enough away to avoid the slight tremor of malignancy that disturbed its surface. Nikki, I figured, had seen much more of this than I had.

"When dad went, it was pretty much just a relief," I told her. "He was laid flat out on the bed and he was breathing hard. I told him that I loved him and that I was sorry he was going away—everything you'd want to say. Everything I'm glad I said. And then he died. The hard thing was believing it, you know? His feet were still there, poking up under the bedsheets. He still smelled the same. My mother just climbed up in the bed and curled up next to him with her arm over his chest and her hair in his face, the way I remember them lying together in bed when I was a kid."

"So what's wrong?" Nikki said. She seemed to be reacting more to the unsteadiness of my voice than to what I'd said. "You were there, you told him you loved him. How could it have worked out better than that?"

"Because I *am* going to miss the guy," I said. "It's not like it was ever exactly boring having him around." I gestured up the hill to where Toby's lights, strung up around the gables of my father's house, were now faintly visible in the daylight. "I'm glad you came. I appreciate the sendoff. It's just that when he goes, you start thinking about all the other people that are missing. You want those other things back, too."

"You're talking about Geanie," Nikki said. "Is that it? Because otherwise, for someone whose father has just died, those all seem like natural things to think."

"I fucked that one up somehow," I said. "Or *we* did, together."

"I always thought it was just the baby," Nikki said.

"Yeah, that's sort of a sign, isn't it?" I said. "You've got to figure things are over when a girl trots straight home and starts a family."

We'd been swinging next to each other in an alternating, lazy rhythm, but when I said this, Nikki's feet scraped the sand.

"I'm talking about when you were at my house," she said.

"So am I. She dumped me right after that."

"She *threw up* twice that day, Jack."

"She was sick," I said. "She had the flu." Something in my expression caused Nikki to get up from her swing set and walk away, as if she were frightened of being close to me. "She went home to her fiancé," I called after her. "That was her choice. You can't put that on me." I'd left my swing, chasing Nikki down toward Prudential Bowen's creek, offering all the logical reasons why Geanie had left—her teaching, her fear of returning to Kansas City, the way I'd forced her decision too abruptly—as if delivering closing arguments not just to her but to the Boccaccio, the Alighieri, and the Cavalcanti apartment buildings across the street, with their soft, yellow-brick façades, their charming gargoyles leering out near the drainpipes.

"I've seen a pregnant woman, okay?" Nikki said when I caught up to her. "Trust me, you learn to notice certain things."

"That's bullshit!" I said. "You haven't talked to her."

Nikki shook her head slowly. The gesture seemed less a response to my assertion than a commentary on my not having considered this possibility before.

"She would've *told* me," I insisted.

"Come on, Jack, whose funeral are we attending?"

"I don't see what that has to do with it."

"Who do you think taught us that a good story could replace a mistake?"

I tried to ignore this echo of the story my father and I had made up for Lonnie but Nikki wouldn't let me. Her almond-shaped eyes tracked me in the soft darkness of the creek as persistently as any gargoyle, though her features—slightly heavier, rounder, more adult—were still familiar as those of the girl who'd crouched next to me in the hedgerows of Kings County. "Come on, Jack. I think you know my brother didn't just fall into that quarry. So how come you never told me what happened? Was it because you hated me? Or was it because you knew it was something I didn't want to hear?"

This last statement was a far more favorable interpretation of my own actions than I would have given for myself—a form of forgiveness, really. I wasn't ready for that yet, at least not on that night. She was wrong about Geanie, she had to be. I would've noticed; I didn't close my eyes to the truth of things. But Nikki had always been a step ahead of me on these subjects and I give her credit for listening to me past the point where my words were only rote, skimming over some worse feeling underneath. By the end I was actually explaining that I remembered seeing a late May issue of the city's society magazine stating that Geanie Bowen had given birth to a baby girl—and then counting backward on my fingers nine months to September, by which time Geanie had long since left me. We were on opposite sides of the small concrete gutter that cradled Brush Creek, and as I spoke, Nikki trailed her bare foot through the water.

"Do you know what I think?" she said. "I think you should check your dates."

Patrician Woods

If you visited my mother's house on Briarcliff Drive today—that is, today in 2002—it would look pretty much the same as the house Nikki and I had returned to that summer evening in 1991. Though the old racial covenants are now "a thing of the past" (they were outlawed by the Supreme Court in 1948, a fact that prosecutors in the area waited until the mid-eighties to begin noticing), the property values of these old Bowen houses have kept pace with newer developments in Kings County. There are several reasons for this. If anything, due to the high housing prices and the failure of the public-school system, the all-white, all-private-school nature of the neighborhood has increased. The cars that you pass on the side streets have Pemberton stickers in their windows. The children and mothers inside these cars are, on a summer's day, very likely to be dressed in swimsuits and returning from either the Mission Hills or Colonial Country Club pools. The fathers, whom you might catch out watering the grass on a Saturday, will be wearing roughly the same Bermuda shorts and collared shirts they've been wearing for most of the last century.

Even the greeting my mother gives me as I show up this afternoon is reminiscent of the greeting she gave Nikki and me that evening, though in this case I am fifteen minutes late instead of several hours. "Where in God's name have you *been?*" she calls out to me. "I was starting to think you'd forgotten me."

"That's me," I answer. "The late Jack Acheson."

"You and your father," my mother says. "How in the world did I raise two men who'd be late for their own funerals?"

"Dad didn't *have* a funeral," I remind her. I have left the anteroom where my father and I once cleaned up after Bobby Ansi's dog and swing through the main hall into the kitchen, where my mother is standing at the counter. "But the after-party was nice."

"That's because *I* was in charge of it," my mother says.

"Then you can organize mine."

"That," my mother says, carrying our plates over to the kitchen table and sitting down across from me, "is why you need a wife."

This is a reference to Mallory O'Neal, whom I've been dating now for six years—and who, with two grown kids from her first marriage, has no more interest in tying the knot than I do. "To bury me? Thanks, I think I'll wait."

My mother is wearing a navy sweater buttoned at the neck (heat is something she doesn't feel, she claims) and picks up her fork and brandishes it at me. "But waiting is the *problem*, ho-ney. How do you think you end up late?"

"Do you know what your late husband's advice was to me?" I ask. "Patience, patience, patience."

"Do you know what my advice is?" my mother asks. "Hurry up, for God's sakes. Arranging one funeral in my lifetime is more than enough for me."

It's an entirely safe way of talking, this sparring business, like the way dogs play in the park, baring their teeth but never biting. The only surprise, my having assumed my father's speaking part, is how much of it must have occupied my parents' lives. Along with the recognition that the source of my love for your mother's smart-assed talk (and Mallory's, in her way) is sitting right across from me, revved up like a puppy.

After lunch she leads me upstairs, though I already know the way. This, too, is exciting for her, walking through that huge empty house *with* somebody instead of alone, as she must do more times than I care to imagine at her age. Her approach to all these empty rooms is different now than it was when she first confronted them as a young woman, immediately after we'd left the Gramercy Apartments. Then they represented the unknown future, the frightening world of possibility; now they are the well-charted though equally vast territory of the past—including the photo of the young golfer down in Texas, a man now some twenty years younger than me. "My God, that man had a beautiful golf swing," my mother says, ritually touching the frame.

We pass my parents' long bedroom and continue up to the third floor, a corner room with slanting ceiling, which has become the de facto library of the King of Kings County. There are stacks and stacks of my father's papers laid out on the floor, the top layers yellowed, like fish fillets set out to cure. A desk, two bookshelves of his old biographies, a pencil sharpener nailed up crookedly to the doorjamb. There is also, on the desk, a nice, flat-panel Dell that I've brought in, whose fan chirps reassuringly as I touch its start button, followed by the xylophone theme of Bill Gates's Office system, whose newness I appreciate, given the surroundings. "I'm taking Shelly Finkel to the doctor from one to two," my mother is saying to me. "Now, Alan"—this is her yard man—"is supposed to get here before I leave, but if he doesn't, do you know what to say?"

"So long as he doesn't come up here, I don't plan on telling him anything," I say. I have my files up on the screen now and am leaning in to read them, detaching myself from her, a procedure that I sometimes have to execute forcefully.

"You're supposed to tell him not to touch your father's tree." This is, of course, the tree that still holds my father's glued-up saw.

"Right, cut down the dead tree."

"No, *don't* cut down the tree, you idiot," my mother says.

"Who said I was going to cut it down?" I say. For my impertinence my mother hits me over the head with the dust rag that she carries in her pocket, and I imagine—it can only be imagination—that the nimbus of particles drifting between my eyes and the screen smells, still, of my father's cigarettes. "Anything else?" I say.

"Do you remember that Elmore is driving us to Kings County this afternoon for out meeting?" my mother asked. "Or did you also forget that?"

It is, as with the tree, the fourth time that she has brought up this topic; however, this time I hear a note of real concern. "Forget what?" I ask.

"I don't know," my mother says. "Something important."

"How do you know it's important if you don't know what it is?"

But my mother is gone by then. I hear her leave behind my back, and I am alone again in my father's study, surrounded by the "untold" story of the building of Kings County and the role he played in it. Were I up here doing what I have told my mother that I am doing—editing my father's own drafts—it would be a daunting task. But this version of my father's history is my own, designed for a private, rather than a public, audience. I do not intend for it to be published anyplace. I do not need notes. I open the window. Down in the garden, I can see the holly bushes; I can see my mother cutting daisies; I can see a dead tree with a saw stuck into it. And for all intents and purposes, except for my blue computer screen, it might as well be the summer of 1991.

It is not so easy as you might suspect to check the birth date of a child that is not your own—or at any rate is not thought to be your own. Hospitals and state offices of vital statistics will give out birth certificates only either to the person whose name is listed on the certificate or to the next-of-kin on the mother's side. Secondly, any request for information must be accompanied by a photocopy of the requester's driver's license, a Social Security card, and a notarized letter. I had none of this material, nor did the birth announcements that I'd looked up contain a specific date, and so I could not call the Mount Moriah Hospital in New Haven, Connecticut, and ask if a girl named Sandra Bowen-McKenzie was ever even born there, whether in May of 1984, or on any other date.

Which is why, about three months after my conversation with Nikki Garaciello, I found myself at the same table where my father and I once sat, underneath the Loose Park pavilion, waiting as the great Henry Bowen made his regular slow shuffle across Fifty-first Street and onto the park's looping sidewalk. Watching him, I experienced all the different emotions that I'd felt about your mother's departure during the intervening years. There was anger, of course—I'd be lying if I did not admit that. I had already tried writing your mother at the University of Connecticut, where I'd heard that she was teaching, and had left several, increasingly terse, voice messages on her office phone, none of which had been returned. Balanced against this, though, was the fear of actually getting an answer to my question. Do not underestimate this impulse—it is, as my father called it, the desire to maintain the dream. It is why, despite my unanswered letters to your mother, it took me so long to go to that pavilion and wait for Henry. It wasn't that I was worried Nikki had been wrong; it was that I feared she'd be right.

It's part of Kansas City life, you understand, the desire *not* to know that you have missed something—*not* to ask why all the people left downtown. Or how, exactly, the Troost Avenue became the city's color line, why the school system failed, or how Lonnie Garaciello ended up in Royce MacVess's quarry. For years people in this city have known how Prudential and Henry Bowen made their money and no one, myself included, has ever publicly contradicted their official history—or written down a chronicle of the entire process, which this manuscript describes only in part. Why, you ask, would an entire city be afraid to do this? Because to have someone else write your story for you is a luxury; it absolves you of responsibility for the role you've played in it. That's what I think Nikki was trying to tell me by the creek. If I'd really been ready to know why your mother left me, I would've asked her at the time. And protesting innocence once the story's written is like betting on a freshman football game at Pemberton and then complaining that it's rigged. By then it's too late to change the ending.

That fall, however, I was ready for an answer. It was in this feeling that I have come closest to understanding my father's contention that bullshit is sometimes the only route to honesty. And so when Henry shuffled through the yellow walnut leaves to my post in the pavilion, I gave him a friendly wave—the same friendly wave I'd been giving him from this same bench, at this same time, for the past two weeks.

"Still there, huh?" Henry said. "They haven't put you to work yet."

"No, Henry, no luck," I said. "You come up with anything?"

Henry showed me, from his pockets, two crushed beer cans, a toothbrush, a handful of bottle caps, and a package of half-smoked Virginia Slims that looked as if he might have taken them from someone before she was actually done smoking them.

"Not much of a haul, Henry," I said. "Don't tell me you're losing your touch."

Henry snorted at this observation, as if to suggest that I hadn't done any better. But he was distracted, too, glancing over the shoulder of his old tweed jacket at his nurse—a bearded man in khakis and a fleece pullover who was idling by a tulip bed, some thirty feet away. "Is that guy bothering you, Henry?" I asked.

"Bothering me?" This comment brought a whole volley of snorts and hollow, nervous sounds inside his chest. Henry began awkwardly buttoning his jacket with his big, trembling thumbs until I reached out and quietly took his hand.

"You want to ditch him, is that it?" I said.

Henry's cheeks were dimpled with anxiety, and he'd begun to quickly lick his lips.

"All right, you just go ahead," I said. "Go ahead and bolt, straight down to the pond. I'll go hold him up, and then, after that, I'll meet you there. Okay? The pond."

Henry had stooped enough in his old age that, as I held him by the shoulders, I looked directly into his watery eyes. Then I clapped his back, and he "bolted" off—a sad, uptempo version of his usual running shuffle, which still moved at a snail's pace.

I'd been working the nurse, too, for the past several weeks, flashing him a business card, dropping a few names, explaining that my deep respect for Henry stemmed from the fact that my father had collaborated with him on several Kings County projects, back in the day. I'd also accustomed him to the idea that I would be perfectly willing—honored, in fact—to walk Henry around the park while the nurse sat at the pavilion and smoked a cigarette—enough so that on this day it was he who said gratefully, "You want to take him? Fine by me," when I came over to shake his hand.

I'd parked my car down by the pond, out of sight of the pavilion, and I had picked Henry's pocket long before he reached it. It isn't hard to pick the pocket of a man with no short-term memory; if he gets nervous, you just put the wallet back and wait for him to forget you took it. This time Henry didn't get nervous, and by the time I'd checked to make sure the documents I needed were there (as they always had been during our "trial runs" over the past week), we'd reached my car. I'd parked next to a trash can, and while Henry was throwing his trash away, I opened the passenger door. Henry was used to having car doors opened for him, and his response was as complacent as I'd hoped it would be. He shuffled over and placed one gnarled hand on the car door, another on the roof, before he cast a suspicious glance at me. "Who're you?" he asked sharply. I had a hold of the outside of his elbow by then, hoping to ease him down into the car. "I'm Jack Acheson, Henry," I said. "Your daughter, Geanie, went to school with me."

"What's that got to do with it?" Henry said angrily.

"Geanie sent me to pick you up," I said. "She's in town, your daughter. She wants to see you. All you have to do is to get in."

He still struggled with me a bit then, swinging his elbow. But this was only because he wanted to get into the car without my help, which he did, slowly and with admirable tenacity, folding his boxy knees up against the dashboard like a crane.

The copy store was only a few blocks away, on Fifty-first and Oak, in a modest, block-long strip of shops that the Bowen Company had built in the early 1940s. I left Henry in the car, the childproof locks engaged, and ran inside to make three copies of his driver's license and Social Security card. When I returned, Henry was repeatedly pulling and releasing the chrome door handle. He glanced up once at me, furtively, then resumed pulling, his shoulders hunched, as if to hide this from me.

I drove Henry back to Loose Park after this. There were other things that I would have liked to discuss with him, subjects that would have taken hours or even lifetimes to cover, instead of the few minutes we had left. I would also have liked to know whether he and his father had really thought Florence was beautiful, even at three-quarter scale. And why, if they thought it was so beautiful, they hadn't—after making their first hundred million—simply gone to live there. I wanted to know whether he'd ever read a book, say, on the Medicis, or studied up on his heroes as my father had. Or whether the empire he'd built, all the streets and houses he'd populated, stretching from here, on Fifty-first Street in Kansas City, clear out to Fairhaven Estates on 119th Street in Kings County, had been the product of deep thought and reflection, or whether it had simply come naturally, like an ant programmed to tunnel away. I would've liked to know what he dreamed.

But Henry was getting uncomfortable with me. His arthritic hands fidgeted atop his thighs, thumbs poked out like a hitchhiker's; he'd tucked his heels tight up against the bottom of his seat. "Here," he said anxiously as we pulled up beside the park. "I want to get out here. What part of that don't you understand?"

I jumped out of the car after that, unlocking the doors, hustling and apologizing around the rear bumper, and continuing my stream of apologies as I helped Henry from the car and to his feet. "I'm sorry, sir," I said. "I'm terribly sorry—and look at all the trash." I collected a patch of discarded Budweiser bottles so eagerly that even Henry, who'd seemed ready to bolt, stopped to regard me with an amused grin on his face. "Sir, I'll have a crew out here in twenty minutes to clean up this place."

Henry watched me do this with an amused, bluff grin as I fumbled with the bottles, dropping one, then stuffing the others hurriedly into my backseat.

"Got your hands full there," he said.

"Sir, I really do. I'm sorry, I've got a thousand things going on today. I'm really not normally this scattered—"

"Do I know you?" Henry said.

"Jack Acheson," I said. "I'm sorry, I thought I mentioned that. My father used to work for you—Alton Acheson, do you remember him?"

"No," Henry said. He gave me one of his hollow coughs. "I'm sorry," he said, waving his hands off toward the Campanile. "We've had a lot of them."

"What about the crews?" I asked.

"What about them?" Henry asked.

I had the letter with me then and spread it out on my car's roof. "I'll need you to sign a work order so they can clean up the park," I said as I handed Henry a pen.

"How many men?" Henry said, looking at it.

"Twenty?" I said.

"Make it thirty," Henry said, signing the letter. "Ten for trash pickup, ten for the lawn cutting, and ten to trim these trees."

"Thirty men, sir," I said. "That's it exactly."

Which was how I got your grandfather to sign your medical release.

You were seven at the time of this conversation; you are now eighteen—a passage of years for which you are owed an explanation, one that may not reflect well on either your mother or me. Perhaps you will think that a real father, a good father, ought to have flown straight out to Connecticut with your birth certificate—which did, as you know, read March 15, 1984. Or that, being a lawyer, I should have begun legal proceedings right then to win visitation rights. I would be lying if I said, in the months that immediately followed my first contact with your mother, that I did not consider all these possibilities. Or if I said that this manuscript was not originally intended, at least in part, to present a version of our separation in which your mother was entirely to blame.

I wanted, in other words, to tell my side of the story right away. I had no interest in your mother's impassioned arguments for why I should wait to contact you until you were eighteen—that you were only seven years old, that you already had a family, as well as a father in whom you believed. That you deserved a normal childhood before someone barged in claiming the whole thing had been a fake. At the start I played along with them primarily because I didn't want your first glimpse of me to be as a litigant. But your mother's arguments were good ones and, having agreed to wait, at least provisionally, I found that my side of the story began to change. Perhaps it was merely hearing your mother's voice on the phone again instead of having her completely ignore me. Prehaps it was hearing her apologize. Perhaps it was the knowledge that she paid a price for her decision to avoid a legal fight, not least, I'm sure, in her marriage. Surely it helps that, with Mallory, I have established a stable life. Whatever the cause, there the pieces were, laid out for me, day after day, week after week, birthday after birthday (both yours and mine, naturally). When you polish a story long enough, you see outlines that you did not expect, divots and surprising flaws that do not fit your version of the truth. Over the years, I've found enough to be glad I did not tell mine prematurely.

In your mother's case, it seems clear to me now that during the summer that we spent together, there were many things I should've done differently. For starters, I had no concept (as I do now) of how she must have felt after her mother's and her grandfather's deaths. Instead, I assumed that her reactions to her family were the same as my own, namely, that her father was a son of a bitch. I should not have thought that Andrew McKenzie, who has raised you—and who has clearly been dealt the worst hand in all of this—could be so easily dismissed. *Who cares what they think?* I would tell her, in an attempt to cheer her up. *They're the ones in the wrong.* No one should ever, ever be allowed to say such things about those you've loved, or tried to love, and the fact that Geanie didn't leave town sooner only shows how lonely she must have been.

As for you, as I tried to imagine telling this story to you, I kept returning to my memory of your mother and me listening down a laundry chute, except that I imagined that girl was you. What would you want to know? What were you out there listening for? How was I supposed to tell you about the world? What was the one thing that nobody would tell you about, the one thing I would tell differently? For me, this was the story of my father and Kings County and of what happened to your mother and me. It is not a story for a seven-year-old, or a twelve-year-old, or even a sixteen-year-old (though I learned it at those ages anyway). It appears neither in the Bowen Company history nor in your great-grandfather's obituary. You won't find much of it in the news clips. But that doesn't mean that it is not worth knowing; you ought to know it, I think. It is, after all, part of your history. And I have tried to show you here the moments when its secrets were opened up for me—there in your mother's bedroom, or the Reserve Room at the Grotto, or sitting at my parents' dining table with Elmore Haywood and Bobby Ansi. It is still there, if you ask me, underneath the Ranch Mart mall and the exits of the highway.

However, growing up around my father, I also learned to value that moment of listening at the laundry chute *before* you hear anything. Had I appeared in your life when your mother and Andrew were still together, I would have started the story too soon, forced you to make choices that you should not have had to consider. And it seemed I would have learned nothing if I made you, too early, an accomplice in my own mistakes.

But there is one other reason I thought you might be interested in the long Acheson-Bowen collaboration in Kings County, other than the effect it had on your mother and me. And so at three o'clock, I flip my flat-screen off and head out to meet your grandmother, Elmore, and Mallory down in the drive. All of us have changed from our original descriptions in the pages that I leave behind. My mother's hands are speckled now and twisted, and, for the first time, I have begun to notice the loose skin of age beneath her chin. Elmore is actually in better condition than he was at the time of my father's death, having had both his knees replaced, though his hair, as he ducks his head to slide into the backseat, has gone completely gray. And then there is Mallory, whom you have not met. She's from Murphy, Arizona, a town that was still just desert when your great-grandfather purchased his first pig farm along the banks of Brush Creek, and she greets me with a flash of high-gummed, Irish teeth and then pats her briefcase as a signal of readiness, since I have asked her to act as my attorney in our meeting today.

The quarry, too, has obviously changed. In fact, forty-five minutes after we leave Briarcliff Drive—the normal time these days, due to traffic, of a trip out to Kings County—I am standing in what looks like a young girl's bedroom, its décor entirely unrelated to the rock walls and dust-colored frogs that once stood in its place. There's a four-poster bed covered by a bedspread in a print of horses and ballet slippers. There is a desk, a chair, a bedside lamp, and, up on the wall, a framed photograph of a gut-strung tennis racket in a wooden press. I have been in this room before, very often after writing you, and every time it haunts me in the same way—it's the theory of a room, your girlhood room that I never got to see, but the memories it ought to hold have been stripped away. When I lift the bed's lace dust ruffle, there are no tennis shoes or old socks or hockey shin guards hidden underneath. Not even dust bunnies. The desk has no papers on it, no carvings, no graffiti, no rocks or marbles or bird feathers in the drawers; the photo of the old gut-strung tennis racket is meant, I think, to be homey and reassuring, but instead it reminds me only of all the games we did not play. And when I search for photos of you, your school pictures, teams or trophies engraved with a name, I find nothing. On every wall it is the same.

A discussion drifts down the staircase from upstairs. I can hear Mallory's clear, blunt voice explaining, "Look, this deal is a slam dunk just on the surface, without any other evidence I could present. The terms of the deed are clear. It says that Alton Acheson, or his descendants, should be notified of and allowed to approve any construction that takes place on this property—and that without such approval the title of the land and its contents will revert back to them."

"That may *sound* simple." These drawling tones come from Mr. Twigg, of Atlanta's Highpoint Properties—which, as you probably know, bought the Bowen Company some five years back. "But if you look at the agreement I've brought here, you'll see that the prior owners of this property, the Bowen Company, assured my company that the title to this land was free and clear. I'll read the language for you—"

"I've read it."

"'The Highpoint Company will retain full rights and control to *all* properties currently titled to the Bowen Company, and accepts the assurance of the Bowen Company that none are subject to lien or other claims.'"

"Caveat emptor," Mallory says, perhaps for my benefit.

"This is a five-hundred-million-dollar company we just bought. Are you telling me that we're supposed to go back and check the title of every eighty-acre scrap of farmland, clear back to the sixties?"

"What you choose to do is not my client's problem," Mallory says. "It was your choice to trust the Bowen Company in this matter, not his."

"What's he think he's going to do with all this land?" Mr. Twigg says, laughing.

"Excuse me, Mr. Twigg, I understand that you're not from Kansas City." This is my mother's voice I hear. "So perhaps you don't understand that my husband invented the idea of building homes in Kings County."

"No disrespect to your husband, Mrs. Acheson, but we've arranged thirty million in financing for this project. Sure, this model home is finished, but without any capital—more capital than respectfully, I, think is available to your family—all you and your son will be inheriting is a bunch of two-by-fours."

As you can tell from this conversation, there is a reason these rooms appear lived in but aren't—nearly any model home you visit in Kings County is arranged that way. It is an attempt to create a feeling of history when the actual history is unpleasant, or inconvenient. But my question is, What else do you expect history to be? I climb the steps and stick my head into the office. Five people glance up: My mother, Mallory O'Neal, and Elmore are sitting in front of a walnut desk. Behind the desk are Mr. Twigg, a good decade younger than me, with his Georgia twang and frosted blond hair, and an assistant. Twigg pokes his finger in his ear and twists it. "There he is, the great developer," he says. "I was just asking your mother how you planned to afford this."

"I hope she gave you an answer," I say. Mallory hands me a brief that we've prepared listing some little-known chapters in the Bowen Company's history. We have determined that my overconfident absence from this process will be more disconcerting to Mr. Twigg than my presence—and also funnier—so I barely glance at the pages before handing them to him. "Are you going to need me for this?" I ask Mallory.

"No, no—piece of cake," Mallory says. And so I leave, chucking Twigg on the shoulder as Mallory starts in. "There are any number of actionable offenses listed in this brief," she is saying. "I would particularly draw your attention to the number of racial covenants, filed between 1950 and 1965, in direct contravention of a Supreme Court decision. Also an agreement by the Bowen Company to purchase this property from Bobby Ansi, a known felon, in exchange for land north of the river and off-the-books payments to family members—can you explain to me, for instance, why

Nikki Garaciello has appeared on your company's books as an employee up until last year?"

I stroll out through the kitchen and into a showroom that has been tacked on to the front house. Curiously enough, it is the only room that appears to be actually inhabited; it's empty now, but there is a real desk, covered with papers, and a working computer with a screen, and a sign on the front of the desk that reads "We do business in accordance with the Fair Housing Act (the Civil Rights Act of 1968 as amended by the Fair Housing Amendments Act of 1988)," followed by a lot of fine print. But the posters are what get me. They cover one entire wall. One of them shows a picture of a tree-lined creek with leaves floating in it and a woman walking along the bank—the same creek that I crossed while chasing after Lonnie, back at our farm party. There is a panel devoted to a hagiography of Thomas French, the "architect" of this model home, and the other, as-yet-unfinished, homes that surround it, which reads "Thomas French has captured the attention of Kings County's discriminating homebuyer in some of the area's most popular patio-home neighborhoods including Willowbrook, Edgewood, Hawthorne Place, Fairhaven, Cottages of Glenview, and now here, in Patrician Woods."

And finally there is a panel describing Patrician Woods itself, which, though unfinished, is apparently the 2002 American Dream Award Grand Award Winner:

> The Cottages of Patrician Woods' prime location is one of the most sought-after in Kings County. Located on the site of the historic Flatrock quarry, residents will enjoy beautiful wooded views, while at the same time being only minutes away from the I-35 business corridor and the many new specialty and department stores available in the exciting developing occurring on both 119th Street and 135th Street. Experience the Maintenance Provided Livestyle! The Cottages of Patrician Woods—*A TRADITION OF EXCELLENCE WITH A VISION OF TODAY.*

The sign displaying the Fair Housing Act, the pastoral photo of the creek where Royce MacVess made his last, defiant stand—these are all absurdities that my father (your grandfather) would have loved, and so I steal paper from the showroom desk and copy down the poster's words because they remind me of the last important thing I have to say. I've named this story for my father because, in the end, he's the one who taught it to me. There's little doubt he would have claimed that it's a poor substitute for your meeting him, but I like to think he would've enjoyed the idea of getting his own biography. He might have regretted how it turned out, he might have involved me too soon, but I know also that he risked my love to tell it to me straight. After all, the stories that we decide to give our children are always more revealing than our dreams.

As for my version, I have no idea how you'll use it. But this account of your mother, your grandmother, Lonnie, Nikki, and Elmore Haywood—the things we hoped for and loved, as well as what we lied about or failed to achieve—is the best I have to offer as you begin to create whatever portrait you will choose to make of me.

Which leaves me, as I wait for Mallory to do her own factual work inside, with nothing to do but rehearse the last part of your letter, which I have yet to write. There is an urgency to this conversation, too. Mallory and I have gone over and over the deed that my father signed with Royce MacVess, and for once the legal language is airtight. I—ready or not—am about to become the owner of this place. But, as Mr. Twigg points out, I don't have the capital to run it, nor do I want to work in real estate. I prefer lawyering. And this is where this message gets complicated, a little bit. It will require a very careful reference to your mother's separation from your stepfather (recent news, for me), one that expresses sympathy but makes it clear this is a business, not a romantic, appeal. It will also have to make clear it is not a bribe; if you and your mother aren't interested, that's fine. But the truth is, the one person I know who does have some capital and might *want* to manage such a property would be your mother. And you, should you choose to accompany her, once you finish your degree. It isn't much, I will say (disingenuously). Eighty acres hardly compares to the holdings your family had before Henry sold the company. But if you have any vestige of that old Bowen gene—and your mother tells me you are an economics major—then you might well be interested in such a project. Prudential started out with less. And besides, eighty acres of prime Kings County real estate are worth $150,000 an acre, which puts the total value of this place up over $10 million, if I have my figures straight.

At any rate, that's how I imagine it as I step outside—the Acheson,

Bowen & Haywood Realty Company, whose sign would replace the High-point sign in front. I imagine this, and I try to keep imagining you and your mother walking with me, as I head down the model home's sidewalk to the street. There are four cars parked there along the curbing, and since there is no sidewalk, I step out onto the asphalt directly. The street is raw and glistening, and it curves off to the right, and as I follow it, there are the frames of houses in bare dirt yards. Thomas French has designed them to be similar, though not exactly the same. Some show the skeletons of broad bay windows and a door to the right; some have frames for skylights that the others lack. One or two will have second floors. The road curves past these houses for a long way, a long and gently sloping cul de sac; the dirt in their front yards is abnormally yellow, having been trucked in and dumped atop the landfill that filled the quarry. After a while I reach a row of houses set along the edge of a hillside, just before a row of trees. One house is finished, a second model; there are cars parked in front of this one, and people leaving, but I don't recognize them, and so when they have left, I cross the lawn and untie the Highpoint sign from between two saplings. Then I circle to the backyard and head downhill through the tree line, thinking of you and your mother and looking for the creek.

The Huntsman

When a young debutante's body is pulled from the Missouri River, the inhabitants of Kansas City—a metropolis fractured by class division—are forced to examine their own buried history. At the center of the intrigue is Booker Short, a bitter young black man who came to town bearing a grudge about the past. His ascent into white Kansas City society, his romance with the young and wealthy Clarissa Sayers, and his involvement in her death polarize the city and lead to the final, shocking revelation of the wrong that Booker has come to avenge. With razor-sharp detail that presents the city as a character as vivid as the people living there, Whitney Terrell explores a divided society with unflinching insight.

ISBN 0-14-200131-7